# Child of Twilight

*Margaret L. Carter*

Hard Shell Word Factory

Dedicated to Catherine B. Krusberg,
my favorite vampire bibliographer and reviewer.

© 2003  Margaret C. Carter
ISBN: 0-7599-3714-1
Trade Paperback
Published September 2003

eBook ISBN: 0-7599-3713-3
Published August 2003

Hard Shell Word Factory
PO Box 161
Amherst Jct.  WI 54407
Books@hardshell.com
http://www.hardshell.com
Cover art © 2003 Dirk A. Wolf
Printed in the U.S.A.
All rights reserved

## Chapter One

*NEVER LET THEM suspect what you are.*

Her mentor's warning, repeated innumerable times, rattled inside Gillian's skull. *What am I, anyway? And aren't I somehow part of "them," too?*

Waving at the van whose lights cut through the sheet of rain, she buried these thoughts beneath the need of the moment. Her mentor had often cautioned her against excessive brooding, too. Cultivating self-doubt would make her vulnerable.

*Not thinking can kill you; on the other hand, thinking too much instead of acting can kill you just as quickly.*

*Oh, leave me alone!* she ordered the ghostly whisper inside her brain. She'd made the considered choice to run away from her guardian, Dr. Volnar; why couldn't she stop thinking of him for more than five minutes straight? At the moment she'd better concentrate on improving her condition—tired, hungry, penniless, and wet. While the December rain didn't chill her, even in a lightweight jacket, she detested being soaked as much as any cat. And the money she'd pilfered from Volnar's wallet had paid for a bus ticket only as far as Richmond.

*Besides, this is supposed to be an adventure.* Her first chance to mix with—*their* kind—without her guardian looming over her shoulder. She'd better make the most of it while she could.

The van screeched to a stop on the shoulder of the on-ramp. When the driver, a lean, middle-aged man with a pointed beard, edged over to peer at her through the passenger window, Gillian heard him exclaim, "My God, it's a kid!"

Opening the door, he shouted to her, "Get in, you're drenched already!"

Gillian climbed into the car, shrugged off her jacket, and dropped her backpack between the two front bucket seats. "Thank you for stopping, sir." She stole a longer look at the driver. He wore a fur-collared leather coat and matching leather gloves. His hair, receding in front, was curly and abundant elsewhere, gray-streaked brown like the beard. She felt indignation mingled with curiosity in the stare he gave her.

The van roared onto Interstate 64. "I'm Adam Greer. Who might you be?"

"Gillian."

"Just Gillian?"

Hands folded in her lap, she kept quiet. The less she revealed the better.

"Good enough—Gillian. Don't you have any idea how dangerous it is for a girl to hitchhike? Especially at night? Good Lord, I could be Jack the Ripper for all you know!"

"Impossible," she said. "He lived in the nineteenth century." Greer's answering chuckle reminded her of another of Volnar's warnings—not to take every statement literally. Fortunately Greer seemed to accept the comment as a joke.

"How old are you, anyway?"

She saw no reason not to answer that question truthfully. As Volnar had instructed her (Why couldn't she keep him out of her thoughts? What kind of independence was *that*?), minimizing the number of lies one had to keep track of made life less complicated. "I'm twelve."

"Tall for your age," Greer muttered.

*And skinny*, she could almost hear the man thinking. Gillian wondered if she'd made a mistake, if she should have claimed to be older. Yet she knew her slim, flat-chested body didn't resemble a teenager's. Better to present herself as an unusually tall pre-adolescent. She ran her fingers through her dripping red curls and sat up straight, trying to keep water off the upholstery.

Squinting through dark-rimmed glasses at the highway, shiny with rain, Greer said, "How far are you going?"

A potential trap? No, what harm could that truth do her? "To Annapolis."

He made a *hmph* sound of acknowledgement. "Heading in that general direction myself. I'm going to a convention in College Park—on the upper side of the Washington beltway, if you don't know the area."

"I have studied maps." The dubious glance he gave her worried Gillian. Her speech must not ring true for a twelve-year-old girl, but how could she remedy that problem when she'd had so little experience yet? *Well, that's one reason I'm here, to get experience.* "What kind of convention, sir?" Maybe she could get him to talk about himself instead of her.

Greer flashed her a smile. "It's a pleasure to meet a polite kid these days, but you don't have to overdo it. A science fiction convention—I'm scheduled to be on a panel about UFOs. I teach sociology at William and Mary, and along with more scholarly articles on the topic, I've published a few popular books on contemporary urban superstitions. Hey, there I go lecturing, as if you'd be interested. Sorry, besetting sin of us academics."

Gillian rummaged through the mental file of her nonfiction reading and came up with a vague picture of what he meant. "But I am interested, professor. Superstitions? Like alligators in the sewers of New York?"

He seemed surprised that she'd caught on so readily. "Right, and the tale of the Hook, the spiders in the imported cactus, the organ-stealing crime ring, and all sorts of wild stories that go around with nobody sure how or where they started. And other popular beliefs that don't strictly fit the *urban* label, like Bigfoot and UFOs full of little green men from Venus."

"There can't be humanoid life on Venus," Gillian said. "It is much too hot."

"Right you are." Professor Greer laughed. "Gillian, you're something else, as we used to say at your age." His amusement faded. "I hate to think of you out on the road alone. I've got a niece not much older than you. Listen, if you're running away, you can tell me about it. I won't turn you in to the cops."

Gillian heard sincerity in the man's voice. The deep pink halo of his aura didn't flicker. Maybe she could tell him enough of the truth, shaded with fabricated details to win his sympathy, to induce him to help her. Either that or she would have to find another ride farther up the highway, and she was so tired already. She hadn't slept all day. "I'm going to visit my father, and I ran out of bus money."

The professor radiated skepticism. "Your parents are divorced?" She nodded. "So why didn't he send you enough money to start with?"

She scrambled for a plausible explanation. One sprang to mind from the soap operas she watched as part of her education. "He doesn't know I'm on my way. I couldn't get in touch with him." She injected a tremor into her voice. "He would have contacted my mother about the arrangements, and if she knew about it—" She paused, pretending to choke on suppressed tears, and watched the man's reaction.

Greer exuded sympathy. Her technique was working. A tiny thrill tingled along her nerves. *So this is what we cultivate them for!* And it wasn't as difficult as she'd feared either.

"She'd stop me. You see, her husband—" Gillian covered her

face with her hands, afraid to volunteer anything specific for fear of striking a false note.

"Poor kid—you don't have to go into details." His voice rough with distress, Greer reached over to pat Gillian's shoulder. A rush of warmth suffused her. For a second she felt energized despite her fatigue and hunger. She wanted more of this!

"I couldn't tell my mother about it. She'd believe my stepfather, not me." Gillian groped for the professor's hand. The touch of his fingers sparked another delightful surge of electricity.

The van swerved. Snatching his hand away from Gillian's, Greer whipped the wheel around to steer the car back into its proper lane. "God, I must be more tired than I thought! Better take a break, get some coffee. I bet you'd like a snack, too."

"I would like a glass of milk," she said.

"Fine, I'll treat you to one." He glanced at the sign coming up. "There's an exit in two miles. Oh, I forgot all about this—" He dug into the pouch below the dashboard between the front seats and fished out a chocolate bar. "Be my guest."

She gave the standard excuse she'd been taught. "No thank you, I'm allergic to it."

With a shrug Professor Greer unwrapped the candy and started eating it. "No wonder I'm beat, grading exams until late this afternoon. Stupid of me not to wait until tomorrow to drive up, but I wanted plenty of time to meet with a few colleagues in the area. And a good thing, as it turned out, or I wouldn't have met you."

Gillian tensed. What did he have in mind? Could she accept help from him without compromising herself?

"I'll take you all the way to your father's. It's only an extra hour of driving time, no problem. You said he lives in Annapolis?"

Gillian decided to accept the offer. Wasn't there a saying about the teeth of gift horses? Once convinced that she was safe with her father, Greer would vanish from her life with no harm done. "Not exactly in Annapolis," she said. "Across the Severn River in an area called St. Margaret's near Route 50."

The van slowed for the exit ramp. "Have you ever been there?"

"Only once, when I was very little, so I hardly remember it. But I have studied—"

He laughed, "Yeah, I know, maps. So you can give me accurate directions?"

"I believe so." She told him the street address.

"Okay, it's a deal." He peered out the windshield at the deserted, wooded county road. The downpour had changed from rain to sleet. "I wonder how many miles to civilization?"

"I don't know how to thank you," said Gillian, quoting a line she'd often encountered in books and TV dramas. She was enjoying the way she manipulated this creature so easily.

With a dismissive wave he said, "Forget it. I'll feel better knowing you're safe. You can thank me by promising not to do anything this dumb again."

"Yes, sir." Partly to divert him from his too-solicitous interest in her and partly out of genuine curiosity, she asked, "Isn't it unwise for you to pick up strangers too? Aren't you afraid?"

"Not of a twelve-year-old—no offense," he chuckled. "And I do carry a pistol in the glove compartment on these trips. Probably against some law or other."

Having read in the newspaper about armed conflict in California traffic jams, Gillian wasn't surprised to hear that the professor had a gun. "How many people have you shot?"

He burst out laughing. "None. I'm not what you'd call the desperado type—" He glanced at her, taking his eyes off the tight curve he was negotiating. At that moment the tires skidded on the ice-glazed pavement. The professor spun the wheel wildly from side to side. Gillian heard his heartbeat shift into overdrive. Her own pounded out of control. The van slid across the curve and onto the shoulder. Its right front bumper collided with a sapling and rebounded.

Gillian felt her safety belt strain against her chest. Greer's panic flooded her. She couldn't gather her wits to brace against the jolting of the car. She felt the brakes catch. The van fishtailed, plowed into a leafless clump of bushes, and stopped.

Gillian's vision went dim. Something more than the wind howled in her ears. Her skin felt on fire. She leaped up, lunging against the belt and barely noticing it snap. Her bones were cracking open, her body turning inside out, her very essence boiling up from her heart and bowels.

She doubled over, forehead on the dashboard. Abruptly the burning pain metamorphosed into a convulsion of ecstasy immeasurably beyond what she'd absorbed from Greer's touch.

It ended too quickly. Her eyes cleared. Meeting the professor's dumbfounded stare, she glimpsed in her peripheral vision what held him transfixed.

She saw the tips of her wings.

What did he see? Only wings? Or also dark fur sprouting on her skin, the fangs and pointed ears of some feral creature from legend?

His terror pierced her between the eyes. Or was it her own? *This can't be—I'm too young—I don't know how!* And then a still more terrible thought hit her: *He saw me change!*

She fumbled for the door handle, jumped down from the van, and launched herself into the air.

Fear-driven instinct made up for her ignorance. Buffeted by wind and sleet, she soared above the trees. Blindly she flew northward until exhaustion forced her to the ground. Landing in a wooded area a few miles from Interstate 95, she huddled in the midst of a stand of evergreens with her head buried in her arms, shuddering with tearless sobs.

When her panic ebbed enough to allow thought, she sat up and craned her neck to look over her shoulder. The wings were gone. *I'm too young for the change! Dr. Volnar was supposed to teach me—later.* A mocking inner voice reminded her, *You chose to run away from him, remember? Isn't there a proverb about making beds and lying in them?*

The back of her blouse hung in shreds, for only a very mature member of her race could include clothing in the rearrangement of molecules. She ached all over. Even though her "flight" was mostly levitation, since the silken wing membrane could not support her weight—despite her being both lighter and stronger than a human girl of the same size—she still had to use hitherto unexercised muscles for balance and steering.

She struggled to bring to mind all she'd been taught about the change. Among their other psychic powers, her people could alter the external shape of their bodies. The change involved no loss or gain of mass, no reshuffling of internal structures. And the shape assumed was fixed in the genes, a cellular memory, apparently, of an ancestral form. What the observer saw, however, depended partly on what he expected to see. And someone with experience and control could project an illusion, making the shapeshift appear more radical than it really was.

This abstract knowledge wouldn't do her much good now. She needed practical instruction. Go back to Volnar and beg his pardon? *Dark Powers, no! Absolutely not!* She'd rather ask her father for help.

Assuming he would help, if he knew how. She'd told Professor Greer the truth about not contacting her father ahead of time. Knowing Roger Darvell hadn't wanted her to be born and hadn't shown any interest in her since, why should she expect him to worry about her now?

*I'll face that problem when I get to Annapolis.*

Meanwhile she had to get there. Several hours of night remained; she'd better travel while she could. The sleet had changed back to freezing rain and slacked off to a drizzle. She would have to walk, staying away from highways and towns. Hitching another ride was out of the question. She knew her ripped blouse would inspire too much curiosity. Besides, the thought of being seen by anyone else terrified her. Suppose the change seized her without warning again? *So much for adventure!*

She started walking north. As soon as she got the feel of the terrain, she broke into a trot, wishing she could run away from her fear. Unbidden, a memory from her eighth year sprang up to torment her.

Dr. Volnar had visited Washington on some sort of business and brought her along. One afternoon she'd awakened early and peeked into his half of the suite to find him still asleep. It had been a cloudy, gusty March day, she recalled. Bored, Gillian had decided to go for a walk along Connecticut Avenue. True, venturing out alone was forbidden, but she knew that as long as she stayed near the hotel the punishment would be slight, well worth the pleasure of the excursion.

She'd put on her sunglasses and straw hat and strolled down the street. In spite of the choking traffic fumes, the spectacle of so many people enthralled her. They frightened her a little, too, making her flinch when one of them passed too close on the sidewalk. Yet nobody gave her a second glance. She didn't stand out as especially odd. What was Dr. Volnar so worried about? After a few blocks she turned away from the hotels and restaurants onto a quiet street lined with gabled and turreted houses. The trees overarching the sidewalk provided relief from the sun that oppressed her even through the cloud cover.

Gillian remembered sitting on the front steps of a brownstone to watch a boy of about ten ride his bicycle up and down the street, making the bike rear up on its back wheel at each end of the block. He must have felt her steady gaze, for after several minutes he stopped in front of her and stared back. "Cool shades," he'd muttered.

Not sure what he meant, she had let the remark pass and said, "You ride very well. I wonder if I could do that?"

"You ever ride a freewheel bike before?"

"I have never ridden a bicycle at all." She'd stood up and sidled over to him, brushing the chrome of the handlebars with her fingertips.

He'd let out a wordless hoot. "You got to be putting me on! Then if you tried this, you'd probably break both legs."

His derision angered Gillian. "I would not! I can do anything I want to do!"

Even then, perhaps, she'd owned a trace of the power of compulsion she expected to develop as an adult, because without another thought the boy had dismounted from the bike and shoved it at her. "Go ahead and try! But if you wreck it, your parents have to pay for it. Dumb girl!"

From watching the angle of the boy's torso and the rhythm of his legs as he'd pumped the pedals, Gillian had rapidly picked up the basic technique. She wobbled up and down the street once, then rode smoothly on the next pass. The third time around she felt ready to practice the stunt he'd performed. After a few false starts she had balanced the bike as deftly as the performer in the circus she'd recently watched on television. Drop-jawed, the boy had watched her ride faster and faster, weaving in and out of holes between parked cars, making the bike jump up and down curbs, glorying in the swift movement and the breeze whipping her hair.

Then a familiar voice had shattered her pleasant trance. "Gillian! Just what do you think you're doing?"

She'd locked the brakes and jumped clear of the bicycle. Striding across the street, Dr. Volnar had seized her hand. After one look at the tall, grim-faced man in dark glasses, the boy had retrieved his bike and fled on it.

"I was only playing," she gasped as Volnar half-dragged her toward Connecticut Avenue. "He let me use the bicycle—I wasn't doing any harm—"

"No harm!" Volnar paused to glare at her, then resumed his rapid pace. "You know very well that you are never to show yourself in public without me."

"Yes, sir, I know." The blaze of his anger blotted out all the joy of her new accomplishment. He'd never reacted this way the other times she'd slipped out by herself.

"And you are never, *never* to show off in front of people."

"Oh. I didn't think—"

"You certainly did not." They crossed Connecticut and walked in the direction of the hotel. "He was only one boy, and when he talks about your—demonstration—his elders will say he's exaggerating. But suppose you'd done something more obviously impossible? Or suppose he had noticed your teeth?" At that stage her dentition had resembled a wolf's more than a human child's. "And what if adults had been present?"

Thoroughly miserable now, Gillian had said nothing.

"Fortunately in most cases people refuse to believe the

impossible. They will deny their own senses rather than let their world-view be overturned. But you cannot count on that weakness. You must never count on it!" He'd punctuated that sentence by grasping her shoulders and spinning her around to stare into her eyes.

"Yes, sir," she whispered. "I'll remember."

"Indeed you will. I intend to imprint it on your mind." Instead of taking her back to the hotel, he had walked her to the National Zoo. Now, jogging through a forest on a December night, inhaling the scent of wet pine, Gillian vividly recalled the ammonia smell of the animal cages stinging her nose.

Volnar had hustled her straight to the big cats and pulled her to the rail overlooking the tiger pen. One of the tigers had lain on his side, motionless except for the flick of his tail, basking in the feeble sun diffused through the overcast sky. The other tiger had paced an unvarying path along the edge of the artificial hill, his muzzle always turned toward the spectators. Gillian recalled a whiff of rotting meat from the tigers' last meal and the shrill cries of two little boys in overalls a few feet away, fighting over a box of popcorn. Their mother had shrieked at them, "You two stop that this instant, or it's back to the car! Come over here and look at Tigger!"

Staggering from sensory overload, Gillian had let Dr. Volnar guide her away. When they'd settled on a bench in the shade, he'd said, "Would you want to spend your life like that—imprisoned, on exhibit, viewed as a rare and dangerous wild beast? Would you want to be responsible for hundreds of your cousins being hunted down and forced to live that way?"

In a quavering voice Gillian had given him the answer he wanted. And then he'd drawn the moral: "Never let them suspect what you are."

And now, reflected Gillian as she maintained her steady trot, Professor Greer knew there was something strange about her. He didn't merely have cause for suspicion; he had *seen* her change. She had broken one of the most vital rules. She couldn't begin to guess how Dr. Volnar would punish her if she went back to him. So she didn't dare go back, not for a long time. Her father, at least, would understand. Maybe.

After a while the rain stopped. Her energy was fading again. Wearing only the remains of a blouse, she found the night chilly and wished for her jacket, which she'd left in Greer's van. Along with the backpack containing extra clothes and everything else she'd paused to grab on her way out of the hotel in Atlanta. She fingered her one remaining asset, the delicate gold cross that hung around her neck. That was worth money, she knew, but she had no idea where to sell jewelry. She wasted little thought on her losses. More important at the moment, she needed food.

Slowing to a walk, she tiptoed soundlessly among the trees, listening and sniffing the air. The wet soil and plants carried odors well. Within a few minutes she scented a rabbit crouched under an evergreen bush. Squatting a few feet away, Gillian focused on the motionless animal. The healthy glow of its aura made her mouth water. Still as a stone herself, with one hand outstretched, she silently called to the rabbit. This talent she had possessed for several years. Unlike her new sensitivity to human emotions, her link with animals didn't overwhelm her and shatter her control.

The rabbit inched from beneath the tangled branches and gave a tentative hop in her direction. Gillian held her breath. She mustn't make a hasty move and scare the creature away. It hopped closer. She encouraged it with a soothing hum. One more hop and it hunched within reach of her hand. She stroked the rough fur on its back until the rabbit's racing heartbeat calmed. Picking it up, she cradled the animal in her arms, exposing the nearly hairless belly.

Its body heat was balm to her cold, aching limbs. With a sigh of relief she sat down against a tree and pressed her mouth to the rabbit's abdomen. The razor-sharp edge of her incisors opened a minute slit in the skin, and she sucked avidly. Her prey sank into sleep, coma, and finally death without the slightest spasm of pain.

Gently laying aside the drained body, she resumed walking. Soon dawn would force her to seek shelter. She couldn't travel any farther without a good day's rest. About an hour later, she came upon a dense thicket of pines tainted by no lingering scent of human intrusion. From the map she'd consulted, she knew this area must be part of a national forest. The trees would screen her from the view of low-flying light aircraft as well as from the sun. With luck nobody would stumble across her hiding place while she slept.

She nestled into a pile of sodden leaves, grumbling at the chill and dampness. All the other times she'd spent the day outside, the excursions had been planned. Volnar had provided her with a sleeping bag and pup tent. How she longed for those amenities now! Tired as she was, though, discomfort couldn't keep her awake for long. Nor could the worries that revolved endlessly in her head. Would her father accept her at least temporarily, or try to send her back to Volnar? She knew her father hadn't wanted a child. He'd been pressured into begetting Gillian. Half-human himself, he had bequeathed human genes to her, traits that made her incomplete, defective—or so she'd heard it whispered for most of her life. On the other hand, human fathers, unlike males among Gillian's mother's people, were supposed to care for their children. Why hadn't Gillian's father defied Volnar's rules to contact her at least occasionally?

She dimly remembered her one visit to Annapolis, sometime in her third year. At that time she'd still been living with her mother, Juliette, who had thought Gillian's father was entitled to a glimpse of the baby he'd sired. During the brief meeting her father had shown polite interest, nothing more. Gillian wondered if this quest would prove a waste of time, if she ought to go straight to Juliette instead. No, Volnar would look there first. Juliette was visiting her literary agent in New York, and Volnar had been taking Gillian there for her semiannual visit with her mother when Gillian had decided to run away. Juliette, who approved of Dr. Volnar's teaching methods, would certainly send Gillian right back to him.

There was at least a chance, Gillian thought, that her father would resist turning her over to Volnar. According to rumor, the two didn't get along well. Comforting herself with that prospect, she yielded to sleep.

GILLIAN AWOKE LITTLE more refreshed than when she'd lain down. She decided sleeping on the bare ground didn't suit her, though she'd heard some of her older acquaintances claim they enjoyed roughing it. Did her distaste for this adventure mean she was flawed by human weakness? Or just sensible?

After catching a squirrel for her evening meal, she resumed her easy lope northward. The closer she got to Washington, the harder it became to avoid people. The constant detours, she knew, wasted time. At this rate she couldn't hope to reach Annapolis under her own power any time reasonably soon. And the longer she stayed on the run, the more likely Volnar would track her down. How, she wasn't sure, but her years with him had taught her to regard her mentor as almost supernaturally powerful.

No choice—she had to risk hitchhiking again.

If not for her torn blouse, she wouldn't have to worry so much about attracting attention. Following the distant sound of traffic, she crept through the woods to the nearest highway. She lay on her stomach on a hillside overlooking I-95 and noted the nearby exit leading to a town. There she might somehow manage to pick up a coat to make her look more suitably dressed for the season.

She made her way down the hill and walked parallel to the side road, careful not to get close enough to be clearly seen by passing drivers. Guided by a scattering of lights, she found her way to a residential suburb of split-level houses and sparse traffic. She hunkered down behind a Dumpster next to a school playground, cogitating over her next move.

In the adventure novels she'd read, runaways and tramps often stole garments off clotheslines. In a neighborhood like this, Gillian knew, people seldom hung laundry outside and certainly not in the winter. The thin layer of snow under her jeans reminded her that she needed a coat for more than appearances. While the cold couldn't harm her, she didn't find it comfortable. She'd have to break into a house.

She catfooted along the street, keeping away from the street lamps. It didn't take her long to find a house with no lights on. She edged over to one of the back windows. Crouching beneath it, she listened. No sound of breathing in the nearest rooms. Gillian stood up and tried the window, pleased that it opened by pushing up, not sideways like some others she'd seen. Locked.

Bracing her legs, she shoved upward with all her strength. The lock broke. At the same time the frame she was pushing on cracked, as did the windowpane inside it. Gillian froze, ears perked. No sound of hurrying feet from either of the next-door houses. The noise of splintering wood must not have been so loud as she'd imagined.

She eased the damaged window open and scrambled inside. She emerged in a musty-smelling bedroom cluttered with several pairs of inside-out jeans and socks. A T-shirt bearing a picture of a dragon lay on the bed. A teenage boy's room, probably, though she knew from fashion ads that one couldn't always judge accurately by clothes.

The barking of a dog interrupted her thoughts. She smelled the animal and heard the click of its claws in the hall. Gillian looked frantically around the room. She'd rather find what she needed here than have to stun or kill the dog while exploring the house. Now the dog was growling outside the bedroom door, fortunately shut. Gillian opened the closet. On the floor a light gray jacket lay crumpled. Excellent!

She snatched it up, put it on, and zipped it. Slightly large for her, the jacket covered her from neck to hips, hiding the worst traces of her rough night. She surveyed herself in the mirror on the inside of the bedroom door. Not bad, except for the dirt smudges on her face. If only she could get to the bathroom and wash up, but that luxury wouldn't be worth leaving a dead or wounded pet as evidence.

The dog's growling rose to a crescendo of frustration. Gillian climbed out the window the way she'd arrived and glided across the back yard. Within ten minutes she stood next to the freeway on-ramp, gesturing with her thumb as she'd seen people do in movies.

This time a trailer truck stopped for her. The driver, a husky black man, gave Gillian the same kind of dubious look Professor Greer had given her. "I'm not supposed to pick up no riders, but what the hell, you look like you really need help. Get in!"

She did, muttering her thanks. The truck's cab smelled like stale cigarette smoke.

Gunning the motor, the man said, "Didn't anybody ever tell you it's not safe for little girls on the road?"

"Yes," she said flatly. The less she spoke to him, the less risk of making another disastrous error.

Shortly he asked, "Where you headed?"

"Annapolis."

"Well, I got a schedule to keep, so I'll have to drop you off in D.C."

"That's fine. Thank you very much." Now the man was lighting a cigarette, whose smoke made her stomach clench with nausea. She gritted her teeth, fighting the queasiness.

After a few more unsuccessful attempts to start a conversation, the driver gave up and switched on a cassette tape of a man bewailing the treachery of his lover—as far as Gillian could make out from the few words she could distinguish. She knew so little of the way people lived. Why had she ever imagined she could get along on her own? Volnar had warned her that soap operas and the accompanying commercials, while they could give her a feel for some aspects of everyday life, were not a totally reliable guide to the outside world. Soap opera—she'd always thought that was a strange phrase, for the actors in those dramas didn't sing their lines, as in *Das Rheingold* or *La Traviata*, and the dialogue seldom mentioned soap.

Against her will her mind flew back to the last time she'd watched a drama with singing. Night before last, in Atlanta, her first experience of live theater. Volnar had arranged a twenty-four hour layover between flights, during which he took her to a performance of *Camelot*. Gillian had never imagined how intense the experience would be, compared to the videotape of the same play.

The story line made little sense to her. All that fuss over a man and woman mating! Why couldn't Guinevere share her favors equally with both Arthur and Lancelot? But then, Gillian understood almost nothing about human mating customs. It wasn't the play that upset her, but the audience's reaction. Caught up in the music, the crowd made her feel as if she was swimming in a river whose current overwhelmed her strength, its foaming rapids sweeping her helplessly toward the edge of a waterfall, the water crashing over her head until she felt near drowning.

And the theater overloaded her outer senses as well as her fresh, raw psychic vision. Perfume, sweat, damp wool, and smoke-impregnated fabric made her stomach churn. The music swelled inside her head as recorded sound never had. The stage lighting dazzled her eyes, but paled beneath the scintillation of the hundreds of living auras around her. Her infrared vision had always allowed her to see the halo of heat radiated by animals, from human beings down to insects. She'd imagined the direct perception of the aura to be similar. She had not expected to see each person surrounded by a corona of rainbow light that pulsed with every shifting nuance of delight, fear, or sadness.

She tried closing her eyes. That retreat only left her inner senses exposed to the full force of the spectators' unbarriered emotions. Like being crushed by an avalanche—

She fled to the lobby, tripping over people's laps in her rush to escape. Volnar had followed her at a sedate pace and led her outside. Even the lights and traffic of a downtown street had seemed restful by contrast.

"I see I've misjudged the speed of your development," he'd said, supporting her with a firm, impersonal grip on her elbow. "I intended gradually introducing you to human society before you reached this phase. It's too late for that." Back at the hotel, he had announced his intention to initiate her—the very next evening at sunset, before catching the flight to New York.

During the day while he slept, she had sneaked out.

What would Volnar do when he caught up with her? Would her father be able to protect her? Would he even want to?

*Don't think about that now. Think about getting from Washington to Annapolis.*

Gillian shrank from the thought of hitching another ride. She'd prefer to take a bus the rest of the way. Where could she get the money? Again she clutched her gold cross and thought about selling it. But she didn't want to attract attention by asking strangers where such transactions could be accomplished.

Besides, she liked the trinket and didn't want to give it up, even though she'd received it as a present from Volnar.

*Sentimental, human thinking.* That was probably what some of the elders who disapproved of Gillian's very existence would say. They constantly hinted at latent human weaknesses that would mar her character and endanger the race. She'd heard such whispers often enough, though Volnar tried to shield her from them.

*I'm not human! If I were, people like this truck driver wouldn't think I'm so strange.* She cringed from the pressure of his curiosity, almost as stifling as the cigarette smoke.

When he exited the freeway and drove into the parking lot of a fast food restaurant on the edge of downtown Washington, Gillian was surprised to notice that the truck's dashboard clock showed only a little after eight. The uncomfortable ride seemed to have dragged on for half the night.

Swinging his door open, the driver said, "Buy you a snack, honey?"

Gillian thanked him as she climbed down from the cab. She swallowed the impulse to protest that *honey*. In the programs she'd watched, that term was used for either very small children or someone with whom the speaker wanted to initiate a sexual union. The word felt inappropriate in this casual context. The last thing she wanted, though, was to fix the driver's attention on her by starting an argument. She simply wanted to slip away from him.

Inside, blinking in the glare of the harsh overhead lights, she scanned the wall menu and asked for a vanilla milkshake. It was just as well that she didn't plan to stay and drink it, for the greasy food odors killed her appetite. She retreated to the ladies' room.

The pungent disinfectant smell didn't bother her as much as it normally would have. Fresh water made up for that. After drinking from the faucet, she wasted valuable minutes scrubbing her face and hands. She stared into the mirror, rubbing her cheeks with a paper towel.

*Dark Powers, what a mess!* A quick wash couldn't repair the effects of sleeping on the ground. She needed a bath. Mud stained her jeans, and the baggy jacket, with the cuffs turned up to leave her hands free, didn't enhance her image. She combed both hands through her tangled mane of short, red curls. Her fingers snagged a dry leaf.

*Who cares what I look like? Time to get moving!*

Emerging from the restroom, she edge to the corner of the wall and peeked in the direction of the counter. The truck driver was paying for his order. Gillian walked rapidly, without quite breaking into a trot, to the door. She held her breath until she'd slipped out.

Logically the man would have no reason to chase her. He'd planned to leave her in Washington anyway. Still, she ran across the parking lot and kept running for another three blocks. No cars slowed down, and the few pedestrians she passed veered out of her way. She switched to a brisk walk, telling herself she had nothing to worry about.

Now for the bus station. She'd tackle the problem of the fare after she'd found the place. Perhaps she could beg for the money, since she knew how to make human adults feel sorry for her. She needed a telephone book and a street map. Volnar had introduced her to these basic skills. Too bad he'd waited so long to teach her about dealing with people.

For half an hour she roamed the streets, not sure what she was looking for. Hunger gnawed at her. A squirrel's blood volume was too small to satisfy her for long. She almost regretted not waiting for the milkshake. The lights of a Seven-Eleven diverted her from that train of thought. Outside the store she saw a phone booth. She flipped through the yellow pages until she found the address of a downtown bus terminal.

Stepping inside the store, she made a circuit of the displays, hands in her jacket pockets. If she had some money, she could buy a glass of milk, not to mention one of the city maps on the rack by the checkout counter. Could she get away with stealing one? When she edged up to the counter, she abandoned that idea. The chunky, gray-haired woman running the cash register eyed Gillian with unmasked suspicion.

Gillian considered snatching a map and running. No, not with two other customers in sight, a slim young black man and a tired-looking blonde in a waitress uniform. Volnar had too thoroughly hammered into Gillian the importance of not attracting attention. An adult of her race could mesmerize the cashier into giving her the map and forgetting about it. Not having learned that skill yet, Gillian was afraid to try; her loss of control with Professor Greer made her frightened of any close contact with human beings.

"Well?" the saleslady snapped. "Do you want to buy something, or not? Sign says 'No Loitering,' and that means you kids."

"No, ma'am," said Gillian. "I only wanted to ask directions. I'm looking for the bus station." She recited the street address she'd memorized.

The woman rattled off an impatient sentence of instructions and told her to get out. Gillian thanked her and left.

Jogging along the sidewalk, a light film of snow crunching under her sneakers, Gillian concentrated on her hope that a bus was scheduled between Washington and Annapolis tonight. She didn't want to travel by day, nor did she relish the thought of waiting in the terminal all night.

Her path took her down poorly-lit streets lined by apartment buildings of dingy brick with the stench of garbage drifting from the alleys between them. Many of the ground-floor windows she passed were boarded up. Occasionally a car rumbled by, or footsteps reached her ears from adjoining streets. At one point a cat darted out of her way and paused to hiss at her before fleeing into an alley. Gillian momentarily considered pursuing the animal. She wasn't used to going hungry—

When she faced front again, four human figures popped up. They had rounded the corner of a building just ahead. Gillian paused, balanced on the balls of her feet, to brush the edges of their minds. Her fear of losing control made her hesitate long enough to let two of them circle behind her before she sensed their belligerence.

Four dark-haired boys, probably a few years older than she, wearing jeans, boots, and heavy jackets. The one directly in front of her, two inches taller than Gillian and twice as broad, said, "What's a little girl like you doing out this time of night?"

Gillian stared back at him without answering. His breath smelled like onions, but the lust emanating from him sickened her more.

"Hey, will you look at that!" The youth next to him, shorter and slightly plump, poked at Gillian's cross. She stepped back, hissing. "Whoa, listen to her!"

"Sounds like a snake," the larger boy said. "Built like one, too. Or maybe you're hiding something under that coat?" He plucked at the zipper of her jacket.

With a snarl Gillian slashed her claws across his face. He flinched back and whipped out a knife. "You gonna pay for that, bitch! First I'll take that thing around your neck, and then we'll see what else you got for us."

The other two breathed hot on the back of Gillian's neck. She understood they intended to rob and rape her. She felt no fear of them—she feared her own anger. The scent of her attacker's blood made her breathing fast and ragged.

*No—I'm too young for human blood!* "Leave me alone," she said quietly, impaling him with her eyes, fervently wishing she could control him as an adult could.

For an instant the compulsion seemed to work. The youth inched backward. The boy next to him, though, remained untouched, for she didn't know how to influence two people at once. The smaller boy tried to snatch the cross from her neck.

Gillian's hand grabbed his arm and squeezed until a bone cracked. Startled by the sound, she let go. The leader's knife swiped at her. The blade slashed the front of her jacket. Dodging just in time to avoid being cut, she felt one of the other boys clutch her from behind.

That violation ignited her rage. All caution consumed by fury, she lashed out. One hand ripped open the leader's throat, while her left fist knocked down the second boy who faced her.

Whirling, she kneed the third boy in the groin, then kicked the last one's feet out from under him. Spinning around once more, she saw the leader doubled up on the sidewalk, clutching his neck. Blood spurted between the fingers. He stared at her, wide-eyed, gurgling.

The boy whose face she had bruised tried to struggle into a sitting position. "You—what the hell—"

Their pain and fear rushed over her like cold fire, setting all her nerves aglow. Involuntary contractions rippled through her muscles. *Oh, no, it's happening again!*

She peeled off the jacket and let it fall. Just in time—the transformation claimed her in an explosion of heat and electricity. Through the red mist over her eyes she saw three of the four muggers lurch to their feet and run away. The one she'd clawed watched her in helpless terror.

The surge of ecstasy faded quicker this time. Gillian set her jaw and focused on a mental image of herself in the mirror, tired, mussed, and outwardly human. With a wrench, her molecules rearranged themselves.

Shrugging into her jacket, she bent over the wounded youth. He gasped and fainted. Gillian rummaged through his pockets until she found a wallet. Without counting them, she stuffed all the bills she found into her pocket and tossed the wallet aside.

Staggering with exhaustion, lightheaded with renewed hunger after exerting that burst of energy, she nevertheless smiled as she loped down the street. She had her bus fare.

## Chapter Two

ON THE SPARSE grass under the leafless tree, the man looked asleep, curled up on his left side, one hand under his head. Except that no respectable, middle-class citizen, as his London Fog overcoat marked him, would sleep on the ground at a freeway rest stop in the chill of a December night. Not even in Nevada. Camille left him there. With luck, no one would notice him, lying outside the range of the building's lights, until she'd covered fifty or a hundred miles.

She hadn't bothered getting his name. She had the cash from his wallet and the keys to his car. When he regained consciousness, he wouldn't remember the woman standing beside an on-ramp next to a "disabled" Mercedes, the tall, attenuated, pale, dark-haired woman he had generously picked up. Nor would he guess why he couldn't remember, why he felt weak and disoriented with no head injury to explain the symptoms. Camille hoped to cross a couple of state lines before the Nevada highway patrol got their act together to broadcast a description of the mysteriously stolen car.

Not that she wasted much worry on the police. She could deal with a would-be arresting officer as easily as she had dealt with the rightful owner of this well-kept sedan. Rolling the window down, she bared her teeth to the cold air whipping her in the face and abandoned herself to the roar of the wind and the purr of the engine. These sensory pleasures kept her from brooding over what she did fear and could do nothing about—the danger that those she fled from would catch her before she reached her destination. Abandoning the Mercedes, she hoped, would extend the time before they tracked her down.

Camille's fingers tightened on the wheel like a hawk's talons gripping its prey. Let them find her—she had little chance of eluding them forever. But let her elude them just long enough. For the first time in her life, she wished she believed in prayer. If only she knew some deity that could ensure her freedom until she reached her goal. Her vengeance on Roger Darvell, her brother's killer.

"HE'S LYING!" BRITT Loren closed the apartment door with greater than necessary force. "Lying through his expensively-capped teeth." She pulled off her damp boots, leaving them on the mat by the door, and draped her coat and scarf over the coat tree in the corner.

With some amusement Roger Darvell noted the frustration she radiated. "Of course he's lying. We both saw that." Years of practice under Roger's direction had bestowed some of his hypnotic skill and empathic perception upon Britt. "But our intuition is not evidence. Why are you letting it upset you so much?" He hung up his own overcoat.

Britt headed through the living room and dining room, decorated in pale blues and greens, to the kitchen. She didn't need to ask whether Roger wanted a drink after more than an hour in peak traffic all the way from Clifton T. Perkins State Hospital, near Jessup. The perpetual construction work on the various freeway extensions only exacerbated an already overloaded system. The two of them, as psychiatric consultants, had been interviewing a murder suspect. Britt shook up a dry martini and handed Roger the chilled glass across the counter separating kitchen from dining room. "I can think of better headache remedies," she said.

"Not now," he said. Already the pain induced by sun glaring off the remains of last night's snowfall was becoming duller.

Britt poured herself a wine cooler and leaned on the kitchen side of the counter. "The man's a classic sociopath if I ever saw one. Hallucinations—uncontrollable impulse—horse feathers! He's been systematically exploiting his stepdaughter, sexually and every other way, for years, and he obviously killed her for the insurance."

"Calm down, colleague," said Roger, smiling at the fire in Britt's voice. "I agree with you. And Captain Hayes should be delighted, since he and the State's Attorney want evidence against an insanity plea." He referred to the county homicide detective who had often recommended one or both of them as expert witnesses.

Britt gulped half her drink, then shuddered at the rush of icy liquid. "You know as well as I do that the defense will bring in their own experts to contest our findings, and there's a fifty-fifty chance of the jury believing them, not us. Come on, I know you don't like it any more than I do."

"Granted. But I must be turning cynical—or realistic—with age. I see no point in getting excited about the situation."

"Roger, sometimes you're no fun to gripe at." With a start, she set down her glass. "Oh, hi, Sigmund." She bent over to pick up the furry creature whose tail had brushed her leg—her aging blue-point Siamese. Rubbing the cat's chin, she went on, "Too bad you couldn't have shelved your scruples and arranged a mysterious death from *anemia*.

The hospital staff would never have noticed a tiny incision on the creep's neck or arm."

Roger stroked the cat's head. Sigmund responded with a hoarse purr. Roger enjoyed the interaction, for most animals recoiled in fear from him. Sigmund accepted him only because of their long acquaintance. "A very unappetizing notion." The cat squirmed to get down, emitting the piercing, child-like cry characteristic of the breed. "Starving your pet again, colleague?"

Britt made a derisive noise. "He knows you're a pushover. You can feed him while I get changed, but no milk this time. I don't need a cat with diarrhea."

While Britt went into her bedroom, Roger took down a can of cat food and began opening it. Sigmund circled his legs, wailing. Switching to the silent communication made possible by their psychic bond, Roger answered: [Yes, I do feel sorry for him, a natural predator never allowed to set foot outside.]

[Predator!] Britt mentally chortled. [If he ever saw a mouse, he'd probably faint! Crickets in the summer are about all the challenge he can handle.]

[Oh, I realize you have to confine him for his own safety. But I still identify with his deprivation.] Roger set down the cat food. Sigmund spared him a cool glance of thanks before digging in.

Roger took the rest of his martini into the living room. Seated on the couch next to the Christmas tree, he listened to Britt unzipping her pantsuit and rattling hangers in the closet. [What about you?] she asked. [There's still some of that *blutwurst* in the refrigerator.] A mental grimace accompanied the words. She often remarked that she didn't see how Roger could eat the stuff. Well, it wasn't his favorite meal, but the blood sausage special ordered from a German deli in Baltimore was useful to keep on hand.

[No, I'll wait until we get to the restaurant.] He sipped the martini, wishing it could banish the headache that still throbbed faintly at his temples.

[You could use more than a lukewarm, bloody steak tonight.] Britt started running the shower.

Roger ignored the hint. Although rare beef wasn't his first choice either, he reminded himself that he was lucky to be able to eat solid food at all. That ability saved him a lot of inconvenience. [What time did you make the reservation?]

[Six thirty. Claude and Eloise are expecting us at the Hilton at six, so that gives us a little while to talk before we walk up to the restaurant. I figured the earlier we started the less crowded it would be—better for you and Claude. I wonder what possessed him to invite us out to dinner in the first place?]

[Something to celebrate, I gather. We'll find out when he wants to tell us.] Roger's half-brother Claude had a sometimes annoying flair for the dramatic. Not surprising, considering he was an actor. He and his wife were in the area for a pair of conferences, a science fiction convention in College Park this weekend and the Modern Language Association conference in Washington right after Christmas. The latter concerned only Eloise, in her role as an English professor; Claude would probably spend that time catching up on sleep. In between their various obligations, the couple would share a leisurely visit with Roger and Britt.

Roger detached himself from Britt's thoughts, except for the wordless bond that joined them constantly. The bond that sustained him even more than the tangible nourishment she gave him. At his insistence they restricted that communion to weekends. On a Tuesday evening he shouldn't be tormenting himself by thinking of it.

Yet how could he avoid thinking of what he craved, when Britt deliberately tempted him to break his own rules? He knew that hint she'd dropped had been only the opening salvo in her attack.

He took the empty martini glass to the kitchen and went into the guest bath to wash up. The cool water felt good. Putting his shirt and tie back on, he checked his appearance in the mirror. He knew his aquiline profile and gray-streaked black hair gave him an air of dignity, which he exploited when dealing with patients. Britt used a less intimidating style, projecting a sort of elder sister persona that induced her patients to open up.

Studying his reflection, Roger noted that he now looked Britt's age or a little younger, though she was forty-nine to his fifty-four. His appearance had not changed since the day fourteen years past when he had contracted to become her associate. His failure to age didn't seem to disturb her. Sooner or later, he knew he would have to make himself look older for his own safety. Fortunately, a man's cosmetic age was expected to vary less radically than a woman's.

When Roger sat on the couch again, leaning back to rest his eyes while waiting for Britt, Sigmund jumped onto his lap. Slowly he stroked the cat, enjoying the ripple of the silken fur. One of the best tranquilizers available.

A moment later he heard Britt returning and opened his eyes to look at her. She wore an emerald green dress—to match her eyes—

with a short jacket. Knee-high boots, more decorative than functional, contrasted with the huge, thoroughly inelegant shoulder purse that she parted with only on the most formal of occasions. She'd restyled her golden-red hair from the tight knot she wore at the office to a softer French twist. "How do I look, colleague?"

"Perfect, as usual." He drank in the vibrant pink glow of her aura, a tranquilizer even more effective than a cat's purr.

She sat beside him and lightly smoothed his hair. "Your head still hurts, doesn't it?"

He couldn't deny that, since Britt shared his sensations at will. "That was a hellish time to be on the freeway."

With a husky laugh that quickened his heartbeat, she said, "You're incredibly spoiled. I could have made you drive, you know." She patted her lap. "Come on, at least I can help you with the headache."

He couldn't resist that offer. Depositing the cat on the rug, Roger laid his head in Britt's lap. Her fingertips traced delicate circles on his temples. He gave in to her invitation and let his tight muscles relax. Inhaling her fragrance and settling into the heat of her body spread a sweet lethargy through his nerves. If only he could rest here for an hour—

Britt picked up the thought, of course. "Why don't I call the Hilton and tell them we'll be late? That session at the hospital was harder on you than me. Trying to shield against all that..." Her sympathy soothed his restlessness, yet made him thirsty for more. "You need—"

"No. Snatching half an hour with you would be worse than nothing."

"Maybe for you. What about me? I can't stand watching you suffer."

He savored her unabashed desire, even though it made him ache for her. "Dear colleague, I'm hardly *in extremis* yet."

"Yeah, I hear you." Britt reached for his hand. He let her slender fingers clasp his—a tactical error, since she immediately began stroking his palm in a tantalizing spiral pattern. The sensitive cilia there tingled in response. Roger suppressed a groan. After fourteen years together she knew his trigger points too well.

"Claude and Eloise wouldn't mind the delay," she said. "They'd understand."

"Yes, and Claude would snicker. No, thank you, I'll wait."

The tapered fingernails of her other hand skimmed along his neck and jawline. He flinched. "If you don't stop that, I *will* bite you, and not gently."

Sensing, as usual, the exact point at which she would be pushing him too far, she suspended her teasing. "Okay, we'll wait—for dessert." At that moment Sigmund leaped onto Roger's chest, curling up as he would on any convenient surface. "Who invited you?" said Britt.

"He doesn't like to share your attention, a feeling I thoroughly identify with. But I suppose we'd better go now, anyway." With a sigh he again dislodged the cat.

Britt bundled up for the short walk from her apartment through downtown Annapolis to the Hilton. In good weather the few blocks between her place, outside the Naval Academy's Maryland Avenue gate, and the hotel near the dock would be a pleasant stroll. This evening they chose to walk simply because finding a parking space in the heart of downtown would take longer than covering the distance on foot. Roger didn't bother with cold-weather gear other than his overcoat, mostly for appearances; at temperatures in the mid-thirties he felt comfortable in a light jacket.

As they started up Maryland Avenue, Britt drew a deep breath of the frosty air and said, "Do you think we'll get heavy snow tonight, colleague?"

Roger sniffed the air, too. "I never claimed to be a weather prophet. It smells like snow, yes, but as for the amount, I'll go along with the newspaper forecast—chance of flurries."

"Unusual to get this much in December," said Britt. "Does it remind you of back home in *Baahston?*"

He acknowledged her imitation of his "accent" with a weak smile. From his viewpoint, of course, she had an accent. But did he try to induce her to say *Bal-ti-moah* rather than *Balt'mr?* Certainly not. The very idea of attempting such a project brought a more spontaneous smile to his lips.

She fell out of step with him to scoop up a glove-full of already slushy snow. "Too soupy to make snow persons with."

He edged away from her, glancing speculatively at the nearest front lawn. "No space to build them, anyway, unless you trespass on your neighbor's property." He collected a handful of snow and began packing it between his palms, eying Britt.

She held up her hands defensively. "Roger Gallagher Darvell, don't you dare!"

He pretended to relax. "I wouldn't think of it, colleague. Like shooting ducks on water." When Britt let down her guard and resumed walking, he pitched the snowball straight at her chest.

With a shriek of outrage she threw one back at him. He dodged. He let her score the next hit and deliberately missed his return shot. A chortle of mock triumph caught in her throat. He saw her slip on a patch of ice.

Instantly he was at her side, his arm around her waist.

"Thanks," she said a bit shakily. "Roger, somebody could have seen you."

"As if your safety weren't more important! Forgive me, I should have thought about the condition of the sidewalk—"

"Will you stop apologizing!" Steadying herself, she lightly held onto his arm. "It was well worth it. When we first met, the word *play* wasn't in your vocabulary."

"Yes, you've corrupted me."

She burst into helpless giggles, clinging to him. "Oh, Roger, I do love you!"

In this position her mouth was perilously close to his. He swallowed the sudden lump in his throat. "Let's go, unless you want to provide a show for the entire block."

"It's dark, remember? We could just move away from the street light." But she complied, her hand sedately resting on his elbow as they continued toward Market Circle and the Hilton.

At the hotel they took the elevator upstairs, since Claude had proposed they meet in the room instead of the lobby. Roger welcomed the chance for private conversation before facing the restaurant ordeal. When Claude opened the door to them, Roger immediately noticed an anomaly in the aura surrounding Claude's wife, Eloise. Nothing that an ordinary man, even a doctor, would have seen—no change in her porcelain-pale complexion or her thick auburn-brown hair, trailing down her back in a French braid—but when she gave Roger a quick hug, his paranormal senses confirmed the curious flicker in the halo of energy she radiated.

Britt sent him a wordless query.

[Eloise is pregnant,] he said.

Britt responded with surprised delight. [Are we supposed to notice?]

[I think they want the pleasure of telling us.]

Roger couldn't help tensing at the sight of Britt greeting Claude with a hearty embrace. Of course Roger trusted his half-brother, yet his instincts screamed in protest at another predator's touching her. And he still, against all logic, felt slightly inadequate beside Claude, who didn't share Roger's half-human heritage. Claude, blast him, always projected such unadulterated self-confidence.

Claude greeted him with a sidelong smile that made plain to Roger how obvious his momentary discomfort had been. "Good to see you, little brother. Sit down, if you can find a place. Before we go to dinner, we've got some good news."

Eloise and Britt sat on the king-size bed, leaving the two chairs for the men. The women made an aesthetically pleasing contrast, Britt slender and too tall for the culture's feminine ideal, Eloise below average height and saved from plumpness only by her liaison with Claude. Yet both shared qualities the average observer wouldn't notice, because few people believed such phenomena existed—skin translucently pale and strangely unmarked for middle age, eyes bright from chronic metabolic speed-up, pale violet shadows from borderline anemia—the stigmata of a long-term donor.

Claude lifted a bottle of champagne out of the ice bucket on the dresser. Dom Perignon.

Britt whistled. "Obviously this is a higher order of celebration than a new movie or book." Eloise wrote novels and literary criticism as well as film scripts, all in the horror-fantasy field.

Roger helped Claude hand out the glasses, regulation champagne goblets, not plastic makeshift. "You couldn't have brought this with you on the plane from Los Angeles—at least, I certainly hope not."

Claude laughed at the outrageous notion. "No, I picked it up at the liquor store across the street when we arrived. Only bottle they had. I didn't ask how long it had been there." He filled three glasses and served Eloise only a token splash. He raised his drink in tribute and nodded to his wife. "*Cherie?*"

She gave a broad smile, and her pale cheeks turned pink. "We're having a baby."

After they'd all drained their glasses, Britt hugged Eloise in a convincing display of surprise. Shaking Claude's hand, Roger said, "Congratulations. But how—?" No male of their species could fertilize a human female, since male potency depended on the female's estrus.

"Artificial insemination," said Claude.

"With you as donor? But how—?" Roger checked himself. Most likely by the same process used when he had sired his own child. A male vampire didn't need physical contact with a female in order to respond to her pheromones.

Claude    grinned    with    what    looked    suspiciously    like embarrassment. "Let's talk about it later." He lofted the bottle. "Refill, anyone? Not you, my love."

Eloise gave him a long-suffering look. "Can't one of you medical experts tell him he's overdoing the clean-living emphasis? A single glass of champagne couldn't be lethal."

"Oh, no, better safe than sorry," Britt said. "Don't you think so, Roger?"

"I have to agree. Since we have no body of clinical experience with interbreeding, we don't know the threshold of possible damage. Better not take chances."

Britt tucked her legs under her and sipped at a fresh glass of champagne. "So, when do you expect to deliver?"

Eloise shrugged. "I'm hoping for June, but that's if the pregnancy follows a human schedule. The idea of an eleven-month gestation period—" She feigned a shudder.

"What are you doing for an obstetrician?" Roger asked.

"That's not one of our customs," said Claude, pouring himself another drink and taking a seat, "and obviously we can't turn to a human practitioner. Fearless Leader is keeping an eye on her progress."

"Volnar?" Roger had troubling imagining the hard, remote Prime Elder functioning as a physician, even though the man did have a legitimate medical degree. "You're letting *Volnar* touch your bond-mate?"

Claude grimaced. "My sentiments exactly. But whatever we may think of him personally, it's a fact that he never trespasses. And the whole procedure was his idea after all."

"What?" Britt looked wide-eyed at Eloise. "Volnar suggested you get pregnant by Claude?"

"Well, Claude mentioned to Dr. Volnar that my one regret about our commitment was that I'd never have a child. Volnar sort of leaped on the idea."

"Pounced like a tiger," said Claude. "You know his obsession with interbreeding, Rodge." Roger certainly did, he himself being the product of such an experiment. Volnar was also Roger's advisor, and the Prime Elder's cold manipulation of Roger's upbringing was one reason he had as little contact with Volnar as possible. "I could practically see him salivating over the prospect of testing his latest brainstorm. I relayed the idea to Eloise, and she wanted to try, so we did. The first attempt failed. The second month, with the reserved— uh—specimen Volnar saved, we scored."

Britt put aside her empty glass and reclined next to Eloise, leaning on one elbow. "How have you been feeling?"

"Well—I'm queasy when I don't eat and when I eat too much, I'm sleepy all day long, and I run to the bathroom three times in every hour."

"Wonderful," said Britt. "Sounds like a textbook normal pregnancy."

Claude smiled at his wife's rueful expression. "I don't mind admitting it's a very intriguing experience."

"Easy for you to say," Eloise shot back. "Seriously, I never expected to be going through a first pregnancy in my forties—I'd given up on the idea long ago—but I'm thrilled."

Roger picked up a tinge of wistfulness in Britt's thoughts. [Beloved, do you wish—?]

[Good grief, no! I made that choice before we met. Still can't help wondering what it would feel like.] She derailed that train of thought and dug into her oversize purse. When she took out a wrapped package, Eloise got up and fetched a similar package from her suitcase.

"Merry Christmas," Britt said. "Or happy Yuletide, I guess."

"By all means," said Claude. "Appropriately pagan." He called himself a rational deist and found Roger's practicing Catholicism amusing.

Britt and Eloise opened the gifts while the two men watched. Britt and Roger always faced the archetypal "man who has everything" problem in buying for Claude, especially with gifts of food out of the question. This time they'd opted for a signed Arkham House first edition obtained through a local rare book dealer. Eloise goggled delightedly at the volume, and Claude made appreciative noises, smiling indulgently at her pleasure. The two of them presented Roger and Britt with a videotape of Claude's latest horror movie, scripted by Eloise, who remarked, "We haven't even seen the finished product ourselves yet."

"Great, we'll watch it at Roger's after dinner," said Britt. "The invention of the VCR must have been a great boon for you guys, culturally speaking. Before, it was crowded theaters or nothing."

Claude nodded. "Not that I'd classify ninety-nine percent of the stuff you see on film as culture." He glanced at his watch. "What time is that dinner reservation?"

Roger stood up and shrugged into his coat. "Six thirty. It's less than a ten minute walk, but we may as well go ahead."

"Yes, let's get it over with," said Claude with an exaggerated sigh.

Britt said, "We don't have to. I can whip up something for us at Roger's."

"Nonsense, I want to treat you ladies to a good meal. And I trust you chose the place well?" He helped Eloise into her coat.

"I like it, anyway," said Britt. "A restored Colonial inn up at the other end of Main Street."

A minute later, they were on their way. Roger noted that even in December they had to dodge a constant stream of pedestrians. He'd never quite fathomed the attraction of a narrow one-way street lined with overpriced shops, many of them chains that had driven out the native Annapolis merchants who used to dominate downtown. At least on Main Street, the city had done a thorough job of clearing the sidewalks, making a safe path for Britt and Eloise. Still, with the impractical mid-height heels on their boots, the two women fell behind Roger and Claude's long strides.

Roger overheard Britt murmuring to Eloise several yards back, "Think we should remind them they're leaving us in the dust?"

"No, I hate to slow them down," said Eloise. "Let 'em race ahead; maybe they'll work up an appetite."

Britt dropped her voice slightly. "I never noticed they had to work at it."

Roger felt himself blushing. "Confound it, women are absolutely shameless."

"You've just got around to noticing that?" said Claude. "And you a psychiatrist. Their appetites are ordinary men's loss and our gain, *n'est-ce pas?*"

"No doubt, but there's a time and place for everything."

By silent consent, they paused to let their companions catch up. "Tell me about this restaurant," said Claude.

"I did my best," said Britt, taking Roger's arm. "It's not Italian, Mexican, or Oriental, and I asked for the non-smoking section. We're early enough that there shouldn't be a crowd, and we'll get in and out quickly."

Once they were seated, the waiter did appear with commendable promptness. Eloise admired the Colonial tavern decor, and Claude pronounced his approval. While the two women ordered every course the menu offered, from cream of crab soup on, Claude performed his usual dining-out evasive maneuver—ordering a couple of light dishes that he would covertly pass on to his wife—and Roger asked for his customary rare steak.

"Why couldn't I have settled into a society that views eating in public as obscene?" Claude sighed after the waiter vanished to fetch their drinks.

"That would certainly save trouble," said Roger.

"Why should it bother you? At least you can eat meat." He absent-mindedly shifted the burning candle from the center to the edge of the table out of his direct line of sight.

"Quit complaining," said Eloise. "You'll get yours later."

"Restaurants really are difficult for them, though," Britt said, glancing at Roger as he took a sip of the martini he'd ordered. Already he needed chemical insulation from the smoke that drifted from the adjoining room. Sitting in a cigarette-free zone didn't provide enough protection for senses as acute as his. Britt said teasingly, "Maybe we should write an article on the covert anti-vampire prejudice in contemporary culture." A passing busboy gave her a dubious look. "Look at the Bible—all those derogatory references to darkness."

The waiter appeared with a tray full of salads, which he passed to each of them. Claude pushed his toward Eloise. "The entire Bible isn't stacked against us. There's a Psalm that compares the Deity's protection to *shadow* and promises *the sun will not strike you by day nor the moon by night.*" Roger always found Claude's knowledge of Scripture incongruous. Like many members of their species born within the past three hundred years, Claude, through overexposure to human superstitions, had developed a psychosomatic aversion to religious objects.

"Not just the Bible," said Britt. She sprinkled oil and vinegar on her salad and passed the decanters to Eloise. "Popular songs are full of that stuff. *You are my sunshine.* And think of ethnic slurs like Count Chocula—degrading stereotype of a minority group."

"Would you include the Count from *Sesame Street?*" said Eloise.

"Oh, I don't think he's degrading. He's actually kind of cute." Britt nibbled thoughtfully on her lettuce before continuing, "I've been thinking of writing an article for the *Journal of Popular Culture* on the monsters on *Sesame Street.* Maybe we could collaborate. The characterization of the Count is very suggestive, psychologically. That obsession with numbers, for instance."

"I wonder if the creators of the show know about the superstition that a vampire can be neutralized by scattering seeds around his grave, so he has to count them until the sun rises?" said Eloise.

"*I* wonder," said Britt, "if they've really thought through the implications of those orgasmic thunderclaps."

Claude stared at her. "Dear lady, you're making that up!"

"Oh, I forgot you don't follow children's public TV. No, it's true. Counting is this character's addiction. When he finishes a number sequence, he's rewarded with thunder and lightning. And if he's somehow prevented from counting, he gets frustrated and twitchy. The thing ought to be rated X!"

Roger said, "Colleague, you must remember that the general public doesn't have minds as devious as ours."

"True." Britt contemplated her half-finished salad with a sigh. "Sometimes I miss real salad dressing." She and Eloise had to stick with plain oil and vinegar to avoid garlic.

Roger switched his untouched salad for Britt's almost empty bowl. "Who's to deliver the baby? Surely not Volnar?"

"Only in case of complications, thank goodness," said Eloise. Conversation was suspended while the waiter came around with dinner plates. Claude had requested soup as his main course, a dish he could dabble in without drawing attention to his lack of intake.

After the waiter left again, he said, "The custom is for a female relative to serve as midwife. The closest we have is Helga, our mother's cousin. She likes you, strangely enough," he said to Roger. "She's also in favor of the hybridization experiments."

"Placing her in a distinct minority." Roger cut into his steak, relieved to see that the chef had prepared it according to his specifications—nearly raw.

"Be that as it may, Helga's solidly behind us, and she happily agreed to deliver Eloise's baby when the time comes. So that's settled."

Later in the meal Britt turned the conversation to the science fiction convention Claude and Eloise would be attending Friday through Sunday. "Isn't it unusual for both of you to go to a con together?"

Eloise said with a teasing smile, "I have to tag along with him sometimes. Can't leave him alone too often with those groupies dying to get their necks bitten."

"Really, my love, as if you didn't trust me!"

"I trust you just fine, it's the fans I don't trust."

Roger knew their banter was just that, for Claude couldn't even be tempted by another woman, however healthy and willing. His bond with Eloise constituted a literal, biochemical addiction, as did Roger's with Britt.

"What all will you be doing at this con?" Britt asked.

"I have the usual panel on vampires in literature, and Claude will do his thing on the horror movie panel. He also has a guest of honor speech at the banquet. I'm giving a writers' workshop Saturday afternoon."

"Also, we'll do a folk singing performance Friday after the Regency Ball," said Claude.

Roger recalled Claude's mention of this act being added to their repertoire, but he'd never heard Claude and Eloise sing. "What sort of folk songs?"

"The standards, slanted toward the darker and gorier specimens from Child's collection. Homo saps can be incredible ghouls, y'know."

"I hate to admit it, but that's what everybody wants," Eloise said. "Incest and infanticide. Tragic deaths and vengeful ghosts."

"Like 'Barbara Allen'?" said Britt.

"Lots of people ask for 'Barbara Allen,' sure, but that's awfully tame. They get more of a kick out of stuff like 'The Well Down In The Valley.' Girl has five babies by an assortment of male relatives and buries them all over the farm."

"Careless," Britt remarked. "Somebody should have given her birth control information. I'd love to hear you two sing."

Eloise blushed. "Well, I could bring the guitar along tonight, if you really—"

"Please do!"

The waiter reappeared, pen and notebook poised. Roger suppressed a sigh of relief. For the past several minutes the heavy perfume of a lady at the next table had been making him feel suffocated.

Britt checked her watch. "We have plenty of time. Couldn't do any harm to peek at the dessert cart—"

Eloise picked up the cue. "Yeah, maybe I could find room for a chocolate mousse—"

Roger glared at Britt, though he knew as well as Claude probably did that the women were teasing them.

Britt threw Roger a wicked grin and said to the waiter, "Just the check, please." To Eloise she added, "There's plenty of ice cream at Roger's, and I get the feeling the guys would rather have—dessert—there."

A few minutes later they separated, Eloise and Claude walking back to the hotel to pick up their rented car rather than riding with Roger and Britt, who walked to Britt's apartment to collect Roger's car. Then they drove at once to his townhouse across the Severn River.

Shortly they pulled up in the parking lot outside Roger's condominium. He changed from his suit into a more casual outfit while

Britt started coffee. By the time he joined her downstairs, Claude and Eloise had arrived. Eloise had exchanged her dress for jeans and a long-sleeved sweatshirt that inquired, "Have you petted your werewolf today?" She carried a tote bag, Claude a guitar case.

"Can you drink coffee?" Britt asked.

"This time of night, I can. But no ice cream yet, unless you really want to. I'm temporarily stuffed." Eloise patted her abdomen.

"How early could you tell she was pregnant?" Roger asked Claude. "As a matter of medical interest."

Claude leaned against the hearth while Roger set a match to the logs already stacked in the fireplace. "A week after fertilization—about the time of implantation, I suppose. If I probed deeply, even then I could sense another life in her body. But not a mind. I still don't sense a separate personality."

"Interesting," said Britt, switching on the Christmas tree lights. Early in their relationship she'd had an uphill battle persuading Roger to indulge in such seasonal decorations.

Claude strolled over to the window. "Coming down nicely, isn't it? I haven't seen snow in months, and I could do with a walk. What about you, Rodge?"

The thought of fresh air and exercise appealed to Roger too. Hesitating only long enough to ascertain that their companions really didn't mind being left, he agreed to Claude's suggestion.

Woods surrounded the townhouse complex, tucked away on a side lane off St. Margaret's Road. For several minutes Roger and Claude walked in silence under the trees through the gentle but steady snowfall. Roger felt Claude's residual tension from the cross-country airline trip fading away. After a while Roger said, "If you want to hunt, feel free. We have deer, opossums, squirrels, raccoons—"

"Enough, you sound like that waiter reciting the day's specials. No thanks, old man, I'll save my appetite for—dessert."

Roger's stomach cramped with hunger in spite of the steak he'd forced himself to finish. "I, too. I wish Britt wouldn't be so outspoken in public." He deliberately changed the subject. "How do you feel about becoming a father? The role is quite alien to you." Young vampires were cared for by their mothers until weaning, then turned over to a mentor for the rest of their education. The male parent played a purely genetic role.

"That's an understatement. Dying to psychoanalyze me, are you? Well, I don't mind talking about it." Claude ducked under a low-hanging branch. When they'd moved on to a clearer path, he continued,

"I'm doing this for Eloise. Having a child means so much to her. I can certainly spare twenty years or so to fulfill that wish. And it will be an interesting challenge." He gave a shaky laugh. "I expected that someday, in the very distant future, I might be assigned as a child's advisor. But not now—and not a newborn infant."

"Being a parent is not the same as serving in a mentor capacity."

"So I gather. Hell, I should be asking you for advice. You were brought up in a human family with two parents—one male, one female. And you've sired a child."

"That doesn't make me a father, only a sperm donor." Roger couldn't keep a trace of resentment out of his voice.

"I hope you don't still bear a grudge against Juliette for that?"

"Certainly not, I never have. It wasn't her fault. Volnar manipulated both of us."

"I've often wondered why you agreed to produce a baby. At first you were dead set against it."

"Believe it or not, it was Britt who convinced me that Volnar had a point about hybrid vigor, my duty to the species, and all that. Only I didn't have a clear understanding beforehand of what the—procedure—would be like. Humiliating is an understatement! But to be fair to Juliette, she hadn't been fully informed of how imperfectly I grasped the situation."

Claude broke into an easy trot. "You'd like Juliette, if you gave yourself a chance to get acquainted with her. She lives nearby, you know—Williamsburg. Teaches English at the college."

"I know, Volnar mentioned that. Also that she writes historical romances on the side, which puzzled me. I've been told so often that our kind aren't creative." He shifted his gait to keep pace with Claude.

"Have you ever read any of those novels? Creativity may be a factor, but it's not absolutely required. There's a formula. The main requirement is knowledge of the period, of which Juliette has an abundance. She specializes in the mid-Victorian era, the time of her own youth. She's a clever lady—minimizes her need for human donors by keeping three Irish wolfhounds, which are devoted to her. She claims they're almost as good as the real thing."

"I had no reason to pursue an acquaintance with her," Roger said. "It was made clear at the outset that I'd have no control over the child's upbringing."

"Have you ever met your daughter?" Claude stopped to lean against a tree, scooping up snow and meditatively packing it as he talked.

"Once. Juliette brought her up for a brief visit when the girl was about three. Really, Claude, I have nothing useful to tell you about fatherhood. What I've learned from listening to my human patients wouldn't help, because you aren't human. You'll have to work out your own pattern."

Claude tossed his snowball at a tree and started walking again, this time in the direction of the house. "The ladies will be missing us— or I devoutly hope so, anyway. You've restrained your prurient curiosity, but I know you want to ask how we obtained the specimen to impregnate Eloise."

"I don't have to ask. It must have been similar to my experience with Juliette. Volnar provided you with a female in estrus to get the— uh—mechanism started?"

Claude nodded. "Most humiliating experience of my entire life."

"But isn't genital sexuality devoid of emotional significance for you?"

Claude said with a rueful smile, "Little brother, this wasn't mating. This was masturbating into a glass container—repeatedly— while the woman responsible sat across the room giggling."

Roger arched his brows in skeptical inquiry. "Really? Juliette wasn't quite that bad."

"Oh, mine didn't snicker out loud, but close enough. It wasn't malicious. The lady simply didn't understand why I chose not to couple with her, using a condom."

"You didn't want to be unfaithful to Eloise."

"Precisely—a concept totally foreign to our kind. And illogical, when you think about it, since I can never share that with Eloise. Not to full consummation, anyhow."

"It may not be logical," Roger said, "but it feels entirely rational to me."

"Perhaps I'm acquiring human traits," said Claude, "after all these years with Eloise." He paused at the edge of the woods to look up into the densely swirling snowfall. "Certainly it's not normal to have such an intense attachment to an ephemeral. Damned if I care. It never gets any less intense It grows more powerful, the longer we're together. Have you found that?"

"Yes." He couldn't tell whether Claude was listening or not.

"You don't know how fortunate you are, Roger. What you stumbled onto with your first long-term liaison, it took me over two centuries to find—a woman who came to me of her own free will with her eyes open and her mind clear. I married her to bind her to me by the laws of her own kind. I never expected the union to become so vital to me. I'll do anything to preserve that."

When they went inside, they found Britt and Eloise drinking coffee in front of the fireplace. Britt had changed into a loose emerald and gold caftan. Candles burned on the mantle. Eloise picked up her guitar as Roger and Claude entered.

"About time you got back," said Britt. "I'm waiting to hear some folk songs."

"Only a couple," said Eloise. "I can't help feeling silly about singing in front of two people." The two women were facing each other on matching love seats in front of the fireplace. After Roger and Claude sat down next to their respective mates, Eloise said, "What shall we start with? Something special for Roger?"

Noting the silent glance Claude and Eloise exchanged, Roger had an unpleasant suspicion of what they were contemplating. "Please, not 'MTA'," he said. "Sylvia used to delight in torturing me with that blasted song."

There was a moment of awkward silence. Sylvia, a young female vampire, had been murdered fourteen years before by one of their own kind. Roger had discovered her body—and had finally destroyed her killer. "Very well," said Claude. "In deference to Sylvia's memory we'll skip the ordeal of poor old Charlie."

"I know the perfect thing," said Eloise. "Also a tribute to your home state, Roger." She strummed a chord, and the two of them launched into "The Ballad of Lizzie Borden."

After three choruses Roger declared abject surrender. Britt's delighted applause didn't help. Relenting, she said, "How about something serious. A vengeful ghost, maybe?"

"I have a better idea," said Eloise. "We've just started practicing 'True Thomas'." She and Claude alternated verses of the ballad of Thomas the Rhymer, with Claude singing the poet's lines and Eloise the Elven Queen's:

> "And see you not yon bonny road
> That winds across the ferny lea?
> That is the road to fair Elfland
> Where thou and I this night must be."

In counterpoint to Eloise's pleasant though not particularly strong soprano, Claude gave a rich Scottish cast to the narrator's lines:

> "It was a mirk, mirk night, there was no starlight;
> They waded through red blood to the knee,
> For all the blood that's shed on earth

Runs through the springs of that country."

At the conclusion of True Thomas' seven years in the realm of Faerie, the four of them sat in silence for a couple of minutes. Claude broke the mood by remarking, "Have you ever considered that Thomas' Queen of Elfland might have been one of us? One of the *longaevi*, neither hellish nor heavenly, never aging nor dying?"

Eloise's eyes lit up. "Interesting—I like that. She's like Keats' Belle Dame Sans Merci, with a taste for poetic young men."

"Yes, she takes more than she gives, yet none of them seems in any hurry to escape," said Claude.

Britt offered refills on the coffee. When no one took her up on that, she proposed they watch Claude's new film.

"Great," said Eloise, "I always like seeing how they fit in the special effects. And Claude enjoys nitpicking his own performance."

"Enjoy?" Claude protested. "*Cherie*, I writhe in agony."

She stuck her tongue out at him. "Don't give me that, you love every minute of it. Some kind of masochism, I guess."

"Naturally one wants to critique one's performance in order to improve it." He stepped over to the window and pulled aside the curtain. "Your flurry has turned into something of a blizzard."

Roger stopped in the middle of adjusting the position of the TV and joined Claude at the window. The snowfall was now so dense that it reduced visibility to a yard or two. Catlike night vision and superhuman reflexes wouldn't make it safe to drive in this. "It's just as well we have a movie to watch," Roger said. "You won't be going anywhere for the next couple of hours."

They settled down on the love seats, angled slightly for easy viewing of the television Roger had wheeled opposite the fireplace. He refused to grant the thing a central place in the living room when it wasn't in use. When he flicked on the remote, Claude said, "Now I can dissect my performance, and Eloise can cringe at the director's pointless shredding of her dialogue."

Eloise punched him in the chest, then curled up against him, his arm around her shoulders.

Britt silently asked Roger, [Why aren't we doing that, colleague?] [In public?]

[This isn't public; it's family. Loosen up!]

He stiffly put his arm around her, trying to act as if he didn't notice when she laid her head on his shoulder. Instead he focused his attention on Eloise's running commentary.

"This is the fairly typical good vampire-bad vampire plot.

Claude's character is trying to stop the evil vampire from continuing his rampage of senseless slaughter—"

"Yes, I've always preferred sensible slaughter," Claude interrupted.

Eloise pretended to ignore him. "Eventually, of course, the villain goes after the woman the hero is in love with. They have a terrific showdown in an abandoned, desecrated church. At least it was reasonably terrific the way I wrote it. I hope the special effects crew didn't screw it up the way they did Varney's suicide in the volcano in *Feast of Blood.*"

After several minutes of watching the villain stalk his first victim along a moonlit country lane, Claude muttered, "Will you look at that idiotic makeup job. Exaggerated—I didn't like it at the time, but I knew better than to say anything. Hoped the photography would soften the effect."

"If you two are going to tear apart every little detail," said Britt, "how are we supposed to enjoy the essential flavor of the story? Get into the mood?"

"I'm afraid the mood's lost on me," said Claude, idly running his fingers through Eloise's hair, which had somehow come unbraided. "Watching one of my films always reminds me of being smothered by the makeup and blinded by the lights."

Britt slipped her hand into Roger's and began caressing him with the ball of her thumb. "You don't get any thrill out of filming the— love scenes, if that's the word?"

"Hardly," Claude chuckled. "Eloise has nothing to worry about."

"Sometimes I regret getting into scriptwriting," she said, "because I don't get turned on just watching him in those scenes the way I did before we met. I'm too busy looking for mistakes. Kind of like what being a writer does to my reading style."

Roger, unfortunately, hadn't developed that immunity. When Claude played his first intimate scene with the leading lady, a tender, tentative approach broken off before his understated artificial fangs pierced her throat, Roger had to force himself not to squirm openly. Britt, blatantly enjoying his discomfort, kept drawing circles on the palm of his hand with her fingernails until he felt like snarling at her.

He did snarl mentally. [Confound it, will you stop that! We have guests, and I'm not prepared to throw them out into the blizzard!]

[Then maybe you should surrender to the inevitable and offer them the guest bedroom.] But she did stop tormenting him, only to stand up and say, "We promised you dessert, didn't we? Anybody for vanilla fudge ice cream?"

Eloise cheered for that suggestion, and Claude asked for a small serving to keep her company.

"Roger and I will get it," said Britt. "Don't bother stopping the VCR. We'll catch up later." She held onto Roger's hand and led him into the kitchen.

Once out of sight of the other two, he broke away from her handclasp. "Colleague, I suspect your interest in ice cream is secondary."

She stood on tiptoe to wrap her arms around his neck. "Perceptive of you."

"This is not a good idea. Why are you upsetting both of us when we can't—" Her supple curves fitted so tightly against him. Yielding, he leaned back against the refrigerator and returned her embrace. He felt the throb of her heart, basked in the heat she radiated. He couldn't resist tasting her mouth just for a second or two.

Some time later they paused for breath, her cheek rubbing his. "Maybe I should have listened to you," she whispered. Her lips brushed his earlobe.

"Stop that."

To his surprise and slight regret, Britt obeyed this time. "We'd better break out the ice cream," she said, breathing unsteadily, "or we'll never make it out of this room."

She opened the freezer and fumbled for the carton, while Roger got out bowls and spoons. With trembling hands Britt served a couple of scoops for Eloise, a smaller portion for Claude. "Here, take these in while I get some for myself. Hurry up before I attack you again."

Restraining himself from giving her one quick kiss, he followed her suggestion. In the living room Claude accepted the bowl of ice cream with an irritatingly knowing look. Roger wished the snow would ease up. He'd lost interest in seeing the rest of the movie.

A knock at the back door replaced his irritation with surprise.

[I'll get it,] Britt told him.

[Let me—you don't know what—] She was already turning the doorknob, though. Roger sensed trepidation, not hostility, on the other side.

He heard Britt open the door. Blank astonishment filled her mind. [Britt, what is it?]

[There's a girl out here—thirteen, fourteen, I don't know. Thin, pale, with huge eyes, red hair, and a ridiculous outfit for the weather.]

Viewing the visitor through Britt's eyes, Roger came to the

obvious conclusion before she articulated it.
    [Roger, she's a vampire.]

## Chapter Three

AT ONCE ROGER knew who the pale, thin girl with gleaming eyes—the eyes of a wild creature poised for flight—had to be. "Come in, Gillian." Before she could think of disobeying he grasped her arm, drew her inside, and bolted the door.

He felt a quiver in the cold flesh under his hand. She boldly met his stare, though. "Good evening, Dr. Darvell. Or should I call you Father?" The tone of the question verged on insolence.

Roger tried to barricade his emotions as he replied, "Since that relationship doesn't exist in your subculture, I don't think it would be appropriate." The girl flinched, a reaction she quickly suppressed. Roger felt a stab of guilt.

Britt said icily, "Well, I hope you aren't planning to make her keep calling you by your title!"

Gillian cast another apprehensive look at Britt.

"This is my associate, Dr. Britt Loren," said Roger, maintaining his grip on the unexpected guest. "She knows about you. Now, isn't Volnar here?" He knew better but hated to concede the fact.

"You want to talk in front of an ephemeral?" Gillian still looked prepared to dash off into the night at the faintest provocation.

Roger struggled to control his impatience with her. "I trust Dr. Loren implicitly. You may discuss anything in her presence."

"But not standing in the middle of the kitchen," Britt interrupted. Roger felt her pity for the child. "Can't you make her comfortable before you start grilling her?" She lowered her voice as she turned to Gillian. "I'll bet you ran away from Dr. Volnar, didn't you?" Roger sensed Britt fighting the desire to touch the girl. A young vampire who knew almost nothing about ephemerals wouldn't readily accept comfort from one.

Gillian nodded, keeping her eyes on Roger. "Are you going to send me back?"

"Not right this minute," said Roger. He led her to the living room.

At the sight of Eloise, Gillian tensed again. "Relax," Roger said. "My brother, Claude, and his wife, Eloise Kern."

Surprise displaced Gillian's fear. "You're married to an ephemeral?" She scanned Eloise more closely. "And she's pregnant!"

Roger strove to hide his amusement at Gillian's shock. Claude didn't even try. "Well, *mon enfant*, you must be my niece. Why does that disturb you so much? You're a product of a similar union yourself."

"I never asked to be!" She glared at Roger, then at Britt and Eloise. "Do you expect me to talk about myself in front of your pets?" Eloise radiated a rueful humor that echoed Britt's.

Roger squelched his impulse to slap Gillian. "Understand, young lady—Dr. Loren and Dr. Kern are not pets. They are our lovers, friends, and equals. You will grant them the same respect you give us."

Gillian visibly wilted. "Yes, sir." She evaded his eyes and turned to Claude, who showed no threatening anger. "What should I call you—Uncle Claude?"

He switched off the television. "No, that title belongs to the mother's brother. The father's has no official status. You may as well keep things simple and address us all by our first names."

"Very well, I suppose that's best," Roger said.

"If that's settled," said Britt with an impatient frown at Roger, "can you stop badgering her for the moment? Sit down, Gillian."

Eloise made room on one of the love seats for Gillian, who gazed at Eloise across the foot of space separating them as if the human female were some sort of exotic beast. As if involuntarily, Eloise's hand stretched out toward Gillian. The girl edged farther away. Projecting disappointment, Eloise backed off.

Britt said, "How long have you been running?"

"Two days and two nights. I left Dr. Volnar in Atlanta." And she looked it. Melting snow plastered her wet hair to her head. Under the damp, mud-splashed jacket, which she had unzipped, her blouse hung in shreds. Her tennis shoes were soaked through.

"How did you get here?" Roger asked. "Did you have money?"

"Not enough." She was beginning to relax now. "I took the bus part of the way and hitchhiked part." A shadow of remembered fear flickered in her eyes. "It was harder than I expected. I slept in the woods today—or yesterday, I suppose."

Britt got up from the other love seat. "Poor kid, you must be exhausted. And starving."

"Dr. Volnar has always told me not to exaggerate," said Gillian. "I am extremely hungry, yes."

She made no attempt to keep from broadcasting her hunger. Roger's stomach cramped in sympathy. Britt was already kneeling beside the couch, pushing up the sleeve of her caftan.

Roger's hand closed on her shoulder. "Britt, no!" In response to Britt's outraged glare, he elaborated, "She's too young for human blood. Aren't you, Gillian?"

Gillian nodded. "I have never tasted it. Dr. Volnar says I shouldn't need it for another two years or more."

"And that's starting young," said Claude. He perched on the arm of the couch next to Eloise, who leaned toward Gillian as if she, too, would open her veins if it were allowed.

Britt stood up, moving toward the kitchen. "Then how about a nice bloody chunk of raw dead cow?"

A flash of injured pride shot through Gillian's exhaustion. "I'm much too old for *that*. I've had my adult teeth for over a year." She bared them, displaying deceptively human-looking incisors and canines.

"Yes, I see," said Britt gravely. "Do you eat vanilla ice cream? Have mine, while I whip up something more substantial."

Since she was thoroughly familiar with the contents of Roger's kitchen, he let her proceed with the job alone while he pulled up a straight-backed chair to Gillian's side. He tried to study her profile unobtrusively. Did she resemble him in any way? All he could see in her so far were Juliette's sharp features and Irish Setter red curls. "Now perhaps you'll tell me why you ran away from your advisor."

After taking a spoonful of ice cream, Gillian said, "He ordered me to bond with him—to exchange blood."

"You knew that would happen eventually," said Claude. "Aren't you rather young for it, though?"

She licked chocolate sauce from the spoon and scooped up another bite. "Yes. I started—seeing—seeing auras, feeling emotions. It came upon me suddenly, in a theater—" She broke off, as if the memory choked her.

Roger felt an unwilling surge of sympathy. He recalled with painful vividness how terrifying his own first experience of psychic perception had been. Would knowing about it in advance make the transition much less traumatic?

Claude said in an even, soothing tone, "Most unfortunate for you, especially since you shouldn't have begun this early. But didn't you realize that bonding with your advisor would ease the discomfort? How else can he teach you to shield against that flood of impressions?"

"Maybe it works that way for real vampires," she said. The bitterness in her voice surprised Roger. "I have human genes. Suppose I can't stand the touch of his mind? Suppose I'm not strong enough?"

"Where the—" An unexpected spasm of anger momentarily silenced Roger. He forced himself to speak calmly. "Where the blazes did you get an idea like that? From Volnar?"

"Of course not. Some of the other elders—I couldn't help overhearing them, sometimes. The ones who don't believe I ought to exist. They think I'm contaminating the gene pool. They are waiting for my—defects—to show. And Dr. Volnar's mind is very ancient and powerful."

"Gillian, that's nonsense." Roger knew neither the words nor the tone would be likely to comfort her, but, damn it, he knew nothing about comforting children. In his psychiatric practice he never accepted patients under age sixteen. He knew that letting her sense his smoldering rage at her being branded "inferior" wouldn't help. "Volnar is my advisor, too. He bonded with me, when I was far less prepared than you are, and it didn't burn out my brain. And I'm more human than you."

She took one more bite of ice cream, swallowing hard, and abandoned the bowl on the coffee table. "What do you care? You never wanted me to exist either."

Roger flinched at the sting of her anger. "Surely you don't take that personally? I didn't appreciate being manipulated into such an important action. It had nothing to do with you. How could it? I didn't know who you would be." *Good God, am I actually defending myself to this vampiric juvenile delinquent?* Yet he couldn't deny that he wanted her respect.

To his relief, at that moment Britt reappeared from the kitchen. She carried a mug from which an appetizing scent emanated— appetizing to Roger and Claude, at any rate. "Best I could do on short notice," she said. "Raw calves' liver, minced, blended with broth and heated to body temperature."

Sniffing the concoction, Gillian said, "I don't like eating dead blood."

Britt, shielding her amusement from Gillian, remarked silently to Roger, [A domesticated predator like Sigmund, hmm?]

Claude reached for the mug. "Until one of us has time to take you hunting, that's all you're going to be offered. If you want to function in human society, you have to accept compromises. But if you're not that hungry—" He started to raise the mug to his lips.

She snatched it from him and drained half of the drink before pausing for breath.

"Slow down or you'll be sick," Claude chuckled. "What have you been doing for the past two nights, anyway?"

Eloise and Britt leaned forward in their seats, eager to hear the story. Gillian gave them each a nervous glance before beginning. "The day before yesterday, as soon as Dr. Volnar fell asleep, I took all the cash from his wallet and bought a bus ticket for Richmond. That was as far as I could afford. That night I found a ride on Interstate 95."

"Wait a minute," said Eloise. "Doesn't your mother live in Williamsburg—Juliette Fontaine, the romance author?"

Gillian nodded. "Yes, that is the pen name she uses. She's Julia Frost to her acquaintances in the area. But she is not in Williamsburg now. Dr. Volnar and I were on our way to meet her in New York."

Britt said, "Obviously you had a reason for not calling her there and asking for help."

Gillian shrugged. "I could have gotten in touch with her through her publisher, I guess. But she would send me back to Dr. Volnar. I thought Dr.—Roger might not."

"I'm suspending judgment," said Roger. "Go on."

Gillian took a sip of her drink. "Now that I think of it, I might have hidden at Juliette's home. The property is large, and the dogs know me. But Dr. Volnar might search there first. So I think I've done the most logical thing. I was picked up by a William and Mary professor named Adam Greer." Roger heard her heartbeat speed up.

"Hey, I know his work," Britt said. "Popular culture stuff on Bigfoot and so forth."

"Right," said Eloise. "In fact, I've appeared on a panel with him. And I believe he's scheduled for Yulecon this weekend."

"He mentioned that to me," Gillian said. "He offered to take me all the way to Annapolis, since it wasn't far off his route. But the car—" She drew a tremulous breath. "He lost control on the ice—skidded into a tree—"

Roger rested his hand on hers, trying to project a calm he didn't feel. Whatever event she was working up to, he knew he wouldn't like it.

Britt mentally cautioned him, [Don't be hard on her. It must have taken incredible nerve and stamina for her to make it here alone. She needs sympathy, not criticism.]

[I'm aware of that, colleague. I just don't know how to give it to her.]

"I changed shape. It never happened before, and I didn't know how to control it. Greer *saw* me!" Gillian ducked her head as if expecting one of them to bite it off.

"Oh, my God," said Roger.

Claude leaned across Eloise to pat Gillian's shoulder. "Brace up, little one, it's not the end of the world. If he's like most Homo saps, he won't believe what he saw. He's probably already edited the memory to death."

Gillian let out a pent-up sigh. Roger heard Britt remark inside his head, [But Greer isn't like most people. Given his area of specialization, he's primed to believe.]

[If true, I suggest we not mention that to Gillian.]

[Of course not, colleague, don't you think I have any tact?]

Claude said, "It's unprecedented for the power to surface that young. Just the opposite of what your background would lead one to expect. Then what? You ran from him?"

Gillian nodded. "When I ran out of energy, I slept in the woods. After sunset I traveled on foot until I could steal this jacket—in an empty house—and then I found another ride to Washington."

"No disasters occurred with that one, I hope?" said Roger.

Claude gestured him to silence. "Less of it, Rodge. Then what?"

"I asked for directions to the bus station. On the way, a group of boys attacked me. I—it happened again." She didn't blush—apparently she hadn't inherited that human trait—but she looked mortified enough. "I had to hurt them."

Britt and Eloise listened with avid interest and no sign of fear. Roger sensed Gillian's surprise at this open acceptance.

"You didn't drink from them, I hope?" said Claude.

Gillian shook her head. She didn't seem to mind the interrogation. Roger supposed Volnar frequently debriefed her in the same way. "One of them was badly injured, though. I took his money to pay for the bus ticket. I rode to the stadium in Annapolis and walked the rest of the way here."

"No wonder you're tired," said Eloise.

Britt got up to reclaim the empty mug. "I hope the one you robbed didn't die—though it would serve him right."

"She probably asked for it, though," said Claude.

Indignation flared from both the women. Roger cut through their mental and verbal protests. "Crass as that sounds, I agree. I know what he means. Britt, don't you remember my telling you what difficulty I used to have in social situations? Even more so than most doctors, I was constantly plagued by people asking for free diagnosis."

Britt calmed down and considered that.

Leaning back against Claude's chest, Eloise said, "Now I think I see. You've complained about the fans mobbing you whenever you let down your guard. It's a kind of involuntary magnetism, isn't it?"

Claude nodded. "*Certainement*. Especially when we're hungry, as Gillian must have been. Transforming drains energy, even more so when you aren't used to it. Gillian, you must learn to turn it off at will."

"Yes, sir. Are you saying that they might have ignored me if I hadn't been—projecting?"

"Precisely. And that's one important skill you need your mentor's guidance for."

"I hope you're not going to start scolding her again," said Britt. "She needs to rest. And I'll bet you'd like a shower, wouldn't you?"

"Yes, please." Standing up, Gillian flashed a mechanical smile. "Thank you."

"Good try," said Claude, "but you'll have to work on it. Ephemerals don't respond well if you look as if you're baring your teeth at them. Oh, don't look so stricken. You'll catch on by osmosis, after you've associated with them for a while. The important thing is not to appear obviously different. If a monkey is dyed pink and returned to the cage, the other monkeys will attack it."

Britt beckoned to Gillian. "Come on, before those two start in on you again. I'll lend you a robe, and maybe we can find a shirt to replace that blouse." She led the way down the hall.

Roger bowed his head on his hands. "Good Lord, what have I done to deserve this?" He looked over at Eloise. "Are you still sure you want one of those?"

Eloise laughed. "It'll be a challenge, all right. Roger, what are you going to do with her?"

"For one thing, I won't force her to go back to Volnar. Not right away at any rate. I understand all too well how she feels."

"If it comes down to that, I sympathize, too," Claude said. "But you're not equipped to train her. She does need his guidance."

"Damn it, I know that. And I have no intention of keeping her, either."

"Are you going to notify Volnar that she's here?"

"Not now," Roger said. "That would destroy any trust in me she might have."

He heard water running in the shower upstairs. Britt walked into the room, came up behind him, and began rubbing the back of his neck. "I feel sorry for the kid. She doesn't know what to make of me. Roger, I wish you hadn't stopped me from giving her a drink. I could *feel* her

hunger—I wanted to help her in the worst way." One of the benefits—
or hazards—of their bond was Britt's heightened sensitivity to all
psychic influences.

Eloise murmured her agreement. Claude, caressing her unbound
hair, said, "Very generous of both of you, but it *would* be the worst
way. Introducing her to human blood before she needs it would incite a
craving that she couldn't easily satisfy, which is hardly doing her a
favor. Besides, when she does reach that stage, starting her off with a
willing donor would be a disservice."

"I don't like it," said Roger, "but I understand. She needs to learn
to hunt."

"Yes. How often can she expect to find someone like these rare
treasures?"

Eloise lightly slapped his exploring hand. "That's almost as bad
as *pet*."

"For that matter, too much exposure to you at this impressionable
phase wouldn't be good for her in any way. Look, *cherie*, if you had an
orphaned fox cub you planned to release into the wild, would you
socialize it to human companionship?"

Eloise's eyes widened in realization. "Oh."

"I see," Britt said. "And I don't like it either. She's been taught
that we're dangerous animals—and for her own good, we can't
undermine that idea too much."

"I don't mean you have to reject her advances, if any," said
Claude. "Just never let her believe you're anything but exceptions."

Roger relaxed into Britt's massage. "How do you account for the
premature—explosion—of her powers? As you said, with her human
heritage one would expect her to start late, as I did."

"Looks like the genes combine differently in each case," Britt
said. "And she's only one-fourth human. Maybe just human enough to
start maturing at twelve, as the average girl would—except that it's the
vampiric form of puberty."

The shower cut off. Claude said, "I do believe you've got
something there, dear Doctor."

"Shouldn't we talk about it some other time?" said Eloise. "She
can probably hear every word we say."

"Of course," said Claude, "so why pretend otherwise?" He picked
up the remote control and restarted the movie. "If you plan to let her
stay here awhile, you'll have to substitute for Volnar—give her a crash
course in blending into human society. Think you can handle that?"

"That's a rhetorical question, I presume," Roger said. "What I'm hoping is to persuade her to return to him of her own free will."

Britt, to Roger's annoyance, sat down on his lap with one arm around his neck. "She certainly won't blend in the way she is now. I can't decide whether she comes across as a precocious ten-year-old or an underdeveloped eighteen-year-old. I hope I'll get some chance to talk to her at length before she's spoiled by too much exposure to us ordinary mortals. For analyzing how vampires think, Roger is practically useless. And Claude—"

Half his attention on his own videotaped image, Claude said, "Analyzing me wouldn't get you very far. I've had over two centuries of corruption by you seductive creatures."

"I was about to say that I've never been able to pin you down long enough. If you'd at least spare me a couple of hours to discuss your dreams—"

"No Jungian archetypes there, dear lady. As you ought to know from Roger, our dreams are deadly dull."

"I have tried to explain that," Roger said. "Very transparent anxiety and wish-fulfillment motifs. Our unconscious conflicts, if any, express themselves through different outlets."

Eloise shook her head in sympathy. "Lost cause, Britt. And hardly worth pursuing, since they don't dream more than an hour or two per week."

Claude scowled at the TV. "Must they overdo the fog effects in those dematerializing scenes?" He broke off as Gillian came into the living room.

She wore a bathrobe of russet terrycloth, too long for her and cinched tight by a sash around the waist. Fragrances of soap, shampoo, and mouthwash had replaced the odors of blood and damp earth that had clung to her a few minutes before. "Is that a horror movie? Dr. Volnar has never allowed me to watch one."

"Good for him," said Claude. "No doubt he explained why?"

Still standing in the middle of the room, Gillian said, "Because we're so adaptable while growing up that we absorb the attitudes and beliefs of those around us, unless careful corrective measures are taken. That is why he prescribes a varied diet of television and reading for me." Her recitative tone softened into one that verged on pleading. "But I'm old enough to discriminate now, aren't I? Isn't that one of your films?"

"Yes, and I doubt that a few minutes of it could hurt you. What do you say, Rodge? You're the authority figure here."

*Not by choice!* "I can't see any harm in it."

Gillian flashed her feral smile in gratitude. "Anyway, I have this to remind me that it's only fiction." She pulled a delicate gold chain out of the bodice of the robe. On the end of it, a small cross glinted in the firelight.

Claude's eyes shifted. "Volnar gave you that? Ingenious idea."

Roger had to admit it was. "The purpose being to symbolize your freedom from human superstitions about our kind? Good—see that you don't forget it."

Gillian sat on the rug, her legs folded under her in half-lotus. While she watched the movie, Roger watched her. *What am I supposed to do with this waif? I can't supervise a child; I don't have expertise or even the time!* Concentrating on that problem helped to distract him from the heat of Britt's strong, slender body and the liquid rhythm of her heartbeat.

When the film ended with the death of the villain at the fangs and talons of Claude's character, Gillian extended her arms in a catlike stretch and stared up at Roger. "I've heard you did that once—you killed a member of our own species."

Roger's jaws clenched involuntarily. Thinking of Neil Sandor, the renegade vampire he'd destroyed fourteen years before, still had the power to elevate his blood pressure. "Did your informants tell you that I killed him in self-defense? And that he had murdered a young woman of our race, not to mention an unknown number of human victims?"

Gillian looked confused. Claude, setting the tape on rewind, interjected, "Sandor was a jackal. Not only did he have sloppy feeding habits, he robbed others of their legitimate prey. Roger performed a public service by killing him."

Roger said, "I wouldn't view it quite that way—"

Claude cut him off. "That is how we view it. A responsible hunter doesn't slaughter indiscriminately. Even human conservationists know that."

Gillian, more perplexed than belligerent now, said to Roger, "You seem to consider it more important that Sandor killed ephemerals."

"I do." He put a possessive arm around Britt's waist to combat the memory of her helpless in the renegade's grip. "Sandor threatened Britt. He would have taken her if I hadn't killed him."

Gillian reclined, leaning back on both elbows, and searched Britt's face. "That would have made a difference to you?"

"Of course. I don't understand exactly what you're asking," said Britt.

"I mean, if someone is feeding on your blood, why should it

matter who?"

Roger felt Britt's bewilderment at that question. "Good grief, I don't know where to begin. It's a special relationship—he isn't a generic vampire to me, any more than all human females are interchangeable to him."

Gillian looked from Britt to Eloise. "It doesn't quite make sense to me. You associate with them voluntarily? Creatures who drink your blood? Why?"

Roger began, "You'll understand better when—"

"Colleague, I don't think it'll help to tell her she'll understand when she grows up," Britt interrupted. "Actually, Gillian, I keep him around to open jars and reach things on high shelves."

"Right," said Eloise. "And he always remembers where I parked the car."

"Also," Britt continued, "he gives the most unbelievably fantastic—"

[Britt!]

"—back rubs," she finished, censoring the bawdy phrase in her mind.

Gillian scanned their faces in confusion. "This is humor, yes?"

Claude unwrapped himself from Eloise and stood up, smiling. "One brand of it, anyway. Roger's correct to some extent; you won't understand until you've experienced a relationship like this yourself."

"Maybe not," said Gillian. "You're bonded with them. You have put your life into their hands, too. That would frighten me."

Claude held out a hand to her. "Come over here, infant, and listen to some facts of life from Uncle Claude."

She got up and stood in front of him, her hands clasped behind her back.

"Relax, you don't have to stand at parade rest. Now, I know you're afraid of bonding with Volnar. Frankly, I don't entirely blame you. Fearless Leader can be—formidable. But you must accept the fact that without that bond, you won't be able to absorb the skills you need." He patted her shoulder. "If you can't bring yourself to submit to your designated advisor, someone else will have to fill the gap. While Roger's detractors were telling you his misdeeds, did they happen to mention Sandor's background?"

Gillian shook her head.

"His refusal to bond with his advisor led to the isolation in which he spent his life. Unguided, he picked up the worst stereotypes about our kind and lived them."

"All too obvious," Britt said, "even from the little I saw of him—trying to overwhelm me with all that *eye of the hawk, soul of the tiger* flamboyance."

"And brain of the great white shark," said Claude disdainfully. "He thought with his appetite. That's what got him killed."

Britt silently protested, [Claude's trying to scare her.]

[Perhaps a good scare, judiciously applied, is what she needs.]

Gillian gazed wide-eyed at Claude. Unshielded, she broadcast her apprehension. "If I have to bond with anyone, I'd rather it be you. Or Roger."

Roger's chest constricted at the thought. What help could he give her? Even Claude would do a better job as mentor.

Claude gave her comforting touch, carefully avoiding the chain that held the gold cross. "No need to worry about it tonight. You can think it over for a few nights. Meanwhile, there are a few skills I can help you with."

Eloise hid a yawn behind her hand. "Not right now, I hope. I'd love to watch, and I don't think I can stay awake much longer. Jet lag and all."

"Tomorrow night is soon enough," said Claude, sitting down and pulling her into his lap. "Gillian needs to rest, and I think she's still hungry, aren't you?"

Gillian hesitated before whispering, "Yes, sir."

Roger sensed her reluctance to admit weakness in front of Britt and Eloise; they had already seen her at too much of a disadvantage. "In that case, I'll take you out now." Britt picked up the cue and got off his lap. "It sounds as if the snow has let up."

"Yes, and I heard the snowplow drive by a couple of minutes ago," said Claude. "We'd better go back to the hotel while we have the chance."

"You'll be here tomorrow night," said Gillian, "to teach me?" She cast an uncertain glance at Roger, as if still wondering whether she would be here the following night.

"Yes, please do," Roger quickly put in. "About six thirty."

He got Eloise's coat from the foyer closet, and after a flurry of goodbyes, Claude and Eloise drove away. Britt stifled a yawn. "Getting awfully late for us diurnal types." Unlike Eloise she was a morning person, who had difficulty keeping up with Roger's preferred hours. "I'm going to bed. See you when you get home."

Her silent promise sent a tingle of anticipation through him. No longer fighting her seduction, he looked forward to the pleasure they would share before dawn.

Outside, the snow had dwindled to an occasional flake. Roger led Gillian through the woods where he and Claude had walked a few hours earlier. She wore her jeans and the pilfered jacket, which had been washed and dried, along with a sweatshirt of Britt's. Since none of Britt's footwear would fit her, Gillian had to hike through the underbrush in her tennis shoes, soaking them all over again.

Once out of sight of the townhouse complex, Roger told Gillian to lead the way. He wanted to discover how well she could function on her own. He watched her sniff the cold air and circle silently, her ears figuratively perked. In a surprisingly short time, she pinpointed a raccoon perched in the fork of a tree no more than three hundred yards from the house.

Roger hung back while Gillian locked stares with the animal and crooned to it in a throaty growl. Roger recognized the sound as an amplification of the low rumble that sometimes vibrated in his own chest when he was sated and relaxed—Britt insisted on calling it a purr. The raccoon succumbed to the lure, inching its way down the tree trunk. Gillian stood frozen in a beckoning posture, her hands held out. As soon as the animal came within reach, she gathered it into her arms. The raccoon jerked once, quickly soothed into immobility by Gillian's hypnotic stroking.

After entrancing the raccoon, she walked over to Roger and silently offered him the furry bundle. So Volnar had made sure respect for her elders was deeply ingrained in her. Suppressing a smile, Roger said, "No, thank you, it's all yours."

She gave him a grateful look and bit into the raccoon's abdomen. The scent of blood made Roger salivate. He didn't want to consume any more bulk nourishment on top of the steak though; he was still saving his appetite for "dessert." While animal blood and milk, supplemented by moderate amounts of raw meat, filled his stomach and enabled him to function, he needed small, frequent doses of human blood, as ordinary people needed certain trace elements in their diet.

Except that the parallel wasn't exact, for human blood—Britt's— meant so much more. Mentally reaching for her, he found her already asleep. If she'd been awake, he might have accepted a taste of the raccoon, after all. When Britt empathically shared his kills, the bond infused animal blood with a hint of her own unique flavor, making it a little easier for him to do without her between weekends.

Gillian took less than ten minutes to drain her victim. Licking her lips with feline tidiness, she laid down the body. "Do we return to the house now?"

"Yes. It's close enough to dawn for us to sleep, I think." He checked his watch—after four. He and Britt had patients scheduled at nine.

Trotting through the woods, leaping fallen branches with the careless ease typical of her kind, Gillian said, "Why didn't you drink? You are hungry, aren't you?"

"One of those things you'll understand when you're older," Roger said. She ventured a smile, comfortable enough to sense he was joking. "I'm—thirsty. I don't need blood as such; I need hers."

After a moment's thought, Gillian said, "You are right, I guess. I can't understand yet. Dr. Volnar has never even let me watch him feed on a human donor."

"In this case, it's much more than feeding." His skin crawled with embarrassment at discussing such intimacies, even obliquely. Gillian must have sensed his discomfort, for she didn't pursue the topic.

Back at the house he waited while she washed up, then showed her to the guest room. Gillian unself-consciously stripped naked and snuggled into the bed. Roger shut the door and lingered outside it until he felt her sink into the deathlike torpor of daylight sleep, a matter of less than three minutes.

*She feels safe here. That's good, I suppose.* She assumed she would be allowed to stay for the next few days at least, and Roger and Claude had tacitly accepted the assumption. *What the blazes am I going to do with her?*

Roger gratefully shed that concern for the time being. Slipping into the master bedroom without waking Britt, he took a quick shower. Awareness of her waiting in his bed made his heart race. Naked, he returned to the dark bedroom and lay down next to Britt.

She slept on her side, facing away from him. Turning back the bedspread and satin sheet, he ran his hand lightly down her side and the swell of her hip. Contact with the silky fabric of her long-sleeved nightgown, warmed by her body, made the cilia in his palm tingle. She sighed in her sleep but didn't wake. As always, he was moved by the way she trusted him so deeply that his touch didn't disturb her. Right now, though, his arousal didn't leave much room for tender reflections.

He would have let her sleep, considering the short time left until they had to get up, if she hadn't spent most of the night deliberately goading him. Still, he paused to savor the peaceful sound of her breathing. So gently that she remained unaware, he slipped into her mind. Having noticed the REM flickers of her eyelids, he wasn't surprised to find her dreaming.

An erotic dream, clearly adopting its manifest content from Claude's film. Roger shared Britt's vision of a tower room with lightning flashing through the panes of stained glass windows. The two of them were locked in an embrace while blatantly symbolic thunder pealed around them. He smiled at her idealized image of him, draped in a crimson-lined black cape, more imposing than he ever managed to be in real life. As in most dreams Britt's picture of herself was blurred.

This dream was disturbingly tactile. Britt's unconscious mind recreated the painless sting of his teeth grazing her throat, the lapping of his tongue, and the rising tension at the core of her desire. He withdrew from direct immersion in her thoughts and skimmed over her body again. One of her hands was nestled between her thighs. He insinuated his own fingers there to caress her liquid heat.

The explosion of her climax woke her. Sharing the ecstatic convulsion sent waves of thirst shuddering over him. He held back, though, giving her his full attention. Breathing hard with the aftershocks, Britt turned in his arms to kiss him. She tasted so delicious that he could hardly resist taking her. But he didn't want to rush the consummation while she was still mostly asleep. Through the cloth he felt her erect nipples against his chest, a sensation that made him ravenous for more.

He tugged at the hem of the gown. "Take off the damned thing."

She let him help her out of it. "What about Gillian?" she whispered, nibbling his ear.

"Asleep. She can't possibly hear us."

"Dead to the world?" Britt murmured. The touch of her bare skin inflamed his sensitized nerves. "You're still cold," she said.

"You warm me, then."

She rose to the challenge with her customary enthusiasm. Being half-human, Roger could attain more than the typical male vampire's partial erection under direct stimulation. Conditioned by years of intimacy with Britt, he became fully hard under the intoxicating caresses of her mind and her fingers. She rolled on her back, inviting him to enter her, both of them delighting in the fact that since he didn't ejaculate, they could remain coupled as long as they wished. But his pleasure wasn't concentrated in that union. Rather, every cell of his body vibrated to the rhythm of her blood. When he pierced her throat, sensation radiated from that point throughout his being and hers, submerging both of them in a tide that flowed on and on until exhaustion forced them to stop.

He lay on his back, her head on his shoulder, his arm holding her close. "Rate it from one to ten?" she murmured, already fading into sleep.

He'd long since discovered that she really wanted an answer, rather than his automatic response of, "Off the scale." He said, "Five or six. It's better when we're both fully awake."

"*Mmm*," she agreed. "Poor Gillian—too young for this." She cuddled closer to him and drifted back to sleep.

Within a couple of minutes he joined her.


THE DESK CLERK at the Holiday Inn didn't enjoy renting a room at four a.m. Camille gave him a ten-dollar bill in compensation and retreated to the room as quickly as she could manage. She whistled under her breath as she deposited the suitcase on its stand, got out a bottle of sherry to pour herself a drink, and flopped across the bed with the glass and her purse. So far, so good. Was it possible they weren't bothering to chase her at all?

*Don't count on that. Concentrate on getting the job done.*

She dug out of her purse the local map she'd bought at an all-night gas station up the road. She unfolded it and set down her glass to open the nightstand drawer. Phone book. She flipped the yellow pages to "Physicians." With an indrawn breath of satisfaction, she zeroed in on the name she wanted. After a minute or two of searching the map's street index, she grinned and folded it open to the relevant sector.

*All right! It starts tomorrow.* She headed for the shower, humming "Mademoiselle from Armentierees" to the empty room.

## Chapter Four

GILLIAN WOKE HUNGRY. Nothing unusual in that; with adolescence, her appetite had become a constant inner demand. After a long, muscle-rippling stretch of arms and legs, she turned to look at the digital clock beside the guest room bed. Not quite two o'clock. She hissed in frustration at the dull hours ahead before Roger would come home to take her out for a meal.

Or maybe Claude. She liked her father's brother. Roger himself wasn't bad, either. At least he hadn't threatened to turn her over to Volnar yet. Gillian lay still for a minute, absorbing the atmosphere of the house. Though she'd been left alone in this unfamiliar place, she felt safe here. The air smelled cool and clean. Heavy green drapes dimmed the room for her visual comfort. Efficient insulation muted the occasional traffic sounds from outside. Within the townhouse, only the purr of the refrigerator and furnace cycling underscored the silence.

Gillian dressed, thinking about what she might find to appease her hunger until evening. Roger must keep milk in the house. Checking the refrigerator, she noticed a package of raw liver. Was she hungry enough to drink it pureed in broth, as she had last night? She decided not. As she'd said at the time, she didn't like the stale, dead taste of supermarket meat, though she had to accept it once in a while. She did squeeze juices from the liver into a mug, which she heated briefly in the microwave before gulping down the nearly tasteless contents. After that she warmed a cup of milk and took it into the living room to drink in front of the television.

On the coffee table she found a note from Roger: "You're welcome to read, watch television, or use the computer. I've left the chess program next to the hard disk. Remember to clean up after yourself. If the paper carrier comes to collect before I get home, pay him ten dollars. If the telephone rings, let the answering machine handle it. Do not under any circumstances leave the house. I'll be home shortly after five." Under the note was a ten dollar bill.

Good enough, she hadn't planned to go outside anyway, not in daylight. She tuned the TV to her favorite soap opera. Since she hadn't watched it in several days, there should have been time for the plot to advance. Maybe today Lila would get around to telling Brad she was pregnant with her cousin Lance's child. Gillian still couldn't comprehend why any man except her brother or uncle would care about a woman's pregnancy. Ephemerals were—different. Intriguingly different. Gillian's limited contact with them so far had only whetted her appetite for deeper firsthand knowledge. Judging from her disastrous experiments with the professor and those boys, playing with their minds could be a delicious pleasure, if only she knew how to control her powers. Claude would start teaching her tonight. She looked forward to that.

With only half her attention on the TV drama, she sipped the milk. Nourishing but far from satisfying. The memory of her attackers' lust and fear made her salivate. *I'm too young for human blood,* she reminded herself. She knew she ought to be grateful for her youth, which kept feeding simple and safe, without the complications of hunting intelligent prey. Sometimes, though, curiosity made her impatient. Four years, perhaps, she'd have to wait to find out what ephemerals tasted like. Or possibly longer, with her hybrid genes. She'd heard from Volnar that Roger hadn't tasted human blood until he was past twenty years old. But maybe he just hadn't recognized the need before then. And Gillian had only half his complement of human DNA; surely she wouldn't have to wait that long.

Curled up on one of the living room love seats, she couldn't help noticing the lingering traces of Britt Loren's scent. To a lesser degree, the presence of Claude's pet—bond-mate—Eloise clung to the room, too. Gillian's empathic perception had already developed far enough that she knew either one of the women would leap at the chance to feed her. Roger and Claude wouldn't allow that contact, of course, and Gillian's better judgment agreed with them. Still, she could fantasize and wish the situation were different.

*Only* fantasize. She sighed, watching over the rim of her mug as, on the TV screen, Lila and Brad flung crystal and china from the dinner table at each other. Never once had Volnar allowed Gillian to watch him feed. Oh, she'd seen the preliminaries, the stalking, the seduction. But he'd always barred her from witnessing the climax. How could she learn what to do if she couldn't observe?

When the soap opera ended, she rinsed out her cup and switched the TV to cartoons. She read Roger's *Wall Street Journal* at the same time, with little comprehension; Volnar hadn't taught her much about finance yet. After a half hour, the program gave way to a *G.I. Joe* episode she'd already seen. She changed the channel to public TV and watched until four. Growing restless, she decided to try out the computer chess game Roger had mentioned.

She'd just booted up the computer when the doorbell rang. Unfastening the deadbolt, she opened the door to face a teenage boy, about her height, with blond-streaked brown hair. To judge from the wind-reddened face above his bulky jacket, he was built lean.

He shoved a folded newspaper into Gillian's hands. "Hi. Collecting." He fumbled with a small spiral notebook. "Hey, I've never seen you here before. Dr. Darvell didn't move or something, did he?"

*Collecting?* Oh, yes, Roger's note mentioned paying the paper carrier. "No, I'm visiting him." Her brain ticked over rapidly. No doubt Roger wouldn't want the curiosity she would excite if she mentioned her true status. "We are second cousins." Considering the inbreeding that the vampires' low population made inevitable, that could even be true. "Please come in, you must be cold." Not only that, the open door was letting in an uncomfortable glare from the snow.

Once the door was shut, the boy trailed after Gillian into the living room. Welcoming the break in her tedious afternoon, she wished she could keep him for a while. "My name is Gillian. And yours?"

"Uh—Alex." He was looking around, openly curious about the furnishings as well as apparently puzzled about Gillian.

She made sure her fingers touched his when she handed him the ten-dollar bill. "Alex." She held his eyes with hers. "Sit down and rest for a few minutes."

"No way, I got a bunch more stops to make." But he automatically obeyed her.

Gillian tingled with pleasure at his instant submission. These creatures were so *easy!* Lightly her fingers brushed his. "Your hands are cold. Why don't you wear gloves?"

"Too much trouble, counting change and messing with the receipt book."

"Let me warm them."

"Hey—" The word of protest trailed off into a gusty sigh.

Sitting next to him, she stroked the backs of his hands to coax the blood to the surface. At once his pulse quickened. By the glow of his aura she sensed warmth suffusing his skin. "Tell me, Alex, what do you like to do?"

He shrugged without pulling back from her touch. "I'm into baseball, but that doesn't start until March. And I like D and D."

"What is that?"

Sinking deeper under her spell, he answered in a dazed monotone. "Dungeons and Dragons, Vampire the Masquerade. Fantasy role-playing games. Some of those computer fantasy games are pretty cool, too."

"I also enjoy computer games. Which do you play?"

He mumbled an unintelligible answer. Dreamily fixed on her eyes, he forgot to keep talking.

Rather than question him further, Gillian basked in the heat he radiated. She felt the stirring inside him in response to her silent urgency. She opened herself to his emotion but felt balked, for it didn't flow rapidly enough. An inspiration from television dramas struck her. She leaned over to touch her lips to his.

At first he stiffened in surprise. She gentled him with her hands until his mouth relaxed. His tongue flicked hers, and a low moan escaped him. Thirstily she absorbed his rising passion. *So this is what ephemerals are for!*

After uncounted minutes of that refreshing stream, over the pounding of his heart she heard a muffled protest. She woke to the realization that she was melting, shimmering—

*Oh, no, not now!*

She drew back from the boy's mouth and forced her transformation under control. Shocked out of his trance, he gaped at her in disbelief. Gillian placed her hands on either side of his head and gazed into his eyes. "Don't be afraid. You didn't see that. You came inside, I paid you, and you left. Nothing else happened. I paid you, that is all you remember. Now you may leave."

With relief she saw the veil descend over him again. "Right, I have to get going," he parroted.

She escorted him to the door and bolted it behind him. A nervous impulse made her secure the chain, too. Her pulse still raced. She spent a moment taming it. When her body's agitation subsided, she returned to the computer. Maybe a challenging chess match would distract her from the hunger that still burned in the pit of her stomach. Playing with the boy had only teased her appetite.

*Maybe I should try to resist the temptation until I learn more control.* That was the echo of Volnar's pronouncements. Irritated with this evidence of his sway over her, Gillian shook off her tantalizing thoughts and focused on the game.

Hardly had she advanced her second pawn when the doorbell rang again. Surely Alex wouldn't come back. Hadn't she wiped his short-term memory well enough?

At the door she unfastened the deadbolt without removing the chain. What she saw out front made her momentarily forget to breathe.

Her highway benefactor, Professor Greer.

"What do you want?"

He gave her a smile meant to be disarming. "You don't have to be afraid of me, Gillian. I just came to return your backpack." He held it up.

"How did you find me?"

"You gave me the address, remember?" So she had; the information hadn't seemed important to guard at the time. "I've been sitting in my car across the street for a couple of hours, waiting for you to show up. Thought you might still be on the road. Then I saw you open the door for the paper boy. Thank God nothing happened to you—hitchhiking's dangerous."

"What do you want with me?" she repeated.

"Just to talk," he said. "Aren't you going to let me in? I can't give you this with the chain on."

The panic inspired by her first glimpse of him faded. She sensed excitement and curiosity in the man, but no hostility. And she could handle him better if she didn't try to talk through a barely-open door. "Very well." She unhooked the chain and stepped aside.

When he handed her the backpack, she tossed it in a corner of the foyer rather than keep it to encumber her. "Thank you. Now you had better leave."

"Don't I get any reward?" He spread his hands in appeal. "I'd just like to ask you some questions. A short interview. Gillian, you must have an inkling of how much meeting a creature like you means to me."

"I don't know what you're talking about." Volnar had advised her that human beings tended to edit anomalous experiences to fit into the "normal" laws of nature, provided further evidence didn't arrive to reinforce the abnormal perception. In any case admitting what she was couldn't help, and denial couldn't hurt.

"Gillian, Gillian—I know what I saw. You changed shape before my eyes. How do you do it? What are you, exactly?"

She folded her arms. "A twelve-year-old girl, as you see."

"You can't convince me I imagined that. I wasn't stoned, and nobody goes nuts on the spur of the moment." He took a step toward the living room. "Couldn't we sit down to discuss this?"

Gillian blocked his path. "No." Buoyed by the residual high from her interlude with Alex, she felt confident of manipulating Greer. She stared into his eyes. "There's nothing unusual about me. Go away and forget you ever came here."

For a second the man's eyes glazed over. Then he shook his head and shifted his gaze to a point beyond her left shoulder. "Damned if I will! So you have some kind of hypnotic power—fascinating. I doubt you're strong enough to make it work on me if I resist. After all, you're just a kid, whatever else you are."

That evaluation stung. She grabbed his arm. "Look at me!"

"Not a chance. Why not make this easy on both of us? Give me the information I want, and I'll leave. Don't worry, when I include you in my next book, I won't print anything that could betray you. I'll disguise the circumstances and your name."

She heard strain in his voice and saw a shift in the hue of his aura with that last sentence. He was lying; he had no intention of protecting her identity. A picture of the caged tigers at the National Zoo flashed into her mind. Fear welled up to choke her. Her hand squeezed harder on his forearm, to no effect. He wore gloves and a heavy coat, preventing the skin-to-skin contact that would have made controlling him easier.

At that moment Roger and Britt walked in.

The gust of cold air that entered with them cleared Gillian's head. After all, what could Greer do to her if she refused to speak? He had no way of forcing her.

Roger grasped the professor's shoulder and spun him around. "Who are you, and what the hell do you think you're doing?"

ALL AFTERNOON ROGER had struggled to ignore his uneasiness about leaving Gillian alone. Surely she had sense enough not to venture out, and what harm could she do inside the house? He declined to speculate on what a bored young vampire might concoct to amuse herself in new surroundings. Aware that children Gillian's age needed more food and less sleep than adults, he had little hope that she would remain quiescent until dusk. He decided against phoning at mid-afternoon to check on her. On the remote chance that she was still asleep, there was no point in disturbing her.

As soon as he opened the door of his townhouse, he sensed Gillian's fear. Already, noting the unlatched deadbolt, he was alert for trouble. Mentally ordering Britt to stand clear, he swooped down on the intruder.

The man's suppressed excitement spiked into fear. Roger didn't feel in the least guilty for enjoying that response. "I—I'm just returning the backpack your daughter left in my van. My name's Adam Greer." He made an unobtrusive and futile effort to ease out of Roger's grip.

Roger scanned his captive—a thin, middle-aged man with sparse gray-brown hair and a pointed beard. "You were threatening Gillian. Why?"

"Not threatening, I wouldn't think of it! Look, I'm a sociologist at William and Mary—" He worked his right hand into a side pocket and pulled out his wallet. Handicapped by Roger's hold on his shoulders, he fumbled out a calling card. "I specialize in contemporary legends and strange phenomena. I'd simply like to interview your daughter. She has some remarkable abilities." He conjured up a feeble smile, which Roger sensed was meant to convey flattery.

"That's out of the question," said Roger. He accepted the card but kept one hand on the professor. "You've committed an unpardonable invasion of privacy."

"I can understand why you wouldn't want a girl her age giving interviews. If I could talk to you for an hour or so, instead—"

Roger cut him off. "You're wasting time. You are to leave here, never contact us again, and don't pursue this matter any further. Understand?" He felt the man's resistance wilt under his steady gaze. Unwillingly he acknowledged the rush of pleasure the small conquest gave him. He could see how, for some of his kind, this pleasure could become addictive, even eclipsing the satisfaction of more subtle forms of communion.

Greer nodded. Roger propelled him out the door. When he was sure the man was heading for his car, Roger locked the door and turned to Gillian. She stood rigidly erect, eying him as if expecting him to lash out at her.

He was tempted to do just that. Instead he kept his voice low. "How did Greer find you? Surely you didn't give him my name."

"No, sir. But I did give him the address. When he offered to drive me here."

Damn it, hadn't Volnar taught her never to volunteer *any* information? "Why did you let him in?"

"I did want the backpack, sir, and I thought once he was inside, I could—manage him."

Roger became aware of another kind of tension underlying her fear. "I think I see. You wanted to experiment on him, didn't you? You thought you could control him."

Gillian nodded, her mouth set in a tight line.

Britt stepped out from the corner where she'd retreated when Roger charged at Greer. "Are you going to try her for high crimes and misdemeanors right here in the entryway? Can't we go sit down first?"

Her voice defused Roger's impatience. "Of course, colleague. No real harm was done, I suppose." He gave Gillian an awkward pat on the shoulder. "Don't worry, he isn't likely to be back."

"Will he obey you? I tried to make him leave, but I wasn't—strong enough." They went into the living room, where she settled in lotus position on one of the couches. Britt, meanwhile, went upstairs to change out of her office clothes. "I tried to tell him to forget about me," said Gillian. "It didn't work. Why didn't you do that?"

Roger sat opposite her and removed his sunglasses. As usual sunlight on the snow had given him a headache. "Too risky. Such extensive memory alteration is apt to backfire. The most I hope for is that he'll accept my suggestion to lose interest in you. Eventually, as the vividness of the memory wanes, he may come to believe he imagined most of what he saw."

"I hope so," Gillian said. "I apologize for my carelessness."

Her chastened tone evoked Roger's pity. "We don't have to discuss it right now. You may as well save the details for when Claude gets here. He'll want to hear about it, I'm sure. What have you been doing today?"

Apparently used to this kind of question, she answered in a brisk tone, "I awoke at one forty-seven p.m. and searched for food. I drank a cup of milk and the juices from a half-pound of calves' liver. You know, sir, cold liver is *mondo* boring."

"Where on earth did you pick up that expression?"

Britt's laughter preceded her into the room. "I think I can guess that," she said. "So, Gillian, what did you do after your boring snack?" She sat next to Roger, leaning against him as if they were alone. He still felt self-conscious about showing affection in front of the child but couldn't deny himself the soothing effect of Britt's touch.

Gillian continued, "I watched Brad and Lila throw objects at each other on *Tomorrow Is Another Day*. She accidentally rendered him unconscious with a serving platter. They are fighting because—"

"Never mind, I don't need a synopsis. I realize you have to learn about human culture in some non-hazardous way, but I do question Volnar's judgment in prescribing soap operas for the purpose."

"He always checked closely to be sure I realized what parts of the program were untrue to daily life. I then watched the *Teenage Mutant Ninja Turtles* cartoon."

"I knew it," muttered Britt. "Bringing up this child on the fast food of popular culture."

"One thing I've been unable to understand about that series,"

Gillian said. "I know it is fantasy, but isn't fantasy supposed to adhere to logic, too? Everyone knows mutagens work on the cellular level, not the gross morphological level."

Britt said, "You know it and we know it, but most elementary school kids don't, and I'm not sure many TV executives know it."

"Did Volnar approve of this portion of your *educational* diet?" said Roger.

"He says it is a refreshing example of mass culture's acceptance of something bizarrely alien as admirable. Most aliens that capture the public's fascination, he says, are either cute or erotically appealing." With a puzzled frown, she added, "I have not fully learned what constitutes cuteness or eroticism. Are turtles not cute?"

Roger rubbed his forehead. "I'm not up to a seminar on the components of cuteness at this moment."

"Perhaps Dr. Loren—Britt—will explain it to me later. After all, she is completely human."

"Certified card-carrying," said Britt.

"I watched a portion of *Das Rheingold* on public television. That was followed by *Sesame Street*. Big Bird visited Gabriella's class at school. Would you like to hear me sing one of the Rhinemaidens' arias? Or 'I Gotta Be Blue,' by Cookie Monster?"

"Maybe later," said Roger. "Did you try the chess program?"

"I began a game, but the paper carrier interrupted me, and then Professor Greer arrived."

"Which brings us back to where we started. I suggest you continue your chess game until Claude and Eloise get here."

Britt said, "Gillian, I picked up some clothes for you on my lunch hour. I left the bag in the guest room."

Gillian acknowledged the gift with a stiff word of thanks. Roger sensed she still wasn't sure how to deal with an ephemeral on equal terms.

He joined Britt in the kitchen to broil a couple of steaks while she tossed a salad for herself. "Do you think you've actually gotten rid of Greer?" she said as she tore the lettuce.

"Probably. And if he comes back, I'll repeat the treatment as often as necessary. What can he do besides make a nuisance of himself? He has no hard evidence, and I'll make sure he doesn't get any."

"Then why are you still tense?"

From his vantage point at the kitchen table, Roger answered her only with a wry smile.

[Because of Gillian?] Britt silently asked.

[I don't know what to do with her,] he admitted. [I don't have the skills or the time to train her, yet I can't betray her trust by throwing her back into Volnar's clutches. As for persuading her to return voluntarily—]

[Besides, you sort of resent having her around, and you feel guilty about that. Right?]

[Colleague, sometimes I wonder why I bothered bonding with you. You read my mind perfectly well without my help.]

The oven buzzed. Britt slid the steaks under the broiler, then sat at the table to slice tomatoes for her salad. [I'm sure this is only temporary. Once Gillian figures out what a dull life you lead, in a few days she'll probably beg to get out of here.]

[But in the meantime—]

Britt put down the knife and gazed at him across the table. [Meanwhile, our vacation is starting day after tomorrow, and there goes our privacy. Right, colleague?] Beginning Friday, a week from Christmas, they would close the office until after New Year's; too many patients took off during the holidays to make it worthwhile to schedule appointments.

Roger nodded. [I do feel guilty for seeing her as an intrusion. But her appetite stimulates mine, which doesn't make things any easier— and children her age are *always* hungry.]

Britt laughed softly. [I noticed. This isn't a breeze for me, either. I can't help feeling that empty space inside her, and I want to *do* something.]

Roger felt jealousy flaring within him and sternly tamped it down. How could he call himself a civilized adult if he perceived a half-grown child as a threat? He got up to remove his steak from the oven, leaving Britt's to cook a little longer.

"I thought about running by the pet shop to pick her up a few rats," said Britt.

"If she stays longer than a few nights, that might be wise. For the moment, I'm sure she'd rather hunt." He salted his nearly raw steak while Britt tossed her salad with oil and vinegar. When her meat was ready, they ate at the kitchen table in comfortable silence. From the downstairs office he heard an occasional beep or fanfare from the computer.

About the time they finished clearing the dishes, Claude and Eloise arrived.

"She's still here, isn't she?" Eloise held up her tote bag. "I brought a computer game she might like."

Gillian emerged from the back room at once. She wore a fuzzy turquoise turtleneck sweater with matching knit slacks, apparently part of Britt's purchase. "Good evening. What did you bring? May I try it now? The chess program defeated me in twenty-seven moves, and I need to think it over before I play again."

Claude greeted her with indulgent amusement. "What happened to, 'How nice to see you again' and 'Did you have a pleasant day'?"

Gillian said with a puzzled frown, "Should I have said that? Those rituals are human custom."

"Yes, and if you expect to mix with ephemerals, you have to practice their rituals, including small talk. Aside from glorious exceptions like Britt and Eloise, they don't perceive emotions the way we do. They need meaningless space-filling noises to reassure each other."

"I will remember," said Gillian. "Did you have a pleasant day?"

Claude and Eloise shed their coats as everyone headed for the living room. Roger took the wraps to hang in the foyer closet. "I'm sure he spent it asleep," said Roger, not attempting to hide the envy in his voice.

Claude, taking a seat near the fireplace, ignored the comment. "Fine, and you?" he said to Gillian.

"She had a visitor," said Britt, "which I think she's supposed to tell us about."

Roger laid fresh logs on the hearth and lit the fire. The room was already more than warm enough for him, but he knew Britt and Eloise liked the atmospheric touch. "Yes, you may as well give us the details and get it over with."

He felt tension emanating from Gillian. "I suppose I must tell you about the paper boy, too."

"What?" Roger heard more sharpness in his voice than he'd intended. Britt, seated next to him, touched his hand in a wordless reminder to moderate his tone. "Gillian, I hope you haven't done anything unwise."

"I didn't think so at the time. I was only—practicing. It almost happened again."

"It?" said Eloise, leaning forward with unabashed curiosity.

Claude said to Gillian with no hint of reproach, "You're speaking of transformation, yes?"

Gillian nodded. "I thought it would be safe to play with him." More words tumbled out, an account of impulsive self-indulgence leading to a loss of control.

"You should have waited and discussed it with one of us," Roger said.

"Yes, sir."

"Isn't this a bit premature for you, anyway?"

Claude answered for her. "Not necessarily. The need for psychic nourishment usually awakens along with the capacity to draw it. Your—gift—awoke in your mid-teens, and you learned to use it soon thereafter, *n'est-ce pas?* Your daughter is merely starting a little earlier."

"I don't understand," said Eloise. "If she's too young for human blood—"

"The craving to feed on human emotion normally develops first, with a possible gap of several years between the two."

*Thank God for that!* thought Roger.

"There you go again," said Britt, "talking about her as if she's invisible. Is that vampire etiquette?"

Claude turned his most charming smile upon Gillian. "Sometimes human customs have reason behind them. We don't intend discourtesy. We're only thinking of your welfare. Please continue with your story."

Roger felt Gillian's self-consciousness at confessing her lack of control with four pairs of eyes fixed on her. She explained how Professor Greer had talked his way into the house and how she had tried to deal with him. Her aura rippled with agitation as she relived the panic he'd roused in her.

"Easy, little one," Claude interrupted. "It's over, get hold of yourself. What's the square root of 11,205?"

Gillian answered instantly, "One hundred five point eight five—"

"That's fine, you needn't bother with any more decimal places. What's twenty-eight times ninety-one?"

"Two thousand five hundred forty-eight." Her breathing had slowed to normal by now.

"Feeling better?" said Claude. "Good, please continue."

Britt silently commented, [Interesting technique. Do vampires always use mathematical drills to calm their children?]

[How would I know?] said Roger.

When Gillian had finished her narrative, Claude said, "This experience should have taught you at least two things—confound it, sit down, you're making me nervous." Gillian settled down on the rug near the hearth. "You need to learn to transform at will, and you need more practice in controlling human minds."

"Yes, I know," said the girl, "but how can I practice without the risk of giving myself away? Professor Greer realized what I was trying to do to him."

"Normally you'd have to exercise your skills on victims with your advisor monitoring. However, in your case I have a better idea." He cut off her questions. "First, how about a few transformation exercises?"

Gillian sprang to her feet. "I would like that very much. Where?"

"Better not try it outside where someone might stumble on you until your skill improves. Right here should do perfectly well, if Roger doesn't mind."

"Certainly not," said Roger. He looked forward to observing the "exercise." Since he lacked the gene for that talent, his curiosity about the change had never been fully satisfied.

Eloise half-rose from the love seat. "Do you want us to leave?" Roger sensed her eagerness to stay and watch. Britt, he knew, felt the same way.

Claude arched his eyebrows questioningly at Gillian.

"I would be glad to have them present."

Roger wondered at her willingness to be watched. Did she, perhaps, luxuriate in the idea of impressing the two human females with her alluring alienness? *I have to stop thinking this way—she's only a child!*

Britt picked up the thought. [Not too much of a child to know what she wants. I'll bet you've hit it, colleague.]

"The first thing we need," said Claude, "is plenty of space." Eloise stood up for a minute to let him move the love seat back from the center of the room. "Take off your sweater," he told Gillian. At the same time he stripped to the waist. Nudity meant nothing to vampires, as Roger knew, but since he'd had little contact with his mother's kind, the casualness still came as a mild shock to him.

Claude and Gillian stood face to face in the middle of the rug. "The next thing you need is an instructor who's bonded with you and can plant the technique directly in your mind. Since you've refused that, you'll have to make do with me."

"Yes, sir." A tremor crept into her voice.

Stretching his arms out to his sides, Claude turned his back to Gillian. "Watch. Not just with your eyes, but with your ears and mind, too. Pay attention to the shade of my aura, the changes in my heartbeat and respiration."

A velvet black growth sprouted on Claude's torso and flowed up his chest, along his arms, and over his face. His ears grew pointed, and he bared his teeth to display fangs that his proper shape didn't wear. Silver-gray wings billowed out from his shoulders. Roger saw him as if through a shimmering veil. Claude's image shifted in and out of focus, doubled like two negatives superimposed on each other. Behind the winged shape, Roger saw the true humanoid form.

He couldn't quite suppress his envy of this power. Because of his human genes, the delirious freedom of transformation and flight were denied him. At the same, time he felt anxious about Gillian. Had she inherited his *weakness?* Would she fail at the change and think herself flawed?

Momentarily slipping into Britt's mind and viewing Claude through her eyes, Roger no longer perceived the shadowy layers of illusion. Through Britt's human vision, he saw the wings, fur, feral ears, and fangs as completely solid, fixed rather than in flux. Part of the change, Roger knew, was a real alteration of surface molecules, while part was a projection that worked on the human mind. Much depended on the viewer's preconceptions.

He heard Britt's breathing quicken. A shaft of jealousy stabbed him. Britt's fingers curled around his. [Scientific ardor, colleague. I was just thinking that next time I want to take his pulse while he's doing that.]

Though the rise in her skin temperature hinted that her ardor was more than *scientific*, he didn't challenge her on the point. Claude again turned to face Gillian. "Now you try it, but don't change completely. Stop short of allowing the wings to materialize."

Gillian drew a deep breath. Roger scanned her thin torso. She was completely flat-chested; secondary sexual characteristics wouldn't develop until her late teens, since her body wouldn't be mature enough to ovulate until about age thirty. The inverted triangle of downy hair extending from her nipples over her ribcage to its apex at the navel was no more than a golden shadow. She inhaled again, and on the shuddering exhalation, the hair appeared to darken and spread. Instead of proceeding slowly like Claude's change, Gillian's transformation engulfed her like flame devouring a dry tree. The wings burst forth like a butterfly emerging in a fast-forward movie. For a second her eyes glowed with the ecstasy of release. Then, recognizing her loss of control, she twisted her body back into human form. Roger sensed the cramp-like pang she couldn't help broadcasting.

Her long white fingers covered her eyes. "Suppose I never learn? What if I'm too human?" She lowered her hands to flash an accusatory look at Roger. "You can't change at all, can you?"

"No. But you clearly don't have that problem." Her anxiety gnawed at him and stirred irrational guilt.

Claude ruffled her short auburn curls. "Brace up, little one. You've hardly begun to try." He guided her hand to the center of his chest. "Let your pulse resonate with mine. Feel the alteration in my cells. See, I can talk to you and maintain this shape at the same time—it isn't that difficult. Now, again—just the hair and the teeth."

In slow motion this time, dark fur—not black, but Irish Setter red to match her hair—crept over Gillian's chest and arms. When she bared her teeth, wolfish fangs protruded between her lips.

"Good," said Claude in a low croon, as if soothing a skittish horse. "Stop there for a minute. The fangs aren't much use for feeding or self-defense, because you'd have to get much older before you could indulge in violent emotion without reverting to human form. But they do serve very well for terrifying an attacker into helplessness." Gillian trembled as if on the verge of an explosion. "Very well, now the rest of it," Claude softly ordered.

Again, her face and ears turned feline, while delicate, pale green wings erupted. Like a Fourth of July sparkler blazing up and burning out, she cycled through the change in seconds and lapsed back into her ordinary shape. Cringing away from Claude's touch, she moaned aloud. "I simply can't keep it stable!"

"This looks exhausting," Eloise murmured.

"I agree," said Britt. "Isn't it enough for one night?"

Gillian, impaled on Claude's direct gaze, didn't seem to be listening. Roger quietly answered Britt, "I'm sure Claude knows what he's doing. He's the only one here with experience."

Claude went on with implacable kindness, "Steady, Gillian—you'll get it eventually. Watch." His wings shifted from silver to green to crimson, finally settling on pearl-gray. To Roger, Claude appeared to stand at the center of a kaleidoscope. "You can't expect to achieve that fine-tuned control in one night. But with practice, you will. It's important that you change voluntarily on a regular schedule, especially at your age. The transforming urge is a drive, a need, and if you don't exercise the power, you'll keep suffering these involuntary seizures."

Gillian nodded her understanding. Holding hands with Claude, she once more turned her focus inward. In a smooth progression of shifts, she first changed her body and hands, then her face and ears, then last allowed the wings to blossom. She stood on tiptoe, breathing shallowly as if afraid she would shatter like crystal. "It feels so—" she whispered. "It's like a burning inside, but painless." Finding that her new form didn't melt away this time, she said in a firmer voice, "But what use is it? Flying is dangerous—someone might catch me."

"It was useful in a precivilized world, no doubt," said Claude. "Now it's purely recreational, and finding a place to indulge safely is just one of the trade-offs we pay for living in this society."

Roger spoke out of his residual envy for this wild talent. "Do you think it's worth it?"

"On balance, yes." He said to Gillian, "And so will you, once you develop your skill. You've had almost enough for one session. Before you shift back, though, I'd like to see whether you can hold steady with someone touching you." He beckoned to his wife.

Eloise stepped to Gillian's side. "May I touch you?"

Gillian nodded dubiously.

"Yes, you're hypersensitive when your molecules are in flux, so you have to be very careful about physical contact," said Claude. "But don't be afraid, Eloise has ample experience."

Blushing, Eloise ran her fingertips along the upper edge of one of Gillian's wings. The girl reacted with a hissing intake of breath. Her aura vibrated with conflicting apprehension and pleasure. "I won't hurt you," Eloise murmured.

"That's right," said Claude. "But never forget how easily someone could. In this shape, you're vulnerable."

"How does it feel, Gillian?" asked Britt.

"As if she were touching me under the skin—touching exposed nerves. It makes me want—" While Gillian couldn't blush, Roger noticed a momentary dimming of her aura that seemed to convey the same meaning.

"Congratulations, you're normal," said Claude dryly. "You'd better stop, love, before you blow her circuits."

To Roger, the air seemed to hum with suppressed excitement. He felt relieved when both Claude and Gillian reverted to their ordinary selves.

"Now, while your problems with Greer are fresh in your mind," said Claude, "there's something else I want you to try." He put on his shirt and buttoned it halfway up, a style that gave him a rather piratical air. "The only way to gain confidence in your control over human minds is through practical application."

"Now?" She paused to pull on her sweater. "But I'm hungry."

"Exactly. For this exercise, hunger will be an asset." He turned to Eloise. "Afraid I can't ask for your help this time. You're too soft-hearted. Britt—"

From her corner near the fire, Eloise said, "I think I'm being insulted."

Britt laughed and said, "I don't know. What does that make me, the cruel witch?"

The point of Claude's remark penetrated Roger's brain. "Wait a minute—are you suggesting Gillian *practice* psychic domination on Britt?"

"Calm down, old man, it's perfectly safe. We're here, aren't we?" Claude resumed his seat next to Eloise, casually draping his arm over her shoulders. "And if Gillian couldn't break down Greer's resistance, do you think for a moment she can override Britt's?" He said to Gillian, "What you need is to build up your mental strength by testing it against an experienced, fully aware target. You've got a rare opportunity here. Usually we're reduced to practicing on unwitting victims, so when we meet any real resistance, it's a shock."

In response to Roger's silent qualms, Britt said aloud, "Stop worrying, colleague, I know she can't hurt me. My problem with the idea is that I'm really not much of a *target*. I won't *want* to fight."

"You're a professional, though," Claude said. "You can understand that resisting her is for her own good. Gillian, go sit beside Britt." Britt moved closer to Roger to make room for the girl. "Excellent. Take her hands and look into her eyes—like that. You said you're hungry—psychic hunger, not merely physical. Your two experiments this afternoon didn't satisfy you. Well, here's your chance. Take what you need."

Roger heard the deliberate taunt in Claude's voice and recognized it for what it was, a ploy to goad Gillian to her best effort. Nevertheless he could barely restrain himself from tearing Gillian away from Britt. *Don't touch her, she's mine!*

Britt's cool amusement washed over him. [Really, colleague, this is strictly for didactic purposes. Now, stop distracting me.]

Rather than trying to evade Gillian's hypnotic stare, Britt met and challenged it. Roger braced himself against the temptation to merge with Britt's mind and help her resist the attack. Aside from the unfairness to Gillian, he knew that if he directly experienced the child's invasion, he wouldn't be able to endure it without interfering. Anyway, Britt needed no help to block the initial attack. Roger felt Gillian trying a frontal assault, which Britt was prepared for. Her barrier held firm. She tossed a side comment to Roger: [This is too easy. I feel as if she's the one you should be helping.]

Soon realizing that brute force wouldn't work against an

experienced opponent, Gillian changed her strategy. Roger felt the energy beating against Britt like waves on rock—*submit, submit!*—dissipate. Instead, Gillian's projected image of herself softened, melted. Her need became a fragrant cloud that enfolded Britt in dreamy warmth. Roger felt Britt relax, reclining on the insubstantial cushion of mist like a swimmer floating on her back in a sun-warmed tide pool—but only for a moment. With no prompting from him, Britt awoke to the seduction and forced herself to vigilance.

Roger felt Gillian's spasm of irritation when Britt snapped out of the nascent trance. The girl immediately schooled herself to renewed calm, however, and tried a slightly different tactic. Still yielding, inviting, she infused her emotional projection with stronger urgency. She bared her hunger to Britt. Within seconds the void within her became so palpable that Roger ached in sympathy. *Damn it, she has to stop this!*

Momentarily Britt leaned toward Gillian as if ready to embrace her, then drew back and shook her head. Across the room Claude and Eloise were intently watching. Eloise inched away from Claude and muttered, "Come on, this isn't fair!"

Britt withdrew her hands from Gillian's. "Damn straight it isn't! Claude, why are you encouraging the poor kid to torture herself and the rest of us, too?"

To Roger's relief the electricity in the air began to fade. Claude exhaled a shaky breath. "You do have a point. She's stronger than I expected. But so are you—you gave her a good fight. Very good for a first try, Gillian. I trust the next time you're faced with someone like Greer, you won't be at a total loss?"

Gillian was breathing harshly, unable to form a coherent answer. Britt said, "Oh, for heaven's sake, this is ridiculous! Contest's over; let's call it a draw." Roger felt an outpouring of sympathy rush from her to Gillian. When Britt reached out to hug the girl, Gillian flinched—naturally enough, the sudden move felt like an attack to her. Britt ignored that response and overrode it with her impulsive affection.

For a minute Gillian returned the embrace. Roger noticed the awkwardness of the gesture, as if hugging weren't in the child's behavioral repertoire. *Probably hasn't been since age three, when she was weaned.* When Britt released her, she leaned back with a long sigh. As the tension in the room relaxed, Roger realized that he'd been clenching his fists to keep from pulling Britt and Gillian apart.

[That wasn't so terrible, was it?] Britt's inner voice sounded a bit tired, but satisfied. [You didn't think she'd drain me and leave me prostrate, did you?]

Roger clasped her hand. Her skin felt cooler than normal. [The child doesn't know her own strength. They're voracious at that age; she might not have known when to stop.] Though fully aware that the energy drain in the absence of bloodletting was only temporary, restorable within an hour or two by ordinary rest, he couldn't deny his irrational fear for Britt's health.

[Well, *I* would've known when to stop,] Britt countered. [Worrywart.]

Claude stood up and finished buttoning his shirt. "Now you'll want some more substantial nourishment, I daresay. It's been dark long enough that we can hunt safely." He directed a questioning look at Roger.

"Yes, you shouldn't have any problem. I won't come with you this time."

Claude shrugged. "Brother, sometimes I worry about this asceticism of yours. Gillian, before we leave, haven't you forgotten something?"

She looked blank.

"When you're dealing with an equal, not a victim, there are social courtesies to be observed."

"Pardon? Oh!" Gillian said gravely, "Thank you, Dr. Loren, that was most enjoyable."

Britt said, "You're welcome," and heroically managed not to laugh.

After Claude and Gillian went out the back door, Eloise said, "What's going to happen to the kid when she has to get her meals from people whose whole idea of vampires is Bela Lugosi? Maybe we really are corrupting her."

"Too late now," said Britt. "Roger, if you didn't want her corrupted, you should never have let her in the house. I wasn't about to sit around and watch her suffer."

"That won't present a long-term problem," he said, "because she won't be staying for long. I fully intend to get her back to Volnar soon, one way or another." Contemplating that prospect threatened to plunge him into gloom. So far, he hadn't hit upon any way of persuading Gillian into that course of action.

Sensing his mood shift, Britt said, "I guess now isn't the time to ask how you're going to arrange that. Eloise, would you like to see my half-finished draft for that article on the *Sesame Street* monsters?"

"Lead on." Eloise took her reading glasses from her purse and started to put them on. She paused, clutching her ribs with a grimace of pain, but waved away Britt's expression of concern. "Just a cramp. Probably ate too much at dinner."

Roger followed them into the office. While Britt was retrieving her file on the computer, the phone rang. Roger wasn't completely surprised to hear Dr. Volnar's voice.

"Where are you calling from?" Roger said. "I don't have to ask why you're calling."

"Oh? I wouldn't expect you to know. Claude doesn't."

"Know what? Aren't you phoning about Gillian?"

"Oh, I see. I'm in New York," said Volnar, "and as a matter of fact, Gillian is not the reason I'm contacting you. You've heard from her?"

Volnar's cool, remote tone seldom varied. Hearing him use that tone in regard to a runaway child strained Roger's self-control to the limit. He reminded himself that flaring up at the Prime Elder never did the slightest good. Sometimes he wondered whether Volnar's emotions had gone into permanent dormancy several millennia in the past. "No, I haven't *heard* from her. She's here. She appeared on my doorstep last night."

"Indeed? Then she has managed to surprise me."

"Damn and blast it to hell! Haven't you even tried to find her?"

"Compose yourself, Roger." The ghost of a chuckle. "You give me very little credit, young man. I assumed Gillian would turn to her mother, if she felt my company had become insupportable. I checked Juliette's home just outside Williamsburg, on the remote chance that Gillian had some idea of hiding there. Not finding her, I went on to New York as scheduled, on the premise that the child had probably joined her mother here. Since that wasn't the case, I'm relieved to learn that Gillian is safe with you."

"What do you plan to do about it? She doesn't want to go back to you."

"There's no reason why she need do so at the moment. She can stay with you for a few nights, since another urgent concern has come up—the actual reason I called."

In his preoccupation with Gillian Roger had hardly noticed Volnar's earlier remark about another purpose for telephoning. "What are you talking about?"

"You know that Neil Sandor had a twin sister, Camille."

The statement fell into a resonating silence. After a moment

Roger said, "What about her?"

"After Sandor's death—quite justified, and the responsible elements among our race support me on that—she petitioned the Council to have you punished. *Executed* was the term she used."

Roger briefly remained silent, choking down his anger. "Why wasn't I told?"

"As they say in government circles, you had no need to know. Camille made irresponsible threats, we placed her in confinement, and there was no need for you to be involved at all."

"Confinement?"

"She might have attacked you. We prevented that. Since your growth was at a delicate stage then, I saw no reason to disturb you with these facts. For the past fourteen years, Camille has been imprisoned—comatose—in a sealed casket."

"Buried alive?" If the cliché *a fate worse than death* had any meaning, Roger thought, that must be it.

"It isn't so bad as it sounds. Within days, or at most weeks, she would have lost consciousness from lack of oxygen."

Volnar's reassurance failed to reassure. Roger's inconveniently vivid imagination hinted at what the woman must have suffered before oblivion released her. "Why are you telling me this now?"

"Her sentence, so to speak, has recently expired," said Volnar. "Frequently, this enforced dormancy has its desired effect, and the—patient—awakens with a new perspective on his or her experience. Camille was released on parole, as it were, on condition that she keep me, through our Nevada headquarters, informed of her whereabouts. Within the past forty-eight hour, she stole a car and disappeared."

"And you're looking for her? That's your urgent mission?"

"Precisely. You now have a need to know—since Camille is probably on her way to carry out her delayed revenge."

"Wonderful." Roger was glad his advisor was well out of emotion-sensing range. He sank into the desk chair and exchanged glances with Britt, who had turned away from the computer to listen to the conversation. "Then why aren't you here instead of dispensing useless warnings by telephone?"

"I have no quick way of finding the woman. The most direct method of capturing her is to bring her advisor into the area. Camille's advisor can use their bond to track her."

"He's in New York?"

"She," said Volnar. "She has had no contact with Camille in many years and is living in England. I've been unable to reach her by phone, so tomorrow I'll be flying to London to see her in person. She may need some direct persuasion, as she washed her hands of Neil and his sister many years ago. Remember, she was of no help when Neil went rogue."

"Meanwhile, what do you suggest I do if Camille descends upon me with a sharpened stake?"

Eloise, who lacked Britt's firsthand knowledge of the other end of the conversation, looked up from the monitor in shock.

"Use your own judgment," said Volnar, "and see to it that she doesn't escape before I get there. If she *is* fool enough to go straight where we'd most expect. And, Roger—this time, try to avoid killing her. It was justified with Neil, but I'd prefer you didn't let it become a habit."

## Chapter Five

THE HARSH WHITE of sunlight on snow, Camille thought, was a small price to pay for the joy of nearing her goal. She spent over an hour parked in a rented car—she had abandoned the stolen one—under the trees across the road from the townhouse complex, waiting for the half-breed to return. She knew he wouldn't be home during the day. Instead of sleeping he was out working for a living like any ordinary ephemeral. The business address below his residence number in the telephone book confirmed that.

A momentary surge of anger made Camille lightheaded. Her years in suspended animation hadn't quenched the fire that smoldered in her when she recalled Neil's murder. To think that the Council of Elders had vindicated that half-breed, who had no right even to exist, and punished *her*!

Now that her revenge was in sight, she didn't intend to hurry it. If possible she would find some way of devastating Roger Darvell's life without endangering her own life or freedom. At least not right away. Since she'd broken parole, she had little hope of eluding the elders' discipline indefinitely. So she would make the most of whatever time she could salvage.

To begin with, she reconnoitered from her position at the verge of the winter-gray woods. Toward late afternoon she was surprised to see the door of Roger's townhouse open to the paper boy's ring. Camille took off her sunglasses and squinted through the slanted sunlight at the figure who answered the door. Not Roger—Camille had never seen the half-breed, but this person was obviously too small and thin for an adult male. A child? The door closed before Camille could sort out the two intermingling auras. With renewed interest she watched until the paper boy left. She noted an unsteadiness in his gait, and examination of the aura of the girl who briefly lingered in the doorway before closing it revealed nonhuman tints.

A vampire girl? Or, Camille wondered, was her perception distorted by daylight and lack of rest?

About five minutes later, someone got out of a van parked several hundred feet ahead of Camille's, opposite the far end of the parking lot. She had noticed the man waiting in that spot ever since she'd arrived but had paid no attention to him. She leaned forward, frowning in concentration, when he walked up to Roger's door.

*Does his house guest always receive so many visitors when he's at work? And who is she?*

Camille's next glimpse of the girl, when she let in the middle-aged, bearded man, confirmed the violet tinge in her aura. Yes, definitely vampiric. And this time Camille noted the auburn hair. Having met Juliette several times, Camille felt confident of her conclusion—this girl had to be Roger's daughter by Juliette. Anger sent a stab of pain through Camille's forehead. Outrageous—that mongrel, chosen to breed! She'd hardly believed it when she'd heard that a sensible female such as Juliette had agreed to be impregnated by the half-breed. Not only that, now it appeared that Juliette actually allowed Roger to interfere in the girl's upbringing.

*So the child lives with him at least part of the time. He must be attached to her, the fool, like a human father.*

That presented possibilities. Camille bared her teeth in anticipation while waiting for the visitor to emerge.

Instead, a gray Citroen pulled into the townhouse's parking space, and Roger stepped out. Camille knew him at once, his aura a chaotic blend of human and vampire. A woman arrived with him, but Camille paid little attention to her. Camille's eyes remained fixed on her target. She felt an absurd sense of loss when he went inside and vanished from her sight.

A moment later, the bearded man rushed out the door. Rather than watching Roger linger in the doorway, Camille turned her attention to the guest. Obviously an unwelcome one—he exuded a cloud of fear and confusion, and he headed for his car as fast as he could without running. Fear implied some knowledge about the inhabitants of the house. Might he serve her purpose somehow? A nebulous plan started to coalesce in Camille's mind.

When the van started up, Camille pulled into the road and followed it. It led her onto Route 50 toward Severna Park. Fifteen minutes later it turned into a motel parking lot in the commercial district on Route 2. Camille parked a few spaces from the van and followed its occupant at a discreet distance into the motel's cocktail lounge.

*Good, he's drowning his humiliation instead of going up to his room.* She was gratified at the chance to approach him in a public setting, where he wouldn't have his guard up as he might if she knocked on his hotel room door. To her advantage, this early on a

Wednesday evening they were the only customers in the dimly-lit room. After ordering a gin and tonic at the bar, she carried it to the corner table where the man sat alone. He was staring morosely at ten-inch goldfish circling in a giant aquarium on the back wall of the lounge.

When Camille sat down next to him, he gave her a bemused stare as if trying to figure out whether he'd met her before. "My name is Camille Kincaid," she said, counting on the introduction to keep his eyes locked on hers. "I think I may be able to help you."

"Adam Greer." He automatically held out his hand, which she clasped a few seconds longer than etiquette dictated. She was rewarded by the way his gaze lingered on her despite the suspicious question that followed. "Help? What are you talking about? Do I know you?"

"Not yet," she said, sipping her drink with a sensuous deliberation designed to hold his interest, "but I believe we have a mutual concern with Roger Darvell."

"Who? Oh, is that her father's name?" The befuddled expression crept into his eyes again. No doubt Roger had tried to dispel Greer's interest in the girl.

"Yes, I noticed you talking to Roger's daughter—what is her name?"

"Gillian." He sipped his drink—Scotch, by the smell—and stared at the fish.

"I have an interest in Gillian too, Adam—may I call you Adam? May I ask what your concern with her is?"

The man's eyes drifted back to Camille's face. His doubts of her evaporated under the pressure of her gaze. "Professional. I'm a sociologist, specializing in contemporary legends and weird phenomena. I've been publishing on UFOs and Bigfoot and such for years. But I never seriously thought anything like that might be real." He fortified himself with a gulp of Scotch. "If I could just talk to the girl for half an hour—"

*A glory-mad scientist! Perfect!* Camille smiled to herself. She'd require very little paranormal skill to bend Adam Greer's obsession to her own purposes. "I've made a study of such things myself. However, my specialty isn't exactly aliens. I concentrate on phenomena that mass culture labels supernatural. For instance—have you ever done any research on vampires?"

He gave a dejected shrug. "I'm familiar with the folklore, and I've read the standard *real life vampire* stories that crop up in all the popular books. Never paid any particular attention to the topic. Have you published in the field?"

"I don't write for publication. This is more of an avocation with me." Her fingers inched across the table to graze his free hand. He didn't notice the contact. "I'm lucky enough not to have to work for a living. I get along on my investments and travel a lot." That was true enough, discounting her failure to mention the recent fourteen-year hiatus in her life. "How would you react if I told you Gillian is a vampire?"

"She didn't burn to a crisp in the sun."

Camille said with a contemptuous smile, "Neither do many of the varieties of folklore vampire, as I'm sure you know."

"She doesn't look dead, either."

"She isn't." Camille modulated her voice to an intimate murmur that forced Greer to give her his full attention. "She was born as she is. That's not unknown in European legend, either. I'm sure you've heard of the *strigoi*, which is one variety of hereditary vampire. Gillian is a member of a nocturnal blood-drinking species—the truth behind the legends."

Greer straightened up, looking genuinely interested for the first time. "How do you know?"

"As I said, I've spent years investigating this kind of thing. Fortunately for us, they're rare, and they avoid conspicuous bloodshed. But that makes them all the harder to track down." She gave him a mental nudge and saw his doubt slide toward acceptance.

"That—that waif is a vampire?"

Camille lightly stroked the back of his hand, where it lay unmoving on the table. "Oh, she has human genes—her father is human." She didn't want to complicate matters by sending Greer on a rampage after Roger. Besides, Roger belonged to *her*. "That doesn't make Gillian any less dangerous, though. She may look like a human girl, but she's still a predatory beast inside. If you want to dig the truth out of her for that book you're probably thinking of, you'll have to make better preparations than just knocking on the door."

"You have an idea about that?"

She glanced around. Several other couples had taken tables in the lounge during the past few minutes. "Adam, why don't we go up to your room where we can talk about this in detail? I think you'll find my experience indispensable."

He stood up, stepping around the table to hold her chair as she rose. "Indispensable for what, exactly?"

"For capturing the child. Isn't that what you want? I can tell you how to catch her and what to do with her."

She held Greer's hand as they walked to the elevator.

WHEN CLAUDE AND Gillian walked into Roger's home office, Eloise stood up to greet them. For an instant she stiffened, gripping the back of the chair, her mouth tightening. Claude was at her side in a couple of steps, his arm around her. "You're in pain, *cherie?* What is it?"

"Nothing. Just a cramp, it's gone now." She relaxed into Claude's encircling arm. "Did you have a nice—outing?"

Roger didn't need to hear Gillian's answer. The rosy halo enveloping her proved she had fed well. From the speed of her pulse, she had apparently gone for a run after her meal. Snow was melting in her tousled hair. Roger half regretted he hadn't abandoned courtesy and joined the hunt.

Gillian said, "Let me show you the new trick Claude taught me." Her form shimmered and vanished. Seconds later, she reappeared.

Eloise clapped. "Way to go!"

"You must be a fast learner," said Britt, "or Claude's an outstanding teacher. I don't know if I'll ever get used to that disappearing act." The invisibility was purely an illusion, a psychic veil, a technique even Roger could handle expertly, though he hadn't learned so quickly and smoothly as Gillian. But he didn't make a habit of doing it for recreational purposes.

Gillian walked over to the computer. "Eloise, may I try your game now?"

"I guess so, if Roger doesn't mind."

Roger motioned for them to go ahead. After Britt saved the text file, Eloise fished the boxed game, with the title "Dragon's Bane" and a garish illustration of a monster spouting flames, out of her tote bag. "The goal of this one is to save your land from the dragon who's destroying villages and devouring the populace." She handed Gillian the basic instructions and took a stack of diskettes out of the box. "This thing has eight diskettes, so it would be a lot more convenient to install it on the hard disk. Roger?"

"How much space does it take up?" He scanned the information on the box. "Very well, so long as it's only temporary."

While Eloise loaded the program, Gillian said, "Could you please define *cute* for me?"

Eloise gave her a puzzled look. Britt explained Gillian's concern about whether turtles qualified as cute. "Well, it's a matter of a complex of traits most all infant mammals share," said Eloise. "Big heads, large round eyes, round faces, pudgy limbs—it's supposed to be a set of visual cues to stimulate adults to take care of them. Right, Britt?"

"That's the theory," said Britt. "My sister says that's God's way of making sure parents don't strangle their babies in the first month of life. It carries over to baby animals, too, and even babyish-looking animals like toy dogs. Of course, some people are immune to it, like my colleague here." She gave Roger a sidelong smile.

"I am not cute," said Gillian. She didn't seem upset by that conclusion.

"Well, not in the conventional sense," said Britt. "I kind of like you."

Gillian appeared confused by this remark. Probably Volnar hadn't given her much experience in dealing with compliments.

"She doesn't have to be," Claude said. "Since we directly experience each other's emotions, our females don't rely so heavily on visual cues in relating to their young."

"Must be nice," said Eloise, "not to have to guess why the baby's crying."

"Well, you shouldn't have to," Claude told her. "You should be able to read our child's emotions as easily as you read mine, perhaps more so."

When she finished transferring the game to the hard disk, Eloise relinquished the chair to Gillian. The girl began sorting out her character's attributes and weapons. "This is essentially a role-playing game?" she said.

"Yes, mostly problem-solving, but with some arcade-type sequences," said Eloise.

Gillian, who seemed comfortable with this sentence that impressed Roger as an arcane dialect, continued her preparations while the adults watched over her shoulder at varying distances. "Ready to shoot them down in flames?" said Claude when the Gillian's computer alter ego left the lord's throne room to begin her quest.

Gillian answered with her usual serious deliberation, "It is the dragon that may shoot me down in flames, isn't it?"

Meanwhile, Claude was rubbing the center of Eloise's back. "Yeah, maybe I should lie down for a little while," she whispered to him.

"Yes, feel free to use the guest room," Roger said. He watched with some concern as Claude escorted Eloise out of the office.

"Now, don't forget to be kind to the creatures you meet on the road," said Eloise to Gillian from the doorway. "You never know who might offer you magical aid."

Roger noticed a trace of blood-scent in the air. A sharp glance from Britt reminded him to squelch his worry.

A few minutes later, Claude reappeared and beckoned him into the hall. Steering him toward the living room, Claude said in a low voice, "Professional opinion, Rodge—there shouldn't be cramps at this stage, should there?"

"In general, no, but it doesn't necessarily indicate a serious problem. I'm no gynecologist, though."

"Eloise doesn't want to consider seeing a doctor. Insists she must be overtired or suffering from indigestion."

Roger didn't mention the unlikelihood of spotting blood from those causes. Instead he attempted to project reassurance to Claude, who thanked him insincerely and went upstairs to Eloise.

[Colleague, what's wrong?] Britt silently asked from her position on the edge of the desk, where she sat bemusedly watching Gillian's fingers dance over the keyboard.

[Eloise is in pain, enough to worry Claude.]

[Then I'd better talk to her,] Britt responded. [If he's anything like you, he'll worry her into nervous prostration and make the discomfort twice as bad.] She got down from her perch and said to Gillian, "Eloise isn't feeling well. We're going to take a look at her."

"I suggest you continue playing," said Roger. He didn't want Gillian overstimulated by pain and blood. Since his tone made the suggestion an order, she nodded without looking up from her game.

When Roger and Britt entered the guest room, Eloise chopped off a groan and tried to smile. She reclined on her back, pillows supporting her, with an oversized towel under her to protect the sheet. [She isn't spotting now,] Roger told Britt. [She's hemorrhaging copiously.]

[Abdominal cramps and vaginal bleeding in the first trimester? Dear God, that's bad.] Britt walked around to the opposite side of the double bed from Claude, who stood holding Eloise's hand. Roger gauged Claude's inner turmoil not only by his heartbeat and the darkening of his aura, but by the white-knuckled grip that was probably adding to rather than easing his wife's pain. Britt, hiding her own agitation like the veteran she was, said, "How long has this been going on, Eloise? Since just before Claude and Gillian came in?"

"Longer. I had twinges off and on for over an hour before that." The free flow of words and the relaxation of Claude's handclasp indicated she was between contractions. "Britt, I don't want to go to a hospital. I won't!" Her anxiety made Claude's fear spike. It scraped on Roger's nerves, already sensitized by the blood smell.

"You will if you have to," said Britt, carefully sitting on the edge of the bed. "Tell me the truth, how much are you bleeding?"

"Enough to soak a washcloth," Eloise admitted.

"Wish I could give you something, but I only use tampons," said Britt. "Listen, we have to get you to the emergency room."

Again that silent shriek of frightened protest. "I told you, I won't go! Can't you examine me right here?"

Britt's voice softened from its tone of brisk authority. "Can you tell me why you're so against the hospital?"

"If I—" Eloise gulped, "—if I lose it, the doctors might notice something—unusual."

Roger understood now; she was afraid of betraying Claude's true nature. "Eloise, that concern is completely groundless. At this stage it would take DNA analysis to find any nonhuman traits in the embryo. Which they certainly wouldn't bother with."

Britt gave him a reproachful glance for his bluntness. "Your welfare is the important thing."

"Of course it is," said Claude. His hand tightened on Eloise's as a fresh wave of pain suffused her. "Do what Roger and Britt tell you."

Eloise shook her head. "You check me, Britt. I trust you."

Roger felt Britt trying to curb her exasperation. "I'm not a gynecologist. I haven't done this since my first year out of med school, not to mention the lack of proper equipment."

"You must have the basics," Eloise said. Her facial muscles were drawn tight from bracing against the cramps.

Britt sighed. "Yes, we should have disposable gloves and a speculum on hand. Not the kind of thing I'd normally need to use. Listen, you need to be seen by a specialist right away, not waste time here."

Eloise's face tensed with pain for a moment. "I want *you*. If you tell me I have to go to the hospital, maybe—"

Britt shook her head at this show of stubbornness. "Very well. Would you bring me the supplies, Roger?"

He went to the hall closet to get his medical bag from the shelf. When he reentered the bedroom, Claude and Eloise's shared physical and emotional anguish struck him afresh. The air was turgid with it. Britt rummaged in the bag for a plastic-wrapped pair of gloves and went into the bathroom to wash.

"Claude, you have to calm yourself," said Roger. "You aren't doing her any good this way."

"I know," Claude whispered through clenched teeth.

Eloise searched his face in a silent appeal he couldn't answer. While Roger felt her pain beating at his mind like the wings of a maddened hawk, it battered him from outside only. Claude, blood-bonded with her, felt every nuance of her suffering as his own. No wonder he couldn't detach himself enough to give her relief.

When Britt came in, gloved, she said to Eloise, "I'll have to examine you in the middle of a contraction, and you aren't going to like it. Claude, she'll need you to suppress the pain and help her relax."

With a grim nod Claude began to massage Eloise's abdomen in gentle circles with his free hand. Feeling superfluous, Roger stepped into the hall to give Eloise a partial illusion of privacy while she stripped from the waist down. Britt's murmured directions followed. A minute later, a moan from Eloise drew him back into the room.

She reclined with her bent knees draped in the top sheet. When Britt attempted to probe with gloved fingers, Eloise stiffened against the invasion. Claude's face mirrored her pain.

"I know it's not easy, but you have to try to relax," said Britt, keeping her impatience out of her voice. "Claude, if you can't help her handle the discomfort, this won't work."

"Damn it, I'm trying!" The low, strangled tone, hardly more than a whisper, intensified the torment he projected.

Eloise flung his hands away from her. "If that's trying, then just stop! You're not helping!"

Claude's impotent anger lashed Roger like a fiery whip. He strode across the room and grasped Claude's arm. "She's right. You're too immersed in it yourself. If you can't do any better than that, you'll have to leave the room."

Claude started to flare up at Roger, then sank into despair. With a wild, helpless look at Eloise, he pulled away from Roger and stormed out. Roger heard him hurry downstairs into the living room.

Shelving his worry about his brother, Roger drew a deep breath to calm his own rioting emotions. Possibly a mistake, since his attention was thereby fixed on the sharp sting of Eloise's blood in the air. An unhealthy scent that couldn't stimulate his appetite, nevertheless, it irritated his hyperacute senses. He forced the distraction to the bottom of his thoughts.

Stroking Eloise's damp hair back from her forehead, he said, "You're going to be perfectly all right. I'm here to help you. Relax, let

your arms and legs go limp, and focus on my voice." At once he felt
her respond to his more impersonal care, where Claude's frantic
urgency had been powerless to penetrate her anguish.

Roger kept up the monotone of soothing phrases, low on content
but useful as a diversion, while his touch laved the tension from her
muscles. He made her gaze into his eyes to keep her from watching
Britt's face during the examination. Imposing serenity on Eloise's near-
hysterical mood channeled his own tension, too. Even amid their
shared anxiety he felt gratified by her response. The familiar sense of
competence calmed him.

Shortly, Britt stripped off her gloves, wrapping them in a paper
towel to throw away. "Well, I won't deny that it doesn't look good. We
have to get you to the hospital stat."

Quiet now, though tears trickled down her cheeks, Eloise said,
"Am I losing the baby?"

Roger cupped one of her hands in both of his, willing her to cling
to this fragile calm. Britt met her eyes directly and said, "You're
dilated between two and three centimeters. You have to be prepared for
the possibility."

Eloise swallowed a sob. "Is there any chance?"

"I can't tell. Whatever chance there is, you'll need qualified care
to maximize it. We certainly don't have the resources here."

"Okay. Let's go."

While Britt found a pair of slacks for her—too large, but they
could be rolled up—and helped her wash, Roger went downstairs to
check on Claude. He found his brother staring into the embers of the
fire in the darkened living room.

"We're taking her to the emergency room," said Roger. He drew
back a corner of the curtain to glance outside. A light snow had started,
not enough to make driving hazardous.

Claude said without turning toward him, "She's shutting me out.
She thinks I deserted her. And she's right. I never thought—never
imagined I could fail her that way!"

"You've hardly *failed.*" Roger's human side wanted to offer a
comforting pat on the shoulder. He restrained himself, knowing Claude
wouldn't appreciate unsolicited physical contact. "It's not your fault
that you couldn't control the pain. She can't blame you for an
involuntary response."

"She does. So do I." He broke off as Britt and Eloise came
downstairs. The two men met them in the foyer and helped them with
their coats. Bundled up in scarf and gloves, Eloise leaned on Claude

without speaking to him.

"Roger, you don't have to come along," said Britt. She knew how he felt about hospitals. "I can drive them perfectly well."

"Of course I'm coming." He took a minute to tell Gillian where they were going. She was still working at the computer, as if focusing on it to shut out the turmoil around her. She barely acknowledged his command to stay in the house.

Picking her way across the thin layer of snow in the parking lot, Eloise conjured up a weak smile. "What, you're not driving the black monster anymore, Roger?"

Britt said, "I convinced him gray was just as well suited to a doctor's dignity, and it absorbs a lot less sunlight than black. So he finally traded in the Whale. I think of this one as the Battleship." She helped Eloise get settled in the back seat.

When Claude started to sit beside her, Eloise silently inched away. Without speaking, Claude took the front passenger seat, leaving the back for Britt. The physical and emotional pain that arced between Claude and Eloise, despite the latter's defensive barrier, made Roger's head pound. He welcomed the need to concentrate on driving.

Behind him he sensed Britt holding Eloise's hand. Now and then Britt winced as her fingers were squeezed. Claude, vibrating with impatience at their slow progress toward downtown, stared straight out the windshield. When they crossed over the Severn River drawbridge into Annapolis, he said, "Shouldn't you have called ahead to the hospital?"

"Pointless," said Roger. "The ER works on perceived need and first come, first served, regardless. Whatever influence I can apply will have to wait until we get there."

The hospital, red brick like most of downtown Annapolis, occupied a block in the middle of the historic district. Five minutes from the bridge, he pulled up to the emergency room entrance to drop off the other three. By the time he'd parked the car and walked back, Britt was seated with Eloise on the hard plastic waiting-room chairs, filling out forms under Eloise's tight-lipped direction. Claude was pacing, oblivious to anyone who happened to cross his path.

Odors of blood, sickness, and disinfectant hit Roger in the face. Breathing shallowly, he assessed the other patients in the room. He glimpsed a gurney being wheeled in from the ambulance bay. Snatches of conversation from the paramedics suggested a stab wound, doubtless the main source of the blood smell. That patient disappeared into the treatment area at once. Huddled in chairs around the cramped waiting room, each hovered over by one or more adults, were a feverish little boy in Disney pajamas, a teenage girl with a bruise on her forehead, and another boy with what looked like a sprained ankle. Roger decided none of them rated above Eloise in urgency.

He strode to the check-in counter. "My brother's wife has a threatened spontaneous abortion. I believe she should be seen at once." He handed the nurse one of his business cards.

The puzzled expression on her face cleared. "Oh, yes, Dr. Darvell, I remember you." Roger recognized her as having been on duty last time he had to visit the ER to counsel a suicidal patient. She dubiously glanced around at the other occupants of the room.

Roger willed her to look at him. When he had her full attention, he said in a lower voice, "They can wait. Take my sister-in-law, now."

"Of course, Doctor." She called Eloise's name and directed her into the emergency room proper.

Britt walked in with Eloise, holding her arm. Claude stopped them with a tentative touch. "Shall I—?" His voice was barely audible. Roger sensed how powerfully the oppressive atmosphere affected Claude, more than Roger himself with his mixed heritage.

Eloise doubled over, clutching her abdomen and Britt's forearm. When she could speak, she whispered, "No, don't come in. You'd only make it worse."

Jaws clenched in frustration, Claude backed off. Britt said, "Why don't you go out for some fresh air? I'll let you know as soon as they've decided anything."

"Excellent idea," said Roger. He headed for the exit, trusting Claude to follow him.

Outside a few snowflakes drifted down. Roger inhaled deeply of the icy air, clean despite the car fumes, compared to what they'd just left. Claude echoed his thoughts. "That place is like the seventh circle of Hell! How can they stand it, even with the sensory fog they wander around in?"

Together they strode along the deserted sidewalk at a rapid pace. "I'm sure it helps to be unable to read emotions," Roger said. "Why do you think I chose a specialty that keeps me out of hospitals most of the time?"

After several minutes of silence—though his jangled aura spoke for him—Claude said, "She's right, I would have made it worse for her if I'd stayed. That room, closing in on me, on top of what she's broadcasting—" An inarticulate snarl escaped him. "But I should have been able to stand by her, help her bear it."

"Should?" said Roger. "Not much logic in that. How can you impose obligations on an emotional response?"

"We pride ourselves on controlling our emotions." He paused at a corner and slammed his fist into the low brick wall around someone's front yard. Roger noticed a web of fresh cracks in the brickwork. "Dark Powers, if she died—!"

"Practically impossible. She's having an uncomplicated miscarriage and receiving competent care."

Claude glowered at him. "Damn it, you can say that! It isn't Britt! How would you react if it were?"

"Probably even more irrationally than you are," Roger admitted. They made a right-angle turn, not wanting to get too far from the hospital. "But you must see that it would help if you'd relax. You and Eloise are reinforcing each other."

"I don't want to relax. I want to kill something."

"Not in the middle of town, please. Wait until later."

"I'd destroy anyone who dared to hurt her. But when I'm the one who's hurting her—" Claude turned on Roger. Pinpoints of red glowed in Claude's eyes. "If I hadn't cooperated with the pregnancy idea, she wouldn't be suffering now."

"She wanted it," Roger said. "Listen, Claude, what's bothering you is something any responsible man who impregnates a woman thinks of—humiliating as it may be to see yourself having human reactions."

"Is this how guilt feels?"

"Yes."

They walked on, with long, ground-eating strides, dodging ancient tree roots that protruded through the sidewalk. "Well, I don't like it," said Claude.

"I gather that's the general idea. Negative reinforcement."

Some time later Claude said, "She's trying to exclude me except for surface thoughts, but her pain still leaks through. I can't escape it, and yet I can't heal it."

"When the first shock passes, she'll open up to you again," Roger said. He felt Claude disdaining that remark for the hollow reassurance it was.

"I never thought," said Claude, "I would envy the human ability to cry."

Shortly, Roger mentally heard Britt's telepathic voice informing him that Eloise's examination had been completed. He passed the fact on to Claude, and they headed back to the ER.

Roger waited in the anteroom while Claude joined Eloise inside. Britt emerged to update Roger on Eloise's condition. "She's definitely miscarried. They're keeping her overnight for a D and C in the morning. Also, there's some worry about her low hematocrit."

Symptoms of anemia weren't surprising, in view of the long-sustained intimacy between Claude and Eloise. Roger hoped that once a blood transfusion raised Eloise's red cell count, absence of further anomalies would quell the hospital staff's curiosity. He joined Britt in the one unoccupied corner of the waiting room. "What about her emotional state?"

"Not good." Britt spoke quietly. "We had a tough time convincing her there was no hope of saving the pregnancy. And intellectually she realizes Claude couldn't control his reaction, but she still can't help blaming him for—well, you know."

Roger nodded. Britt only confirmed what Claude had said outside. A minute later Roger heard Eloise's voice raised to such a pitch that his inhuman ears couldn't help picking up the words: "Get out of here and leave me alone! You never wanted the baby in the first place!"

No answer from Claude. He emerged, grimly silent, and walked out the door. After Britt popped in for a quick farewell to Eloise, she and Roger followed Claude to the car.

The snow had stopped for the moment. On the way home, Britt, from her place next to Roger, twisted around to face Claude, sitting alone in the back seat. "Want to talk about it?"

After a drawn-out pause Claude said. "I did want the child—for her sake. I never claimed I wanted it for my own. But I was sincerely happy, happy in her joy."

"And yet—?" Britt prompted.

"You're too perceptive by half, dear lady. I admit one part of me didn't care for the change. We've had to—cut back."

"And after the baby came, it would've drained more from her, leaving even less for you."

Claude made a wordless sound of acknowledgment. Roger felt, like an itching at the nape of the neck, Claude's discomfort at exposing himself this way to an ephemeral, even a close friend. Britt must have intuited that too, for she suspended her inquiry, gazing out the window as if the white-on-black landscape visible to her human sight held absorbing interest.

When they reached the townhouse, Roger heard Gillian's slow respiration as they opened the front door. He went to the office to check on her. As he'd expected, she was still playing the computer game. Roger heard her heartbeat accelerate when Claude walked in behind him. Gillian spared them a quick glance. "Eloise?"

"Hospitalized until tomorrow," said Roger. He saw Gillian's shoulders slump in relief, probably at the news that she wouldn't have to deal further with human sickness tonight. No doubt she'd never seen it firsthand before. Claude's anguish seemed more than enough disturbance for her to handle.

Sounds of cabinets opening and ice clinking in glasses came from Britt in the kitchen. "How about a drink?" said Roger.

In the kitchen, dimly lit only by light spilling from the adjacent dining room, the three of them sat around the circular redwood table with tall glasses of Scotch and soda. Roger made sure Claude's ran heavily to Scotch. Alcohol couldn't affect their kind as strongly as it did human drinkers, but enough of it might blunt the edge of Claude's grief.

"What now? How long do you think they'll keep her?"

Britt made an impulsive gesture in response to the weariness in Claude's voice but stopped short of touching him. "If there aren't any complications, they should release her shortly after the D and C. Miscarriage isn't normally physically debilitating. Women can go back to work the next day."

Claude rubbed his eyes and took several sips of his drink. "But she might already be *debilitated*. She's built up an energy debt, so to speak."

"True," said Roger. "I wouldn't worry about it. They'll transfuse her, and that should take care of any problem."

Britt expressed one worry that might have been on Claude's mind. "Think the anemia will make them suspicious?"

"I doubt it," said Roger. "The resident on duty will simply assume that she lost a large quantity of blood before he examined her."

Claude stared into his glass. "She did, but over the long term, and not the way they think. Could that have caused it?"

Britt looked blank.

"Could my demands on her body have weakened her so much that she couldn't carry to term?"

Roger felt Claude's anxiety like a raw wound in his own flesh. "Put that out of your mind. Anyone who saw her aura could tell she was healthy."

This time Britt did reach across the table to clasp Claude's free hand. "Listen, any number of things can cause spontaneous abortions.

Most of them are never explained, and they very seldom have anything to do with external trauma. Contrary to the pop image of Scarlett O'Hara falling downstairs, you'd have to practically kill the mother to dislodge the embryo."

Claude seemed only marginally reassured. He gloomily drained his glass. Shortly Roger poured refills for all of them, and they drank in silence for some time. He felt Britt's fatigue, but she answered his silent query with a refusal to go to bed and abandon Claude.

Abruptly Roger realized that he'd just heard, but not registered, the front door opening and closing. He stood up to listen, sniff the air, and extend his preternatural perception. He mentally probed the various rooms as he might have flipped through the pages of a book.

"Gillian isn't in the house."

Claude roused from his apathetic stillness. "Probably couldn't stand to be under the same roof with me another minute. That's understandable."

Roger saw no point in offering a polite counter-argument. The vibrations of anxiety and grief must feel like searing flame to Gillian's newly awakened psychic powers. "Confound it, I don't want her wandering out there alone," said Roger. "I'd better go keep an eye on her."

Claude stood up. "No, I'll find her. I could use the fresh air myself." When Roger started to protest, he said. "Please. I need to be alone." He forced a smile. "Lick my wounds, eh?"

After he went out, Roger took Britt's hand and kissed the tender skin on the inside of the wrist. The throb of her pulse against his lips comforted him, even though he couldn't act on his hunger at the moment. *This is no time to think of yourself, and you shouldn't need it tonight anyway,* he admonished himself. "Colleague, you can see that Claude doesn't need us right now. Hadn't you better go to bed now?"

She brushed the back of her hand across his cheek. "What about you? Will you come up soon? You need to get at least a couple of hours' rest before work." She sighed. "Thank heaven it's our last day until New Year's. This has been a heck of a week."

Roger couldn't agree more. "Yes, I'll try to sleep a little. Soon. Now, you go ahead."

That was when he heard the gunshot.

## Chapter Six

DRIVEN BY CLAUDE'S unshielded agony, Gillian rushed out into the night. Fresh snow swirled in her face. She welcomed the sting of wind on her cheeks and needed no warmth aside from the long-sleeved pullover she wore.

So intimacy with a willing ephemeral didn't guarantee unadulterated pleasure; observing Claude showed her that truth. With the fading of the exhilaration she'd enjoyed when touching Britt, Gillian's qualms about the sudden awakening of her psi talent returned. Now that she craved contact with human minds, she couldn't isolate herself from them, these volatile creatures who assaulted a thirsty predator's exposed nerves with storms of emotion.

She jogged around the perimeter of the parking lot, an exercise that scarcely altered the rate of her respiration and pulse. Slipping on an icy patch, her legs recovered almost before her brain registered the lapse. Exertion twice as demanding wouldn't have shut down the turmoil of her thoughts. Could Claude and Roger really provide her the necessary training? Or should she submit to Volnar's age and authority?

*No! Not yet anyway. Not until I've proven I can function on my own.*

The wind dumped snow from a branch of a young tree onto her head. Gillian shook it out of her hair without breaking stride. How long would Roger let her stay? She couldn't help noticing that he found her an inconvenience.

On her second lap, at the far end of the lot from Roger's unit, a van with its motor running and parking lights on penetrated her anxious concentration. The illusion of eyes on the car's grillwork jolted her into awareness that living eyes were watching her. The driver's door opened.

Just before he stepped out, Gillian recognized the van as Greer's. She froze a few yards from him.

He took a cautious step toward her, both hands in the pockets of his heavy, fur-collared jacket. "I just want to talk to you, Gillian," he said softly. "What's the harm in that?"

"I already answered you," she said. "And my father told you to stay away."

A step closer. "But I'm asking you, not him. Maybe you don't agree with his rules."

She stood poised to dash away. "I can't tell you anything."

"You could tell me so much if you wanted to." She sensed the fear behind his wheedling tone and noticed how he avoided her eyes. "You want to learn about people—human beings—don't you? Let's learn from each other." One more step. "I won't take much of your time."

Despite the transparent ploy, Gillian was tempted. She'd enjoy testing her strength against a victim who, unlike Britt, was ignorant and unwilling. Hadn't she learned a lot since confronting Greer the previous afternoon? *Watch out, that's overconfidence. That's what Claude and Roger would say!* Gillian shook her head, impatient with the drift of her thoughts. Had she fled from Volnar to accept someone else's command so readily?

While she debated with herself, Greer took a final stride toward her. His left hand flung the contents of a small jar in her face.

A stinking powder filled her eyes and nose. Garlic! Retching, she doubled over. Blinded, her windpipe clogged, she heaved up her last meal. The acid of half-digested blood burned her throat. She hardly felt Greer's fist slamming into her temple.

Greer's hand clamped on her arm. Through a mist of tears and snow, she saw his other hand holding a gun before her eyes.

"You know I could destroy your brain with a well-aimed bullet," he whispered. "But I don't want to hurt you. I just want my questions answered."

He jerked her arms behind her back. Still paralyzed, she couldn't resist. Her fogged brain registered with humiliation the fact that he wouldn't need the gun to keep her helpless. She felt the cold metal of cuffs being fastened on her wrists.

A curse from Greer made her look up. Lightly running footsteps on the snow-sprinkled blacktop—glowing eyes—it took Gillian a second to realize that Claude was bounding toward them.

Greer let go of her to throw open a side door of the van. He picked her up by her sweater to shove her inside. At that moment Claude let out a lupine howl—and changed.

Gillian saw an apparition of gleaming fangs and wings undulating like smoke. She had no way of knowing what Greer saw. The vision horrified the man into an inarticulate gurgle. He whipped up the pistol and fired.

Gillian caught only a glimpse of Claude collapsing to the pavement. The sight paralyzed her with fear. *Claude—!* Greer flung her into the van, where she rolled over and hit her head on the leg of a bench-type seat. She heard the doors slam, then felt the motor rumble as they roared away.

WHEN ROGER DASHED outside, he saw Claude lying on his side in the middle of the parking lot. He heard a car's engine out of sight down the road. Pursuing it had to take second place. He turned Claude over. Fresh blood stained Claude's cream-colored turtleneck shirt.

Roger hastily scanned the facade of the townhouse. No curious neighbors were coming out to investigate or peering through their windows. Fortunately, anyone who heard the shot must have mistaken it for a car backfiring or the sound track of a TV show. He lifted Claude in his arms. Thank God for the gentle snowfall, which would soon hide the traces of blood on the blacktop.

Britt was waiting in the foyer. For once, she'd behaved with proper caution instead of rushing to follow him outside. He carried Claude up to the guest room, where the medical bag still sat open on the dresser. Britt had covered the sheet with clean towels. Roger deposited his brother on the bed face up and stripped off the shirt with Britt's help.

He was alarmed to note that the wound still bled. Britt immediately applied pressure with a gauze pad, but external measures couldn't do the job as well as the vampire's own willpower could. Was Claude too far gone to suppress the flow? Roger sharply spoke Claude's name. The wounded man's eyes opened.

Roger tried not to let his relief show. "Listen, Claude, you have to stop the bleeding. You can't afford to lose any more."

Claude gave a minute nod. His eyes momentarily unfocused. When they cleared, Roger removed Britt's hand from the improvised dressing. Blood had stopped leaking from the wound underneath. "Good," he said. "I didn't see an exit wound, so we'll have to probe for the bullet. Can you tell me what happened?"

"Greer. Shot me. Took Gillian." Claude spoke in a strained whisper.

Britt's eyes widened in shock. "He's got her?"

Roger leaned over Claude. "How? Didn't she resist? Tell me what you saw."

"Good grief, don't badger him now!" said Britt. "Can we give him anything for the pain?"

"I don't know of any drug that wouldn't be useless or harmful. He'll have to depend on his own ability to control it." Roger didn't bother asking how the patient felt. No sense in belaboring the obvious—pain radiated from Claude like heat from a furnace. "You'll have to draw on Britt for support." Roger disliked making this suggestion, but he couldn't let groundless jealousy cloud his judgment. "Use her as a focus to shut off the sensations. Otherwise you're likely to experience some discomfort when I remove the bullet."

Britt scowled at him. "Forget the bedside manner, colleague, it's not your strong suit. Claude, this is going to hurt like hell unless you let me help you."

Claude's mouth twisted in an attempt at a smile. "Well put. All right."

Britt drew a chair up to the bedside and gazed into Claude's eyes. He turned his head to focus on her. Roger felt the immaterial pressure on his own nerves lighten with the fading of Claude's pain. The patient's breathing slowed and deepened, merging with the rhythm of Britt's.

Roger silently reminded himself not to project an uneasy possessiveness that might shake Britt's concentration. Instead he channeled his thoughts toward the surgery at hand.

Immersed in a light self-induced trance, Claude held all physical sensation at bay and simultaneously shunted blood flow away from the puncture that Roger's instruments opened wider. Roger allowed himself a twinge of envy for such refined control of autonomic functions. To his relief the slug had missed the heart as well as both lungs. He informed the other two of that fact. "You were lucky. Too bad you don't believe in anyone you can thank for it."

"You," Claude responded in a distant murmur, keeping his eyes fixed on Britt's. "Say it for me. Couldn't hurt."

Given the accelerated healing of vampire flesh, stitches would be superfluous. Roger closed the wound with gauze and tape. He and Britt together rolled Claude to one side, eliciting a groan from the patient, to replace the towels under him and strip off the rest of his clothes. Roger was dismayed to notice Claude's eyes drifting shut.

"Wake up! You can't lose consciousness yet. Britt, hold his hand and make sure he doesn't."

Taking him literally, Britt resumed her seat by the bed and cupped one of Claude's hands in both of hers. "Why not? Is there any danger—?" Her reluctance to speak the words, in contrast to her usual candor, showed the extent of her anxiety.

"Of his dying? I don't think so. As far as I know, an injury kills us outright or not at all." A minuscule nod from Claude. "My concern is that the energy drain might send him into a coma so deep he couldn't revive on his own. And I wouldn't know how to awaken him safely."

"Okay, I'll keep him alert," said Britt.

Roger left the room to clean his instruments and repack his bag. He had to get blood into Claude before dawn, since sunrise would certainly force the injured vampire into the deathlike daytime sleep. Reluctant though he was to take the risk, Roger knew he would have to contact one of his infrequently-used illicit sources. Over the years he'd cultivated several unscrupulous hospital and blood bank employees for this very purpose.

When he reentered the bedroom for a quick check on his patient, he saw Britt pressing her wrist to Claude's mouth. Claude hadn't accepted the invitation, but that didn't temper Roger's reaction. He sprang across the room and grabbed Britt's arm.

"Colleague—" Her warning tone made him realize how hard he was squeezing her forearm.

"Sorry." He relaxed his grip. "Britt, you mustn't, it's too far dangerous."

"Claude? Dangerous?" Her voice was as harsh as Roger's own.

"He's desperate. He could drain you without meaning to."

"The hell with that! Roger, he's hurting—I can feel it! And you want me to *ignore* it?"

Her selfless courage shamed him. Imagine putting his own need ahead of a patient's, and that patient his own brother. "Very well, do what you can for him."

Claude moved his head in a slight negative gesture. "He's got a point. Not sure I could stop."

"No, Britt is right," said Roger. "You need living nourishment. Excuse me, I have to make some phone calls." He'd just as soon not watch Claude feed on Britt. True, Roger had once drunk from Eloise, with Claude's permission, during a long separation from Britt. Soon thereafter, they'd tasted token sips from each other's lovers to provide for just such an emergency as this. Normally, Claude, in this weakened state, would have been unable to accept any donor other than Eloise, because of their fixation on each other. Thanks to their precautions, now Britt was an acceptable substitute.

But the preparation didn't make the act any easier for Roger to tolerate.

He went downstairs, well away from the bedroom, to use the

office telephone. The first two contacts he spoke to made excuses, insisting they couldn't obtain blood for several hours at the least. The third, an orderly in a hospital near Baltimore, said, "Man, I wondered if you'd ever call again. I got a dozen units in the freezer I been holding onto, just in case."

Roger approved of the man's foresight. No doubt he'd filched the supplies bit by bit over a period of months, from blood due to be discarded. Roger asked for six units.

"That'll cost you."

Roger wasn't surprised at the exorbitant price quoted. After all, one expected to pay for high-risk services. He agreed to the deal and set terms for a meeting.

"You don't care what type? What do you do with the stuff, anyhow?"

"You don't need to know." Doubtless his suppliers suspected some underworld connection.

"On second thought, guess I don't want to." The man hung up.

Roger went upstairs to tell Britt and Claude he was leaving. He found Britt leaning over the patient, who obstinately turned away from her. "Roger, he won't take it."

Striding to the bed, Roger looked down at his brother. Claude's eyes glowed with hunger in the deep shadow, for Britt had switched off the lamp for his comfort. "Oh, yes, he will. Listen to me, you. Stop trying to act noble. It doesn't suit you. Besides, you're making Britt feel rejected."

Claude's gaze shifted from Roger to Britt. Again she placed the pulse point of her left wrist against his lips. Roger felt her silent invitation, like a fragrant cloud that lulled all resistance to sleep. After a shuddering moan, Claude surrendered. His mouth fastened on her flesh.

Britt, sitting on the edge of the bed, closed her eyes and swayed toward Claude. Though the emotion that flowed from her with her blood was nurturing, not erotic, Roger could hardly bear it. He stared at his watch.

At the end of five minutes he placed a hand firmly but gently on Claude's shoulder. "That's enough. Stop."

Claude's eyes dreamily drifted open. Removing his mouth from the incision, he pushed Britt's arm away.

"No, he's not satisfied," she said. "Colleague, I'm fine, I can give more."

Pressing on the tiny wound to stop the flow, Roger guided her from the bed to the nearest chair. "You're experienced enough to know that your feelings aren't reliable right now. You're letting empathy undermine your judgment."

Britt rubbed her forehead. "You could be right. I do feel a little dizzy. Interesting sensation—nothing sexual about it, a pure emptiness begging to be filled."

"*Merci*," Claude whispered.

Britt smiled weakly. "Anytime. But you do need more."

"I've arranged for six units of whole blood," Roger said. "In fact, I promised to meet my source in less than half an hour, so I'd better go."

"What about Gillian out there with Greer?" Though Britt kept her voice even, she couldn't hide her anxiety. "Every minute he may be taking her farther away. Isn't there anything you can do?"

"Such as?" Roger said. "I'm worried, of course, but it's realistic to suppose that she's in no immediate danger. If he wanted to kill her, he would have done it, not kidnapped her. He'd want a healthy hostage—or research subject." Britt nodded but didn't look wholly convinced. "I'll be back as soon as possible. Keep the doors locked, and don't let Claude sleep."

"Aye, aye, sir," said Britt.

Silently apologizing for giving unnecessary orders, Roger went into his bedroom to get cash from a small safe in the back of the closet. One precaution Volnar insisted on was keeping ample amounts of money in the house. While Roger normally led a civilized, unadventurous life, occasionally he'd had cause to appreciate his mentor's advice on that point.

Thoughts of Volnar reminded him of their recent conversation. With the hectic night, Roger had found little time to spare for considering Volnar's news. Now, driving toward Severna Park, he pondered it. Would Sandor's twin sister risk her own freedom to wreak vengeance on him? Did Claude know anything about her? Roger decided to question him as soon as he could talk halfway comfortably.

Roger had chosen the far end of a shopping mall lot for the rendezvous. Less likely to be monitored by police than a convenience store, less suspicious for a motorist to visit at night in midwinter than a public park. In his upscale vehicle he might pass for a very early commuter waiting to meet his car pool at the Park and Ride lot. Seven minutes after his arrival his contact drove up in an aged but well-polished blue sedan. The supplier, a stocky black man, handed over the frozen blood and accepted the payment with only a subdued grumble about being dragged out of bed to drive around in the snow. Obviously the roll of fifty-dollar bills made up for the inconvenience.

Roger waited for the other man's car to vanish around a corner before he pulled out. His infrequent suppliers knew neither his name nor where he lived, a situation he intended to maintain. On the way home, he extended his thoughts to touch Britt's mind. No change in the patient's condition, Roger was glad to learn. God, he was tired. The smudge of gray lightening the eastern horizon invited him to sleep. No time for that, with Claude to consider.

As soon as he got home, Roger defrosted three of the six plastic bags in the microwave. Carefully squeezing out ice crystals and shaking the bags to homogenize the contents, he transferred two of them to pint beer mugs to finish heating. While stored blood lacked the vital spark of fluid from a living body, and quick thawing further diminished the quality, it was a good deal better than nothing. Ordinary people had to put up with the mediocrity of processed foods; why should vampires expect to be exempt? With a momentary flash of humor, he visualized restaurants serving blood—categorized by type and Rh factor, of course, guaranteed free of drugs or garlic, and maintained in thermal cups at precisely ninety-eight point six degrees.

In the bedroom Britt helped Claude sit up, braced with pillows. Only a tightening around the lips betrayed the pain this effort cost him. "Damn, I hate this. Takeout breakfast? Thanks." He accepted one of the mugs from Roger and started gulping the contents.

"Slow down, you'll make yourself ill." When Claude obeyed, Roger sipped his own drink and said, "Do you feel able to talk? What exactly happened with Gillian?"

"Don't, colleague," said Britt.

Claude cut off her protest with a languid gesture. "No, it's all right, I'm ready to talk. Not much to tell, actually. I saw her doubled over on the ground with a man—Greer, I assumed, from her earlier description of his van—holding onto her. Odor of garlic in the air. No doubt that's how he rendered her helpless. I charged him, thinking to scare him into letting her go. I transformed. Instead of panicking and running for it, he panicked and shot me. I heard the car drive off, and that's about it until you carried me in here."

"I'm surprised you changed," Roger said, "considering how cautious you people generally are about displaying that ability. Didn't you think it might be dangerous?"

Claude grimaced. "Didn't have much time to think, old man. One advantage—seeing me transformed, he couldn't recognize me later.

And how the hell was I supposed to know he had a gun? Not the most typical reaction to the impossible, to go blasting away at it." He finished his drink.

Roger took the empty mug and handed it to Britt. "Could you refill this, colleague?"

On the way into the hall, she paused to say, "What about Gillian? If he shot you, having her in his hands is pretty frightening."

"Oh, he wouldn't harm her," said Claude. "Prize specimen—wants to keep her intact. From what you told me, all he wants is an interview."

"That's all he wants *now*," Roger said gloomily. "Too bad you couldn't have noted the license number of the vehicle."

"Of course I did. What do you take me for? Light green Chevrolet van, Virginia plates." Claude recited the number. "Since he's passing through, that may not be of much immediate help." Roger noticed that he already spoke with less strain, now that the first unit of blood had fortified him.

A minute later, Britt appeared with the refilled mug. "Claude, how did Eloise react to your getting shot?"

"She slept through it, thank Providence. They've got her heavily sedated. Postponing the inevitable—I don't look forward to telling her about this tomorrow."

Britt took the chair next to the bed, while Roger leaned against the dresser slowly drinking from his mug. "I agree that Greer won't harm Gillian unnecessarily," he said. "But I don't have much hope that he'll simply let her go when he's finished interrogating her."

"She may very well escape," said Claude, "or he may contact you when he discovers that as a child, she can't satisfy his greed for the esoteric. Either way, I'm sure she's safe for the time being."

"Much as I hate to admit it," said Roger, "I don't see that we can do anything about it today."

Britt scanned Claude, displaying an avid interest in his rate of healing that Roger could hardly blame. "Think it's safe for him to sleep yet?"

"I'd say so. Claude?"

Claude gave the empty mug back to Britt. "I should wake normally at sunset."

Roger examined his aura, which had brightened measurably in the past fifteen minutes. Yet the effects of the massive energy drain he'd suffered couldn't have passed away so quickly. "I don't like leaving you alone."

"Maybe I should stay with him," Britt said.

"I don't like to ask that."

"You aren't, I'm offering. And doesn't it make sense? I can do more for him than you can."

True, Britt's mere presence would offer Claude strength. "Yes, there's something in that. But it's unfortunate that you'll miss your last appointments before we shut down for the holidays."

"I'll call in and order them cancelled." Roger could have given their receptionist that direction, but he agreed with Britt that there was no point in flaunting their off-duty association at the office. "I'm sure the patients won't object, and I won't in the least mind an early vacation from my Thursday ten o'clock session. Thirty-year-old playboy—I wouldn't mind him coming on to me, that's textbook normal, but he acts as if I should be flattered. Half the time I feel like laughing in his face, and the other half I want to strangle him."

Claude smiled weakly at this image. "I daresay you could do it. Thank you for giving up your day for me, *ma belle-soeur*."

"No problem. Lie down and stop trying to talk."

"Yes, Doctor."

She followed Roger to his bedroom. "Will you go check on Sigmund for me? Refill his dry food, and open a can for him."

He stopped her from reciting any more of the familiar routine. "Yes, I know. And I'll call the hospital to find out when Eloise will be released. You should be resting as much as possible. I'll stay out of your way."

"What are you talking about? I assumed you were going to work as usual. No reason for both of us to stay here," said Britt.

He suppressed a sigh. He should have expected this contrary attitude. "I don't want to leave you alone. Claude is certainly no protection."

"I don't expect to need protection." Impatience cut through the fatigue in her voice. "Greer, or Camille if she's nearby, is just as likely to contact you at your office as at home. In the middle of the day, maybe more so. Besides, I thought you didn't want to advertise our relationship. How will it look if we both take the day off at a moment's notice?"

Aware that he couldn't shake her determination without a tiring argument, and struck by an unpleasant image of Camille looking for him at the office and deciding to victimize Marcia, the receptionist, Roger gave in. "You can give me a telepathic call if anything happens—and see that you do, instantly."

"Of course, I'm not stupid. It's okay for me to sleep a while, isn't it? I don't think I can hold out much longer." Britt sat on Roger's bed watching him choose a fresh suit and accessories.

"Yes. In fact, it might help if you'd lie down with Claude."

Her eyebrows arched in mild surprise. "That's a switch."

"Don't be too hard on my instinctive possessiveness, colleague. He's obviously no threat to you, and more than likely, he'll remain unconscious until I get home anyway." He undressed, hanging up items or dropping them in the hamper as necessary. No matter how harried he might be, tidiness came naturally to him.

"All right, will do."

"And if Gillian, by some chance, does escape from Greer and telephones for help, the answering machine will be on."

Britt drooped back onto the pillow. "Oh, Lord, I hope she does."

After his shower, he came out of the attached bathroom to find Britt tucked into the queen-size bed. The clothes folded on the chair demonstrated that she was naked under the covers. One of many traits he valued in her, she shared his ingrained habit of neatness. She drowsily held out her arms to him.

"God, don't tempt me, or I'll never get out of this room." Nevertheless, he did sit on the bed and give her a tentative embrace.

"You can do better than that," she murmured into his neck.

"Not if I plan to see patients today."

"On second thought, maybe you should stay home. You look exhausted."

"No, that's one reason I shouldn't. Claude will be draining energy from you, and I don't want to add to the stress." He resolutely untwined her arms from around his neck and stood up. "One thing— before you join him in there, please put something on."

"I thought you'd given up being jealous," she teased. "Idiot, of course I will. Now, go feed my cat."

"Certainly." The sooner he got moving, the less likely he would succumb to Britt's allure and forget the whole thing. "By the way, be sure you don't forget to eat, too."

"I won't. Worrywart." She sat up, arms wrapped around her knees, to watch him leave.

Driving across the bridge into Annapolis, he hoped he was successfully concealing the worry that most plagued him, leaving her alone while two different enemies potentially lurked in wait to descend upon his home.

WHEN ROGER CALLED the hospital at mid-morning to check on Eloise's release, he discovered that the resident on duty wanted her to stay an extra night because of her inexplicably low blood count. Switched through to Eloise herself, Roger found her in a foul mood over the delay.

"I don't need to be monitored, and I feel all right. Physically, at least. I want *out* of here! Can't you come over and do something? Convince them to let me go?"

"That probably wouldn't be wise." Roger leaned back in his swivel desk chair and flipped open the file on his next scheduled patient. "I understand they have you set up for another transfusion, which strikes me as a good idea."

"I don't like that either. It takes forever, lying there staring at the ceiling, and the last one left me feeling woozy."

"Shall I come by and see you on my noon break? Anything you'd like me to bring?"

"No, there's no reason for you to drive at that time of day if you don't have to. I'll probably spend the afternoon napping anyway." Her apathetic tone worried him. She hadn't even asked about Britt.

"Then we'll visit you this evening, and tomorrow morning we'll take you home. Home to my place, if you like, instead of the hotel."

"That would be nice," she said dejectedly. "I tried to reach Claude, but he's asleep. I didn't mean to hurt him, honestly. And I know he didn't wimp out on purpose. But I can't seem to *feel* it."

"Give it time," said Roger, wishing they were face to face so he could use his psychic influence to loosen the knot of her misery. "You can talk to him tonight." This didn't seem the right moment to hit her with Claude's injury and Gillian's abduction.

Eloise's condition preyed on his mind throughout the afternoon, except when he shunted the problem aside while interacting with patients. He'd had decades of practice at such compartmentalizing. A couple of people commented on the icy streets. After the night's flurries had blown over, the bright sun had melted the top layer of snow just enough to refreeze when the temperature dropped in the afternoon. Roger's last session of the day called in to cancel on account of the hazardous roads. He was unsurprised—she was a mild agoraphobic who regularly seized upon any excuse to skip appointments—and, on the whole, grateful for the chance to get home early. Even if that meant driving while the sun was still above the horizon.

After wishing the receptionist an advance Merry Christmas and

Happy New Year, he packed his briefcase full of case notes and income tax records and started for home. Awareness of Britt waiting there for him lifted his spirits. They'd agreed living together full-time would be unwise, but an occasional interlude like this could be a great pleasure. Despite a severely wounded visitor and a host of other troubles lurking on the sidelines.

Roger popped a Handel cassette, in deference to the season, into the car's tape deck and hummed along with it. He'd checked on Britt several times during the day. She'd slept until about one. Since then, she'd occupied herself with light housecleaning—though he'd urged her not to bother—and the ordeal of a pile of Navy Tricare forms she'd brought from work the previous day. Her telepathic grumbling had made him smile in spite of his worries; he, too, would prefer the most intransigent case of schizophrenia over insurance claim documents.

Pulling into his parking space, he allowed himself a moment of envy for Claude, sharing a bed—however innocently—with Britt this morning. Sleeping with a vampire, literally dead to the world, was no fun for the human partner. For the nonhuman beneficiary himself (or herself), though, contact with that warm, vital presence bestowed the deepest and most invigorating rest. Roger felt sorry for most of his compatriots, who could never bring themselves to trust an ephemeral that far.

Britt met him at the door without offering a welcome-home kiss. She knew he preferred to do without such indulgences when they didn't have time or privacy to do it right. "Not a peep out of the phone all day. I halfway expected Greer to call, given that he's probably not getting any satisfaction out of Gillian."

"What about Claude?" Roger said, hanging up his coat.

"He just woke up."

"This early?" They headed for the stairs. "What is he doing?"

Britt smiled. "Trying to charge in all directions at once. I ordered him to stay horizontal until you've examined him. I don't feel I have the proper training to prescribe for this case."

"What makes you think I do?"

"I was about to warm some dinner for him when you got here."

"Fine, exactly what I would have suggested." Roger went up to see Claude, leaving Britt to defrost *dinner*.

Claude half reclined, both pillows rolled to support his head and shoulders. "That partner of yours is a flaming tyrant. I'm perfectly capable of walking."

"I don't consider you qualified to make that judgment. How do you feel?" Roger pulled a chair up to the bed and sat down.

"Rotten," said Claude cheerfully. "But not half so bad as I would've otherwise. Thanks—to both of you."

"Don't thank me. If it weren't for me, you wouldn't be in this situation to begin with."

"Good point. Maybe I'll take it out of your hide later. Seriously, old man, I'm sorry I botched it with Gillian."

"We'll discuss that after a while." Roger scanned Claude's aura, which had shed most of the murkiness of the previous night. The slow, steady heartbeat was equally encouraging. When he ran his fingers lightly over the wound, Claude winced. "Prepare yourself. I have to change the dressing." As soon as Claude's eyes glazed over in a light self-induced trance, Roger peeled off the bandage. As he'd expected, the entry wound appeared to have been healing for at least a week. Another day or two, and no mark would be visible. Clearly, however, Claude was still paying for the extreme energy drain he'd suffered.

Having replaced the dressing, Roger lightly tapped Claude's wrist. Claude's eyes focused on him. "Do you need to get up?"

"Not now. And if I did, I'd rather lie here and suffer than ask Britt."

Roger had expected the negative answer. In the normal daylight dormancy, a vampire's kidneys virtually shut down along with other metabolic functions. "Then ask me, when necessary. I won't have you keeling over and risking a concussion or a fracture."

"Come on, Rodge, you exaggerate the danger. I'm practically recovered. By the way, when you visit Eloise tonight, would you please tell her that? She doesn't believe me."

Britt stepped into the room, carrying a pair of mugs on a tray. "Goodness, I wonder why? So she's speaking to you?"

Claude's expression darkened. "Only on a superficial level. Like talking on the blasted telephone—she won't let me inside. But she's upset about what happened, and I need you to convince her I'm fine."

"Lie, you mean," said Roger.

Claude summoned up a smile. "Right. Knew I could count on you." He chose a mug from the tray Britt set on the nightstand. "She said they're releasing her tomorrow. By then I should be on my feet."

Britt, curling up in an armchair across the room, looked skeptical. "You think so, colleague?"

"I don't have much basis for comparison. It's possible." Roger picked up the other mug and drank a few swallows of the warm blood before changing the subject. "Claude, have you ever met Neil Sandor's twin sister?"

"Camille? *Certainement.*"

"Why the blazes haven't you ever mentioned her?"

Claude seemed mildly surprised by the angry response. "Why should I? The subject never happened to come up. I hardly know the woman. Haven't seen her in years."

"Was she—is she like her brother?"

"A sadist and suicidally reckless to boot? Not so far as I could tell, but as I said, I've never seen much of her. I didn't care for her style. Why?"

Roger repeated what Volnar had said in the previous night's long-distance conversation.

Claude frowned into his mug. "Bloody hell! That explains why she dropped out of sight about the time Neil—died. No, I didn't hear about her imprisonment, or I certainly would have told you. Twins are close, that's to be expected, so I can understand she'd bear a grudge against you, but to make threats wild enough to get herself condemned to *that*—Can't be sure what effect the punishment had on her. It might have cooled her off—or it could have changed her personality for the worse."

"What do you know about her?"

Claude took a moment to gather his thoughts. "Aside from a few casual meetings, I visited her apartment near San Francisco once. Happened to be in the area for a film, and she invited me to join her regular weekly soiree. At that time, she had a select circle of acquaintances—human—that she had over for sedate parties. Sedate until the end, that is."

"Well, what did she do? Host orgies?"

"Hardly. She accepted donations."

Roger stared at him. "Are you saying these people knew what she was?"

"No, that was the clever bit. She posed as a blood fetishist."

"Say what?" Britt exclaimed.

"That's right, she professed to be a blood fetishist who enjoyed playing the role of a vampire. Held court in a crimson-lined black cape with ghastly white makeup, the whole stereotype. She'd built up a stable of followers who got a kick out of enacting their vampire fantasies by giving her a few ounces of blood. She made sure she rotated the privilege, never taking from one donor too often, to minimize the chance of addiction." Claude shook his head, chuckling. "Damned ingenious, I must admit. But I left as soon as the fun started.

She'd invited me to partake and couldn't fathom why I declined."

"Why did you?" said Britt.

"It may have been all very well for her, but I had to think of my reputation. Suppose I'd been recognized, and one of the tabloids had picked it up? Besides, exhibitionism makes me uncomfortable. It can backfire so readily."

Roger marveled that Claude didn't class his own flamboyant film career as exhibitionism. "So she enjoys manipulating people and taking risks," he said. "If the—punishment—hasn't cooled off her rage over Sandor's death, she probably won't hesitate to come after me."

"If she's got any sense, she'll forget the whole thing and enjoy her freedom. Volnar and the Council won't aggressively pursue her unless she causes trouble."

Britt thoughtfully leaned her chin on her clenched fists. "I can't believe she'd let it go without a fight. The sibling bond is important, isn't it? And you said twins are especially close. She sees Roger as her brother's murderer, I suppose."

Roger felt Britt's eyes, shadowed with apprehension, on him. "Well, now that we're forewarned, she won't take us by surprise. And in any case, there's nothing I can do until Camille shows herself. More immediately, what about Gillian?"

"You think there's anything you can do about her?" Britt said.

Claude emptied his mug and replaced it on the tray. "We'll have to. The longer she stays in Greer's hands, the more likely she'll end up giving him information about our species. Remember, she's only a child, and at a vulnerable stage."

"He already knows more than he should," Roger said. "More than he did when he forced his way in here, I think. He used garlic against her, and he wasn't too paralyzed with fear to take a shot at you."

Britt nodded. "Interesting point. How did he make such good guesses—or get so well informed so fast?" She stood up to collect the empty cups.

"We do know some things about him," Roger said. "Not only his appearance and where he comes from, but the description and license number of his car."

Balancing the mugs on the tray, Britt said, "You're thinking of Captain Hayes?" She alluded to their contact in the county homicide division.

"If approached the right way, he might be able to track down Greer's present whereabouts. Or where he's officially staying, at the very least."

"Yes, and Hayes did say he owed us for our prompt, detailed report on that suspect the other day, didn't he?" She left to take the used cups downstairs.

"Police?" Claude frowned dubiously.

"If we do ask for his help, of course we won't tell him why," said Roger. "We'll put it as a favor."

Claude tried to push himself into a sitting position, grimacing at the strain on his wound.

"Careful! Didn't I warn you not to do that?"

"Well, I need to get up now. Damn, I hate feeling helpless! Remind me not to get shot again in the near future."

As much as Roger sympathized with Claude's feelings, he didn't let his brother attempt to stand without support. An attack of vertigo convinced Claude that Roger had reason on his side. In the bathroom Roger helped Claude with a sketchy wash at the sink, cut short because of the patient's limited strength.

Back in bed, he said, "When do I get a shower?"

"Tomorrow, if you're lucky."

Britt reappeared. "We have to go see Eloise soon. Are you planning to phone Captain Hayes first?"

"Probably you ought to do that. My special ability is useless over the telephone, and he likes you better than he likes me."

"Now that I can understand," Claude put in. "She does everything she does so consummately well. If I weren't committed elsewhere, I'd challenge you for her."

Roger was dismayed to feel a growl rising in his throat.

"Take it easy, little brother, I said *if*." His mocking smile faded. "Damn, I can't imagine life without Eloise. Does she honestly think I don't care? Can she blame me that my grief isn't as intense as hers?"

Britt stepped over to the bed to clasp his hand. "I know she'll see things clearer when the hurt isn't so sharp."

"Maybe," said Claude. "How can I get through to her? She'll mistrust any overture I make as manipulative."

"If necessary, I'll talk to her later." Sensing Claude's discomfort at baring his emotions to her, Britt withdrew to make the phone call to Captain Hayes.

"If you insist on chaining me to this bed for the night," Claude said, "how about bringing me something to read?"

"Certainly." Roger went down to the office to gather a selection of books. He found Britt re-dialing; obviously she'd had to call Hayes at home.

Roger overheard Hayes' friendly tone shift in the direction of caution after Britt detailed her request. "Doctor, I'm due to retire next year. You wouldn't want to screw up my pension, would you?"

"It's a simple thing to ask," said Britt in a more persuasive manner than she'd ever bother to use with Roger. "You can run a check unofficially, just to find out where this man is staying. He must be registered at a local hotel."

"Unofficially—sure. How do I explain it if somebody happens to notice this unofficial inquiry?" Hayes' long-suffering voice indicated that he didn't expect an answer. "You won't tell me why you want to find this Adam Greer person?"

"Sorry, I can't. It's confidential. Come on, how often have Roger and I asked you for favors?"

"Want me to start counting?" In fact, they'd seldom had occasion to use their police contacts this way, so Hayes' protest lacked force.

"He's a sociology professor at William and Mary, probably between forty and fifty years old, brown hair and beard with some gray. I don't know about his eyes." She described the van and dictated its license number to the officer. "All I want is the word on where he's staying, or was staying last. Roger and I need to talk to him."

"Something to do with a patient?"

"It's confidential," Britt repeated. The word would reinforce Hayes' assumption that her concern was medical. "Didn't you remark just the other day that you owed us one?"

"Guess I did," the officer sighed. "Okay, I'll see what I can dig up. Now, could I get back to my dinner?"

After telling him to call Roger's number with the information, Britt thanked him and hung up. "Colleague, we could've made that simpler by telling him Greer has been harassing you."

"Not with Gillian to consider. If the police discovered her in Greer's clutches, they might get some idea of why he captured her—her unusual qualities. And if they arrested the man, for either harassment or kidnapping, they'd wonder why I declined to press charges."

"Which you couldn't—same problem about exposing Gillian's true nature." Britt shook her head, running her fingers through her unbound golden-bronze hair. "This secret identity of yours makes some things unnecessarily complicated."

"Secret identity?" he dryly repeated. He took her into his arms, no longer able to resist the comfort she offered. "If I were Superman, dear colleague, I wouldn't have most of these problems." He felt her drooping with fatigue as she leaned her head on his shoulder. "You need to rest."

"Shouldn't. I slept half the day."

"With Claude continuously drawing on your reserves. I didn't realize it had been such a drain on you."

"I don't mind. A good night's sleep will fix it, isn't that what you always say?" She straightened up. "Let's go see Eloise. She's the one who needs help."

## Chapter Seven

HANDCUFFS CHAFED GILLIAN'S wrists and ankles. To minimize the discomfort she had stopped struggling an hour previously. To keep the van's motion from aggravating her residual nausea, she stared out the window at the eddying snow. Deep breathing might have helped, but she inhaled as little as possible because of the garlic grains that clung to her shirt.

She'd temporarily resigned herself to her inability to break the shackles. They must be made of some extra-tough alloy. Greer was thorough. About a mile away from Roger's place, the professor had pulled over to cuff Gillian's ankles together. Then he'd used another two pairs of cuffs to fasten her to the legs of the van's middle seat by her hands and feet. Lying on her side, free to do no more than squirm in place, she noticed Greer glancing back at her every few minutes. Probably, Volnar could have broken these bonds. Maybe Claude or Roger—she had her doubts. She herself couldn't. Once convinced, she decided to conserve energy for later.

The vision of Claude falling beneath Greer's bullet haunted her. If a mature vampire could so easily be struck down by this mere mortal, what chance did she have?

Screaming never occurred to her. In the unlikely event that someone in the passing traffic heard her cries, the potential rescuer would be human. And exposing herself to human view was what had caused this disaster. At his destination, Greer would have to unfasten her, and by then her strength would have returned.

Once, when he stole a glance at her, she asked him where they were going. He hastily turned his eyes back to the windshield. Her abraded nerves felt his trepidation. So he was afraid to meet her gaze? That realization gave her a scrap of confidence.

Glimpses through the window showed her trees and an occasional overpass. Linking those observations with the car's speed, she concluded they were driving along a freeway. When the van braked and lurched around a curve, she knew they'd taken an exit and must therefore be reaching the end of the trip. Though the snow had almost stopped, the professor peered anxiously through the windshield and muttered a curse now and then. Several times the tires slid on patches of ice. Inadequately cleared back roads, Gillian guessed. She made no conscious attempt to memorize the turns, which would imprint themselves on her brain without effort. In any case if she managed to escape, she wouldn't need to follow roads. Her innate directional sense would lead her straight to Roger's home across whatever terrain intervened.

Roger—how long would it take him to find her? Or would he bother searching? And how badly hurt was Claude?

After a while, Greer parked the van and got out, taking the keys with him. With the motor off, the windows quickly fogged. Gillian made her arm and leg muscles go limp, trying to ease the cramps from lying for over an hour in this unnatural position. Shortly, the professor reappeared, carrying a key and a grocery bag.

"We're almost there," he said. "Sorry I had to leave you that way for so long." He sounded sincere.

He started the engine and turned the heater on again. She wished he had left it off; the warm air blowing at her from the floor vents distressed her already unsettled stomach. A few minutes later, he stopped once more. By the decisive way he pocketed the ignition keys, she knew they'd arrived.

"Where are we?"

Stooping a bit, he stood over her. "What difference does it make? Somewhere we won't be bothered. Excuse me a minute." He got out of the car. Gillian heard wind but saw no more snow falling.

When Greer came back and knelt beside her, she bared her teeth at him. "I'm going to let you walk now," he said. "You won't give me any trouble, will you?" He switched the handcuff keys to his left hand and drew the gun from his belt with his right hand.

"You wouldn't kill me," she said. "I wouldn't be able to answer your questions then."

"No, but I could shoot to disable, and you wouldn't like that, either." His expression softened. "Look, I don't want to hurt you. Knowledge, that's all I'm after. This," he gestured at the cuffs, "is only to protect myself." He gingerly leaned over to unlock the shackle attaching her arms to the bench leg. His eyes shifted, as if he saw something in her face that scared him. "On second thought, I'd better let you shuffle along with your feet locked together. Don't worry, I won't make it worse on you than I have to."

She watched him fumble with the other cuffs, until she was free of the seat's frame but still hobbled. The gun's muzzle never pointed away from her. "Now I'm going to pull you upright," he said. "You will cooperate, won't you?"

Gillian slumped, feigning even more dejection than she felt. For the moment, let him think her utterly tamed.

WHEN ROGER AND Britt stepped off the elevator at the OB/GYN ward and checked in at the desk, he paused to lock eyes with the nurse on duty. "Please see that we have complete privacy during our visit."

The nurse acknowledged the command with a dazed nod. Satisfied, Roger took Britt's arm for the walk around the corner to Eloise's room. Not that his associate needed guidance—rather, he needed support himself. Sheltering within the circle of Britt's aura and clinging to her warm flesh gave him some armor against the pain, the tumultuous emotions, and the chemical odors of the hospital. In the distance his inhuman ears picked up the wailing of babies in the nursery.

Eloise had been assigned a private room well removed from the new mothers and their infants. The visitors found her slouched on the bed watching television, with pillows wedged behind her. She clicked off the remote control and removed her glasses when Roger and Britt walked in. "What's wrong with Claude?" she asked at once.

"It's sort of complicated. But he'll be fine." Britt leaned over to hug her gingerly, while Roger pulled the door shut. "How do you feel?"

Eloise shrugged. "Physically okay. Thank goodness they're letting me out tomorrow morning."

Grazing the edges of her consciousness, Roger found that she was telling the truth about the absence of bodily pain. Her emotional numbness, though, disturbed him. "We'll pick you up, of course." After placing the room's single chair by the bed for Britt, he leaned against the window sill. "Would you like to come to my home rather than the Hilton?"

"Yes, thanks. Might as well stop by there to check us out, since we're registered at the convention hotel starting tomorrow night."

"You're still going?" said Britt.

"Why not? I'm capable, and it'll take my mind off—everything." She straightened up, a stubborn light in her eyes. "Besides, I've never reneged on a commitment in my life. And I don't want to have to explain why. Questions, stares, pity from strangers—no thanks. Now are you going to tell me what the heck happened to Claude, or do I start throwing pitchers and trays?"

Heartened by the tiny smile that accompanied this threat, Roger said, "You recall Gillian's mentioning Adam Greer, the man who gave her a ride? He came back last night and abducted her." He kept his voice low for fear of chance listeners in the hallway. "Claude surprised him in the act, and Greer shot him."

With a stifled gasp Eloise pressed her knuckles against her mouth.

Britt patted her other hand. "Listen, it's all right. He's recovering normally."

"What about Gillian? Roger, aren't you *doing* anything?" She choked on a sob, then gave up and let the tears flow.

Britt put her arms around Eloise until the upsurge of grief wore itself out. Roger answered Eloise's accusing stare with the same explanation he'd given Britt earlier.

Eloise nodded acceptance, though her doubts remained obvious. "No wonder Claude didn't push too hard for closer contact, the rat! Did he think he could keep me from knowing?"

"He didn't want you to worry."

Eloise stared vaguely for a few seconds. When she focused on Britt again, she said, "I guess he doesn't sound too bad. You took care of him. Thanks."

"My pleasure," said Britt.

Eloise looked over at Roger. "You, too. I know what it meant to you. He needed someone, and I couldn't be there."

"Tomorrow you can. He needs *you*," said Roger. He couldn't help sympathizing more with Claude, though he hurt for both of them.

She swallowed a couple of times, as if fighting a fresh outburst of tears. "I want to open up to him, but it's not that simple. After last night, I don't trust his feelings or mine. Any emotion he shows to me could be manipulation. After all, he's an actor, on top of the other thing."

Roger couldn't suppress a flash of anger. "For a single involuntary lapse—"

"Colleague." Britt gave him a warning glare. "Eloise, you may not be ready to think about this, but you can always try again. I'm sure Claude would be more than eager, which would put your doubts to rest, wouldn't it?"

Eloise was shaking her head before Britt completed the question. "I've already decided not to try again. We don't know enough about interbreeding." She lowered her voice in response to Roger's uneasy glance at the door. "The genetic mix may have been incompatible to start with. I won't risk repeating the mistake."

"But we know it can work. Roger and Gillian—"

Eloise said to Roger, "Your father was human, and you're half human. Your mother—and Gillian's—weren't. Maybe human females can't safely carry hybrid pregnancies to term."

"We have no evidence for that," said Roger. "Too small a sample."

"We have no evidence against it, either. As you just said, not enough cases to judge from." She folded her arms. "Let somebody else be the lab mouse. I won't risk conceiving other babies just to have them die. And my age is a strike against me, too. Subject closed. What about Gillian?"

Britt explained how she'd asked for informal help from their county police contact. "Aside from that we can only hope Greer will call Roger when Gillian turns out to be a disappointment. I've read a couple of the man's articles. He doesn't sound like a complete lunatic."

Eloise said with a wan smile, "What unprofessional language. From what I've seen of him at conventions, I'd say this is out of character, too. If you don't hear anything by tomorrow, I have an idea. Talk about it later." She eased lower on the pillows. "I do feel a little better now. A micron or two's worth anyway. Think I'll try to sleep."

After Britt gave her a farewell peck on the cheek, Roger stepped over to clasp her hand and gaze into her eyes, imparting a subtle suggestion of tranquility. Eloise didn't resist. Apparently her new wariness of vampiric "manipulation" applied only to Claude.

"Colleague, was that strictly ethical?" Britt asked, half-seriously, in the car.

"I forced nothing on her," Roger said. "It wasn't like influencing an ignorant victim. She knew what I was doing and could have countered it."

"Still, maybe you offered a temptation she'd rather have been spared. Maybe she'd have preferred to be left alone with her feelings, even if unpleasant."

Since Roger had already considered that point, he didn't enjoy having his conscience pricked by suggestions from Britt. "Then next time, I'll ask permission," he snapped.

They'd crossed the Severn River and were now driving through a wooded portion of the St. Margaret's area. "Pull over," Britt said.

As soon as they reached a widened section of road, designed for U-turns, Roger complied. Suspecting what Britt had in mind, he turned toward her with a wry half-smile, his right arm stretched along the back of the seat. She scooted over to lean on his shoulder. He lightly put his arm around her. "Colleague, we're too old for amorous dalliance in a parked car."

"Don't be stuffy." She cuddled closer to rub her cheek against his. "You're tense. You need it badly, and you wouldn't make love to me with Claude in the house, would you?"

"No, it would be discourteous, to say the least." Especially with Claude in his present borderline condition.

"Also, I'm still keyed up from this morning." Britt nibbled at Roger's ear. "Does that make me disgracefully amoral, getting turned on by serving your brother in desperate straits?"

Her teasing tone defused the jealousy Roger couldn't quite extinguish. "Trick question, colleague? You know perfectly well that it's a normal biological aftereffect of an adrenaline high. Morally neutral." She reached up to scratch the nape of his neck, a caress he enjoyed as much as her cat, Sigmund, did. "You have a talent for undermining my better judgment. After your donation this morning, I shouldn't touch you for at least a week."

"I'll eat an extra half-pound of liver." She nipped the side of his neck. Her fingers skimmed with pretended casualness along his thigh to his lap. Though his arousal wasn't centered there, he was human enough to respond to her intimate touch.

He traced the familiar contours of her breasts. He had to contend with her winter coat, under which she wore a heavy wool sweater. "Beloved, you've spoiled me. I want complete skin-to-skin contact."

"That's my first choice, too. But this is better than nothing, hmm?" She arched her back as his hand stroked down to the juncture of her thighs.

"Oh, God, yes." Already his jaws were aching, his teeth tingling along with the heat-sensitive cilia in his palms. As she often did, Britt had picked up his urgency before he'd recognized it himself.

When she reached her peak, he held back, though trembling with eagerness. As her climax faded, he renewed his caresses and leaned over to kiss the softness of her throat. He didn't begin to drink until she spiraled up to a second explosive release.

Long minutes later, she lifted her head from his shoulder. "I guess we have to go home now."

He kissed her fingertips. "Yes, your breathing has leveled off enough that we won't be blatantly flaunting it in front of Claude." The car, Roger noticed, was becoming chilly. With the heat of her passion expended, Britt would be uncomfortable soon. He switched on the engine.

"Oh, you—" She lightly punched him, but her playful mood

quickly faded. "I feel sorry for those two, and exasperated on top of it. I wish we could shove them together and force them to make up."

Roger gave her a sidelong look. "And you criticized me for using a bit of subtle persuasion on Eloise."

"Oh, I know we can't. *A man convinced against his will is of the same opinion still*—goes double for a woman whose feelings are bruised. But you know I have this urge to fix people. That's why I'm a psychiatrist."

"Yes, the temptation can be strong," Roger agreed. "What I'm counting on is that when Eloise comes face to face with Claude, his debilitated condition will rouse her nurturing impulses and break down that barrier."

When they got back to the townhouse, however, Claude appeared less debilitated than he had an hour before. Even Roger was surprised at the vitality that shone in his aura. The patient sat straight up in bed, reading an Agatha Christie classic, visibly chafing at the confinement.

"No telephone calls so far," he said. "I'm quite sure I can walk now. How long are you going to keep me immobilized?"

Britt checked his pulse. "Too bad you can't really pass on this stuff with a bite. I wouldn't want to live forever, but I'd love to have your stamina and repair speed."

"Let's give it until midnight, at least," Roger said. "I prefer to err on the side of caution."

Claude bared his teeth at him. "You would."

"Why not? Were you going somewhere?"

"Not until tomorrow night. I telepathically overheard Eloise say she's still planning to attend the convention. Best thing for both of us, I suppose."

"What about you?" said Britt. "Could you possibly be well enough?"

"No question about it." He shifted restlessly.

Noting that the movement didn't seem to cause pain, Roger said, "Much as I dislike admitting my first estimate was off, I have to agree. Another day of rest should do it."

"Oh, that won't completely make up the energy deficit," said Claude, "but I'll be able to function all right." He added morosely, "If I don't expire of boredom first. Damn, I wish I could *do* something."

To distract him from his worries, Roger unearthed a deck of cards, and they played several rubbers of three-handed bridge. Well before midnight, though, Britt surrendered to a backlog of fatigue and retired to Roger's bedroom.

Not quite tired enough to sleep in the middle of the night, Roger caught up on professional journals while Claude returned to the mystery novel. Neither could sustain much interest in his reading matter.

"You're worried about Gillian," Claude observed after a while.

Roger switched off the reading lamp for the comfort of their nocturnal vision. "Yes. Odd, since I was hardly aware of her existence three days ago."

"Human trait, I suppose, to feel responsible for your offspring. I'm not sure I could have learned that." Lying back with his hands behind his head, he stared gloomily at the ceiling. "Perhaps this development is for the best. I might have proved a totally inadequate father. Do you know, I even missed Eloise having a regular monthly cycle? How would I have dealt with the larger sacrifices I would've had to make?"

Roger tried to keep his impatience out of his voice. "I assure you, there's nothing unique about those qualms. All human fathers feel some jealousy, even resentment, of their own children. All couples with infants have to adjust to that change in patterns of intimacy. Fatherhood isn't instinctive. It's a culturally conditioned role." He said with a self-conscious smile, "There, I'm lecturing, and I know how little faith you put in psychological theories."

"I'm willing to accept some validity in them. It's just damned unfair to Eloise—this was the one thing she wanted that I couldn't give her, and I thought we'd overcome that problem. Now—well, I tuned in to her conversation with you. I couldn't help it. She's afraid to try again."

"Understandable at this time," said Roger. "She may change her mind later, when she's recovered emotionally."

Claude shrugged. "Doubtful. Not so long as she doesn't trust my affection for her. I'm beginning to feel that I've chained her in this relationship that can never satisfy her fundamental needs."

Roger stood up to pace across the room and back as he talked. "Confound it, you think I've never worried about being unfair to Britt? She's brilliant, beautiful, self-assured. She could have had a complete relationship with any man she chose, a normal marriage with someone she wouldn't have to explain away to her relatives. If she weren't bound to me, she might even have chosen to adopt a child. I've cut her off from all that." Listening to himself, he was surprised at his heated tone.

"She's never complained, though? Never expressed any doubts?"

Roger acknowledged the fact with an impatient movement of his head.

"You see, I'm not so fortunate." Claude hoisted himself back to a sitting position and turned on the bedside radio, tuned to a classical station. "We are a pair, aren't we, reinforcing each other's depression! You'd better leave me alone for a while."

In full agreement, Roger went outside for a walk in the woods. He didn't bother with a coat; the sting of the cold air refreshed him.

Before eight the next morning, he received a call from Captain Hayes. The hope he felt at the sound of the police officer's voice was quickly demolished. "I've got the info for you on where your friend, Greer, was staying. But he's not there anymore." Hayes named the hotel.

"Was he alone?" Roger asked.

"As far as anybody knows. He paid for a single, and he was alone in the lobby when he checked in. He left night before last. No forwarding address. You ever going to tell me what this was about?"

"I'm sorry, it's a confidential matter. Thank you for your help."

"Yeah, right," said Hayes with a sound close to a snort. "Just keep in mind, if this guy turns out to be an ax murderer or something, I'll be seriously pissed off."

Roger assured him that wasn't the case and asked him to keep his ears open for any further news of the professor. After hanging up, he turned to Britt, who stood listening at his elbow. "Not too encouraging," she said. "Are you going to interview the motel clerk to dig for details he might have forgotten he noticed?"

"That would probably be futile," said Roger. "If Greer relocated because he knew he would need a safer place to hide Gillian, he's not likely to have talked about it." He sat on the edge of the office desk, rubbing his forehead.

"Go upstairs and get some sleep," Britt said, "before I take drastic measures to make you. I can collect Eloise by myself."

"I dislike letting you go out alone."

"What on earth are you talking about?" He felt her bristle at the hint of overprotectiveness. "Greer has Gillian, so how could he possibly threaten me?"

"I'm not talking about him. Camille is out there somewhere, and it troubles me that she hasn't shown herself. She could very well strike at me through you."

"If she even knows about me, which is unlikely. Stop being paranoid." Britt reached up to put her arms around his neck. "Come on, colleague, she's probably decided to be reasonable and run in the opposite direction. Why should she risk her freedom just to pay you back? Claude's mentioned to me that sensible vampires don't go in for revenge—waste of energy."

"What makes you think this woman will behave reasonably or sensibly?"

"Well, don't borrow trouble." Britt kissed him on the cheek. "Now, good night—or good day, I guess."

He gratefully took her advice and went to bed, but in spite of their pleasant interlude of the night before, his sleep was ravaged by dreams.

*FROM THE CENTER of a black cloud, Britt was calling to him. He could barely see her through the thick miasma. Though her pain and fear cried to him for rescue, he couldn't move. His heartbeat raced out of control—*

He opened his eyes to find Britt sitting on the bed, leaning over him. "Bad, colleague?" she murmured.

He nodded, reaching out to fondle her unbound golden-red hair.

"You shouldn't be dreaming at all. I thought I took proper care of you last night. Must be slipping." She laid her head on his chest, radiating a calming warmth. After several minutes, she withdrew from the embrace and said, "Claude's been awake for half an hour. I took off the bandage, and he didn't need another—amazing. As far as I can tell, he's up to par. No trouble moving around."

"That's to be expected, I suppose, though I haven't gotten over being astonished myself." Roger sat up and reached for the clothes he'd left on the nearby chair.

"He and Eloise have a plan to deal with Greer. They want to discuss it with both of us together. So hurry up."

Roger didn't bother to ask whether she'd received any significant phone messages, since she would have mentioned that right away. As soon as he'd washed and dressed, they joined Claude and Eloise in the kitchen.

Eloise sat at the table eating a bowl of granola, while Claude drank warm milk. Britt handed Roger a mug of milk she'd preheated for him. At once Roger saw that Claude and Eloise hadn't reconciled their estrangement. Though they behaved politely to each other, visible strain—literally visible in their off-color auras—vibrated between them in place of their usual easy companionship.

Eloise fortified herself with a drink of orange juice and said, "Adam Greer is supposed to be at the convention starting tonight.

That's your chance to worm out of him what he's done with Gillian."

"But will he attend?" said Britt, pouring herself a glass of juice. "Won't he be pretty distracted by this new—project?"

"I don't think so," Eloise said. "They've got him lined up for two panels, one tonight and one tomorrow. He'll make it to those at least, if he possibly can."

Claude put in from across the table, "In his unaccustomed role as a kidnapper, he may believe it necessary to keep up his normal routine to forestall suspicion. The wicked flee where no man pursueth, as the proverb says."

"Logical," said Roger. "Eloise, what do you have in mind?"

"Well, you don't want to approach him, because he knows who you are." She thoughtfully dabbled her spoon in the cereal bowl. "I considered questioning him myself—"

"I'd rather you wouldn't," Claude interrupted.

She gave him a cool stare before continuing. "I wouldn't do it because I don't have the skills. Britt, you've studied hypnosis, haven't you? Any chance you could get the facts out of Greer without letting him remember much of what he's told you?"

"More than a chance," said Britt. "I've managed to learn some of Roger's tricks. He says I have a trace of natural psi talent in that direction, and constant association with a vampire tends to amplify it. I couldn't pick someone's brain as thoroughly as Roger or Claude can, but I could interrogate Greer and easily make him forget the whole thing, as long as he doesn't have his guard up."

"Okay, I'll introduce you to him. We've been on panels together at other cons, so he'll remember me. You've read some of his stuff, haven't you?"

"Sure. Nothing would be easier than to get him talking about his work. Then I invite him to my room for a quiet conversation—for that we have to get a room. Would that pose a problem?"

"No more so than getting last-minute convention memberships for you and Roger," said Eloise. "After all, this is hardly Worldcon."

Now Roger was becoming apprehensive. "Colleague, I don't like the idea of your being alone with this man."

"Don't be silly, what could he do to me? We'll be talking for a few minutes in the middle of a crowded hotel."

"He shot Claude," Roger said.

"Not relevant. That was a fluke." Britt turned to Claude. "Sorry, I don't mean to make light of it."

"Don't apologize, you're absolutely right."

Britt said, "What I'm concerned about is that he'll recognize me as Roger's associate. He did see me that afternoon when he came looking for Gillian."

"Not in any sense that matters," Roger said. "I had his full attention from the moment we walked in. I doubt that he even noticed you."

"In that case I don't see a problem," said Britt. "Unless he recognizes Claude from the other night."

"Impossible," said Claude. "He didn't see me as I normally look. He saw a monster."

"All right," she said. "Let's do it. When do we start?"

Claude glanced at his watch. "Eloise and I had better leave now. You two should arrive in a separate car, since we don't want Greer to notice any connection between us and Roger."

"I'm not happy with the plan," Roger said, "but I'll cooperate. I suppose once we're there, Britt and I shouldn't be seen together." While he knew how remote any risk of harm to Britt was, and anyway he would keep constant watch over her telepathically, he still felt uncomfortable about letting her confront Gillian's kidnapper.

She silently chided him, [Colleague, you're thinking irrationally again. The man is hardly a desperate criminal. Didn't Eloise say the way he behaved the other night was completely out of character?]

[Was it really? Then what pushed him into it?]

"ARE YOU HUNGRY? Anything I can get for you?"

Gillian glared up at Professor Greer. He stood in the doorway of the windowless bathroom, while she sat on the closed lid of the toilet. He'd shackled her by one leg, with a pair of handcuffs linked together into a chain, to the sink's exposed drainpipe. Prolonged experimentation had convinced her that she didn't have the strength to rip the pipe out of the floor.

He'd brought her to a cabin in the woods sufficiently isolated from those nearby that screaming wouldn't do much good even if she became desperate enough to call for human aid. Besides, as Greer had made a point of mentioning, at this time of year, few people were eccentric enough to vacation in a forest hideaway. Hunters, maybe, but deer season was over. On the way in, Gillian had surveyed the limited confines of the cabin—two rooms, a small kitchen and a living room with a fold-out sofa bed. Since Greer hadn't shut the bathroom door all the way, she'd been able to watch him lie down for a nap after he'd washed up, judging from the sounds, at the kitchen sink. He'd left her hands free with the warning, "Don't bother trying to attack me, because I won't come near you with the keys in my pocket. If you kill me, no telling how long you'll be stuck here."

Yet he seemed sincere with his assurances that he didn't want to hurt her. At her request, before he went to sleep he'd taken away her garlic-sprinkled shirt (with a puzzled stare at her gold cross) and given her one of his sweatshirts. And now he was offering to feed her. Gillian dismissed her first impulse to ignore him. What would be the virtue in starving herself? She needed to maintain her strength and alertness to have a chance of escape. "Milk," she said.

"All right," he answered softly. "You wouldn't rather have blood?" He began rolling up his left sleeve.

Startled by the offer, she blurted out, "I don't drink human blood."

Greer's eyes widened. "So you do drink animal blood? I'll try to get you something—maybe from a pet shop—if you'll talk to me."

Gillian inwardly cursed herself for confirming his guess. It had to be a guess; how could he know anything definite about her nature? After they'd stared at each other in silence for a moment, Greer withdrew from the doorway out of her sight. Shortly he reappeared with a paper cup. "Here's your milk." Without stepping into the bathroom he reached out to set the cup near her feet.

She drank the milk, then rinsed the cup to fill it with water. Drinking directly from the faucet was a slow, messy business.

Watching her, Greer said, "Give me that. I'll bring you a clean cup—sorry I didn't think of it before."

She crumpled the empty container and tossed it to him.

Again he left, this time returning with the promised cup. "You see, I want to make you comfortable, aside from this." He gestured at the cuffs. "Tell me what I want to know, and you can go back to your father."

Insincerity crept into his tone at this point. "No, you won't send me home. You'd be afraid to." Greer's almost imperceptible flinch confirmed that intuition. "What do you really plan to do when you're finished with me?"

He only stared at her, his eyes cloudy with confusion. So he hadn't thought out his plan to the end.

Gillian fixed her gaze on him. Her hypnotic power had almost ensnared him before. Surely, given enough time to work on him, she could override his will. His weariness after only a few hours of sleep worked in her favor. He swayed on his feet, and his eyes momentarily glazed over. Recollecting the danger, though, he wrenched himself away, shaking his head.

"You almost had me that time." He actually smiled, as if pleased to watch her talent in operation even at risk to himself. "But what's the point of fighting? Listen, I've already seen you change into—whatever that was. Show me that again. I know about it, so what could it hurt?"

Gillian sat on the floor, her back against the wall and knees drawn up to her chest, and looked away from him.

He disappeared again, making her think he'd decided to leave her in peace. Instead he dragged the worn, floral-print armchair from the living room to the bathroom door. He sat with a portable tape recorder in his lap and a Polaroid camera on the floor beside him. "Talk to me, Gillian. It's a couple of hours before dawn, and I'm not expected anywhere until tonight. I've got plenty of time."

When he started working through an unwritten list of questions, she ignored him. Since he didn't want to damage her, what was the worst he could do? Bore her to death?

Once he'd apparently reached the end of his mental list, he got up to fix himself a drink. She heard him puttering in the kitchen, dropping ice cubes into a glass and pouring liquid. He sat down again, sipping a beverage that smelled strongly of alcohol, and resumed the interrogation. This routine went on for hours, with Greer taking occasional breaks to step outside, until Gillian felt the weight of the rising sun through the trees and the walls of the cabin. Fatigue dragged at her. At this rate, the man *would* bore her to death, or at least to raving madness. Fortunately, she could escape him in sleep. She curled up in fetal position on the hard tile and closed her eyes.

"Wake up!" Greer barked at her. She incuriously looked up at him. "I'm not letting you sleep until you give me something. One day of staying awake won't hurt you, and I can hold out as long as you can."

She displayed her contempt by closing her eyes again. She soon realized, though, that he could fulfill his threat. When he discovered that talking alone wouldn't prevent her from dozing off, she thought he might try shaking or slapping, thus giving her a chance to work on his weak human will through touch as well as eye contact. But he proved too cautious for that. Instead, he got a broom from the kitchen and poked her under the chin with the straws whenever she closed her eyes. She began to feel like the performing lions she'd seen in circuses on television.

"What's the point of this stonewalling?" he said in a coaxing voice. "I told you, I don't like giving you a hard time. Just do one thing for me, and I'll let you rest until tonight." He picked up the Polaroid. "Let me photograph you changing shape."

Gillian wondered how much good such a picture would do him. While part of the shape-change involved real shifting of molecules, a large portion consisted of illusion. She stretched her cramped arms, scowling at Greer from beneath her brows. Suppose she projected an illusion without transforming at all? Would the resultant failure to photograph the change convince him that no real change had ever occurred, that it was all a form of hypnosis?

"Very well, I'll show you what I can do, if you promise to leave me alone after that. I make no guarantee about the results."

"Wonderful!" Animation returned to his tired face. "I knew you'd see reason eventually. You won't regret this." He centered her in the camera's viewfinder. "First, let me get a picture of your normal appearance." Gillian winced as the flash went off. "Interesting, your eyebrows actually grow together above your nose." She'd been too preoccupied over the past few days to pluck them and had forgotten how less human the bushy growth made her look. "And in this dim light, your eyes glow. Now, please, the transformation."

Gillian turned inward, concentrating. Could she project a false image of herself without getting carried away and physically changing? She visualized what she wanted the professor to see—pointed ears, a feline muzzle, fangs, a pair of bat wings, velvety fur shading from tawny red to glossy black. At the same time she folded her legs beneath her and wrapped her arms around herself, gritting her teeth with the strain of leashing the wave of power that swelled within her. Faintly, she heard Greer's heartbeat accelerate. The camera clicked over and over. Confident of her control now, she opened her eyes to gaze at him. But she couldn't entrap him, because the camera blocked eye contact.

"Beautiful, beautiful!" he whispered. She smelled the sweat of excitement on his skin. "I'd love to touch you this way—but not now. Maybe when we trust each other more." His voice quavered with a trace of fear behind the excitement. "Those teeth—Maybe I'll bring you a present, see what you can do with those teeth." He was muttering more to himself than her. Finally he said, "That's enough for now."

Gillian relaxed, lightheaded from the sustained effort. She watched Greer gather up the snapshots the Polaroid had ejected. His euphoria faded into anger. "What the hell is this?"

*Excellent, I did it!* Her joy at mastering the skill equaled her pleasure in tricking the man. "I told you I didn't guarantee satisfactory pictures. You saw what my mind projected into yours. How could a camera record that?"

He shuffled through the photos. "There's something here, though. Kind of a fogging effect. And that gleam in your eyes shows up great." He held up one of the pictures in her line of sight. She saw that a luminous halo outlined her form. And the red glow did visibly smolder in her eyes. "Too indefinite to prove anything, though," said Greer.

Remembering books she'd skimmed dealing with creatures such as Bigfoot and the Loch Ness Monster, Gillian said, "What if you did record on film what you thought you saw? Would others believe in it? Wouldn't they say you faked the pictures?"

Greer's shoulders sagged. "They might. God knows special effects can do a lot more impressive things. Well, I'm going to come up with something that will convince people, and you damn well better decide to cooperate. I've been generous, letting you have the facilities to yourself. Maybe I should chain you on the porch instead. Nobody's around to notice, and why should *I* have to go outside and freeze my butt off?" He collected his paraphernalia and moved the chair away from the door. Before leaving Gillian alone, he gave her a pillow, which she accepted with a dry word of thanks.

She drifted into sleep, still meditating on the subject of illusions. With her skill sharpened by desperation, she ought to be able to weave some mirage that would lure her captor within her grasp—something to lull his resistance until she could trap him in her mesmeric web. She gnashed her teeth like a lion that had its trainer between its jaws.

## Chapter Eight

*I'LL VANISH. THAT ought to shock him into dropping his guard.*

Gillian had no clear plan for implementing that inspiration. Proud of her new accomplishment, projecting an illusion of invisibility, she had a notion that it could prove useful against Greer. Surely the impossible sight of an empty room where he'd left her chained would lure him within her grasp. Then—Her brain stalled at that point. Killing or disabling him would, as he'd made a point of warning her, leave her with no access to the keys, since he didn't keep them on his person.

Gillian had awakened well before sunset from a restless sleep hag-ridden by dreams of futile escape attempts. She'd found herself alone in the cabin. Now, with the early twilight of winter closing in—though she couldn't see the windows from her position, thickening shadows in the living room confirmed what her vampire time-sense told her—she expected him to return soon. Knowing Gillian would awaken as dark approached, he would want to check on his captive. Probably he was gearing up to nag her with a few more hours of questions.

No, he'd mentioned that he had somewhere to go this evening. So if she wanted to try hypnotizing him into releasing her, she'd better prepare to make her move as soon as he walked in.

Hunger cramps distracted her. If she were older, she could accept Greer's blood. Drinking from him would give her a stronger chance at controlling him. Even if she accepted his offer, though, would he follow through on it? She sensed in him a fear out of proportion to the meager threat she presented.

Idle speculation wouldn't help her master her own fear. She diverted her thoughts to practical matters. After all day on the floor she felt dirty as well as sore and stiff. The cuffs were too short to let her reach the shower stall. Peeling off the sweatshirt, she washed at the sink. In the absence of a towel she waited for her skin to air-dry. Meanwhile she ran through a series of stretching exercises to limber her aching muscles. When she put the shirt back on, she felt slightly cleaner but not much. The desire to make Greer pay for this humiliation preyed on her like a physical thirst.

*No, revenge is a waste of energy. That's what Lord Volnar would say, and so would Claude. Have to concentrate on getting away from here.*

Why hadn't Roger or Claude shown up searching for her yet? Had Greer covered his trail that well? Or did her father simply not care? Were they so angry at her for endangering Claude that they would cast her off? Her head ached with emotions that her kind could not relieve with tears.

She reclined on the pillow, calmed herself with slow, deep breathing, and recited logarithmic tables in her head.

Some time later the sound of the front door broke her self-induced trance. A gust of cold wind and Greer's footsteps on the hardwood blew toward her. Anxiety made her heart race. No, any emotion might unravel her control. She submerged herself in the quiescence required to project her illusion. She visualized a dazzling cloud around her body. She imagined it bending light rays around her, fracturing and scattering the professor's mortal sight. She envisioned herself secure within this cocoon of mist until she chose to reveal her presence.

Greer's voice floated to her. "Gillian, I brought you a present. Want you to keep your strength up so we can work together."

She scented rodents. Again, her heartbeat accelerated. Saliva trickled into her mouth. She knew she mustn't let the sensory input distract her. Slowing her pulse, she sank deeper into the sheltering cave of her invisibility. She heard Greer pause to shed his coat and gloves before approaching the bathroom door. He carried a cubical, plastic cage.

"What the hell—!" Setting the cage on the floor, he stared at the *empty* shackle. He blinked as if he thought the dimness deceived his eyes.

Gillian kept a tight curb on her excitement. She couldn't lose her grip on the illusion. *Come on*, she silently urged her captor. *Come over here and investigate.* Greer took half a step into the bathroom. He goggled at the spot where Gillian should be, as if his gaze could make her reappear from thin air.

"This is stupid," he muttered. "Not unlocked or broken, so how—? She can't really dissolve into mist, can she?" He cast bewildered glances around him. "Gillian?" He moved closer and knelt on the floor, staring at the handcuffs.

*Touch me*, she willed. *Put yourself into my hands.* She struggled to keep her fingers from elongating into claws at the image of his flesh in her grasp.

He slowly reached toward the place where her ankle should have been. When his fingertips brushed the metal of the cuff, she knew the moment had arrived. She couldn't maintain the psychic veil while his sense of touch contradicted what his eyes told him. She allowed the mirage to melt away. At the same instant she clamped one hand on his outstretched wrist, and with the other she stroked the side of his neck.

Before he could break the paralysis of shock, Gillian caught and imprisoned his eyes. She willed her own to glow crimson in the unlit room. *I did it, I have him! If Volnar could see this!* She *could* learn her race's survival skills without a blood-bond.

The professor's groping fingers went slack. Gaping at her, he didn't resist the massage of her thumb along his jawline. His pulse under her hand made the cilia in her palm bristle.

"You're mine now," she whispered. "You don't want to confine me this way, do you? Would you not prefer to observe me in my natural state, free and wild? Let me go, and I'll answer all your questions."

"Yes—" His voice trailed off. His head lolled to one side, inviting her to continue massaging his neck.

"I'll give you more of this, as much as you want," she said, cued by his rising excitement. "First, get the keys and unlock me. Then we can share—observations—in comfort."

He answered her with a lethargic nod. "Do it now," she whispered. He pulled himself to his feet and shambled off.

A few seconds later he returned with the keys. "I shouldn't do this," he muttered. "There's a reason why I shouldn't do this." His muddled eyes, faintly accusing, sought hers. "You're a dangerous animal."

"Oh, no, you can't really believe that." Holding his gaze, she disarmed him with the purr of her voice. "You want to give me pleasure. You want to set me free."

Clutching her ankle again, he fumbled with the key. Spasms shook his hand as he tried to insert the key into the lock. His eyes constantly drifted away from hers; she had to struggle to lure them back. Again she rubbed his neck and chin, counting on the physical contact to undermine his will.

His trembling hand dropped the key, which clinked on the tile. He started at the sound. Eyes widening, he cringed back. "No—mustn't do this—dangerous—"

Exasperated by the sudden resistance, Gillian raked her nails across his throat. Luckily she didn't succumb to all-out rage, and Greer was backing off at that moment, so her claws inflicted only superficial scratches. Four raw scrapes oozed blood. The scent made her head spin.

Snatching up the key, Greer leaped out of range and slapped his palm to the side of his neck. "You little she-devil—" He held out his hand to stare at the flecks of red.

Gillian wanted to scream with frustration. Only pride stopped her. *How can he resist? What makes him so strong?* Added to her bitter shame at her impotence was the realization that if she'd planned her attack instead of lashing out in random anger, she could have Greer disabled and the key in her hand at this moment.

He'd left her alone briefly. Now he was back, with the camera. "There's your supper." With his foot he pushed the plastic cage toward her. It contained a pair of white mice. He held up the Polaroid, poised to snap.

Gillian snarled at him. Let him photograph her feeding? But when he made it clear that he would wait for hours if necessary, hunger defeated her pride. The smell of his blood tormented her. She drained both mice, hardly bothering to soothe their panic first, while he took picture after picture. Still hungry, she fractured the bones and sucked out the marrow.

Openly gloating over this performance by his specimen, Greer tossed her a paper sack and a wet rag. Much as she hated helping the man in any way, he'd correctly gauged Gillian's distaste for the mess. She cleaned up the mouse fragments and wiped the tile floor.

Shortly, the professor, calm and freshly washed, announced that he was leaving. "I've got to attend a convention, so I've taken a room at the hotel. But don't worry, I'll be back to check on you. Think about what you're going to say for our next conversation." He scanned her without looking directly into her face. "That couldn't be comfortable. You must be getting pretty sick of it."

He left her alone with her dismal reflections. Bitterest was the knowledge that Volnar and Claude had been absolutely right about one thing. If she'd accepted a blood bond with one of them—with any adult, including Roger—she could be broadcasting her location at this instant.


AT THE HOTEL in College Park just off the Washington beltway, Roger dropped off Britt and waited for her to pass through the lobby before entering himself. Inside scents of sweat and perfume assailed him. The sensory assault grated on his nerves. He threaded his way past a knot of people in pseudo-medieval dress, who seemed to be arguing about the convention schedule. At the far end of the lobby two women sat behind a table littered with index cards, name badges, and flyers. Heading in that direction, Roger noticed that the front of the table bore a banner trimmed with sprigs of fake mistletoe: "Welcome to Yulecon."

He purchased a membership from a plump blonde in red satin, who wore a lapel pin that proclaimed, "I'm not born again, my Mother got it right the first time." *Good God, neo-pagans!* He might have been amused if he hadn't been concentrating so hard on blocking out her fruity cologne. Pinning on his name tag, Roger proceeded to the next step, renting a room. The Christmas tree next to the registration desk was real. Its pine fragrance provided a welcome antidote to the artificial smells that hung thick in the overheated air. As Eloise had predicted, the hotel had vacancies, and within minutes Roger was in the elevator, key card in hand.

On the way up he mentally reached for Britt, informing her of the room number. Two minutes after he'd entered the room, heavily curtained with forest green drapes, and lain down on the king-size bed to savor the quiet, she tapped on the door. He got up to let her in.

"Clandestine assignations," she said after bolting the door behind her. "What fun!" She plopped down on the bed and patted the mattress. "Sure you don't want to take time out to make proper use of this?"

"Time we don't really have." Roger treated himself to a leisurely inspection of Britt. Following advice from Claude and Eloise as veteran convention-goers, she wore an emerald green three-piece pantsuit with dangling earrings in the shape of holly sprigs—a gift from one of her nephews—to foster the carefree image of a fan indulging in a weekend of revelry. A pendant Roger had given her, a large, teardrop-shaped emerald, hung between her breasts. With their peaks clearly visible beneath the clingy knit fabric, she did look tempting—almost too tempting to allow within any other man's reach. "Aside from health considerations—yours—you know hotel rooms make me nervous." Taking a seat in one of the armchairs by the coffee table, outside temptation's range, he scanned the furnishings. "I don't care for the idea of your bringing our target up here alone."

"What do you suggest I do, hypnotize and interrogate him in the bar? Don't be silly."

"He could easily misinterpret your motives."

Britt countered with a long-suffering sigh, "Come on, colleague, I've been handling men well over half my life. In the unlikely event he gets pushy, I can deal with it. Good grief, do you expect him to knock me down and ravish me?"

Roger's lips tightened with disapproval. "Don't." The thought was too alarming to entertain, even as a joke.

"Don't worry, Eloise says that at things like this, a hotel suite isn't a bedroom, just another kind of meeting lounge." Digging in her oversize shoulder purse, Britt produced a couple of lapel buttons. When she'd pinned them on her jacket, Roger saw that they read, respectively, "If you're not part of the solution, you're part of the precipitate," and "Blood is thicker than water—and much tastier." A sentiment he endorsed but hardly wanted publicized. "You should have one of these pins," she said. "Since you won't wear a costume, you need something to make you blend in."

"I dressed the way Claude said I should." Roger glanced down at his outfit—a black pullover, charcoal gray casual slacks, and loafers.

Britt shook her head. "There's something about the *way* you wear it—better than a suit, but you still look like you wandered over from an AMA conference. Eloise gave me another button—" She rummaged through her bag again and took out a third metal disk. "Here, this one's perfect for you!"

Roger accepted the button and grudgingly pinned it on: "Don't tell me what kind of day to have, dammit!" Well, he couldn't deny it encapsulated his mood. "You and Eloise seem to be in charge of strategy. What now?"

"I hang around with Eloise and Claude, while you lurk in the background until she hooks me up with Greer." Britt fished a program out of her bag and scanned it. "He's on a panel with Eloise and three other people at eight. *Bigfoot in Fact and Fiction.* At the end of that session she'll introduce us, and I'll lure him up here. You can listen in telepathically, if that'll make you happier."

"I fully intend to," said Roger. "No point in my having to get the results from you secondhand. Besides, you can draw on me to enhance your hypnotic influence over him."

Britt nodded. "Sounds good. Okay, I'll sneak out, and you follow anytime you think it's safe." She gave him a brief, emphatic hug before leaving.

Five minutes later, Roger took the elevator down to the mezzanine, intending to check the dealers' room before catching up with Claude, Eloise, and Britt. He kept abreast of trends in vampire fiction, on the grounds that he needed to be aware of how the largely unsuspecting human world regarded his race. Eloise's critical judgment forewarned him against the worst excesses of bottom-of-the-barrel horror fiction. Half the recommended books bored him senseless, anyway, but Britt liked to keep up with the field, too, so he humored her by collecting the stuff.

The dealers' room proved to be uncomfortably crowded. Roger couldn't help brushing against other shoppers as he made the circuit of the tables, and each contact made him flinch, as his unruly instincts interpreted it as an assault. When he involuntarily bared his teeth at a robed, cowled teenager who blundered into him, he decided it was time to get out. He quickly stopped at the largest book display to buy three new paperbacks on Eloise's recommended list, then headed for the exit. Beside the door he noticed a glass case full of jewelry that held some promise of quality. A bronze dragon-paw necklace with a large opal in its claws caught his eye. That might please Britt. After a brief inspection, he bought it for her.

Judging that he'd stayed away from Britt long enough to avoid giving the impression that he was deliberately trailing after her, he followed her mental traces to the main ballroom. Convention volunteers were in the midst of clearing the back half of the hall for a Regency dance that, according to the program, started at eight. Meanwhile, up front Claude and Eloise, seated on folding chairs in a friendly, informal style, were rendering folk songs to the accompaniment of Eloise's acoustic guitar. Thirty to forty people comprised the audience. Britt sat at one end of the front row listening. Roger took a chair at the opposite end.

Claude was outfitted in his complete vampire regalia—ruffled white shirt, ruby stickpin, high-necked, black, crimson-lined cape. The two front rows, Roger noted, ran heavily to young women whose rapt gazes never left Claude's face. Eloise wore an empire-style dress of royal blue velvet, cinched tight beneath the bustline with silver embroidery. A matching silver snood confined her chestnut hair. She was finishing up a song in which she seemed to enact the role of some sort of shape-changing water sprite.

A muted patter of applause greeted the conclusion. Claude's eyes lingeringly traveled over the small audience. "Any requests?"

A babble of phrases answered him. Claude nodded affirmation to somebody's shout of, "Sweet William's Ghost." He and Eloise sang in dialogue form about Sweet William and his Lady Margaret, who "ran over the hills on a cold winter night in a dead man's company." As soon as they fell silent, the babble resumed. Holding up a hand for quiet, Claude said, "How about another nice, gloomy, romantic ghost story?" He exchanged glances with Eloise, who strummed a chord in response. They launched into a ballad, reversing the previous one, in which Claude played the part of a bereaved man and Eloise his dead sweetheart:

"I'll do as much for my true love
As any young man may.
I'll sit and mourn upon her grave
For a twelvemonth and a day."

At the end of a year and a day the ghost begged her lover to leave her in peace, while he demanded a kiss from her "clay cold lips." Roger recognized the archetypal folklore motif of excessive grief binding the dead to the earth. Eloise sang the ghost's quasi-vampiric response:

"I fear if you kiss my clay cold lips,
Your end will not be long."

As the ballad unfolded, Roger sensed the appeal, more than audience-directed drama, that Claude projected. Eloise, under the mask of the lyrics, answered him with cool remoteness. When the song ended with the spirit's withdrawal to a higher plane and the lover's acceptance of loss, the listeners applauded enthusiastically. Claude's genuine emotion, modulated to the requirements of the performance, communicated itself to them.

Roger had seldom seen Claude "on" like this. It was interesting to observe how the actor-vampire played to his public. While he didn't ignore the male spectators, careful to toss out witty replies to their shouted jokes and comments, Claude focused most of his attention on the women. His eyes caressingly brushed each one he spoke to, the second or two of contact designed to leave her with the impression that if only he were free, she would be his companion for the night. Roger found himself hoping Claude wouldn't turn that teasing sensuality in Britt's direction. The air seemed permeated with a rosy, sweet-scented mist. Roger began to grasp how Claude endured these overcrowded surroundings. Able to gather and mold the emotions of his audience, he thrived on the tumultuous responses Roger shrank from.

Eloise, joining Claude in a duet of Kipling's "Female of the Species," sang in a brittle, ironic tone. She couldn't be oblivious to Claude's toying with the audience; no doubt over the years she'd learned to distance herself. Roger could hardly blame Claude, whose aura showed that the residual hunger from his recent ordeal remained unsatisfied, yet the behavior did seem tactless in Eloise's presence.

Finally Claude refused any further song requests, announcing that he had to move on to a scheduled autograph session. "We'll be singing at nine, after Eloise's panel, to warm up for Mock Turtle Soup's concert. See you then, *n'est-ce pas?*" The majority of the audience, of course, trailed after him in search of autographs.

While Eloise packed up the guitar, Britt talked quietly with her. Roger wandered into the hallway, since he didn't need to be within earshot to listen telepathically. Britt remarked that Eloise looked as if she needed a break and invited her to grab a drink in the cocktail lounge before the panel.

"We've got fifteen minutes," Eloise said. "I guess that's enough time." Now that she didn't have an audience to perform for, she let her voice quaver with fatigue.

Roger decided to follow up that suggestion himself. He couldn't watch the panel discussion on Bigfoot, since Greer might notice him, nor could he return to the bedroom, which Britt would need later for her hypnotic session. With various con activities diverting fans in all directions, a dark corner of the bar might afford as much peace as he could hope to find in this setting. Once Britt and Eloise were safely ensconced in a booth in the lounge, he came in, took a corner booth on the other side of the room behind a hanging fern, ordered a brandy, and leaned back with his eyes shut to follow their conversation.

ORDERING A SOFT drink for herself, Britt watched with concern as Eloise asked for a gin and tonic. "Should you—"

"What possible difference could it make now?"

The flat tone of voice worried Britt. "I was only thinking that you still have a long night ahead of you, and you're already stressed."

Eloise shrugged. "I'm okay." After the drinks came, she said, "You can really do this? Hypnotize the guy as well as Roger could?" She kept her voice down, and Britt had made sure to choose a booth in a sparsely occupied section of the bar.

"Almost. I've been practicing for years. It helps with patients— I've reached the point where I can even tell when they're lying or evading. I used it on a murder suspect at the state hospital just the other day."

"Wish I could do something. I feel so useless." She swirled her drink, making the ice tinkle. "What do you think I should do about Claude—our relationship?"

*At least she's willing to talk,* Britt thought with a loosening of tension. "Whom do you want, the sister or the shrink?"

"A little of both, I guess. You know what worries me? I don't have anything to hang onto. I'm beginning to wonder if any of the love

I thought we shared was ever real."

Britt kept her tone even, concealing her distress at this statement. "You do love him, don't you?"

Eloise gave an impatient toss of her head. "Sure, if you mean do I feel the emotion. But did I have a choice about it? You know what he is. He could have made me feel any damn thing he wanted me to."

"Do you believe he did that?" Britt asked softly.

"That's just the point, I don't know what to believe! How can I trust any of my own perceptions? Look, you know how we met, don't you?"

"Parts of it. You'd been corresponding about your work, and he'd tentatively agreed to use your *Varney* script for a film he wanted to finance. And then you met at some horror awards banquet, right?"

"Right." Eloise sipped her drink, her mouth twisting as if it tasted bitter. "I'm a pushover for that lethal charm like everybody else. There he was in the black cape and the whole nine yards, my fantasy in the flesh. He took me up to his hotel room to discuss the script and—well, I don't have to draw you a diagram, of all people. He made me forget it completely."

Britt started to understand Eloise's belated misgivings. "Do you remember it now?"

Eloise shook her head. "Not long after that I accepted his invitation to his place in Big Sur, and while I was there, he told me the truth. Before that, he did it again—the first night, while I was asleep. Those were the only times—or so he claims. Since then, he's tried to reactivate the memory of our first night together. But it hasn't worked. Frankly, I don't think he's really trying."

"Can you blame him?" said Britt. "He may consciously believe he wants you to remember, but on an unconscious level he's probably holding back. Once he discovered he loved you, he could very well have been ashamed of taking advantage. They're not immune to those emotions, you know."

"They aren't? How do we know, really? Maybe Claude's not capable of love—he didn't have Roger's human childhood. Maybe what he and I share is just mutual addiction. Since he'd already had me before I fell in love with him, how can I ever know?" She gulped her drink, shivering as the cold liquid went down. "He might even think he really cares for me, but how can *he* know? Maybe I'm nothing but a convenience. A drug."

Britt inwardly shuddered at the labyrinth of doubt layered upon doubt that Eloise unfolded before her. She reached around the scented candle in the middle of the table to clasp her friend's hand. "How can any of us be sure of our feelings? Or our lovers' feelings? Eloise, when it comes down to it, we simply have to have faith." *Doing great, Doctor, keep feeding her the trite truisms.*

"I know. But I seem to have mislaid mine." Eloise checked her watch. "Good grief, I'm one minute late for the panel already." She scrambled to her feet. "Thanks for trying. I'll think about it—honest."

Britt followed her down the hall to the conference room designated for the Bigfoot panel. Finding a seat near the front, she watched Eloise take her place at the long table with Greer and three science fiction authors, two women and one man. In the back of her mind, Britt felt Roger silently absorbing everything she perceived. [I'm really beginning to worry about Eloise, colleague,] she told him.

He expressed agreement. [How is Claude supposed to defend himself against that kind of charge? How can he prove his love if she won't believe he knows his own mind on the subject?]

Britt mentally shrugged. [I hope the sheer passage of time will convince her. She's not in a normal state right now.] Britt turned her attention to the moderator's introduction, already in progress.

Familiar with most of the reported Sasquatch sightings and the evidence—generally tenuous—of the creature's existence, Britt didn't concentrate very hard on the discussion. Professor Greer played the role of tolerant skeptic and genial debunker in counterpoint to the more credulous stance of the other panel members. Someone in the audience brought up the case of a man who had claimed the entire Bigfoot phenomenon was a hoax based on evidence he and his friends had fabricated. That topic led to an acrimonious shouting match, until Eloise diverted the group to speculation about whether Bigfoot, if real, should be classified as human and what rights he would be entitled to. Somehow the conversation meandered onto the intelligence of dolphins and the ethics of rumored Navy experiments on them. Eloise, Britt was glad to note, abandoned her apathy and gleefully plunged into this impersonal argument.

At the end of the session, Britt wormed her way up to the table, as she and Eloise had planned. Meanwhile Eloise hovered next to Professor Greer to forestall any escape he might try. "Adam, I have a friend who wanted to meet you," she said as soon as Britt came within speaking range. "She's had some stuff in the *Journal of Popular Culture*, too. Dr. Britt Loren, Dr. Adam Greer."

Shaking hands with the professor, Britt didn't see any flicker of recognition in his eyes. He wore a tweed jacket with no tie, studiedly casual. She thought she noticed red streaks above the unbuttoned shirt collar. "I was intrigued by your article last year on UFO abductees," she said.

"Yeah? Thanks, it's always a thrill to hear somebody actually reads the stuff."

Britt laughed. "I know exactly what you mean. The most we can usually hope for is to be cited in a footnote or two."

Side by side they drifted toward the door. "Your name rings a bell," said Greer. "I know—didn't you publish a thing on archetypal patterns in Anne Rice's books? Perceptive. You don't get a fresh viewpoint on vampirism too often. All the same old Freudian oral-sadistic readings, until you could scream."

Too bad this guy was a kidnapper; Britt felt that in different circumstances she could get to like him. "Do you have time to talk? I didn't have anything planned for the next hour."

"Sure, I'd like that." He checked his watch. "I'm free for a while." As they walked down the hall, Britt sneaked a closer look at her companion. Her first impression hadn't been wrong—he did have scratches on the side of his neck. Fresh ones. Her incipient pleasure in his company went sour. "What are you a doctor of?" he asked.

"M.D. Psychiatrist. What about you?"

"Ph.D. Sociologist. College professor." He paused to turn toward her with a nervous laugh. "Okay if we call each other Adam and Britt?"

*Good, he's attracted to me. I can use that.* She felt Roger in the back of her mind bristling at the thought. She ordered him to calm down and quit distracting her. "Would you like to come up to my room, Adam? That way, we can hear ourselves think."

Greer glanced at a swarm of Klingons who marched down the center of the hall singing 'Banned from Argo.' "Anything would have to be a major improvement over right here," he said. Britt's worry that he might perceive her as too forward was quickly dispelled. "Sounds fine, lead the way."

In the elevator, Greer leaned against the back wall, hands in his pockets. Britt wondered how much his loose-jointed relaxation owed to chemical influence. When they'd shaken hands, she had caught a whiff of alcohol on his breath. "You know, Adam, I got the impression that you were exaggerating your skepticism about Bigfoot just a wee bit." By discussing questions of belief, she hoped to nudge him toward the topic of vampires.

"Every panel needs a devil's advocate, and listening to the rest of them, I figured I was elected. Off the record, I wouldn't rule out a clan of gigantopithecines surviving in some relatively unexplored corner of the world."

"People don't realize just how much of our planet, even nowadays, has only been mapped from the air." Britt led the way from the elevator to the room she and Roger had rented for the night.

"Yeah, there's a lot of woods out there." Inside the tweed jacket, no doubt chosen for professorial effect, his bony shoulders lifted in a shrug. "But what do I know? I don't specialize in prehistoric man." He smiled an apology behind the neatly-trimmed beard. "Excuse me, prehistoric hominids."

"Drink?" said Britt. At her suggestion Roger had provided a bottle of sherry, which she held up for Greer's inspection. When he nodded acceptance, she poured each of them a glass. She waved the professor to one of the twin chairs, glad neither of them had to sit on the bed. That might indeed give the wrong impression, and while she was certain she could handle a seduction ploy, she didn't want to be sidetracked.

Lounging in his seat, Greer imbibed a large swallow of the sherry. Encouraged by this further evidence that his guard was down, Britt pulled her chair around the coffee table to sit a foot or two from him, at an angle where she could meet his eyes. She took a minimum sip of her drink. "So you suspend judgment on the paranormal?"

"Depends how paranormal you're talking. All those UFO stories, for example, sound like science fiction written by people who've never read any."

Britt leaned forward, chin resting on her hand. In her other hand she held the chain of her pendant, which she idly twirled. The teardrop emerald sparkled in the light from the overhead hanging lamp. She'd left it at the dimmest setting and turned off all the other lights in the room to create a circle of illumination in which to work. "And the other stuff? Ancient astronauts? Feral children? Poltergeists?"

"I'm more interested in how people react to the phenomena than in whether they're real or not. People who read the tabloids and actually believe Noah's Ark ran aground on Mount Shasta." He stifled a yawn.

*Did he stay awake all night with Gillian? I hope she wore him down good and proper!* "But you must have some opinion yourself—off the record, as it were. Ever seen anything you thought qualified as supernatural?"

He paused for a second in lifting his glass. Drawing strength from

Roger, who watched through her eyes, Britt brushed her fingertips over the back of Greer's free hand. She felt the tension melt from him as he drained his sherry. When he set the glass down, she unobtrusively filled it. "Can't say that I have," he said. "Not unambiguously."

"Drink up," she said, modulating her voice nearly to a croon. "Relax, you must have had a hard week, driving up from Williamsburg in the snow. Time to take it easy." She increased the rate of the emerald's spin. While she couldn't order him to watch its motion, a crude approach that would alert him to her attempted hypnosis, the sparkle of the gem automatically drew his eyes. His lids drooped. "That's right, you feel better already. Have a nice drink." He obeyed. When he'd half emptied the glass, she said, "Now put it down and let your hands go limp on your knees. I'll bet they're cramped from driving. Now breathe deeply, expel the tension left over from the panel. Good, isn't that relaxing?" His slow, even respiration rewarded her efforts. She felt Roger's silent applause. "Adam, in the last few days you came across something that looked supernatural, didn't you?"

He answered with a drowsy nod, marred by tense creases in his forehead.

"That's all right, stay calm, you can tell me about it. I'm a fellow professional. You can tell me anything." Greer's frown smoothed away. "Tell me, Adam, how long have you been interested in vampires?" She thought a "have you stopped beating your wife" question would stir less resistance than a yes-or-no query.

"I never was, before. The subject was too much of the same old thing over and over."

"But now you are. What did you see?"

"A girl with wings." He shifted his feet, and his fingers clenched on his thighs.

"Very interesting." Britt stroked each of his hands in turn until they relaxed. "Don't worry, I believe you. It's perfectly safe for you to tell me this. What did you do about it?"

"I wanted to talk to her."

"Why? To write an article?"

"Maybe a book. Incredible. She changed shape. And her eyes glowed red." He gave Britt a misty stare. "Do you believe me?"

"Of course I do. What did you do with this girl?"

"Took pictures. They didn't come out—mind control. How can I make people believe what I saw?" He breathed slowly through his mouth, his words becoming slurred. "Why's she afraid? Won't hurt her, just wanta talk. She hurt me—dangerous beast."

"You have her hidden somewhere?"

"Right. In a cabin. She can't escape—I'm careful."

"Tell me about this cabin." Britt softened her tone still more to counteract the urge to scream at and shake him.

"Campground, less'n an hour away. Nobody's renting cabins week before Christmas. Perfectly safe."

"Tell me where. How do you get there? What freeway exit?"

"It's in Prince George's County. Y'take ninety-five east from here—" With an occasional prod from Britt, he recited the route.

Britt thanked the Lord she was dealing with ordinary human senses. If Greer had been able to hear her heartbeat, its triumphant spiking would have penetrated even his alcohol- and hypnosis-induced fog. [Did you get all that, colleague?]

[Certainly. I'm not asleep down here.]

For a moment, Britt debated whether to give Greer a post-hypnotic suggestion to release his captive. She decided not to push her luck. Even a vampire's power of compulsion, let alone her merely human skills, might fail against Greer's obsessive drive to unearth Gillian's secrets. "Adam, it's getting late, and you're tired. You'd better go rest now."

He fumbled the cuff of his jacket up to reveal his watch. "Yeah, there's somebody I'm supposed to meet."

"Good, you do that." She let go the pendant to dangle on her bosom. "You've enjoyed our little talk, and you feel relaxed and pleasantly drowsy. But you can't quite remember what we talked about. It was nothing important. By the time you get out in the hall, you'll forget everything we said. By the time you punch the elevator button, you won't remember anything except that we drank sherry, and you had a pleasant time, but you don't especially want to see me again. Got that?"

He nodded.

"Fine, you can leave now."

Greer stood up. "Well, I'd better be going. Been a long day. Thanks for the drink. I had a pleasant time."

Smiling at this parroting of her suggestion, Britt shook hands with him and walked him to the door. She lingered to watch him shamble to the elevator and push the Down button.

Roger, his mental voice vibrating with excitement, told her, [If you can do it without being noticed, follow him. I'd like to be sure he's safely occupied before we go after Gillian.]

[We?]

[Claude insisted on coming with me, remember? I suppose he has the right, considering Greer almost killed him.]

Britt caught the next elevator down to the lobby. She emerged just in time to see Greer exiting through the main plate glass doors. Following him at a discreet distance, she hunched her shoulders against the cold night air. Why hadn't she delayed an extra thirty seconds to snatch up her coat? For that matter, why was Adam Greer running around coatless on a sub-freezing night?

[At least this probably means he's not taking off to check on Gillian,] Britt speculated to Roger. [He mentioned meeting somebody. Most likely he'll intercept whoever it is in the parking lot and bring them inside.]

Shivering, Britt crept along the side of the building, both to minimize the chance of being seen and to get a slight shelter from the breeze. The parking lot lights showed Greer walking down the middle lane. A woman emerged from the driver's side of a dark sedan and strode toward him. Britt caught a flash of crimson from the woman's eyes. The average observer would have mentally edited that anomaly and dismissed it. Britt, with her specialized experience, noted and understood.

[Roger, he's meeting a vampire.]

[So I see. I wish you had my night vision, colleague.] Since he was limited to seeing through Britt's senses, he couldn't gather the information he could if he'd been present in the flesh.

[Shall I get closer to them?]

[No, she might notice you. Certainly would, if you approached close enough for her to hear how fast your heart's probably beating.]

For a couple of minutes Greer and the female vampire stood in the middle of the parking lot talking. Britt deduced that fact from their attentive posture and Greer's arm-waving. At this distance, she couldn't hear more than an undifferentiated murmur, almost submerged under the traffic noise from the adjacent highway. Folding her arms against the cold, Britt watched the woman take Greer's arm. They strolled to another car, a pale-colored compact, and sat down. Since it happened to be parked under a light, Britt could see the silhouettes of the two occupants even after they closed the door. Greer's head lolled against the window on the driver's side, and the woman moved close to him, embracing.

[Somehow, I don't think they're just kissing,] Britt remarked.

[He is occupied,] said Roger, [which is the important thing from our viewpoint.]

Huddled against the wall under the eaves, Britt watched the car for about five increasingly cold minutes. The windows quickly fogged, depriving the scene of whatever limited interest it may have held. At the end of that time the compact's engine roared to life, and the couple drove off the hotel grounds together.

Britt gratefully retreated into the lobby, where Roger met her. "Excellent job, colleague." He rested a hand lightly between her shoulder blades, a rare liberty in public. "This is where I take over. I'll collect Claude, and you get some rest, or join Eloise for—whatever one does at these affairs." He waved vaguely in the direction of the ballroom.

Britt felt his relief that her part in the quest was finished. "Not fair, cutting me out of the rescue mission," she teased.

"We already agreed on that. We wouldn't want the slightest chance of his discovering that you tricked him, would we?"

"Agreed. Not that there is any. The lady in search of a liquor-flavored snack came along just in time, didn't she?"

"A little too opportunely." Roger steered Britt out of the main traffic pattern. "Too bad we couldn't get a closer look at her. At any rate, she did get the man out of our way."

Britt lowered herself into a damask-covered armchair beside a potted palm. "Right, why count your gift horses before they hatch?" After a pair of blue-haired angels passing nearby had moved out of earshot, she said, "At the risk of sounding like Miss Kitty, for heaven's sake, be careful."

"When am I not?"

"By yourself, sure. But you're taking Claude along." Britt's stomach twisted at the memory of Claude's gunshot wound. "He has a motive to act a bit more recklessly."

## Chapter Nine

HAVING PROMISED TO let Claude join him on any "rescue mission" for Gillian, Roger now regretted that promise. Teaming with his brother meant an annoying delay. He had to return to the ballroom, where Claude and Eloise were winding up their last set of the night in preparation for the main event, a band called Mock Turtle Soup. Lurking at the edge of the audience, Roger caught Claude's eye. No words were necessary to telegraph the reason behind Roger's impatience.

Claude made a hasty farewell to the audience, left Eloise to a more leisurely departure, and strode down the side aisle to Roger. "Britt got some answers out of him?" said Claude as they hurried through the hall, dodging streams of other pedestrians with preoccupied ease.

"He told her where Gillian is being held. Less than an hour's drive."

"We should take my rental car. Your gas-guzzler is too conspicuous." When the elevator didn't respond instantly to Claude's emphatic jab of the button, he led the way to the stairs. "First I have to shed this outfit. I'd rather not have my departure noticed. I never know when some idiot fan might decide to follow me for a lark."

Roger paced while Claude flung off the cape and changed the ruffled white shirt for a more conventional plaid sport shirt. While waiting he told Claude about the woman Britt had seen with Greer.

"Could it have been Camille?" Claude tossed his car keys to Roger. "You may as well drive—your territory. You didn't get a firsthand look at this woman?"

Roger shook his head. "Only what Britt was able to distinguish. Tall and dark, which aren't much help."

"Stretches coincidence to think another female vampire just happened on the scene tonight. But how did she know you'd be here, do you suppose?"

"Followed me from home, perhaps?" The idea gave Roger a chill. He thanked God he'd carefully avoided being seen with Britt in public. If Greer's companion was Camille, she mustn't learn of Britt's importance to Roger.

Leaving Claude's room, both men made themselves unnoticeable. Not quite a veil of invisibility, but a more tenuous psychic shield that would cause any observers to dismiss them as unimportant. Now that Claude had discarded his trademark costume, he could manage that deceit. "Tell me, Roger," he said, "if it is Camille, do you seriously believe that she just happened to be cruising for dinner and picked your professorial acquaintance by sheer chance?"

"Not for a minute."

Claude waited until they were in the car before he said, "Nor do I. fancy she was watching your house. How else could she know Greer has a connection with you?"

"If she saw him enter and leave," Roger speculated, "maybe she thinks he has useful information about me, and she enticed him in order to question him." *And in that case*, he thought, *it could be Greer she followed to the hotel, not me. If she followed me, she'd have noticed Britt, too.* He kept that thought to himself, as if speaking it aloud would invoke misfortune.

After they were well launched onto the beltway, Claude broke his gloomy silence. "If Greer turns up while we're liberating Gillian, he's mine."

Roger shot a dismayed look at him. "I won't be an accessory to murder."

Claude flashed him a smile before resuming a steady gaze out the windshield at the light-speckled freeway. A clear night had displaced the snow clouds of the past few days. "Compose yourself, *mon frere*. I haven't taken leave of my senses completely. Revenge is a waste of effort, and the man isn't worth the inconvenience of killing. But he does owe me."

"I suppose I can't argue with that."

Claude shifted in the passenger seat, projecting a restlessness that affected Roger like a gnat buzzing in his ear. After drumming his fingers on the armrest for a minute, Claude took cigarettes and lighter out of the breast pocket of his windbreaker. In reply to Roger's disapproving glance, he rolled down the window. "Sorry, I need this."

Claude used that vice to mute the demands of unsatisfied hunger. Roger couldn't fathom how he could stand to smoke at all. "I thought Eloise would have taken care of that. She refused you?" He rolled down his own window. The cross-draft made the cigarette smoke barely tolerable.

"Not at all." Claude emitted a humorless laugh. "She offered—in a teeth-gritting, *close your eyes and think of England* manner. I turned her down. I'd rather starve than be treated as an unpleasant obligation."

Though a vampire couldn't starve, he must be feeling that way with the void generated by his rapid healing unfilled. The shadow of that need turned Roger cold inside. He couldn't imagine that kind of rejection from Britt, another ordeal that would give substance to the cliché, *a fate worse than death.* "That explains your behavior with those female fans."

"Oh, you noticed?" said Claude. "When they make themselves so blatantly available, it's hard to resist playing with them, even though I've absolutely no intention of following through." He blew smoke rings out the window to be shredded by the wind.

"That's no way to advance a reconciliation with Eloise." A psychiatrist shouldn't give advice, but this was his brother, not a patient.

"Dash it all, I can't help it—habits of a lifetime, and all that. My self-control isn't up to par this weekend."

"I can't believe you get much satisfaction from that—flirting." In accordance with the directions Britt had wormed out of Greer, Roger exited the freeway onto a wooded county road.

"Not much." Claude exhaled a gust of smoke. "The difference between starving in the wilderness and eating grass, I suppose."

Despite their errand, Roger welcomed the dark, deserted highway, peaceful after the crowded hotel, its atmosphere dense with noise, smoke, alcohol, and sweat. He was tempted to rest his eyes by turning off the headlights, which handicapped his superhuman night vision. He left them on, though, for fear of a collision with a driver who lacked his advantages.

When the car slowed to a crawl on the winding gravel road that led into the resort described by Greer, Roger did extinguish the lights. The less attention they attracted the better. Claude threw away his cigarette stub and perked up, his nostrils flared as though he could scent their quarry from this impossible distance.

Within less than five minutes, Roger parked the car a few hundred yards from the clearing where Greer's cabin ought to be. Careful to walk on loam rather than gravel, Roger and Claude crept soundlessly toward the house. Claude sniffed the wind. "A vehicle was driven through here a very short time ago," he whispered too low for anyone but Roger to hear.

Roger nodded agreement. He, too, smelled fresh engine fumes ahead of them. When they stepped into the clearing, he saw the professor's van parked to one side of the wide, gravel-surfaced driveway. The cabin door stood open. A body lay face up near the van.

Claude trotted over to the supine form and knelt to examine it. Right behind him, Roger recognized the professor. No other living presence rewarded his mental probe. "He's alive," said Roger. To confirm the diagnosis Greer let out a groan as Claude's hands clutched his shoulders.

"He's been hit on the jaw," said Claude, "but he's coming around well enough." He shook the half-conscious man. "Wake up, damn you!"

The professor's eyes opened. At the sight of Claude's eyes glowing crimson in the night, he moaned again and closed his. Claude ripped open his collar button to reveal a small wound. "Losing a bit more won't hurt him."

"Unwise," Roger said. "He'll make you sick."

"I won't allow that to happen. I'll take it easy, and his being half out of it helps." He shoved the professor's head back to further expose the throat.

Roger didn't care to watch. Though he felt that the cabin was deserted, he went inside to search. Gillian's metallic scent lingered. She must have been there until only a few minutes ago. In the bathroom, where her scent clung most heavily, he found material evidence—handcuffs. They were unlocked, not broken. A growl rumbled in his chest. *Maybe I should encourage Claude to kill the bastard, after all.*

In the living room, he found a Polaroid camera. Alarmed by the implications, he ransacked the two rooms until he unearthed a pile of instant photos of Gillian. He held onto them for destruction at the earliest opportunity.

Outside, Claude crouched over his quiescent prey. Roger noticed Claude swallowing repeatedly, as if fighting nausea. No random victim, even one too shell-shocked to emit discordant mental static, could nourish him comfortably while he remained fixated on Eloise. He glanced up at Roger. "He's been drinking too much."

"I tried to warn you."

Claude shuddered, pressing his lips together. In control now, he impaled Greer with his gleaming eyes. "Wake up. You're going to answer a few questions."

The professor's glazed eyes stared up at Claude.

"Very good. Where is Gillian?"

"Don't know. She gone?" The words came out slurred.

Claude tried a different tack. "Who hit you?"

"Camille."

Roger stiffened. Claude prompted in the same smoothly compelling voice, "Why?"

"Don't know. Thought she liked me. Told me how to catch the girl. Kissed me—wild." His voice remained flat, but his aura momentarily flared a deeper red.

"Yes, and then?"

"Scratched her neck. Made me lick the blood. Then we got out of the car, and she knocked me down." His eyes rolled. "Where's rental car? She take it? Bitch." He spoke the word as dully as if reciting from a script.

"So. Interesting." Greer's head slumped to one side. Grasping his hair, Claude pulled his head up to make him look forward. "Listen carefully. Forget I was here. You arrived with Camille. After she hit you, you fell unconscious. That is all you remember." Greer attempted a sluggish nod. "Good. Now go to sleep." He let the man's head drop to the ground.

"She exchanged blood with him," Roger said. "Normally she'd have found that extremely—distasteful."

Claude stood up, brushing at the damp spots on his trousers. "Yes. So she must expect to have some future use for him. One reason I made sure to obliterate his memory of me."

"Camille took Gillian. Obviously she planned the whole thing and used him to get at the child."

"Logical conclusion." Claude started for the car.

"You're planning to leave him this way?"

Claude turned to give Roger a puzzled look. "Why not? I said I wouldn't kill him, but I don't have any incentive to pamper him."

"With the blood loss in this weather, you'd be condemning him to hypothermia." Though he loathed the man too, Roger's conscience wouldn't allow him to kill outside the heat of battle. "That's tantamount to murder."

Claude shrugged. "Do what you like with him."

Roger hauled Greer inside, dumped him on the couch, and shut the door.

As he started the car, Roger said to Claude, "Feel better now?"

Claude overlooked the caustic tone. "As a matter of fact, yes. Marginally."

A little later, Roger said, "What do you think Camille plans to do with Gillian?"

"Not kill her, certainly, or she would have done so at once. Nor do I think Camille would risk a death sentence that way." Destroying one of their own kind constituted the ultimate crime.

"What would you do in her place?"

Claude stretched, his long legs trying for a comfortable position in the medium-size sedan. "I'd never have absconded with the girl to begin with."

"Did she go willingly, I wonder?"

"You didn't see any signs of a struggle, did you?" Roger admitted the fact. "However willing or unwilling she may have been," said Claude, "I don't give her long before she'll be under Camille's wing one hundred percent. Remember, she's at the most impressionable age."

"If Camille presents herself as Gillian's rescuer—" From what he recalled of Camille's late brother, Roger shuddered to think of what Gillian might learn from the woman.

Claude seconded his thoughts with an emphatic nod. "Vampire version of the Stockholm syndrome."

"I WISH YOU had let me kill him." Gillian gazed sideways at the pale, dark-haired woman who propelled the compact car along the twisting lanes as if the campground were a race course.

"I might need him again in the near future. Besides, didn't they teach you not to leave bodies lying around that can be traced to you?"

"Yes, but what he did—"

"For the present, losing his treasure—you—is a fitting punishment." The woman began to sing, the draft from the open window whipping her unbound hair:

"Oh, what are we going to do with Uncle Albert?

A bloomin' stallion

Is Uncle Albert!

When he goes out strolling in the park,

Watch your step, girls, especially after dark—"

She broke off, glancing at Gillian. "What are you thinking, with that earnest, wide-eyed stare?"

"Who are you? Did Roger send you?"

The woman quizzically arched her brows. "My name is Camille. Of course Roger didn't send me. Why would you think so?"

Now Gillian grasped the meaning of the human idiom *her heart sank*. No doubt Roger had been glad to get rid of her. "I thought he might feel some—obligation." The woman's name suggested something to her, but she was too agitated right now to scour her memory for the reference.

"Because he let you live with him? He might have acted like a human father, but you couldn't expect the pose to hold firm under pressure." They'd left the resort area, and Camille was now driving the stolen car at about seventy along the traffic-free county highway.

"I didn't live with him." Gillian felt a flicker of something like surprise from Camille. "I ran away from Lord Volnar, and I'd been with Roger only two nights. I suppose I shouldn't have expected him to feel responsible for me."

"I see." Gillian couldn't read Camille's reaction. The vampire woman had firmed her psychic shield, which etiquette didn't allow anyone, especially a child, to challenge.

"How did you find me? And why?"

"*Why* should be clear enough. I couldn't allow a man like Greer to hold one of our young captive, could I? As for how, I followed your sire to a convention and became acquainted with Greer. I'd noticed his interest in Roger and wanted to question him about it. As you'll find out, tasting a human male's blood makes him highly suggestible. He spilled the whole story of the exotic beast he'd captured. So here I am."

*Exotic beast!* Gillian's anger at Greer flamed afresh. There was nothing she could safely do to him, though; Camille spoke wisely on that point. "Thank you. I'm most grateful. Where are we going?"

"Are you hungry?"

"Yes!" Camille could have read Gillian's unshielded desire but instead chose the courtesy of asking, a bit of consideration that made Gillian feel gratifyingly adult.

"Then after we've found a place to stay, we'll find you a meal." Another brief but probing look. "You don't take human prey yet, do you?" To Gillian's silent negative, she said, "Soon, though. I sense you're growing into it."

A ripple of excitement stirred beneath Gillian's fatigue and hunger. *Soon!* She stretched, then curled sideways in the bucket seat, luxuriating in the freedom of movement she'd lacked for so many hours. Along the highway the wooded landscape was now varied by gas stations, convenience stores, the occasional cluster of houses. A few minutes later Camille slowed for a motel sign with *Vacancy* illuminated in red. When the car turned into the parking lot, Gillian saw a one-story semicircle of units with a door at one end of the arc labeled *Office*. A window next to that door showed a desk clerk in the rectangle of light. Except for the green doors to the guest rooms the building was white, its paint streaked and peeling. Mounds of grimy snow dotted the partially cleared lot, occupied by a panel truck and four cars.

"The management should be glad to see us," Camille remarked. "Wait here."

Through the windshield, Gillian watched her rescuer enter the office and negotiate with a stout, gray-haired woman. Red and blue lights blinked on a scrubby Christmas tree beside the counter. Camille, Gillian noticed, handed over cash, not a credit card.

Returning to the car with a key in hand, Camille said, "Neither the comfort of a Holiday Inn nor the quirky charm of the Bates Motel, but it'll do until we have time to find something better." She drove to the other end of the lot.

"Bates Motel?"

"You've led a sheltered life, haven't you?" said Camille, pulling into a parking slot and killing the engine. "Haven't you been allowed to watch horror movies yet?"

Gillian shook her head.

"Sheltered. You're mature enough to handle the exposure, I'd think."

*Mature.* Gillian basked in the word's implications.

Inside, Camille sat cross-legged on the double bed, leaving Gillian the one chair, fake leather, with stuffing poking out of the cushion seams. The smell of chlorine bleach from the bath permeated the room. Camille didn't bother to turn on a light. "Volnar was your advisor? Why did you run away from him?"

"I didn't feel prepared to bond with him." Gillian narrated her experience at the play, the flood of emotions that had overwhelmed her. "Everyone says I can't learn the full range of adult skills without a blood-bond. I don't want to accept that."

"Nor should you," Camille said. She combed out her windblown hair with splayed fingers. "I don't in the least blame you for being reluctant to bond with Volnar. I wouldn't care to place myself under his dominance, either." She frowned in thought for a few seconds. "Gillian, I have an idea. Why not let me teach you—it would be my pleasure. And I give you my word, I'd never think of forcing a blood-bond on you. Your mind would remain entirely your own."

An unrecognized tension that had been squeezing Gillian's ribcage loosened. "Would you? I know I do need a mentor—but not him."

Camille's eyes gleamed red in the darkness, relieved only by a pale glimmer from the far end of the parking lot. "Excellent decision. I won't force any act upon you against your will, and I won't restrain your growth. Sometimes, the elders are a little too cautious, don't you think so?" She sinuously unfolded herself from the bed and went into the bathroom for a glass of water. "Now, shall we hunt?" She refilled the glass and offered it to Gillian.

The water had a strong mineral flavor. She didn't mind; every area's water tasted different, but not necessarily unpleasant. The trace of salt titillated her blood-thirst. "I'm ready."

When they left the motel room, the light in the office had been turned off. "Good, she won't notice our driving away later," said Camille as they walked around to the back of the complex. "I need a meal too, and animal blood won't be enough."

"Didn't you have the professor?" Gillian said. Like Camille, she automatically spoke in a near-whisper. "I thought I noticed the mark in his aura."

"Very good observation. But I also expended energy in subduing him. At any rate, why should we deny ourselves full and frequent satisfaction? Too many of our kind drag themselves around half-famished, out of exaggerated caution."

They picked their way across a trash-strewn back lot into the sparse woods behind the motel. Intermittent traffic sounds drifted to them from two directions. "Lord Volnar says two or three times per week should be sufficient."

Camille cast an amused glance at her. "He's conservative. As Prime Elder, that's his job. The rest of us can recognize that in this society, we can feed as often as we choose without arousing suspicion. Nobody believes in us."

Gillian's nostrils flared, catching the spoor of squirrels, skunks, and raccoons. "What about Greer?"

"How did he come to suspect you?"

Still abashed by the memory, Gillian told her as briefly as possible.

"Witnessing a transformation is a far cry from something as indefinite as a mysterious attack of anemia." Camille gestured for silence. To ambush their prey they needed quiet.

With Camille in the lead, they backtracked along the trail of a raccoon, which they found perched in the fork of a tree. Like Roger, Camille hung back to allow Gillian to lure the creature down. She ensnared its glittering eyes, reveling in its obedience to her call. The snarl in the animal's throat died as it inched down the tree. By the time Gillian gathered her victim into her arms, its heart and hers were beating in perfect synchronicity. Unlike Roger Camille claimed a token sip before letting Gillian drain the raccoon.

"Now for the main course," said Camille as they returned to the motel. "I'll let you help me with the hunt. That will be good practice."

Gillian tingled with pleasure. Though Volnar had often let her watch the preliminaries, he had never enlisted her aid. Of course, then she'd had none of the necessary skills. Now, so short a time later, she did. "Where are we going?"

"Washington." After a stop at the room to pick up the car keys, they were on the road again.

Gillian rode with the window open, enjoying the wind in her face. Doubts still nibbled at the back of her mind, though. "Now I remember," she said when they pulled onto the freeway. "Lord Volnar has mentioned your name. You had a brother, Neil. Roger—destroyed him."

A flare of anger from Camille, instantly quenched. "Yes." The word was nearly a hiss. "He killed one of our race. That is the kind of creature he is." She shot a smile at Gillian, her mental barrier so strong that Gillian couldn't sense the underlying emotion. "But *you* needn't be like that."

"Lord Volnar said your brother—that is, he's spoken of as a renegade."

For a moment, Camille's fingers tightened on the wheel, and her breath came shallow through gritted teeth. Once she'd calmed herself, she said in a neutral tone, "Many of our people reject Volnar's judgment. Even some on the Council of Elders. Don't believe everything you hear, Gillian." After a while, she took an off-ramp toward downtown Washington. Apparently having forgiven Gillian for broaching the offensive topic, she began to sing again:

"It was a hell of a war as I recall, *parlez-vous,*

It was a hell of a war, as I recall, *parlez-vous.*

It was a hell of a war, as I recall,

But still it was better than none at all—"

She turned to look at Gillian, who shyly stared at her. Humming along with an opera tape was the only musical self-expression Volnar ever indulged in. Camille said, "You don't know this song, do you? Want to learn it?" Gillian nodded. "Fine, repeat after me: Mademoiselle from Armentieres, *parlez-vous...*"

The car crawled through a section of Washington Gillian had never seen on her visits with Volnar. Rows of graffiti-marked brownstones, many boarded up, lined the streets. Camille and Gillian rolled up their windows to shut out the stink of garbage. The setting reminded Gillian of the street where the boys had attacked her a few nights ago. Noticing her nervousness, Camille inquired the reason, and Gillian recounted her experience.

"This time I'll be with you," said Camille. "And soon enough, you'll have the strength to handle a minor challenge like that on your own."

"Losing control was the worst part. Will you help me work on my transformation?"

"Of course. Didn't I promise to train you?" Camille's tone seemed to reproach Gillian for doubting.

"You can do it without the blood-bond?"

"As I said before, the Prime Elder's way is not the only way." Since Camille seemed impatient with the questions, Gillian dropped the subject. Instead she surveyed the neighborhood they were traversing. A few people were afoot on the cracked sidewalks—a stout black woman at a bus stop, three boys in their late teens a block farther along. Picking a moment when nobody was in sight, Camille turned into an alley and switched off the motor. "Parking here is probably illegal, but we won't be gone long, I hope—and anyway, the penalty would be a ticket, not a tow, and the car is rented in Greer's name."

Gillian got out and stretched while Camille locked the car. "Why here?"

"I notice a soup kitchen a block up the street." Camille tucked the keys into the Velcro-zipped pocket of the tightly-fitted silver-gray slacks she wore. "Not that locking it will do much good if someone decides to smash the windows. Well, let's go."

Dodging patches of dirty ice, Gillian followed her along the sidewalk. "What do you want me to do?"

"By this time, people should be lining up for free breakfast." The night had flown faster than Gillian, in all the excitement, had realized. The sky she glimpsed between buildings was fading from black to gray. "I plan to send you in as a decoy. You look very young in human terms and vulnerable because of your thinness." She paused to clasp Gillian's elbow and look her over. "It's a good thing we didn't stop to get you some clean clothes. A veritable waif. Exploit that appearance as long as you can. You'll outgrow it all too soon."

Sure enough, five people were clustered on the concrete steps of the two-story building with the wooden, white-painted, green-lettered sign announcing three meals a day for all comers. A few more shabbily dressed customers drifted up as Camille and Gillian watched from half a block away. "I don't want to be seen," Camille said in a muted tone, hardly more than subvocalizing, audible only to another vampire. "Let me think—that one looks like a good prospect. Undernourished but still basically healthy. You can pass for about her age." With an unobtrusive gesture she indicated a black girl with corn-rowed hair, bony arms sticking out of a red sweatshirt torn at the elbows.

Though Gillian didn't know much about human growth patterns, she suspected the girl was under sixteen, Volnar's prescribed minimum age for victims. This didn't seem the right time, however, to mention Volnar to Camille again. Watching the girl hug herself, shivering, Gillian marveled at how delicate, how susceptible to ordinary weather variations, these ephemerals were. "What do you want me to do with her?"

"Approach her in your own way," Camille said. "I'd like to see how you work. Cut her out of the flock and bring her to me—the details are up to you." Camille sidled into the nearest alley out of any casual passerby's sight.

Gillian's heart raced with excitement. She focused inward for a few seconds to slow it. Only ephemerals let their emotions rule their physical reactions. Ambling over to the group by the front steps of the mission, she congratulated herself that no one paid special attention to her. She must have imitated the appropriate body language adequately. When she joined the others waiting in the predawn cold, she did provoke a couple of curious glances, which she decided sprang from her being the only light-skinned person present except a bearded man who reeked of smoke and alcohol.

Falling into place beside her target, Gillian ventured a tentative smile and a "Good morning."

The other girl, petite in height as well as overly thin, dubiously looked up at her. "Yo. Ain't you cold?"

"Not very." Gillian decided it was too late to fake shivering.

The other girl scanned Gillian, her eyes lingering on the designer jeans. "You on the wrong side of town, girlfriend. You run away or what?"

"Yes. My name is Gillian." She offered her hand.

The black girl hesitated long enough before accepting it to tell Gillian the gesture had been out of character. "Bonnie. This my Aunt Loretta." She jerked her head to indicate a middle-aged woman leaning against the railing nearby. "This your first time here, right?"

"Yes. Is the food good?"

Bonnie laughed. "Who cares? They give you plenty, anyway. But you don't want to go in there without no adult." She stressed and drawled out the first syllable of *adult*. "They call the child welfare on you, for sure."

"Then what can I do?" Gillian was reluctant to entice Bonnie away from the group with her aunt standing by. The woman would surely interfere. Maybe if she flocked inside with the others, she could sneak out with Bonnie unnoticed during the meal.

The girl shrugged, then tapped her aunt on the arm and spoke to her in a rapid undertone. While Gillian had trouble following the dialect, she gathered that Bonnie was telling Aunt Loretta about her. After a whispered discussion, Bonnie turned back to Gillian. "You can be our *guest*." She grinned at her own joke. "We say you my girlfriend staying with us."

"Thank you very much." Standing in line with the growing crowd of ephemerals made Gillian uncomfortable. Except under Volnar's protection, she'd never mixed with large groups of them. Their cold, hunger, and low-level fear battered her imperfectly developed psychic shield. She found herself edging closer to Bonnie to immerse herself in the relative cordiality of the girl's aura. The sign announced that breakfast started at five thirty. Gillian had no watch and hadn't checked the time recently enough to be able to estimate it now. She felt the pressure of Camille's attention.

Finally, the door opened and the line of people filed in. The cafeteria-style room smelled of disinfectant and stale cooking aromas. The rectangular Formica tables were adorned with potted poinsettias. Homemade posters of butterflies, crosses, and slogans such as *God don't make junk* relieved the starkness of the whitewashed walls. Over the background odors Gillian smelled eggs and some kind of frying meat.

The preoccupied woman at the window between kitchen and dining hall didn't question Aunt Loretta's claim to be Gillian's escort. When the three of them had collected their trays, Gillian made a stab at separating Bonnie from her aunt. As the woman headed for a table in the center of the room, Gillian said, "Bonnie, why don't we sit near the window instead? We can see out while we're eating and have some fresh air."

"Fresh air?" the girl hooted. "You some kind of Eskimo, or what?" On reflection, Gillian thought the proposal sounded rather weak herself, but she'd managed to get Bonnie staring into her eyes. On this young and totally unsuspecting victim Gillian's new-fledged power worked like the flick of a switch. "Sure, why not? You crazy, but I like you." She relayed their intention to her aunt, who mumbled something about eating *her* breakfast where icicles wouldn't sprout on it.

At a table against the front wall Bonnie dug into her scrambled eggs and two slices of ham. Gillian had accepted a tray rather than arouse suspicion by refusing the meal she'd waited for. She slowly drank the milk that came with it. After Bonnie had gobbled her food, Gillian pushed her own plate over. "You take this. I can't—I am allergic to eggs."

Bonnie's shock at this prodigality shifted to delight. "You sure? Thanks!"

Nervously checking on Aunt Loretta, Gillian was glad to see the woman lingering over a cup of coffee. Gillian forced herself not to fidget while waiting for Bonnie to devour the second breakfast. As soon as the other girl wiped her mouth for the last time, Gillian said, "Let's take a walk. It's no fun sitting here."

"Walk? Girlfriend, do I gots to keep telling you it's freezing out there?" When Gillian reinforced the suggestion with a light touch on the girl's hand, Bonnie said, "Okay, whatever. Aunt Loretta, she sit there drinking coffee until they throw her out." After dumping their plates in a bin up front, the two girls strolled out to the sidewalk. Gillian made no attempt to rush her companion for fear of attracting attention.

A block from the mission, Gillian gently took Bonnie's hand. Bonnie started to jerk loose, but when Gillian gazed into her eyes, she forgot her qualms. "Girl, you weird," she murmured. "Thought you say you not cold—you feel like ice."

"I know somewhere we can get warm without having to stay in that roomful of people." Questing with her psychic perception, Gillian sensed that Camille had moved farther up the street. Approaching the alley where they'd left the car, Gillian sensed the vampire woman's presence. "Come along, Bonnie, I'm to meet someone here. She'll be glad I've brought you."

"She? Huh?" Bonnie's vague doubts were no match for the hypnotically-induced trust she felt toward Gillian. She allowed Gillian to lead her into the alley.

Warmth flowed through Gillian from the clasp of the other girl's fingers. Somehow the idea that food she had provided, indirectly at least, was even now nourishing her prey gratified Gillian. She soaked up Bonnie's friendliness, however artificial, like a plant's roots groping for water.

When Camille stepped out of the car, the red glint of her eyes startled Bonnie. The girl let out a squeak of alarm and tried to pull away from Gillian. "It's all right, I know her," Gillian said. "She's a friend."

Before Bonnie could decided whether to believe, Camille's mature power drowned her will. The black girl wobbled on her feet. Camille scooped the victim up in her arms and, crooning, bent to her throat.

Gillian felt an irrational urge to protest when Camille claimed the prey *she* had captured. *Bonnie's mine. She likes me.* For the moment it was easy to forget that the liking was largely her own creation. Shaking her head to throw off the confusion, Gillian reminded herself that she was too young for human blood, and that she'd only been acting as a decoy for her new mentor. *I'm not even hungry. I've fed well.*

Once Camille paused in her feast to glance up at Gillian, licking her red-stained lips. "Wonderful. You've primed her perfectly." Placing the half-conscious girl on the hood of the car, Camille leaned over her to drink deeper.

After a while Gillian had to stop watching. If she wasn't hungry, why did this spectacle make her feel hollow inside? Finally Camille said, "That's all. We'd better dispose of her and get clear of the area."

"Dispose?" Gillian glanced around the alley. Not a visible speck of blood on the pavement or the car; Camille was as neat as any adult vampire ought to be. But Bonnie—For a moment Gillian couldn't accept what the girl's fading aura proclaimed. "She's dead!"

"Dying," said Camille in an indifferent tone. "Amounts to the same thing. She won't regain consciousness."

"You killed her," Gillian whispered.

"Accidents do happen." Laughing, Camille shifted the body for easier carrying. "Don't tell me you have scruples? Surely Volnar wouldn't let you pick up silly ideas like that. Considering the life she was probably headed for, I did her a favor. Not that I meant to drain her, but she tasted surprisingly good. And I've had a strenuous night." Camille trotted to the far end of the alley. Gillian watched her deposit her burden in the shadows next to a Dumpster.

"But it's forbidden to kill—"

"Conspicuously. There's no way this death will be identified for what it is, much less linked to us. Come along, we'll go back to that roach motel and get a good day's sleep."

Gillian kept quiet during the drive, glad Camille didn't start a conversation either. What the woman said made sense, from a certain point of view. Yet Gillian knew what Roger or even Claude would have said about this night's work.

## Chapter Ten

WHEN ROGER AND Claude got back to the convention hotel, Britt and Eloise waited together in the latter's top-floor suite. "Manning the barricades?" said Claude. "Any fans lay siege to you?"

Eloise shook her head. "The hotel is nice about protecting your privacy, thank goodness. The room number doesn't seem to have gotten around. We watched *Silence of the Lambs* in the video room, then made it up here with no problem."

"Good research," said Britt, "but you'd have found holes to pick in it anyway, colleague."

"Precisely why I haven't cared to see it," Roger said. He surveyed the sitting room for something to drink.

Guessing what he wanted, Claude detoured into the bedroom for a bottle of brandy, from which he served all four of them—generous glasses for Roger and himself, single shots for the women. "Good decision. Eloise dragged me to the blasted thing, and it gave me nightmares."

On the basis of what he'd heard about the story, Roger found that puzzling. "I wouldn't expect you to be squeamish about flayed corpses, particularly when they're just special effects."

"It isn't that." Claude sat on the couch near Eloise, carefully not touching her. "It's the incarceration scenes. I thought I had no imagination, but it was painfully easy to visualize myself in that fix." He sipped the brandy as if to counteract the vision. "Our ultimate nightmare. If you're confined and fed, yet deprived of human prey, you go raving mad. Only a matter of time." He stared into space for a moment, then shook off the image. "So. You two observed what we found?"

"Britt did," said Eloise, "and she told me. I'm surprised you didn't try to follow Camille and Gillian."

"Good thing Roger *didn't* go charging after them. Yes, I know you wanted to," Claude said to Roger. "By the time we'd finished with Greer, they could have vanished in any direction. And if by chance you'd run across them, suppose Camille had decided a threat of death—or torture—against Gillian was the perfect way to bring you into line?"

"I see what you mean," Roger said. "Have you any suggestions?"

"Other than waiting for Gillian to come to her senses and flee that woman like the proverbial pestilence?" Claude said. "Considering you don't even have the license number of the rented car she appropriated, finding her presents a problem."

"I'm sorry about that," said Britt. "The light hit the plates at the wrong angle for me to make it out. I have these inconvenient human limitations."

Roger, in a chair next to hers, said, "Probably just as well I wasn't following Greer myself. Camille would certainly have noticed a vampire watching her."

Claude nodded. "Too true. Your attention on her would have been like shooting up a flare—*Here I am, let's fight!* Think you could enlist that police captain friend of yours?"

"Not much he can do for us at the moment," said Britt, "especially since reporting Gillian as kidnapped is out. I'll call him again and drop a few hints, though."

"*Is* she kidnapped, really?" Eloise mused. "After what Greer must have put her through—like what you mentioned a minute ago, Claude, she must've been terrified—a woman of her own race would have been the answer to her prayers. If vampire kids pray."

"Yes, we considered that," Roger said. "If she's using Gillian, somehow, to get at me, corrupting the child might be part of her plan."

Britt said, "I think we made a strong impression on Gillian in that brief time, though. Maybe she'll weigh the alternatives and come back to Roger."

"Which is one of many reasons why we should return to Annapolis as soon as possible." Roger polished off his brandy and set down the glass, wearily contemplating the prospect of another hour's drive. At least it would all be in darkness.

"Guess you're right," said Britt. "Not really anything else we can do here." She stifled a yawn.

"Perhaps you should report to Volnar," Claude suggested to Roger.

"I don't have a contact number for him. Juliette might, if she's still in New York—I'll consider getting in touch with her."

"You will keep us posted?" said Eloise. "I'm worried about her. I hate to think of an innocent kid in the clutches of somebody even remotely like that Neil Sandor person."

*Interesting,* Roger thought. *She seems to take Gillian's plight personally.*

"YOUR'RE RIGHT. I do feel confused about my reaction to Gillian's disappearance," Roger said to Britt as they turned onto St. Margaret's Road an hour later. "She's a responsibility I never wanted. Did I neglect some precaution that would have saved her from getting abducted in the first place? Naturally, there's some guilt."

Britt, her head in his lap, rubbed drowsily against his thighs. "I feel a little of that, myself. We were all preoccupied with Eloise's condition—rightly so—but we never stopped to think how the turmoil affected Gillian. And now that she's with Camille, you're ambivalent about trying to get her back, aren't you?"

Roger admitted to the charge. "Part of me questions why Camille should be any worse a teacher than Volnar. We don't know that the woman shares her brother's antisocial tendencies."

"Antisocial for a vampire," said Britt. Unspoken was the axiom that by the standards of the gregarious human race, all purebred vampires were antisocial.

"Yes. If Gillian *wants* to stay with Camille, and Camille does nothing to prove herself unfit—"

"You think the child should have a choice." Britt sat up, brushing her disheveled hair out of her eyes. "And in order to determine her choice, you have to find her. So just letting the matter drop is out of the question."

"Exactly," said Roger, pulling into his reserved parking space in front of the townhouse. He appreciated Britt's skill at articulating his problem so succinctly. "I have to confront her with the alternatives, and I have to find out—and prove to Gillian, if necessary—what kind of person Camille is."

Inside Britt sprawled on the couch as if she hardly had the energy to drag herself to the bedroom. "I've got to get a few hours of sleep. As soon as the civilized world's day starts, I'll call Hayes again. I can't stay in bed much past eight a.m., anyhow."

Though he disliked the idea of her waking up so early after their crowded night, Roger knew she spoke the truth about her relentlessly diurnal circadian rhythm. And the prospect of a full day of rest beckoned him as an irresistible seduction. "What are you going to tell Hayes? We don't need Greer found anymore."

Britt shrugged off her winter coat and the green jacket under it. "No, but it won't hurt to ask the captain to keep an eye out in case Greer gets into some kind of trouble. I'll say we're worried about him, without specifying why. The condition Camille left him in, I'd guess there's good reason to worry." Roger nodded. "Also, what if Camille is like her brother—in her attitude toward us mere mortals, anyway? I'd like to get the word on any unexplained deaths, especially of people who wouldn't be missed much."

"Good thinking," Roger said. He took Britt's coat and jacket to hang them up. For once she didn't offer a teasing protest at this "sexist" gesture. "Go to bed, colleague, before you fall asleep on the spot and develop a backache."

"Yes, Doctor." Britt stood up and wrapped her arms around his waist, leaning on him. "Oh, Lord, that feels good. I was worried about you, going after the professor." She chuckled softly at the silliness of the idea. "As if you and Claude couldn't handle six or ten of him. Poor Claude and Eloise, depriving themselves of this."

"How is she coming along?" Roger's arms tightened around Britt. He basked in her warmth like a plant rotating toward its own private sun.

"After the movie she told me she's afraid Claude is only playing a role as her lover. After all, he's an actor. I didn't know how to answer that. I don't know him that intimately—maybe he is."

Roger thought over the question, choosing his words with care. "In a sense everything he does—any vampire does—in human society is role-playing. But don't forget that we, more so than human beings, tend to become what we simulate. It's a distinction without a difference."

Britt shook her head. "Eloise doesn't see it that way, and in her place I'd have a little trouble with the concept myself."

"He cares for her as deeply as he's capable of, and he's doing his best." Roger felt a twinge of impatience with Britt—she ought to understand, even if Eloise, awash in a tide of grief, couldn't. "He has my complete sympathy. You would never shut me out that way."

"*You* never wimped out on me when I was in pain." The edge in her voice surprised him. "If you had, I might've developed some doubts, too."

He almost returned a sharp answer. Struck by the absurdity of the conversation, he stopped himself just in time. "Colleague, are we appropriating their quarrel?"

Britt laughed softly. "I guess so. And I'm too tired to analyze why right now." She eased out of his embrace. "Tomorrow—or today, I guess—I'll have to go home. My apartment is collecting dust, and Sigmund must think I've forgotten him."

"You'll come back in the evening?"

"Sure, after supper, about seven thirty."

Feeling unreasonably deprived, though they'd spent more time together than usual this week, he watched her go upstairs. *Juliette,* he reminded himself. He was supposed to contact Juliette to ask whether she had a current number for Volnar. *Tomorrow afternoon.* His only way of reaching Gillian's mother was through her agent, who certainly wouldn't be answering his office phone at this time of night.

That scheduling problem left Roger to the inadequate distraction of journal articles and insurance claim forms, while he brooded over Gillian's disappearance. *Where is she now? What is Camille doing with her? And do I really want the girl back?* What he wanted scarcely mattered, though; he couldn't abandon her.

AT FOUR IN the afternoon on Saturday, Roger made the necessary call to New York. Waking up early didn't prove to be as much of a chore as he'd feared, since he wasn't sleeping well anyway. No messages on the answering machine, to his regret. Phoning the literary agent's office, he got forwarded to the man's home. Years ago, on the remote chance that they might sometime have to consult about Gillian, Juliette had added Roger's name to the select list of people to whom her agent had permission to divulge her current location. Roger got the number of Juliette's Manhattan hotel from him.

Juliette answered sleepily after five rings, but the sound of Roger's voice brought her fully awake. "Volnar told me Gillian was with you. What's going on?"

Roger hadn't spoken to Juliette since she'd brought Gillian up from Williamsburg for a brief visit when the child was three. Before that, the only contact he'd had with the woman had been the night Gillian was conceived. Unlike a human female, Juliette displayed no self-consciousness about that night thirteen years ago. To vampires, reproduction was enviably free of emotional complications. Well aware that this was no time to let awkward feelings distract him, Roger plunged directly into the current problem. "She isn't with me now. She was abducted." He summarized the events of the past few nights.

After a moment of silence Juliette said, "That's not good. I didn't know about Camille's punishment, either, but from what little I've seen of her in the past, she's not the type to emerge from it a better person. By our standards *or* the conventional ones."

The judgment confirmed Roger's fears. "Then I think it's past time for Volnar to take a direct hand in the situation. Do you have a number for him in London?"

"Oh, he isn't there. He hasn't been able to leave. The airport is snowed in—haven't you read the papers lately?"

"I've been otherwise occupied," Roger said dryly.

"No reason for you to bother calling him. I'll pass on the message as soon as possible. I'm sure he'll get back to you if there's any change."

"You're saying we're on our own down here?"

"I wish I had better news," said Juliette, "but contrary to *Dracula*, we can't control the weather. I'd drive down myself if it would do any good. Only it wouldn't—I'm not telepathically bonded with her, either. Mothers and infants don't do that. Children aren't capable of it before adolescence." She sounded genuinely worried. So the vampire pattern of child-rearing didn't mean mothers lost all interest in their weaned offspring. "For what it's worth, Roger, I've been thinking about asking Volnar to let Gillian spend some time with you. She needs exposure to the human viewpoint. However, I'd rather have waited until after she passed this developmental crisis."

"Thank you for your confidence." He meant it, though he couldn't quite keep a sarcastic edge out of his voice.

Shortly after he broke the connection with Juliette, the phone rang. Roger was surprised to hear Professor Greer's voice. The man sounded hoarse as well as exhausted. "Dr. Darvell, I have to talk to you."

"Go ahead, then." Roger kept his tone flat. He didn't want to give away anything until he had some idea of what the caller intended.

"I mean in person. I feel nervous about discussing all this on the phone."

"This?"

"You know—your daughter." He did sound nervous. "How specific do I have to get? Listen, I'm sorry I did what I did to her. It was all a mistake. I want to help you get her back."

"Do you know where she is?" Unless Greer had picked up some new information since Claude questioned him, the answer would be no. But Roger saw no reason to reveal the extent of his own knowledge.

"No, but I know who—" Greer broke off, as if he expected someone to overhear him. "When can I see you?"

"Give me a number, and I'll call you back." Roger wanted to think over this change of heart at leisure, and he also wanted reinforcements. Besides, it would do no harm to make the man suffer a bit.

Under protest Greer recited a number, begging Roger to return the call as soon as possible. Guilty conscience? Or did he expect Camille to be shadowing him? Roger thought he heard fear in the man's voice.

After a few minutes' consideration Roger telephoned the convention hotel and asked for Claude. Fortunately, Eloise happened to be in their room and relayed a telepathic message to him. After a brief wait Claude picked up the phone.

When Roger had informed him of Greer's message, Claude said, "Glad you told me. I'll be more than pleased to help you wring him out. Just one thing—I hope Camille wasn't listening in on the entire conversation."

"What? How could she—oh, damn."

"Exactly. Remember, she formed a bond with him. We can only hope she's too busy to keep a constant watch on him."

Roger ordered himself not to succumb to discouragement. "After only one exchange, the bond couldn't be strong enough to alert her automatically, could it?"

"Probably not. And if she's at all like her brother in that respect, she won't want to touch his mind any more often than necessary. Well, this is no place to discuss such matters, and I have to be somewhere in five minutes. I should be able to get away from here by eight. Tell Greer to be at your place at nine thirty."

They agreed on that plan, and Roger phoned the professor to make the arrangements. Greer seemed on the verge of hysterics at the enforced delay. Intriguing response. Roger hoped the intensity of it wouldn't draw Camille's attention.

CLAUDE ARRIVED A few minutes after nine, having left Eloise to cover for him at the convention. "My scheduled appearances are over for the day, so they can get along perfectly well without me. She can appease any fans that come stalking after me, and the less she's directly involved in this mess, the better."

"If I were Eloise," said Britt from her favorite seat near the fireplace, "I'd object to that."

"So would she, ordinarily," Claude said. "However, our present circumstances aren't ordinary." He spoke with a bleak absence of expression that stirred an echo of pain in Roger.

"While waiting for you, I thought of a problem," Roger said. "If you help me question Greer, he'll know what you are—exactly what you don't want in view of your notoriety."

"I don't anticipate any trouble there." Claude, dressed tonight in blue slacks and a turtleneck sweater of a lighter blue, took possession of the love seat opposite Britt. "I look quite different from the way I do at conventions or in publicity photos. Furthermore, I've already established some influence over him. If both of us keep telling him he's never seen me before, I daresay he'll believe it."

Roger turned to Britt. "What about you, colleague? Perhaps you'd better stay out of sight."

She started shaking her head before he finished the sentence. "And miss all the fun? Forget it. This is a rare chance to see Claude in action. Since there won't be any reason for me to work on Greer again, it doesn't matter if he knows I'm connected with you."

*I should have known she wouldn't let me steer her out of harm's way.* "Very well. How do you suggest we go about this, Claude?"

"I'll prepare him, and you act as chief inquisitor." Claude's aura pulsed with anticipation. *God, he must be famished, if playing with Greer's mind for a minute or two looks good to him!*

They agreed on that procedure. Britt excused herself to start coffee. She'd just returned with the pot and four mugs on a tray when the doorbell rang.

Greer's hollow eyes and uncombed hair underscored the anemic hue of his aura. Shaking the visitor's hand, Roger touched skin almost as cool as his own. When he took Greer's overcoat to hang in the foyer closet, Roger cringed from the odor of Scotch. Though not quite drunk, the professor must have been imbibing off and on ever since waking from last night's ordeal.

Guiding the visitor into the living room, Roger made no introductions. The room was almost dark except for the fire's glow and the light seeping from the entryway. Greer's eyes locked on Britt, who poured coffee and pretended not to notice his reaction. He sank onto one of the couches. "I think I've been had."

"Don't expect us to apologize," Roger said. "Consider yourself fortunate I didn't report you to the police."

Britt passed around the coffee, which Roger and Claude accepted for the sake of appearances. Before exerting their paranormal powers on Greer, they planned to question him conventionally. Putting him at ease with social amenities might facilitate the process. He took a generous gulp of the coffee despite its scalding heat, then bowed his head on his hands. "Okay, I deserved that. Circumstances weren't what I thought. That woman, Camille, told me—"

"Begin at the beginning," Claude interrupted. "How did you meet her?"

Greer turned a puzzled stare upon Claude, as if trying to identify his face.

"No, you don't know me," said Claude with a subtle psychic nudge. "Tell me about Camille."

"How I met her?" Greer gazed vacantly at the fire for a moment, as if he had to fumble for the memory. "She saw me here the other day, and she followed me to the motel where I was staying. Said she knew about your daughter. Vampire. Don't know why I believed her so quickly."

"But you did," Roger said. "And she encouraged you to abduct Gillian?"

"Encouraged, hell! She talked me into it. Told me exactly what to do, gave me a crash course in Gillian's strengths and weaknesses." Greer shook his head. "I can't believe I went along with her just like that. She even told me to have my gun handy."

"Did she say why?" Roger struggled to keep his rising anger reined. He was becoming more and more convinced that this man wasn't its legitimate target.

"Dangerous monster. She said Gillian was dangerous." Greer brushed a limp strand of hair off his forehead. "I think she was lying. The kid sure didn't look or act like a ravening wild beast. Oh, Christ, I didn't mean to hurt her! I never meant for all this to get so out of hand!"

Claude gazed steadily at him until he calmed down. "Do you remember what happened last night?"

"Camille is one herself. She must be." Behind the beard, the professor's mouth twisted with revulsion. "I think she bit me. Why else would I feel so weak? I could hardly move when I woke up this morning. And she definitely made me taste her blood. I remember that."

"How did it feel?" Britt asked.

Startled, Greer looked at her as if he'd forgotten she was there. "Interesting." He flushed. "Quite a turn-on, to tell the truth. Then we got out of the car—this was at a cabin where I was holding the girl. Camille knocked me out. Next thing I knew, I was waking up on the couch this morning. She must have taken the kid. I don't know why." His voice rasped even more now. He drank the rest of his coffee and held out the cup for a refill.

"Why did you come to me?" Roger said.

"To make up for what I did." The statement rang false. Greer shifted his eyes from Roger's. "Well, not only that. I want that woman, Camille or whatever her real name is, to get what's coming to her. And

I don't claim to deserve your gratitude or anything, but I'd still like to have that interview from you."

"I'll try to forget you said that." Roger kept his voice icy to counteract the impulse to throttle the man.

"Oh, hell, I do feel terrible about how I treated the kid, and that's the truth." He added in a less defensive tone, "And to top it off, Camille must have stolen the pictures I took of Gillian."

"Don't worry about them," Roger said, reinforcing the command with a small mental shove. He'd shredded and burned the photos an hour ago after displaying them to Britt's avid examination. "There is a possible way for you to help us find Gillian. We're going to hypnotize you."

Greer turned paler than he already was.

Britt silently remarked, [Looks like you may get some resistance.]

[No wonder,] Roger answered, [after he's been subjected to that from you, Camille, and Claude, all in one night. On the other hand, he should be softened up so thoroughly that he shouldn't be hard to mesmerize.]

"Does it have to be that way?" said Greer.

"You do want to help, don't you?" Claude asked in a dangerously quiet voice. When the professor nodded, he said, "Through your mind, we may be able to get a fix on Camille's location. Will you cooperate, or must I force you?"

"I'll try to cooperate. But how—"

Claude cut him off. "The less you know the safer you will be. I don't even intend to let you remember what you tell us." Getting up from the love seat opposite the one occupied by Greer and Britt, Claude pulled up a chair to a spot where he could gaze into Greer's face at close range. Greer flinched. Though Roger couldn't see well from his position on the love seat across the room, he suspected the angle of the firelight from Greer's vantage point brought out the gleam of red in Claude's eyes.

Claude brushed his fingertips across the professor's forehead. "Relax. You're safe here under our protection, and we mean you no harm." He took the coffee cup from Greer's hands, which immediately went limp. With admiration, and a touch of envy, Roger watched Claude send the subject into a trance with a few light strokes along temples and shoulder blades, augmented by a couple of minutes of meaningless patter in an almost inaudible voice. Greer's heartbeat slowed, and the agitated fluctuation of his aura stilled. "Now you will answer our questions in a calm and unworried manner," said Claude, "and when I awaken you, you'll remember nothing of what we've said to each other." He moved his chair aside to give Roger an unobstructed view of the hypnotized man. "He's all yours."

Britt leaned forward for a better look. Skirting the coffee table, Roger walked over to stand in front of Greer. "You have the ability to reach out to Camille and link with her mind. I'm going to use that ability to locate her, through you."

Claude softly interrupted, "I suggest you use a hit-and-run technique. We want to avoid catching her attention."

Roger nodded. He said to Greer, "First, I'd like you to tell me whether she is watching you at this moment. Think of her—not as you last saw her, but as she looked the instant before she kissed you. Hold that image in your mind. Now, reach out to Camille. Do you have contact?"

Greer nodded, heavy-lidded. "I see her."

"Delicately, please—watch her from outside only. Where is she?"

In a distant monotone Greer said, "On the freeway."

Roger silently cursed. To discover Camille's present lair, if she had one, they had to catch her when she wasn't on the move. "Does she feel your presence?"

The professor's brow furrowed. "No."

"Disengage from her. Come back." Greer nodded slowly. Roger continued, "What freeway? Did you see?"

"Fifty west."

Roger mulled over the information. Suppose Camille was heading out of the area altogether? She could drive beyond Greer's range in an hour or two. "Rest and renew your strength," he ordered. "You'll be aware of nothing until I speak to you again." Greer closed his eyes and slumped back on the couch.

Britt said, "Van Helsing made it sound a lot easier, didn't he?"

"All I can do," Roger said, "is continue checking periodically until she arrives at her destination, if that happens before she gets out of reach."

"I agree," said Claude. "Which, with a new, untested bond, won't be long."

"How encouraging," said Britt. She fingered Greer's wrist to count his pulse without inducing any reaction from him.

After a five-minute wait Roger sent Greer into Camille's mind again. "Is she still driving?"

"Yes. The highway looks so light—like dusk, not the middle of the night."

"Still the freeway?"

"Yes."

"Does she feel you in her mind?"

"No."

Roger decided to risk further probing. "Is she alone in the car?"

"No. A girl."

"Look closely. Is it Gillian?"

"Yes." Greer's head shifted on the cushion. "We're slowing down. The car's on a curve."

"Is it an off-ramp?"

"Yes."

"Where? Read the sign." Roger strove to keep his voice even and avoid agitating the hypnotic subject.

"Bowie," said Greer.

"Very good. Get out, come back, and rest again."

"That's good, she isn't planning to drive forever," Claude said. "Logical. If she wants to strike at you, clearing out of your territory isn't the way to do it."

Britt asked Roger, [What is your territory, anyway? How many square miles are you allotted?]

He dryly answered, [I don't know, I've never gotten around to staking a claim.] A few minutes later he said to Greer, "Go back to Camille. Are you with her?"

"Uh-huh."

"Good. What is the car doing now?"

"Turning onto a divided roadway. Lights. Used car dealers. Motels. Slowing at a motel."

"Read me the name."

"Pine Tree Lodge. Got a Quality Court seal." Greer exhaled a long, shaky breath. "She's pulling into a parking space. Her fingers feel cramped from holding the wheel. She turns off the engine and opens the door. Cold air feels good. The kid opens her door. Asks where they're going for dinner. Camille's hungry—no, more like thirsty—"

An urgent whisper from Claude: "Pull him out, now!"

Greer muttered, "I should be with her—but I don't want her to—"

Roger gripped the man's shoulders and ordered him to open his eyes. "Look at me! She has no power over you. Get away from her. Come back to this place and time."

"Yes." Greer's eyes rolled. Roger sensed a slackening of the pressure that had built over the past minute or so. The link had been inactivated once more, though it remained present, ready to be awakened.

"That was becoming entirely too intimate," said Claude. "Much more and she would certainly have noticed his attention."

"Now we know where she is," Britt said.

"Yes, we can get rid of him, and not a minute too soon for me," Roger said. He turned Greer over to Claude, who ordered him to forget what had transpired and roused him from the trance.

At the door Roger tried one more command. "You must go back to your normal activities and forget your interest in me and Gillian. Meddling with us is dangerous. It's brought you nothing but trouble. You don't want to pursue it any further."

"Right," said Greer. Still dazed, occasionally shaking his head like a swimmer with water in the ears, he staggered across the parking lot to his van.

"What do you think?" Britt said when they'd regrouped in the living room. "Will that stick?"

"Unless Camille interferes with him again, we can hope so," Roger said. "I wish I dared try to wipe his memory of us altogether, but—"

"Best not to," said Claude. "One of the elders could pull it off, maybe. You or I would probably end up with a psychotic on our hands."

"I wouldn't be surprised if he came around again," Britt said, "eventually, when his fear of you wears off. I understand what drives him. You think I wouldn't slap you between the covers of a book at supersonic speed, if I didn't have personal motives for keeping your secret?"

Roger returned her affectionate smile. "I'm incredibly fortunate that it was you who unmasked me, not someone less understanding."

"In my profession, I live on the edge of that possibility night after night," said Claude, "so I have a personal stake in your keeping him in line. I assume you'll head for that motel in Bowie at once? Shall I come along?"

"I'd be grateful," Roger said. Before Britt could speak, he told her, "You stay here." He cut short her protest with, "As much as you may dislike the fact, you'd be a liability. If you stay behind, you're our backup in case of disaster."

"Oh, all right, I won't argue." She gave him her word to stay put, monitoring their progress telepathically. Despite Claude's presence, Roger kissed her goodbye with unaccustomed thoroughness before they left.

ONCE INSIDE THEIR new motel room with Gillian, Camille didn't feel the security she had hoped for. They'd transferred here from last night's no-frills roadside lodging after the predawn meal and settled in for a full day's rest. In the evening, Camille had taken the child with her to Annapolis to pick up the luggage she'd left at the Holiday Inn there. She didn't yet trust Gillian alone. Suppose in Camille's absence, the girl's loyalty wavered back in Roger's direction?

Gillian did venture to ask whether she should call Roger to let him know she was safe. Camille had squelched that idea at once. "What makes you think he cares? And you do want to stay with me, don't you? Roger would make that difficult. He probably has distorted ideas about my character."

To Camille's relief Gillian accepted the argument without much resistance. Unpacking her suitcases at the new motel while Gillian bathed, Camille pondered what to do with the child. Since her original belief that Gillian lived with Roger as his daughter had been disproved, Camille couldn't be sure that destroying or corrupting the girl would hurt Roger as badly as she wanted to hurt him. She still planned to convert Gillian into her adoring disciple, though. There must be some way she could use a converted Gillian against her enemy. Meanwhile she rather enjoyed watching the girl exercise her new abilities. After all, Camille would probably never have a child of her own to train.

On the drive to and from Annapolis, Camille had drawn Gillian, with a few ostensibly casual questions, into discussing her father. Camille now knew that Roger possessed a human pet he treated with an absurd degree of fondness. Maybe Gillian, once trained, could be used to strike at Roger through that female. What deliciously apt justice if Roger's lover became his daughter's first human victim!

Although Camille hadn't firmed her plans yet, these speculations gave her great pleasure. Her immediate worry was not how to use Gillian, but what to do about the warning prickle she'd felt inside her head at the moment she drove into the motel parking lot. She felt a nagging desire to check on Adam Greer.

The thought was distasteful to her. She didn't enjoy the prospect of rooting around in an ephemeral's mind, what there was of it. When she'd forced Greer to taste her blood, she'd viewed the bond as purely an emergency precaution. If he was daring to poke into her head, though, she would have to discipline him.

In the bathroom, the water stopped running, and gentle splashing noises drifted through the closed door. "Don't bother me for a few minutes," Camille called to Gillian. "I need to concentrate."

Sitting cross-legged in the middle of one of the double beds, Camille closed her eyes and cleared her mind. Though she'd never bonded with anyone but her advisor, whose thoughts she had not touched in decades, she remembered how to make contact. Some things the nervous system never forgot. She invoked a memory of Greer, the scent of his skin, the bristle of his beard against her cheek, the taste of his blood. With no more effort than slipping on a coat, she glided into his mind.

Through his eyes she saw a nearly deserted highway unrolling before him. His head ached, his throat was sore, and a drained weariness dragged at his limbs.

[Adam!] she silently called.

He jumped, jerking the steering wheel sideways.

[Don't do that! Get control of yourself.] Under the pressure of her will he steered the car off the shoulder and settled back to a steady speed. [That's better. Tell me, Adam, where are you going?]

[I'm not hearing you. You aren't there. I'm losing my mind.] Her silent insistence weighed upon him until his resistance caved in. [I'm going back to College Park for the rest of the convention. What do you want?]

[What have you been doing? Where did you go this evening?]

[To Annapolis to see Dr. Darvell.]

Camille hastily withdrew from his mind, afraid her rage would wreck her precarious control over her victim. So Roger had been at him! So the half-breed—hell devour him—knew Greer was linked to her! He must know—that must have been the meaning of the fleeting mind-touch she'd felt in the parking lot. So Adam Greer was no longer an asset but a liability.

No ephemeral could be allowed to remain a chink in her armor. Calming herself, she reached for Greer again. [Adam, I'm sorry I had to hurt you. But I did you no real harm, did I? And you enjoyed what we shared, didn't you?] She planted in his mind an image of their embrace. She felt his lust rising, his self-contempt helpless against the lurid memory.

[You don't want to go back to the convention,] she told him. [You want to come to me.]

A tortured *No* rasped from his hoarse throat, yet his inward self screamed *Yes*.

[Keep driving westward. I'll find a place to meet, and I'll guide you to it.] Satisfied of his submission, she withdrew from his brain, all except a tendril of contact to monitor his progress.

Uncurling herself, she plucked her discarded shoes off the carpet. "Hurry up and get dressed," she called to Gillian. "We have to move."

Water gurgled down the bathtub drain. "Pardon? We just got here."

Camille began tossing clothes back into her suitcase. "No matter, we have to be elsewhere. Someone we don't want to see knows where we are."

Used to following orders, Gillian made little protest. A few minutes later, they were packed and driving away. They no longer had Greer's rented compact, which they'd abandoned in a convenience store lot before switching motels. Camille had lurked in wait for a solitary customer to emerge, car keys in hand, and had hypnotized him into unconsciousness before taking his keys and cash. She trusted that the change of vehicle would make her almost impossible to trace by mundane means.

Fifteen minutes east on Route 50, Camille checked into another mid-priced motel, grumbling to herself at the annoying expense of three rooms in a twenty-four hour period. She would have to get possession of more cash, since credit cards would leave a trail. Noting a restaurant across the street whose cocktail lounge had a separate entrance, she reactivated the bond with Greer.

[Adam, I know you betrayed me to Roger Darvell.] His start of alarm confirmed her hunch. [I've forgiven you for that. I know you're only human and can't resist his power. You want to be with me again, and I'm ready. Come to me here, now.] She gave him directions to the restaurant and ordered him to meet her in the bar.

"Gillian, I have to go out," she said, stripping off her slacks to change into a dress. "You're to stay in the room, understand?"

Gillian, subdued by Camille's atypical grimness, said, "Yes, of course. Where—"

"I'll talk to you when I get back." She dressed quickly and hurried out, slamming the door behind her. She could hardly contain her anger at the man. Her prey, turning against her, a tool for her enemy! She knew she had to channel the rage into a simulation of passion, or she could frighten him away before he swallowed her bait.

In the lounge, Camille ordered a frozen strawberry daiquiri, both to calm herself and to give herself an excuse to linger until Greer showed. He couldn't be left on the loose for Roger to use in tracking her. Roger would betray her to Volnar, and the Prime Elder would condemn her to captivity again.

Her imprisonment, the brief parts not obliterated by suspended animation, was mercifully vague in her memory. But she recalled enough—the unprecedented terror of absolute darkness in a casket too tight to admit the least ray of illumination, the agony of thirst and suffocation before she fell into coma, the scars on her hands from pounding and scratching at the wooden lid, the bitter taste of her own blood, the blinding shards of light that lacerated her eyes each time she was half-awakened for testing by one of the elders.

This last time, finally, after fourteen years, she'd convinced them of her surrender. Her rehabilitation! Well, maybe they *had* broken her, but only temporarily. A few feedings had restored her spirit and enlivened the memories of her outrage. Once revived, she'd managed to maintain the submissive pretense long enough to get free of the watch set over her.

*And I'll stay free. Before I'd go back to that, I'd let them kill me!*

Chapter Eleven

EVERY TIME FOOTSTEPS sounded in the corridor outside the room, Gillian's nerves twitched. Why had Camille left so abruptly? Why the secretive manner? The woman allowed no crack in her mental barrier for emotion to seep out. True, Volnar kept himself shielded, too, but that behavior was expected of an elder. Camille wasn't at all like him otherwise.

As soon as Camille had left, Gillian had stripped off her filthy clothes and taken another bath. Afterward she sat naked on the bed watching television, which soon lost interest for her. She flipped between a stand-up comedy show whose jokes made no sense to her and a *Masterpiece Theater* rerun of "I, Claudius."

When Camille's key turned in the door, a glance at the clock radio told Gillian that she hadn't been left alone as long as her subjective time sense perceived. Camille stepped inside, bolted the door, and transfixed Gillian with eyes as cold as a reptile's.

"What happened?" Gillian whispered. She used the remote to flick off the TV.

Blinking, Camille looked at Gillian as if noticing her for the first time. "Adam Greer threatened us. I got rid of him."

"How?"

"You don't need to know."

Though Camille's icy stillness troubled her, she persisted. "I want to know. I have to learn how to handle—threats."

"Very well." Sitting against the headboard of the other bed, Camille continued in her normal voice, "I summoned him to me and commanded him to destroy himself. He betrayed me. It would have been too dangerous to let him live."

"But the rules—"

"Rules!" Camille scornfully bared her teeth. "I didn't break the spirit of their rules. I haven't lost all regard for my own safety. The man died in a way that won't be linked to us."

"Are you certain he's dead?"

"Of course. I stayed inside his mind until the last possible moment. I withdrew, naturally, an instant before the impact." She briefly closed her eyes as if to shut out some intolerable image. "Never let yourself experience their death. Remember that."

Gillian nodded. At the thought of facing something that frightened this bold woman, the hair prickled at the nape of Gillian's neck.

"After I was certain it must be over, I reached for his mind again. Nothing. So he's most definitely dead. Dismiss him from your thoughts."

"Yes, ma'am," said Gillian. She strove to shield her emotions, for she didn't want Camille to suspect how much this killing disturbed her. Gillian was developing a tentative appreciation for Volnar, who always recommended solutions short of death. If bonding was as cataclysmic an experience as Claude and Roger made it appear, how could Camille bring herself to destroy a bond-mate? Even one she regarded only as a tool?

With an ironic smile Camille said, "Watch your language. I don't expect you to treat me like an elder." She scooped Gillian's dirty clothes off the floor. "I saw laundry equipment down the hall. After I've washed and dried these, we'll go out to obtain a more varied wardrobe for you."

"But clothing stores aren't open this late."

Camille shook her head in mock despair. "You do have a lot to learn."

An hour later, luxuriating in clean clothes, Gillian watched Camille maneuver along the four-lane highway, busy despite the late hour. "Saturday night," Camille remarked. "Good time to catch a victim at a nightclub or a movie theater. But that's not what we're after just now." She seemed to have shed the grim mood induced by the confrontation with Greer. She sang an interminable song called "This Land Is Your Land" and taught Gillian a few verses.

After a while she turned at a stoplight into a strip shopping center. Driving behind the stores, Camille waited several minutes in the back lot with motor and lights off before getting out of the car. "The coast looks clear. Prepare boarding party." She grinned as if excited by the risk. Gillian followed her to the rear door of a boutique called Beyond 2000. "Since they probably have a silent alarm, we must act quickly. I assume you know your sizes?" Gillian nodded. "Then once you're inside, grab an armful and run."

At the moment Camille's hand gripped the massive metal latch, headlights shined around the corner of the last building in the row. "Vanish!" Camille said in Gillian's ear.

Calming her heartbeat and drawing upon the memory of her

practice with Claude, Gillian veiled herself. She felt Camille's hand on her shoulder but saw nothing except a pale blur of an aura outlining the space where the woman should be. Around the building crept a police car. It rolled to a stop next to the car they'd arrived in. The officer opened his window and aimed a flashlight at Camille's stolen vehicle. When no movement responded to the light, he switched it off and drove away.

Camille oozed back into solidity. "Routine check. You can be visible now. After I've opened the door for you, I'll fade again and wait for you by the car." Both of her hands closed around the latch. With no appearance of strain, she twisted it. The lock popped open. "Now hurry," she whispered.

Gillian darted inside. From the corner of her eye, she glimpsed Camille's image thinning to a wisp of light. After emerging from the stockroom to which the back door led, Gillian surveyed the store display in the darkness that was a pastel landscape to her eyes. She dashed for the underwear counter and snatched up a package of briefs and two pairs of socks in her size, then ran across the room to a rack marked *14 Long*. In the distance a siren wailed. Unable to tell whether the noise signaled a response to the alarm Camille had predicted, Gillian rushed anyway. After grabbing three pairs of jeans and four shirts, hangers and all, she raced out the door, slamming it behind her.

The car was already running—with, to a superficial glance, no one at the wheel—and the passenger door opened just as Gillian reached it. The ululation of the siren pierced her ears. She tossed her booty into the back seat, dived for the floor, and gathered her psychic veil around her quaking body.

Her vision misted from the effort of making herself look insubstantial, she vaguely saw Camille's form waver into focus. The car moved—not at top speed, as Gillian expected. Instead, Camille drove no more than a block and pulled in behind a closed, deserted gas station.

"The last thing we want to look like is a pair of criminals fleeing the scene of a burglary," said Camille before smoothly vanishing again.

Sometime in the past minute or so, the siren had cut off. "They'll be searching the store and the parking lot now. Wish I could see their faces when they examine that lock," said Camille in a murmur like a breeze rustling distant pine boughs. "Calm yourself, concentrate, and lend me your strength."

Gillian forced her taut muscles to loosen and her pounding heart to slow almost to immobility. She extended tendrils of psychic energy to Camille. For a while, she felt as if she floated in one of those sensory deprivation tanks she'd read about. She didn't know how long it was before Camille said, "Wake up. It's safe to leave now. They drove past and didn't notice us."

Unfolding from her crouch on the floorboards, Gillian massaged the kinks out of her legs. "Didn't even notice the car? How could that be? Surely you can't make the car invisible, too?"

"No." Camille chuckled. "However, I can divert their attention from it. I projected a suggestion that nothing of importance was in this spot, that they ought to look in the other direction and feel absolutely no interest in this car. Unless they were questioned directly on the point, they'd hardly even be aware they saw a vehicle."

Gillian fell silent with admiration for a few blocks. But she couldn't help thinking this kind of escapade could become hazardous. "Wouldn't it be simpler and safer to use money?"

"True. But I'm running low on cash, and places like that don't sell their merchandise cheap. Tomorrow night, we'll replenish our wallets."

"How?"

Camille flashed her a smile as they drove at scrupulously legal speed toward the motel. "Our hypnotic power is good for more than ensuring an easy meal. I know you've already engaged in a little casual robbery yourself." Gillian had told Camille the high points of her adventures while fleeing from Volnar.

"Yes, but to make a habit of it—that goes against what I've been taught." While she didn't want to annoy Camille with petty arguments, she felt impelled to air her misgivings. "Is it wise to use ephemerals that way constantly?"

"What else are they good for? They're put on earth for our convenience—tools, toys, and food." Camille made the pronouncement with casual assurance, as an unquestionable fact.

"Like Professor Greer? When he wasn't a useful tool anymore—" She hesitated, not wanting to goad Camille into the forbidding mood she'd displayed earlier.

"I disposed of him, yes." Camille showed no anger now.

"But are they all good for nothing else? Aren't there exceptions?"

Camille gave her a sidelong look. "Such as?"

"Roger's bond-mate and his brother Claude's wife. Roger and Claude seemed to treat them as friends—equals."

Camille's lips twitched in a snarl of disdain. "No superior being can accept an inferior as equal. Roger and Claude may want their pets to *believe* in that phantom equality. They're simply using those women for their own gratification, though. It has to be that way. Otherwise, if you seriously tried such an impossible relationship, you would be yielding yourself into an inferior's power. Never forget that."

Gillian nodded, raising her mental shield to hide the confusion she no longer wished to lay bare to her strange new mentor. *Maybe she's right. But when I saw Britt and Eloise, it didn't look that way at all.*

ON THIS EXCURSION, Roger drove his roomy Citroen. They had no special reason to avoid bystanders' notice this time. What mattered was separating Gillian from Camille long enough to let the girl make an unfettered choice.

Riding with his window open, enjoying the wind that would have left a human passenger numb with cold, Claude started to light a cigarette. Roger's glare changed his mind. "So if she wants to stay with Camille, you won't force her to come with us?"

"What good would that do?" Roger said. "You wouldn't forcibly override Eloise's will. I certainly can't see doing it to one of our own kind."

"No, I wouldn't." Claude's fingers clenched and unclenched on his knees, a movement he seemed unaware of. "Yet it's a tempting shortcut—if I could just get deep into Eloise's mind for a minute or two, she'd realize my sincerity. But it's her doubt of my feelings that makes her keep the gates barred."

"You can't be certain a telepathic merging would satisfy her doubts, anyway. In her present state of mind, she might fear that even the communion was a lie."

Claude said with a despairing headshake, "Granted, I've played roles for her benefit. But it was never a lie—all I've tried to become for her, I've done because her happiness is the most important thing in my life."

"You don't have to convince me," said Roger. "I know." He thought of the potential routes to happiness Britt had denied herself for him. Could any male of their race be everything a human woman needed? Britt insisted he was all she wanted, yet how could she know what she had missed? Roger cut off that line of thought. *Claude's mood must be infecting me.* "And yet touching Greer again made you hungry," he observed. "Good thing Eloise wasn't there to notice."

"Damn straight it did." Claude's tongue skimmed his bared teeth. "I've tasted him once—unsatisfying as it was. The flavor of his emotions naturally stirred my appetite. Purely physical and involuntary. Eloise would understand."

*Normally she would*, Roger thought. He didn't want to aggravate Claude's depression by discussion Eloise's abnormal state of mind any further.

Claude, however, wasn't ready to let the subject drop. "I wonder if Eloise knows—or Britt, for that matter—can any of our human lovers really fathom what we need them for? Through her, I experience a vast range of human sensations and emotions I would never taste without her. Maybe that doesn't apply so much to you. You're half human."

"I do know what you mean," Roger said. Without Britt's flesh and senses to mediate for him, most foods would remain no more than insipid or nauseating lumps of matter he couldn't digest, the sun and salt air on a beach at high noon only a blinding torture.

"And my pleasure in that experience isn't merely a mask I wear to please her. I *need* it." Claude's fingernails scored parallel gashes in the leather of his armrest. Startled out of his passionate abstraction, he ruefully examined the damage. "Oh, damn, I'm sorry. I'll pay for the repair."

Roger waved away the apology. Better a few rips that could be fixed than cigarette smoke, which would've clung to the upholstery for months.

After a silence of several miles, Claude said, "I've been waiting for a chance to mention this—if you comprehend something of how I feel, if you can see that even that idiot professor—attracts me, you must realize what a temptation Britt could become." Roger involuntarily tensed. "Yes, you see what I mean," said his brother. "She'd appeal to me anyway, because she's not only been fed from innumerable times, she's undergone it willingly. On top of all that, she nourished me when I was desperate. Powerful combination, that. I could easily transfer my fixation to her."

Roger struggled to control his breathing. His fingers, clamped on the wheel, ached. "Why are you belaboring the obvious? I'm not worried. You never trespass."

"Not worried, eh? Then why are you an inch away from strangling me? I'm asking you to warn Britt—make her keep her distance. If that generosity of hers overwhelmed her better judgment, and she caught me alone—well, I'm not sure I could resist."

Roger reminded himself that Claude was *not* threatening to seduce Britt. On the contrary, Claude's insistence on spelling out the danger proved his honorable intentions. "All right, I'll caution her." Claude's perception of Britt's extravagant generosity was all too accurate. "Now, haven't we discussed this enough?" He turned on the cassette of Handel's "Messiah" to fill the silence. Then he remembered Claude's religious phobia. "You don't mind, I hope?"

"Like you and cigarettes?" Claude forced a smile. "No, it's all right. Hearing the oratorio performed in a church by a full choir would bring me to my knees in agony, but fortunately, I can enjoy the recording with no trouble."

To Roger's relief, the music displaced further conversation until they arrived at the motel in Bowie, Maryland, where Greer had telepathically seen Camille and Gillian. To begin with, Roger made a sketchy survey of the parking lot. While he didn't come across a car he could definitely identify as the one Camille had driven, he didn't let that negative fact discourage him. Since Greer had seen the vehicle only from inside, in brief glimpses, Roger couldn't have made a positive identification anyway. He knew it was a light-colored hatchback, and that was about all. He parked the Citroen in a remote corner of the lot.

This area had been efficiently cleared, leaving no ice patches to hinder them. Claude led the way in a tightly controlled stride like a compressed steam valve ready to blow. Roger decided to handle any necessary questioning himself.

A fragrance of pine and gingerbread met them in the lobby. The Christmas tree near the registration desk was decorated with real cookies. Approaching the counter, Roger began to weave his spell even before he spoke.

The clerk, a trim woman of about thirty with a spray-lacquered cap of brown hair, faced him with a heavy-lidded gaze. Waiting until a couple across the lobby had entered the elevator, he held the woman's eyes while his fingers grazed the back of her hand, lying slack on the counter. "Good evening, Marian," he said, reading her name tag. "I want you to tell me about a guest who registered here tonight or possibly last night or this morning."

The clerk nodded. Otherwise she remained still. The combination of her sex, relaxed mood, and ignorance about his nature made her completely receptive.

"A tall, pale, dark-haired woman who may call herself Camille. She has a twelve-year-old girl with her."

Marian nodded again. "I've seen them." Her breath came softly through parted lips. Though Claude stood motionless, his face composed, beside Roger, Roger heard his heartbeat accelerate.

"Tell me their room number," Roger said.

"They aren't here. They checked out an hour ago."

Careful to remain outwardly calm, Roger said, "Are you sure?"

"I was on duty. I saw her pay and leave."

"How did she pay?" Claude asked.

The clerk turned her head sluggishly toward him. "Cash." For a second she blinked, stirring from the trance, but Claude captured her attention. "Computer said she paid for one day this morning when she checked in, so we charged her for tonight when she checked out. Funny."

"Describe her car," said Claude.

"I didn't really look at it."

"You must have glanced out the front door at some time during the transaction. The doors are plate glass. Did you see this woman get out of or into a car in the breezeway?" He reinforced the mental pressure by stroking her forearm.

Though uneasy about letting Claude take over the interrogation, Roger didn't interfere. Claude seemed to be getting results.

"Yes. The girl stayed in the car, and the woman came in to pay for the room. It was a hatchback."

"What color?"

"Hard to tell in that light—medium blue, I guess."

"Now place yourself back in that moment. Did you watch the vehicle drive away?"

"Yes," the clerk said in a dreamy voice. Her pulse quickened in response to Claude's touch. "We weren't busy, and I thought it was strange, them leaving at this time of night."

"Look at the rear bumper of the car. Do you see the license plate?"

Marian nodded.

"Read me the number." Marian recited it. "Excellent. We're going now. Forget what you've told us. We asked about a friend, and she wasn't here. Now you can get back to work."

As Claude and Roger walked out, the clerk was drifting over to the computer keyboard like a swimmer treading water.

Roger felt Claude's agitation like lava simmering under a thin crust. He'd been looking forward eagerly to a clash with Camille, Roger suspected, and sucking energy from the motel clerk to fortify himself. In the car, Roger waited for Claude to cool down before speaking. "We've confirmed that Gillian was with her."

"And willingly," said Claude as they reentered the traffic stream. "Otherwise she wouldn't have been left alone in the car. Missed them by an hour, damn it to hell!"

Though equally frustrated, Roger pointed out, "Clearly we never had a chance. Camille fled immediately after we talked to Greer. She must have sensed his probing of her mind."

"Logical deduction. *Et maintenant?*"

"We do have another vehicle description—thank you for thinking of that, by the way. I'll pass it on to Captain Hayes, though there's a limit to the extent of payback for past favors we can claim."

"You may have to invent a story for him," Claude said. "Runaway patient or something of the sort."

Roger began to speculate whether he shouldn't, after all, take the risk of telling the county detective that his illegitimate daughter was missing. If he rendered a convincing imitation of an embarrassed professional desperate for confidential help—Could be worth a try.

After they reached Annapolis and Claude returned to his convention, Roger discussed the fresh information with Britt. "Lord, that's frustrating!" she said. "If Gillian's hopping all over the county with Camille, it couldn't be against her will. If she wanted to get away, wouldn't she have tried to reach you by now?"

That discouraging hypothesis harmonized with Roger's own fears. "Even so, I have to find her."

Britt, cuddling into the circle of his left arm as they sat together by the fire, murmured agreement. "Do you really think it's safe to level with Hayes? Or pretend to, rather?"

"A selected piece of the truth should convince him I had sound reasons to be evasive in the past." Disengaging from Britt, too preoccupied to respond to her pang of disappointment, he paced across the living room and back. "It's not midnight yet. I suppose I could call the captain at home without destroying whatever rapport we have left."

"Since you won't settle down until you've done it," she said crisply, "you'd better go ahead."

He retired to his office to make the call. The sleepy grumble in which Captain Hayes answered the phone wasn't encouraging. When Roger identified himself, Hayes said, "Yeah, what now?"

"I have another vehicle I'd like you to check on."

"Can it wait till Monday?"

"No, I don't think so." Roger described the hatchback Camille had been seen driving.

"Do I have to remind you, Doctor," said Hayes in a long-suffering tone, "the Anne Arundel County Police Department is not a private detective agency? Especially not for free. I don't go an inch farther with this until I hear an explanation. And make it good."

Roger commenced his embarrassed pillar of the community act. "I assure you, I have vital reasons not to discuss my—what's behind these inquiries."

"Your reasons don't mean diddly-squat if you're not prepared to explain them. And don't give me that *confidential* bull again. If you've got a patient who's a danger to the public, or you two are covering up a crime—"

"Damn it, Captain, that's not it!" Roger allowed a tension-laden pause before continuing. "This matter is strictly personal."

"Yeah?" The officer's voice carried no sympathy.

"My daughter, who is visiting from out of state, has disappeared." Roger used a hesitant tone that made it clear how much he detested volunteering that fact.

"Daughter? I didn't know you'd ever been married."

"I haven't." Roger growled the words, as if angered by Hayes' obtuseness.

"Oh." A hint of interest crept into the officer's voice.

"Dr. Loren knows, and that's all. Surely you can understand that I don't want the matter publicized. I value my privacy."

"For Christ's sake, if you think the girl's been kidnapped, are you going to let that stop you—"

Roger cut off the indignant protest. "No, I don't think she was abducted. That is why I haven't reported it officially. She ran away of her own free will."

"With that Adam Greer? Why haven't you reported her as a runaway? Or brought charges against him for contributing to the delinquency of a minor?"

"That's irrelevant, because to the best of my knowledge, she's no longer with him. Listen, Hayes, I came to you because we've worked together many times. I hoped you would understand." Hesitancy, with an underplayed note of paternal anguish. "The girl and I aren't—close. I can't make an official report and send the authorities after her. One glimpse of a police uniform would send her running in the opposite direction. And she'd never trust me thereafter."

Hayes heaved a sigh. "So what do you want from me?"

"Just the information Dr. Loren and I are asking for. If Gillian is found, I want to confront her in my own way."

"The kid's name is Gillian? Hang on, let me get a notepad." So he hadn't even bothered to write down the data on the car! Roger heard rummaging sounds on the other end, and murmured words of reassurance, apparently from Hayes to his wife. "Okay, give me her age and other statistics."

Roger described Gillian. "I think she's now traveling with a woman, first name Camille—unless she's adopted an alias—tall, pale, dark-haired."

"Alias? You know of any crime this woman's committed?"

"Not to my knowledge."

"Say, what does this have to do with that earlier question about peculiar deaths in the Maryland-D.C. area?"

Roger sidestepped the question. "I'd appreciate it if you would follow that up, too."

"Hell, I should know better than waste time trying to get a straight answer out of you. Tell me the license plate of that blue hatchback again."

After Roger had given all the details he felt safe in revealing, Hayes said, "Damned if I can figure out how you know so much but don't know where your daughter is. I'll get right on it. Unofficially."

Roger gave him an effusive and completely sincere speech of thanks. He only hoped Hayes would keep the inquiry unofficial, treating seriously the plea to refrain from sending uniforms in pursuit of Camille and Gillian.

Finding Britt half-asleep in his bed, he sought distraction by giving her a massage for the nagging ache in her legs. "I should know better than to run the perimeter of the Academy after skipping so many days," she said.

"Don't tell me you've been jogging in this weather."

"Why not? For goodness' sake, the sidewalks are clear. Especially on Navy property." Lying on her stomach, she raised her head to give him a drowsy smile over her shoulder. "You give a fabulous aerobic workout when your heart's in it, but it can't substitute for a five-mile run."

The teasing remark augmented the delicious frustration of stroking her when he'd promised himself to abstain from anything more intimate. He pointedly changed the subject. "You listened to my conversation with Hayes?"

"Uh-huh. Wonderful. You're becoming as good an actor as Claude."

"Not entirely an act. I *am* worried about Gillian, and I *was* reluctant to tell him about her."

"Do you think she'll come back to you?" Encroaching sleep slurred Britt's voice.

"Questionable. She hardly knows me, and God knows what ideas Camille has been feeding her."

Britt turned on her back, her eyes drooping shut. "That really upsets you."

"Yes, now that you mention it." Roger was bewildered by his own reaction. "Yes, if she rejected me, I would be hurt. Strange."

"Another of the hazards of being human," said Britt. "Try not to worry. Physically, she's bound to be okay. If Camille actually is trying to corrupt the kid, she'll pamper her, not abuse her."

"I'm trying to keep that in mind." He stroked Britt's hair back from her forehead. "Go to sleep, beloved."

He left her to rest undisturbed, while he faced the yawning void of a night of inactivity.

Hayes' return call came at five a.m., just as Roger was considering trying to snatch a bit of sleep before church.

"You have some information for me?" Roger said, injecting the proper note of strained urgency into his voice.

"Trivia first," said the detective. "That hatchback you mentioned? It was reported stolen yesterday. The owner, thirty-seven-year old office worker on a trip to—" Roger heard pages rustling. "Well, you don't care about all that. Guy stops at a Seven-Eleven to pick up coffee and doughnuts. This was approximately six thirty a.m. yesterday, Saturday. He exits the store and passes out—apparently. He can't remember a thing until he woke up—get this—in the back seat of a rental car he'd never seen before."

Since Hayes appeared to be trying for a dramatic pause, Roger interjected an impatient, "Well?"

"The precinct contacted the rental company and determined that the car was signed out to your friend Greer. Tried to track him down to ask why he hadn't reported the vehicle missing, didn't have any luck. Now here's the punch line." Another pause. "About an hour ago, Greer's van was found totaled at the bottom of a ravine under a Route 50 overpass."

"Good God Almighty."

"Waiting on the autopsy, of course, but we strongly suspect DUI."

"I see." Roger didn't have any thoughts on the subject that would be safe to share with Hayes.

"Are you sitting down? There's more." Further rustling of pages.

"You and Dr. Loren asked about unexplained deaths, especially of—how did you put it?—people who wouldn't be missed. The D.C. police got a report of a body, black female, age thirteen, no obvious marks of violence. Discovered around noon yesterday, next to a Dumpster in an alley. Girl lived in one of those downtown welfare hotels with her aunt, who'd last seen her when they had breakfast at a soup kitchen a couple of blocks from the death site. The aunt assumed the girl had run off with her new friend, so the aunt just went on to work, waitressing on the early shift at a diner."

"What drew your attention to this death? You said no obvious marks of violence." Roger wondered about less than obvious marks, such as a small incision on the neck or arm.

"Autopsy indicates massive loss of blood. No sign of internal hemorrhage, no wounds other than a scratch on the neck." Weariness competed with suspicion in Hayes' voice. "Dr. Darvell, this sounds awfully familiar, and I hate *déjà vu*. What do you know about all this?"

"Nothing, really. It's only vague conjecture." He wished he had the detective face to face, where he could use his paranormal influence to derail the conversation.

"Well, one thing makes me real curious. The dead girl's new friend, who ate breakfast with her at the soup kitchen, was a skinny redhead who called herself, Gillian. No woman with her, dark-haired or otherwise, by the way."

"Oh, my God!" Roger scrambled for the proper response. "I'm sorry for the other girl, but thank the Lord, Gillian didn't run into the murderer, too."

Hayes' tone softened. "I can imagine how worried you must be. Don't you think it's about time to file a formal missing child report?"

"No!" Forcing himself to speak calmly, Roger repeated his earlier argument. "She wouldn't cooperate with the police. She'd just lose herself permanently."

"I can't force you," said Hayes, "but I think you're making a hell of a mistake."

Roger feared the officer might be correct, but not in the way he meant. Perhaps it had been a mistake to mention Gillian at all.

As Britt remarked when Roger discussed the situation with her on the way to church, at least confessing about his illegitimate child had elicited the detective's help. Roger tried to wipe the whole mess from his mind and cast his thoughts into a proper frame for worship. Since Britt always attended Mass at St. Mary's with him on Christmas Eve, he reciprocated by joining her at St. Anne's, the restored Episcopal church in the middle of the historic district, on the fourth Sunday of Advent. At this early morning hour, they managed to preempt a parking space on State Circle across from the capitol building, a short walk to St. Anne's on Church Circle. In the foyer they separated, since Britt had duty as a chalice bearer this Sunday.

Roger preferred the early service, not only because it left more of the day free for sleep, but also because it was less crowded and featured fewer hymns. For his hyperacute hearing and perfect pitch, congregational "singing" meant minor torture. The prayerful (or at least groping toward prayerful) concentration of the worshipers, most of them elderly, cushioned the discomfort a vampire invariably felt in large groups of people. Unlike Claude, with his religious phobia, Roger found this kind of service restful and nourishing. As compensation for the lack of Britt's presence within arm's reach, he enjoyed watching her in the white lay reader's robe and listening to her read the lessons in her rich alto. Though she couldn't carry a tune, she had a sensuous speaking voice.

When the priest descended into the aisle to read the Gospel, Roger deflected his thoughts from the inappropriately carnal detour Britt's voice had lured him into and made a sincere effort to listen. The familiar reading from the first chapter of Matthew described St. Joseph's dilemma, whether to marry his pregnant fiancée or divorce her quietly. All his life, Roger had been taught to revere the Blessed Virgin's spouse as the paragon of earthly fatherhood.

*Quite a standard to live up to.* Faced with the crisis, Joseph had made the divinely inspired choice to embrace responsibility for the child he could have repudiated. *Fine, but I haven't heard an angel speaking yet.* Nevertheless, Roger knew he couldn't evade his duty; the *natural light of reason* he'd learned about from his parochial school teachers decades ago offered guidance he couldn't ignore.

He heard little of the sermon, which he gathered dealt with the topic of faith and risk. *I've got more risk than I can handle, thanks, but I could use an extra portion of faith.* By the time the rest of the congregation filed to the rail for communion—which he was too much of an unreconstructed pre-Vatican II Catholic to partake of—that natural light shone upon him with dazzling clarity.

The vampire community's attitude toward fatherhood ought to make no difference in his behavior. *To hell with their customs—I have to live by what I've been taught. In this respect I'm human, and I have to act like a human father. Gillian belongs to me, too, and I won't lose her without a fight.*

He made a mental note to drop in at his own church later and light a candle to St. Joseph.

*INSIDE A CABIN like the one where she'd been imprisoned by Greer, Gillian was screaming. Roger raced to the door. Suddenly at his feet, a serpent appeared—at least twice the length of a man's height, emerald green, with glistening, golden eyes. Its coils blocked the doorway. Raising its head to hiss at him, it displayed three-inch fangs.*

*Roger grasped the thing's head in both hands and squeezed. Its coils whipped around him. His accustomed strength melted away. The snake's body compressed his lungs, suffocating him.*

*Gillian shrieked his name. The snake disappeared, and Roger rushed inside. On the cabin's scuffed hardwood floor lay Gillian and Britt. The serpent stretched across them, daring him to advance closer. The suffocating pressure paralyzed him again. Gray fog thickened before his eyes—*

He was jolted awake by the telephone jangling next to the bed. His hand shook as he picked up the receiver. "Yes?" His own harsh breathing rasped in his ears.

"Roger, this is Gillian. Please come and pick me up." She spoke low and rapidly.

He had to tame his heartbeat before he could listen to her over its pounding. "Yes, of course. Where are you?"

"At a motel off Route 50 near Bowie, with Camille. I don't feel—right—about her. She kills." A long, indrawn breath, followed by an explosive rush of words. "She called Professor Greer to her last night, met him in a restaurant, and made him kill himself. I'm not sure how."

"I have some idea," Roger said. In view of Hayes' information, he could visualize Camille pouring alcohol down the professor and commanding him to drive off an overpass. Even if the man had survived the crash, with luck he would have been incommunicado long enough to ensure her safety. "Gillian, give me the precise location of that motel. I'll be there in less than an hour."

Gillian rattled off the directions. "Please hurry. She's still asleep now, but—" A gasp, a muffled shriek, and the telephone connection went dead.

## Chapter Twelve

GILLIAN FELT THE lash of Camille's rage a second before the door of the phone booth opened. She barely had time to cry out before Camille simultaneously clamped a hand over her mouth and slammed the receiver into its cradle.

Wedging her against the wall of the booth, Camille whispered between ragged breaths, "We're going back to our room now. You *will* appear to come with me of your own free choice."

Gillian nodded. Camille's nails gouged her forearms, and the woman's wrath made her head throb with pain. Grasping Gillian's left wrist, Camille led her from the parking lot of the convenience store where she'd made the phone call, across the street to the motel. Aware of Camille's adult strength, Gillian didn't try to wrench her arm free. Nor did she consider screaming for help. Camille's mature powers would swamp the will and cloud the mind of any bystander who might venture to interfere. Worst of all, the volcanic heat of the woman's anger terrified her into paralysis. Inside, she writhed in humiliation at her own impotence.

*I was certain she'd sleep longer. It's only four thirty in the afternoon!* Perhaps an intuition of Gillian's absence had penetrated Camille's day-sleep.

Camille hustled her into the elevator and up to their room. Once she'd bolted the door, Camille flung Gillian onto the nearest bed. "You treacherous little beast!" The woman's eyes glowed in the shadows of the heavily curtained room. "Ungrateful brat! I thought you appreciated what I've done for you. I thought you were loyal to me." With her fingers curled like talons, she pounced on top of Gillian.

Gillian's struggle didn't last long. She flailed her arms and flexed her legs like a cat trying to disembowel an attacker, to no avail. Within minutes Camille had her pinned to the mattress, her legs trapped by the woman's, both her wrists shackled above her head by one of Camille's hands. Camille's breath blew hot in her face. The woman's flesh scorched wherever it touched Gillian's skin.

*What does she want? What is she going to do to me?*

The bared teeth answered Gillian's question a second too late. They slashed the side of her neck. While vampires were immune to the anesthetic in their own saliva, Camille could have reduced the bite to a nearly painless sting. She didn't try. Gillian's back arched as the pain ripped through her. Camille's mouth scalded her throat.

*She can't kill me—she wouldn't destroy a child of her own race—Dark Powers, no!*

The suction at the wound went on and on, until Gillian felt the marrow was being drawn from her bones. Uncontrolled energy coursed through her, as her body tried to deal with the trauma by transforming. At last the pressure slackened. Rubbing her wrists, she opened her eyes. Camille, sitting astride her legs, stared down at her. Gillian hesitantly covered the incision with one hand, afraid any movement might set off her attacker.

The woman peeled off her shirt. Braless, she now wore only a pair of knit slacks. Sometime during the fight, she had kicked off her shoes.

Gillian watched, puzzled. *What is she up to now?* She understood when Camille rolled to the side, reclined on one elbow next to her, and scored her own breast with a claw-like nail.

*No, she promised! Never this!*

Gillian leaped off the bed and sprang toward the door. Instantly Camille was there, blocking the exit. Gillian threw a wild glance at the window.

"Don't even think it!" Camille panted like a wolf at the end of a chase. "You're too young to jump three stories down. And I'd get to you—long before—you could—open it or break it."

Camille's hands shot out to grab Gillian by the shoulders and force her to her knees. In the same inexorable motion Camille knelt too. Her arms wrapped around Gillian and wrestled her into an embrace with the strength of animate stone. Gillian felt smothered against the woman's cold bosom.

Like all female vampires, like Gillian's mother Juliette, Camille had small breasts. The incision she had made bisected one of those spare curves. Gillian, her eyes closed to shut out the violation, her mouth involuntarily flattened against the thin slash, experienced a sudden rush of tactile memory. Until the age of three, she had fed on her mother's blood as well as milk, in this very position. Since Juliette had never sampled from her veins in return—mothers and infants didn't bond that way—weaning had meant an irreversible break. Gillian allowed herself to remember, for the first time in years, the tearless sobs that had burned her eyes when Juliette had announced it was time for them to part, for Gillian to move on to the next phase in her growth.

Beads of Camille's blood oozed between Gillian's lips. She couldn't stop her tongue from lapping the wound. A black void opened to swallow her. Beyond thought, she clung to the woman as she had once clung to her mother.

Gillian whirled in a maelstrom of nothingness. After an immeasurable time, a sound reverberated through the dark. A pounding. A heartbeat? No, two heartbeats synchronized. As Gillian floated to the surface of the whirlpool and reawoke to her own identity, she realized the paired pulses were hers and Camille's. The woman's blood tasted bitter, and the touch of her mind seared like acid.

*Alone, forever alone. My twin, my other self, annihilated. Outcast, untouchable, bad blood. Never a mate, never a child. Nothing but darkness, cold, starvation, emptiness. Fill the void—devour them, devour all of them. They exist to fill me. Life, hot, sweet, rich fountain of life.*

Dimly Gillian realized that she was sharing the trauma of Camille's imprisonment. She ripped her mind free of the memory's talons. [No! I am not you. I am myself, Gillian! And we aren't locked in a casket. We're free! Your hunger does not have to go unsatisfied.] She groped in Camille's mind for an image of their animal prey of their first night together and projected that image back at the woman.

Camille's passion dissipated, and she replied in a mental voice not too different from her audible one: [Nice try, child, but not good enough. It's not raccoon blood I'm thirsty for.] She ravished Gillian with the girl Bonnie's last breathing moments, with the flavor of the victim's blood, the heat of her flesh, the vibrant life-force she'd radiated.

Thirst overwhelmed Gillian. Mindlessly she clutched Camille and drank as if the vampire woman could nourish her. Then somehow she found herself flat on her back on the floor. Camille stood in the alcove outside the bathroom, washing up at the sink.

Suddenly cold, Gillian hugged herself. The motel room seemed two-dimensional and monotone-hued after that shattering exchange.

"Don't pretend you're too weak to move," said Camille with an air of tolerant amusement. "Thanks to what you've done, we can't stay here. Now that there's no chance of your betraying me again, it's safe to leave. You're hungry, aren't you?"

Gillian squeezed her eyes shut as if to blot out her humiliation. "Yes."

ROGER STARED AT the telephone, emitting a dial tone that mocked him. Britt, across town in her apartment, spoke inside his mind: [You're going to her?]

[Of course. But I'm terribly afraid it's too late.] While answering Britt, he was already collecting his jacket and car keys.

[A little while ago, I spoke to Eloise on the phone. Now that the convention's over, I don't see any point in their going back to the Hilton, so I invited them to stay at my place until Christmas. They agreed—subject to your approval—and they're headed here now.]

[My approval?]

[Obviously, I'd have to move in with you.]

[I already surmised that.] Roger locked the front door behind him and sprinted to his car. [I suppose I have no choice, and I won't deny I'll enjoy your company. I just don't know whether I'll be able to handle the constant temptation.]

Too anxious about Gillian to toss him a light comeback, Britt silently lingered in his mind as he accelerated away from the condominium. The image of Gillian in Camille's grip both frightened and angered him more than he would have expected. He gritted his teeth in frustration when he thought of how futile this excursion would probably be. It seemed unlikely that Camille would wait around for Roger to track her to her lair.

*Unless she's lying in wait with Gillian as hostage.* The thought chilled him. Would a frontal attack, as Claude had suggested, endanger the child? *I don't necessarily have to attack. I can decide on tactics when I find them.*

He maneuvered the car toward Route 50 as fast as traffic would allow. At twilight on a Sunday evening, the highway wasn't overcrowded. Thankful for the continued clear weather, he set the cruise control at eighty on the freeway. He wished he dared to drive still faster, even as the rational part of his brain reminded him that Camille and Gillian had probably moved elsewhere.

Gillian wanted to return to him. That news lifted the weight of indecision and freed him to act. He only prayed Camille hadn't warped the girl's mind too badly in the short time they'd spent together.

Forty minutes after leaving home, he screeched to a halt in front of the motel Gillian had described. Since she'd given him the room number, he didn't bother entering the lobby. All the suites opened directly onto outdoor breezeways, so he went directly to the door.

The curtains covering the picture window were shut. Not reckless enough to charge up and knock, Roger crept silently to the door from the side opposite the window. He pressed his ear to the hinge. No sound of breathing, no vibrations of a living presence in the air.

*Gone.* Then another possibility hit him. Suppose Camille had murdered Gillian and left her body here? *Nonsense. That would be utterly irrational, even for Sandor's sister.*

The image wouldn't leave him alone, though. Wrapping his handkerchief around the doorknob, he wrenched it open.

The cool, dusty smell of the dark room, with only a fading trace of Gillian's scent, reassured him. Nevertheless, he made a quick search before withdrawing. On closer inspection, he picked up a faint tang of blood. But no smell of death. Camille had left nothing tangible behind. Well, he'd hardly expected such convenient carelessness.

Pulling the door shut to look undisturbed, Roger hurried around the empty swimming pool to the lobby. At the front desk he latched onto a young man with black hair and moustache, who offered no resistance to a straightforward hypnotic assault. Roger wasted no time on subtlety. If the woman talking on the telephone at the other end of the counter happened to notice her coworker's dazed manner, Roger was prepared to overpower her, too. "The woman and girl in room one-seventeen," he said as soon as he'd cast his target into a receptive trance. "How long ago did they leave?"

The clerk answered in a subdued mumble, "Maybe twenty-five minutes."

*Damn, so close!* Roger kept his own voice low to encourage the man to remain quiet. "Did the woman say anything about her next destination?"

The man shook his head. Roger had expected no different.

"What kind of car was she driving?"

"Blue hatchback." Good, she hadn't replaced it yet.

"Did you get a look at the girl with her? Did the child appear healthy?" That trace of blood he'd scented in the bedroom worried Roger.

"Pale, skinny kid. She hung around just inside the door while the lady checked out. The kid looked okay, except she wasn't dressed right for this cold weather."

"Very well. Forget I mentioned them. If anyone asks, I only wanted directions." Roger quickly walked out, not trusting himself within reach of innocent bystanders. His head was pounding.

*I refuse to give up this easily.* Camille had less than a half-hour start on him. If she had stopped somewhere within a few miles, for whatever reason, a systematic search might stumble upon the car. It

202          Margaret L. Carter

could do no harm to try. He drove around the block, then commenced to crisscross the area in a steadily expanding grid.

TO GILLIAN, CAMILLE'S presence felt like a wasp buzzing inside her skull. Huddled against the right-hand door of the car, Gillian said, "Why did you do this to me? You gave your word."

"Circumstances change." Camille's lips curled in a humorless rictus. "Do you think I wanted to be tangled up in your mind this way? I had to, because you betrayed me. You won't do that again, will you?"

Gillian said nothing. A cooperative answer would be a blatant lie, yet she didn't want to antagonize Camille with open rebellion.

"How could you turn on me that way? We belong together now. I took risks to free you from our late friend Adam."

Gillian sensed that Camille's expectation of gratitude was sincere. "Only because you wanted revenge on Roger." How she wished she had the strength to eject Camille from the inside of her head.

"That was my original motive. But now I've decided that we should stay together. There's so much I can teach you, and I'll never have a child of my own."

Gillian felt the bitterness and recalled the cryptic fragments of thoughts during the blood-exchange. "Why not?"

"You have no concept of what your—father—stole from me!" Camille revved the accelerator, making the car leap forward and whip around an eighteen-wheeler they'd been following. "Not only my brother's life—and fourteen years of my own life—he made me an outcast, too! Not officially, but enough that it makes no difference. People who should be my peers are wary of me, don't want to get too close—after all, I'm unstable. And no male would consider siring a child on me. Not with my brother's *taint*—it might be hereditary!"

Gillian didn't grasp how Neil Sandor's taint could be blamed on Roger. She said timidly, "But your brother did kill a woman of our race, didn't he?"

"Which he never would have needed to do, if Roger hadn't identified him to the police in Boston. Betrayed one of his own kind to ephemerals!" Camille's fingers flexed on the steering wheel. "True, I didn't see much of Neil during his last two years of life. He was becoming careless about how and where he fed. But in our early decades we were very close. After he rejected our advisor, nobody else would associate with him." Her thoughts grazed Gillian's in a phantom caress. "You can understand that, can't you? You ran away from Volnar."

Gillian tried to shield her thoughts, though she doubted Camille could sift much sense out of their confusion anyway. True, Gillian could sympathize with Neil's reluctance to bond with his advisor. *Especially if it has to be like this!* On the other hand, "careless" seemed a feeble term for the slaughter the renegade had supposedly indulged in.

Gillian kept quiet until the car abandoned the freeway for two-lane rural roads. "Where are we going? I thought you were looking for a new shelter."

"Not yet. I want to show you some of the advantages of pairing with me." Shortly, Camille parked on a dirt road marked *Private Drive*, under a concealing overhang of pine trees. "Unless the owner happens to drive past, the car should be perfectly safe here."

When she got out, Gillian followed without bothering to ask questions. Since the fight in the motel had left her ravenous, she hoped this was a hunting foray.

Camille sensed the desire and answered it. "Maybe later. I'm not sure whether you've been punished enough yet." She no longer radiated anger, just a gloating delight in her power over Gillian. When they reached an area where the trees grew sparsely, she faced Gillian and held both of her hands. "Look at me. Let my thoughts flow into yours. No, I'm not planning to hurt you again."

Wearing a blouse and sweatshirt without a coat, Gillian flinched from the frigid night wind. She forgot any discomfort, though, when Camille began to dissolve from human shape into the form of a gigantic, black she-wolf. [Do as I do. Be my mirror.]

Atavistic instinct stirred in Gillian's viscera. With Camille's thoughts and hers intertwined she could channel that tingling electricity under her skin. She willed molecules of skin and enamel to rearrange themselves, allowing fangs and fur to sprout, and had no trouble stopping there. For the rest, she molded her outward appearance into the same lupine illusion Camille projected.

Camille's illusory beast-form melted from wolf to panther. Resonating to the silent chord, Gillian followed her lead. When Camille segued from cat to winged monster, Gillian did the same. The wings of spider-silk lightness and strength were real, and their eruption from her shoulders—she had automatically wriggled out of her upper garments without conscious thought—shot spasms of ecstasy through her.

Camille levitated toward the treetops. [You know the real truth behind the mirror legend, don't you? Not that we have no reflections, of course, but that a mirror reflects our natural appearance. Illusions don't work in mirrors. Remember that.]

Gillian wordlessly acknowledged the advice. She floated, shivering with pleasure at the wind that tickled her wing membranes. Trailing over the woods in Camille's wake, she used the wings only to steer and balance. They were, of course, too flimsy to support her weight.

Camille said, [After a few weeks of practice, you'll have the skill to levitate and maintain the transformed shape at the same time without my guidance. It's like swimming; you have to develop it into a system of learned reflexes.]

Though she begrudged the fact, Gillian had to admit that changing and flying were easier with direct telepathic help from an adult. Would Volnar's initiation have been so violent? Surely not! She hastily buried the thought for fear of angering Camille with it.

Such conflicts were easy to forget in the glory of flying. Gillian savored the crisp chill of the night, the sharp scent of pine, the glitter of the stars in the cloudless sky. Only the gnawing of hunger marred her pleasure.

[Would you like to get dinner less strenuously this time?] Camille asked. [I notice a house with a barn over there to the east.]

The house stood near the road in a field of several acres, partly grass, partly dried remnants of corn stalks. Camille alighted at the edge of the woods, flowing into her natural form. When Gillian did the same, her naked arms and chest prickled with the cold.

Camille grinned and licked her lips. "Chilly? A drink should fix that." She sniffed the air. "No dogs roaming outside tonight. Horses in the barn—three, I think."

Veiling themselves against a casual glance from the house or a passing car, they walked across the open field to the barn. Camille paused to listen. "We're in luck. I don't think anyone is home."

Gillian gave her a sidelong look. Could the woman really distinguish life or the absence of it in the house at this distance? Together they silently opened the unlocked barn door and slipped inside. The horses, alarmed by the inhuman scent, stamped and snorted. Camille led the way to the nearest stall. A brown mare, teeth exposed and nostrils flaring, backed away from the intruder.

Camille vaulted over the chest-high stall door. Leaning on the partition, Gillian watched her mentor stalk up to the restive beast. Gillian was glad to see Camille take the lead, for she herself wouldn't have cared to approach those hooves. Projecting confidence, Camille gentled the horse with a tuneless hum. The glitter of hostility faded from the brown eyes, and the laid-back ears perked forward. Camille stroked the broad neck until the mare stood still, head drooping.

The woman nipped through the tough hide and sipped the trickle of blood. Its metallic tang mingled with odors of manure and horse-sweat. Gillian didn't mind the smells, which were clean and natural compared to the pollution generated by human beings. She felt too dizzy with hunger to care about her surroundings anyway.

After a couple of minutes Camille licked her lips clean and beckoned to Gillian. Concentrating to make her body momentarily lighter, an abbreviated version of the levitation she used to fly, Gillian sprang over the barrier. She hugged the horse's neck, weak with gratitude for the life-essence flowing into the hollow place within her. She burned with more than physical hunger, for she had partaken of the emptiness at the core of Camille's being. Gillian feared animal blood could never fill that void.

Camille's hand on her shoulder shattered her feeding trance. "Listen, someone's coming."

Gillian shook her head, but the mental prodding that accompanied the words wouldn't let her return to her meal. Outside, she heard a car pull up the driveway and decelerate.

[They've come home,] Camille said. [We'd better leave.]

[But I'm not finished!] Gillian's silent wail went unheeded. Following Camille's example, she made herself invisible, drifted out of the stall, and edged through the barn door. The door, left ajar, banged shut as they glided across the field.

[They'll probably think it was left unlatched, and the wind opened it,] Camille suggested.

Behind her, Gillian heard the car door slam, followed by uneasy murmurs and running feet. She swallowed her fear, the better to focus on keeping herself unnoticeable.

Once under cover of the trees Camille shifted to her winged form. Though she had to do likewise to keep up, Gillian had misgivings. [Aren't we supposed to avoid changing so close to human habitation?]

Camille's words sounded like a ghostly echo inside her head. [Cub, you worry too much about what ephemerals think. They exist to provide for us. Why should we let them rule our lives?]

[But doesn't our freedom depend on keeping them ignorant of us?]

[What kind of freedom is that, pussyfooting through life to guard yourself from your inferiors? *This* is freedom.]

Immersed in the exhilaration of soaring above the trees, Gillian couldn't produce a credible counter-argument.

A few minutes later, they dropped to the ground and walked the rest of the way to the car, where Gillian retrieved her blouse and sweatshirt. "Listen, child," said Camille as she started the engine, "what they witness doesn't matter nearly so much as Volnar made you think. First, they won't believe it. Their own aversion to the bizarre and impossible makes them reject the evidence of their senses. Second, if it comes to the crunch, we can always mesmerize them and revise their memories. Now we have to get out of here, before whoever owns this place drives by and wonders about this strange car parked in their lane."

After they'd traveled a couple of miles, Camille said, "That was just an appetizer. Now I need dinner."

*What about me?* Gillian thought but did not project. The energy drain of flying had sharpened her appetite.

"Furthermore, we need to ditch this car," her companion went on. "Roger probably knows about it. This time we'll try a freeway rest stop. I've had good luck with them in the past."

Camille sang as they cruised Route 50, this time "The Battle Hymn of the Republic." Gillian preferred the *a capella* entertainment to conversation. While the woman was singing, she might not notice Gillian's ill-suppressed rebellious emotions. They didn't stop on 50, instead turning north on Interstate 95. Gillian was having an increasingly hard time controlling her impatience by the time they pulled into a rest station.

Camille dropped her off at the bottom of the ramp, before approaching the brightly-lit brick shelter that held the restrooms. "Wait here while I check out the prospects. I don't want us seen together."

Gillian retreated under a tree and faded into the shadows. By now, she was confident that she could maintain the psychic veil; no ephemeral would see her unless she wanted him to. Since she hadn't been ordered otherwise, she linked telepathically with Camille to watch the woman's reconnaissance.

After washing her hands in the ladies' room, Camille got a drink and lingered by the water fountain to observe people passing between the shelter and their cars. She fixed on a young couple, an elfin-faced blonde in a fur-collared coat and a husky, chestnut-haired man who clasped the woman's hand as they studied the Maryland map on the wall. Camille listened to their murmured conversation "—about another hour and a half to your mom's, think we should call? Nah, we're ahead of schedule, no reason she'd be worrying."

[Vacationers,] Camille remarked to Gillian. [We'll take them. You're going to serve as bait.] Through Camille's eyes Gillian watched the couple walk toward a four-door compact in the parking lot. [Quickly, Gillian, get to the other end, where you can intercept them before they speed up at the on-ramp.]

Still veiled, Gillian rejoiced to find she could sprint at better-than-human speed without losing her grip on her invisibility. When the target couple's car accelerated out of the parking lot, she was ready for them. Out of direct sight of the other cars at the rest stop, she flickered into full visibility soon enough to catch the driver's attention, but not close enough to let him be sure she'd appeared out of nowhere.

The young man braked when she waved. Before he could change his mind and move on, she lurched to the car and leaned on the driver's window. She made herself breathe hard.

The man rolled the window down a few inches. He was cautious. Gillian silently ordered him not to notice the crimson pinpoints at the centers of her eyes. "Help me, please!" She injected a sob into her voice.

"What's wrong?" The man spoke in a rumbling bass that made her diaphragm flutter. Gillian felt his gaze on her. Once again she was fortunate to be without a coat, since she looked more pathetic that way.

"Please get me away from here!" She gulped, as if choking down tears. She felt Camille mentally applauding the act. "I was hitchhiking, and this man—he—" She projected terror, drawing upon the memory of the frightful instant when Greer had seen her change.

[Easy,] Camille reminded her. [Don't get so carried away that you lose control and do it again.]

Gillian's simulated desperation had its effect on the woman in the car. "You poor thing! Frank, pull over!"

Gillian stepped back to allow the car to park at the curb. The man, Frank, moved the gearshift to neutral, a good sign. The blonde woman scooted over to the center of the front seat. "Get in, you must be freezing. It's a tight squeeze, but it's warmer up here."

Gillian accepted the invitation before Frank could express his doubts. "I don't know about this, Jan," he said after Gillian closed the passenger door. "Sure, we should help, but—what happened, exactly?"

"This man in a truck gave me a ride. When we stopped here, he tried to—And then I slapped him and jumped out. Please don't make me talk about it!" The fewer details, the less her chance of striking a false note, Gillian thought. She focused on Jan, the more susceptible of the two.

"Isn't there somebody you can call?" said Frank. "I'd be glad to walk you over to the phone booth."

Gillian shook her head. "There's nobody." She clasped one of Jan's gloved hands. When the woman's face softened with increased pity, Gillian wrapped her arms around the woman's neck.

Startled, Jan stiffened for an instant. Gillian's fingers stroked her hair so delicately she probably didn't notice the touch, while Gillian murmured meaningless pleas for help into her ear. Exulting in her new power, Gillian felt the woman's muscles relax as she returned the hug.

Gillian heard a bewildered "Hey" from the man. She ignored it.

"I'm so cold," she whispered. And she was. She needed this woman's body heat to alleviate a chill beyond the below-freezing outdoor temperature. She couldn't help realizing that Jan had responded with kindness before the psychic compulsion had lulled her into a trance. *And I'm just supposed to turn her over for Camille to drain?* Gillian felt a wild impulse to drive off with these people this very moment, before Camille could interfere. With Frank and Jan's hypnotically-induced cooperation Gillian could be at Roger's townhouse in less than an hour.

Then she heard a strangled gasp from Frank. *Too late!* A mental sting from Camille demonstrated that she'd sensed Gillian's intent. Jan stirred, trying to look around at her husband. "It's all right," Gillian whispered. "Don't worry, Frank is fine. I'm freezing—hold me."

Vaguely she sensed Camille ensnaring the man's will and ordering him out of the car. She led him away from the curb to a cluster of pines, where she made him lie face up on the winter-brown grass. [Put the woman to sleep,] she told Gillian.

Gillian obeyed, surprised at how easy the maneuver turned out to be. Jan's sympathy and Gillian's imbibing of her life-force, even without shedding blood, had forged a link that enhanced Gillian's influence. The woman exhaled a long sigh and slumped against Gillian's shoulder.

Again Camille spoke: [You've been a big help, so I'm going to give you a treat. Join me.] She flung open the gates to her mind. Gillian plunged in. Her earlier immersion into those depths had horrified her, but hunger and curiosity dominated over fear.

Her senses exploded. A rich stream of lust and power poured into her. The victim's heartbeat and breathing sounded like the roar of the ocean; his aura incandesced behind her eyelids; the heat of his flesh licked over her skin like painless fire. She was drowning and didn't care whether she ever touched bottom or rose to the surface again.

Abruptly she was thrown out. She landed with jarring force in the heaviness of her own body. [Never share their death,] came Camille's icy command. [You're too young. It would devour your mind.]

Gillian clung to her only consolation, the woman unconscious in her arms. Her mouth was an inch away from Jan's throat. The synthetic fur of the coat collar tickled Gillian's nose. It would be so easy to fold back the collar and satisfy her thirst.

[No, you aren't ready,] Camille told her. Gillian sensed Camille releasing the man, whose life was seeping away into the frigid night, and walking back to the car. Slipping into the driver's seat, Camille said, "I'll take her now."

Gillian noticed Camille pocketing a handful of paper money. Putting an arm around the unconscious woman, Camille said, "Hand me her purse."

Chilled by the loss of her prey's warmth, Gillian leaned over the seat to pick up the purse. Camille rummaged in it for a wallet, from which she extracted all the cash. She then placed her fingertips on Jan's forehead. "Look at me." Gillian felt the atmosphere grow turgid as Camille gathered her strength for an illusion. Lambent flames haloed the head of a glossy black panther with glowing eyes. Gillian knew the image she vaguely glimpsed would appear twice as real to Jan, who sat paralyzed beneath Camille's dominance.

"Forget you saw us," Camille said. "You don't know what killed your husband. It's so terrible you want to forget it. Get out of the car and lie down under the trees. You want to go to sleep so you can forget."

At Camille's mental command Gillian moved to allow Jan to obey. The woman staggered across the lawn, her eyes glazed, and stretched full length on the ground. Meanwhile, Camille extracted the car keys and unlocked the trunk. She pulled suitcases out and dumped them on the ground along with the woman's purse. "No reason to clutter it up with identifiable items we don't need. We may want the space for something else later. Hurry up, let's go."

Gillian regretted the loss of the clothes in the hatchback. Now they'd have to buy or steal fresh supplies. Camille took as disconcertingly casual an attitude toward material possessions as toward her prey. An attitude Gillian still wasn't reconciled to. "You killed him," she whispered as they sped down the freeway.

"You're on that again? Don't try to claim you've got some kind of purity, cub. You weren't in any mood to stop me."

Shame suffused Gillian at this reminder of the thirst that still burned in her. "But this time it's sure to be identified as murder. And what you showed the woman—"

"Better than letting her have a good look at my normal appearance. Also, terrifying her out of her wits minimizes the chance of her telling a straight story. And it's *fun*." Impatient with Gillian's persistent qualms, she said, "Granted, I took a risk killing the man. The elders would call it reckless self-exposure—as if I cared. So would you rather I'd have killed her, too, without even hunger for an excuse?"

Gillian shook her head, more confused than ever. How much of this irregular behavior was justified in the name of self-defense? Camille's attitude had an insidious sort of logic that undermined Volnar's doctrines. Yet this time, as Camille herself admitted, she'd trespassed beyond all bounds. The elders would never accept her now. But Gillian couldn't keep her mind on abstract questions. The mention of hunger reminded her of her own. Somehow she knew animals would no longer satisfy it. "When will I be allowed to drink human blood?"

"When you prove yourself worthy."

Chapter Thirteen

THE URGENCY THAT drove him had long since died, leaving Roger to pursue his quest out of a sense of duty. After cruising central Maryland for several hours he'd given up hope of running across Camille and Gillian. Nor did his vague notion of making himself a target in the conspicuous Citroen with the hope of drawing Camille's fire make as much sense as it had at the start of the evening. *She can find me at home whenever she wishes anyway. But why hasn't she made contact yet? She must be planning to; why else is she hanging onto Gillian?*

Having worked through a wearisome assortment of motels and gas stations without a glimpse of the blue hatchback, he'd switched to rest stops. Just two more, he decided, and he would head back to Annapolis. Already he'd driven halfway to Baltimore with no idea of what direction his quarry had taken. Doubtless he was simply wasting time.

*Suppose Gillian calls again, and I miss her? Or Camille does, and she gets angry when I'm not there to answer?*

Driving north on 95, he took the off-ramp for the next rest stop. When he pulled into the parking area, he thought for a moment that fatigue and hope were making him hallucinate. A medium blue hatchback sat at the end of the row. Roger had to shake his head to clear the mental fog before he could check to confirm that the license number was the one he'd memorized.

His heart racing, he parked beside the hatchback and got out. Already he'd seen that it was unoccupied. While he strode rapidly toward the restrooms, he extended psychic tendrils, searching for any hint of a nonhuman presence. He felt none. Well away from the car, he flared his nostrils and picked up no trace of Gillian's scent. So they'd been here, but they had switched vehicles and fled again. Somehow, Roger wasn't surprised to arrive too late once more.

As soon as he'd reached that conclusion, he consciously noticed for the first time that a revolving red light was casting lurid shadows on the other end of the parking lot. He stalked toward the light and the babble of voices that surrounded it. Three police cars, two from the state highway patrol and one from Anne Arundel County, lined the curb at the beginning of the freeway on-ramp. A ribbon marked "Crime Scene—Do Not Cross," stretched between a pair of sawhorses, blocked access to the grassy buffer zone between parking lot and freeway. Several uniformed officers were clustered nearby, one of them taking photographs. A plainclothes detective paced over the grass, occasionally pausing to make notes. Not Captain Hayes, Roger noted with relief.

A faint effluvium of blood and death hung in the air. Roger's night vision distinguished a crushed, darkened patch of grass where a body must have lain. His chest constricted.

The police had apparently impressed bystanders with the need to stay clear of the crime site. The few people watching did so from a distance, hovering near the brick shelter. When Roger walked up to the barrier, one of the officers intercepted him. "You'll have to stand back, sir. There's nothing to see now, anyway."

"I'm a doctor," Roger said. "I wondered if I might be of some help."

The rather illogical offer, in view of the conspicuous absence of an ambulance, won him a direct but non-hostile stare, which had been the object of the remark. "Thank you, doctor, but as you can see, the victim has already been transported to the hospital."

Roger didn't touch the man for fear of triggering trained defense reflexes. The hypnotic process was working well enough without physical contact. "Who was the victim? Tell me what happened here."

"Between ninety minutes and two hours ago, a female Caucasian in her twenties wandered into the ladies' room, traumatized and apparently delirious. Two women who were present persuaded her to sit down and called 911." The policeman was conveniently suggestible; he recited the facts as smoothly as if delivering an official report. "Upon arriving at the scene, state police personnel found the body of the first victim's husband lying under a tree. No obvious cause of death was immediately discernible. Questioning revealed that the couple's car had been stolen. However, the contents of the vehicle, including the woman's purse, had been left beside the road. Several hundred dollars in cash had been removed from the purse and the man's wallet."

When the officer paused for breath, Roger interrupted the recitation. "How long ago did the assault take place?"

"The wife was incoherent, so she wasn't able to say what time she and her husband arrived here. The medical examiner's initial estimate is that the man had been dead at least two hours."

Roger shoved aside the discouragement this information

produced. "You say she was delirious and incoherent. What did she tell you?"

"She was raving. Made no sense. Something about a monster with fangs. If not for the car and all their cash being missing, I'd think they'd been taking some kind of crap that killed him and drove her out of her head."

Roger wished that explanation would hold up. How neat—while drugged, the couple had succumbed to a random robbery. Unfortunately the post mortem would reveal the absence of drugs in the man's system. Camille was becoming reckless; she'd taken care to pump Greer full of liquor first.

"Describe the stolen car."

The officer flipped open a notebook and reeled off the description, including license number. Roger guessed the woman must have carried that in her purse, for she could hardly have remembered it while delirious. Just then, one of the other policemen called, "Gonzalo, what's going on over there?"

Roger captured Gonzalo's eyes to focus his wavering attention. "Thank you for your help. I offered my services, and you declined. You didn't tell me anything of consequence."

Roger turned and walked away with a purposeful but outwardly unhurried gait. Behind him he heard Officer Gonzalo shout back, "No problem, just getting rid of a sightseer."

Having fed, Camille would probably go to ground. Roger had no heart for any further useless wandering tonight. He drove up the highway to the next exit and circled back toward Annapolis.

Knowing Britt was at her own apartment, he went directly there. He found her dozing on the couch, while Claude sat across the living room flipping through the latest Tom Clancy thriller by the glow of a single dim lamp. Eloise had gone to bed. Britt, more than half asleep, silently greeted Roger when he walked in. [I've behaved myself, colleague. I haven't so much as touched him once.]

Roger commended her restraint in view of the urgent need Claude radiated. *How can Eloise possibly resist that?* Claude plopped the book down on the rug when Roger entered. "Bombed out again? I'm damn sorry about all this. If I'd reacted faster the other night, Gillian wouldn't be in this fix to begin with."

"Apologizing?" Roger said as he hung his coat up. "That isn't like you. And unnecessary—if Greer hadn't succeeded in capturing Gillian, Camille might have still managed to lure her away."

Claude's attenuated aura confirmed the message of his body

language. He drooped, that was the only word for his posture. Roger had never seen him in such a bleak mood. "Yes, I know I look like hell," said Claude, correctly interpreting Roger's expression. "Believe it or not, I've never been this seriously injured before. It's like being ill—the way I imagine illness must feel. Extremely unpleasant."

"You've overextended yourself." Roger cut off the lecture he'd been about to deliver. Midnight Sunday was a bit late to tell Claude he should have cancelled the convention appearances. "So has Eloise. I hope she's resting comfortably?" He took the remaining armchair, low and angular like the couch.

"As well as can be expected." Sigmund padded into the living room and jumped onto Claude's lap. Obviously having made the cat's acquaintance already, Claude mechanically stroked the cream-colored fur.

"Is she still determined not to conceive again?"

Claude nodded. "I'm more than willing to try, but she's adamant. Can't blame her for being afraid, I suppose. And in a way, I'm relieved. I detest the thought of putting her through that agony again."

Britt sat up, raking her fingers through her tousled hair. "One instance doesn't necessarily constitute a pattern, you know."

"Try to convince her of that." Claude's mouth was set in a grim line. "And I understand her feeling—even if she doesn't believe I can. It was a gamble to begin with."

Roger went into the kitchen to pour himself a glass of milk. He did the same for Claude, spiking it with brandy. As an afterthought he added a shot to his own glass, too. He realized that he hadn't eaten since the previous night.

Claude grimaced at the offer of cold milk but drank it without verbal protest. Like Roger, he was doubtless too hungry to care. "We'll be going now," Roger said, "and let you rest."

"Wish I could do something else to help," Claude said. "But to tell the truth, old thing, I've hardly got the energy to move from here to the bedroom when the sun rises."

"Yes, you need sleep. You've been up for two days straight; even we can't go on like that indefinitely."

"Sounds good to me too," said Britt. "Unlike you guys, I'm only human." She yawned and reached for the coat she'd dropped at the end of the couch, the stretch pulling her sweater tight across her breasts.

Claude said with a wry smile, "Yes, little brother, get her out of here before I forget whose she is. I'm not made of stone."

On the way home Roger tried to enjoy having Britt cuddle up to him without letting the contact whet his appetite. He was too tired for such strenuous doublethink. Impatient though he was to pursue the search for Camille and Gillian—*how? if the woman wants to mock me by strewing a trail of victims and making herself impossible to find, what can I do about it?*—he knew he would have to sleep through the day also.

After he'd sent Britt to bed alone over her protests, he checked the answering machine. Captain Hayes had called to pass on the information about Camille's latest crime, which Roger had discovered on his own. The second message he played back was from Juliette:

"Hello, Roger, it's midnight, Sunday. Since I haven't heard from you yet, I guess Gillian is still missing. Volnar's flight finally got off to London. I'm driving down to Maryland tomorrow night if I don't hear any news by late afternoon. Don't know what I can do, but I have to try."

Roger's stomach churned at the prospect of facing Juliette after his carelessness had made their daughter a victim. On the other hand, the meeting would offer him a chance to persuade Juliette that he should have a role in Gillian's upbringing, when they got her back. *If this episode doesn't convince Juliette of my total unfitness. If Gillian ever comes back at all.*

Of course she would. He'd make sure of it, if he had to trade himself to Camille for her freedom.

*You're not thinking straight*, he told himself. *Why would Camille be fool enough to accept an offer like that? Gillian gives her just the leverage she wants.*

"WHY DO YOU waste emotion on the deaths of ephemerals?" Camille said as they drove down 95 South. Gillian found herself getting very tired of riding in cars. "They all die eventually. Considering how short their lives are compared to ours, what's a decade or two more or less?"

Gillian shrugged. An unexpected side effect of the forced blood-bond, she reflected, was the improvement in her mental shield over the past few hours. She had a strong incentive to block random leaks, though she didn't flatter herself that she'd be able to hold out if Camille really wanted to read her mind. Camille's arguments had a skewed logic that Gillian had trouble refuting, yet she knew Roger and Claude would disagree. Why? Gillian couldn't conjure up a reason. There was hardly a current shortage of human prey.

"I don't make a habit of torturing them the way Neil did. Granted, that was unwise of him. We feel our victims' emotions, so invoking pain is like torturing ourselves. But Neil was a little—strange. I never denied that."

Surprised to hear Camille speaking of her brother calmly, Gillian took advantage of the moment. "Why was he that way?"

"After he refused to bond with our advisor, he seemed to need stronger, harsher stimulation from his prey. I tried to steer him away from the worst excesses, and until the last couple of years, he listened to me." A tinge of bitterness seeped into her voice. "But his behavior didn't justify Roger killing him. Or our advisor turning her back on both of us. I'm not responsible for what Neil did. *My* victims, if they die, die happy." Camille seemed to make a deliberate effort to lighten the mood. "You know that firsthand now. You felt it."

Gillian's stomach cramped at the memory. Yes, Camille had given that man ecstasy his normal life would never have held. Gillian yearned to plunge into that flood again. She made no attempt to hide her desire from Camille.

Camille's amusement rippled the air in the car. "I know what you want. Maybe if you behave yourself, you'll get it soon. Tell me about Roger's pet."

Confused by the apparent change of subject, Gillian described Britt's physical appearance. "And she isn't afraid of us. She enjoys giving to him."

"That attracts you, doesn't it? How would you like to have her?"

Gillian quivered with excitement at the expression of this forbidden desire. "That would be trespassing. She belongs to Roger."

"You told me she offered herself to you. That negates his right to forbid the act."

Gillian's newborn lust warred with the remnants of her lifelong training. "Lord Volnar said—"

"Forget about his decrees!" A flare of anger from Camille stung Gillian like a slap on the cheek. "You are my child now. You live by my rules."

*Her child?* The words lanced through Gillian like an icy blade. Yet Camille's regime had its seductive aspects. Apparently these rules meant Gillian could do anything her appetite and curiosity impelled— as long as she didn't anger Camille. The prospect held a dizzying blend of excitement and terror, like flying in a thunderstorm.

[You'll never lack excitement with me, cub. All you have to do is break those rusty old chains.]

After they'd left the interstate for Route 50, Camille detoured off the freeway until she came across a picnic ground where she could park inconspicuously. The two of them washed up with handfuls of snow from under the leafless trees, then strolled on a carpet of brown pine needles. "Enjoy the exercise," said Camille, "because we can't linger very long. This car will be reported stolen. We need to find a place to hole up."

"Where?"

"I'm heading back to Annapolis. By now I think we've teased Roger enough."

"Teased?" Gillian plucked a twig from a low-hanging bough and twisted it in her fingers.

"Yes, why do you think I've been chasing all over the Maryland-D.C. area instead of confronting him straight out? I wanted to get him good and frustrated before closing in for the kill—so to speak. And I'll bet keeping you just out of his reach has done a terrific job on him." Camille grinned as if expecting Gillian to share her delight in the scheme.

In that instant Camille's mind was open and unguarded. Gillian saw the truth—that Camille had incited the professor's actions and planned all along to *rescue* Gillian. *I'm a toy to her, a weapon to strike at my father!* Gillian felt herself dissolving under the force of the shock.

"Stop that!" Camille's nails, gouging her wrists, aborted Gillian's involuntary change. "Yes, that was my original plan. But I didn't know you then. Now I want to train you. We can have a wonderful time together."

Hurt and anger at how she'd been used swamped Gillian's fear of Camille. "Why would I want to do anything with you? Why should I ever let you touch my mind again?"

"Because you don't have a choice—except to relax and enjoy it or fight and get hurt." Camille brushed aside Gillian's mental assault like a toddler's tantrum. "Given an alternative, I'd rather not cause you pain. They condemned my brother to death, made my advisor renounce me as a lost cause, stole fourteen years of my life, and destroyed my chance of ever having a child. You can make up to me for some of that."

Gillian felt that Camille was sincere, on one level. Yet the woman was holding something back. Between pleasure in the mentor role, lust for excitement, a hunger strangely intense for a mature vampire, and hatred of Roger, Camille's mind was so clouded with static that Gillian couldn't sift truth from lies.

"Let's go." Camille led Gillian back to the car, as if afraid her pupil would try to escape. "We've spent too long in one place. I hope you're working up a hearty appetite, because tomorrow, if you behave yourself, I'm sending you to your first human—donor."

*She means victim. Her revenge on Roger will be to give Britt to me. And Britt is exactly the one I want!*

Gillian's head ached with confusion. The moment she'd decide to hate her self-appointed mentor, the woman would tantalize her with a promise that she couldn't ignore. Camille subjected her to discomfort, uncertainty, and danger, yet the last couple of nights had held a seductive excitement, too. Beginning to wonder whether Camille lived in this haphazard style all the time, Gillian asked, "What do you normally do? As an occupation, that is?"

"You mean work?" Camille gave a harsh laugh.

"Yes. Roger is a psychiatrist, Claude is an actor, my—Juliette writes novels, and Lord Volnar spends his time trouble-shooting—is that the word?—for our people. Don't you do anything in particular?"

With an exaggerated sigh, Camille said, "I can't believe you've been corrupted by the human work ethic. Surely you didn't get that from Volnar. I don't need to work for an income. Over the decades, with my investments under various aliases, I've accumulated enough wealth to live comfortably. And when I can't get at it, such as my present predicament, I can always take contributions from my victims. What else do they exist for?"

Gillian didn't express her misgivings about the hazards of this lifestyle, since by now she knew what answer she'd get. The idea of wandering around with no fixed goal or regular avocation, though, sounded boring to her. The excitement of hunting could fill only so many hours per night.

Picking up that thought, Camille said, "There are other things we can do with unlimited leisure. After all this is settled with Roger, we'll establish a permanent home, and you'll find out what I mean."

That idea wasn't totally unattractive to Gillian. But she wanted no part of helping Camille settle with Roger.

When Camille finally stopped the car again, they were near Route 2, Ritchie Highway, north of Annapolis. Even in the predawn hours, traffic on the four-lane highway was constant. "This isn't a good place to be in a stolen vehicle," said Camille as she turned off the highway in search of a less traveled area. After a period of apparently aimless driving she found a forested stretch of road that seemed to satisfy her wish for isolation. Leaving the car, they hiked through the woods for a couple of hours.

Only once did Gillian venture to ask what they were waiting for. "Daylight," Camille said. The tone didn't encourage further questions. She wouldn't allow Gillian to hunt. "I don't want you to lose your edge." The comment was a depressing reminder that Camille's friendliness was a mask for the desire to shape Gillian into a weapon.

At seven a.m., both of them squinting in the sun, for they hadn't had a chance to pick up dark glasses, Camille drove to a complex of drab buildings that sprawled beneath a self-storage billboard just off Route 2. Leaving Gillian in the car outside the gate, Camille rang the bell to summon the manager from his cottage at the entrance. Gillian watched her fill out a form and hand over cash.

Slipping into the driver's seat a moment later, Camille said, "We now have a place to sleep for the day."

"Here, in one of those—closets? Not a motel?"

"Too many people see us at motels," Camille said, backing up to turn around. "Thanks to your misbehavior, we have to be more careful."

Gillian understood that the new hiding place was partly designed as a punishment. "Why did you pay for it, if we're only going to sneak in anyway?"

"So the man won't rent it to someone else who might stumble on us, of course." Camille parked the car on a side street about a block from the storage complex, in front of a used-car lot that was deserted and apparently closed.

"Didn't he ask for identification when you signed the papers?" Since Camille carried no wallet, that request would be hard to answer.

"No, I pulled an Obi-wan Kenobi on him. Told him he didn't need to see my identification." Walking around to the trunk, Camille pulled out a rolled-up blanket. "Lucky this happens to be here. I wouldn't enjoy lying on a bare floor."

"Obi what?"

Camille arched her eyebrows. "Dark Powers, your education *has* been neglected! Volnar didn't let you watch science fiction films, either? What did he think, that you would develop delusions of being a Wookie?"

"Pardon?"

"Next time we have access to a television, I'll rent—" Camille broke off, staring at a police car that crawled along the narrow street. "Blast, we can't vanish when he's looking straight at us," she muttered. "Perhaps he won't stop."

He did, however. The patrol car drew level with them and halted.

The officer, a tall, wiry black man with a bushy moustache, walked to within a yard of Camille and said, "Ma'am, this car has been reported stolen. I'll have to see your license and registration."

"Why, I can't imagine what you mean," said Camille in a breathy voice. Her eyes wide in simulated fear, she continued, "There must be some kind of computer mix-up. Just a minute, and I'll get my ID."

When she walked to the driver's door, the policeman followed, as Camille had doubtless planned. Edging out of the way, Gillian watched from the sidewalk. Instead of opening the car door, Camille leaned against it and waited for the policeman to approach. "Your license, ma'am," he repeated.

She spread her hands in an appealing gesture. "Please, officer—" The words drew his eyes to hers. From that instant, he was lost. Unheeded, Gillian slid into Camille's mind. The lust that stirred in the man when the hypnotic spell overcame him made Gillian salivate. When Camille's teeth nipped his skin, his ecstatic convulsions rushed over Gillian like a gale-force wind. She doubled over, blinded and deafened by the sensations.

After the wave receded, she saw the man staring at Camille in a wide-eyed trance. Camille's fingers fluttered like insect wings over his face. "That was exhausting. You're very tired and not worried about anything. Get into your car, forget about me, and drive onto Route 2. You can't keep your eyes open. Once you're on the highway, you will fall asleep."

The officer nodded thoughtfully, as if she'd proposed that he head to McDonald's for a quick breakfast. A moment later, he was gone.

*But he could be killed!* Gillian knew better than to voice the protest. Camille didn't care. *That's what she is hiding! She doesn't care!* Camille made light of the risks because, deep inside, she didn't expect to survive this escapade. Sooner or later, she'd end up back in captivity—or dead, like Neil. Her mental barrier slammed shut before the two of them started walking away from the car, but Gillian knew she hadn't imagined that revelation.

All the talk about building a new life together in a simulated mother-daughter relationship was only a fantasy. Camille might believe it herself when she said it. But a deeper layer of her mind was bent on cramming the maximum gratification into what she expected to be a brief period of freedom.

Gillian strove to shield her thoughts as they headed for the storage complex, their psychic veils in place. If the manager chanced to peer out of his office, he wouldn't notice them strolling through the open gate and slipping under the barrier that limited access for cars. Sun glared on the pavement and the cinderblock rows of sheds. Camille led the way to the one she had claimed. Gillian scanned the new lair dispiritedly as they closed the door to shut out the day.

Thirsty, frustrated, unbathed, and frightened, she didn't relish sleeping in a five-by-eight-by-eight-foot cube on cold concrete. They had to brush away cobwebs before spreading the blanket. "If you please me tonight," Camille murmured as she lay down on her half, "tomorrow will be entirely different."

Gillian curled up on her side as far from the woman as possible. Fleetingly, she thought of escaping while Camille slept. But she knew the futility of that notion. Because of their bond, if Gillian ran away, if she so much as called Roger again, Camille would be instantly alerted.

*Or maybe not.* Gillian forced herself to remain half-awake while Camille succumbed to fatigue and fell into suspended animation. Slowly Gillian stood up, afraid to twitch a corner of the blanket, much less make noise. She clung to the memory of her exercise with Britt, imitating the human female's mental shield. Surely as a vampire, Gillian thought, she herself could block her thoughts better than an ephemeral. She visualized a smooth metal shell around her mind, as impregnable as a bomb-proof vault. Not a single wisp of thought must leak out.

The door of the shed didn't creak when she opened it just far enough to creep through. Nor did Camille's thoughts flare into wakefulness.

Breaking into a trot, Gillian headed for the gate. She'd noticed a pay phone by the entrance, and she had loose change in her jeans pocket. She dialed Roger's number, got the answering machine, and recited a quick message. With every second, she was terrified of Camille's waking and catching her. When she slipped back into the temporary lair, though, the woman still slept.

*I'm chained to her.* Though comatose, Camille held her prisoner. Against expectation, despite her fear, Gillian sank into oblivion. But the welcome darkness didn't last long. She dreamed of Juliette, of being torn from her mother's breast and flung onto the scorching heat of a sun-baked slab of rock.


JUST AS SHE finished playing the recording on the telephone, Britt heard the doorbell ring. For an instant she thought she was imagining it. Retying the sash of her robe, she went to the door, opened it with the chain on, and peeked out.

The fuzziness left from too little sleep cleared the moment she saw Eloise. "You're supposed to be at my place with Claude. What's up? Is he all right?"

Eloise stepped into the foyer, shutting out the cold. "Sure. He's dead to the world." She folded her arms when Britt tried to take her coat.

"So is Roger. Come into the kitchen." Though Britt hadn't expected Roger to sleep well today, considering the tension of the past weekend, exhaustion had plunged him into the normal daylight coma.

"Good, because they'd try to stop me." Eloise perched on the edge of a chair at the kitchen table. "I'm going to look for Camille and Gillian."

Britt froze at the counter with a hand on the coffeepot. "How?" Not that it mattered, given the message she'd just heard.

"And don't you try to talk me out of it. I came to ask you to go with me."

Pouring two cups of coffee, Britt said, "For heaven's sake, take off that coat. We aren't rushing out this instant, regardless."

With open reluctance, Eloise shrugged out of her heavy coat and draped it over the back of her chair. "I don't want to waste any time. I can't believe those two are sleeping away the entire day!"

"They're superhuman, but they aren't machines."

"Granted," said Eloise with an impatient shrug. "All the more reason why we should make use of the daylight hours. They're planning another visual search the way Roger did last night, aren't they?"

"They won't have to," Britt said. "Listen to this." She pushed the *Play* button on the answering machine.

"Roger, this is Gillian. Camille's rented a storage shed in a place just off Route 2 in Severna Park. Please hurry, before she wakes up. I can't talk anymore."

Eloise sprang to her feet. "Then what are we waiting for?"

"Hold on a minute. Have you eaten this morning?"

"Sort of. Orange juice."

"Insufficient," said Britt. She took two cups of strawberry yogurt from the refrigerator and plunked one in front of Eloise. "Doctor's orders."

"I don't feel like—"

"Have to keep up your strength if you want to be any use to Gillian."

Eloise picked up her spoon and dabbled in the yogurt. "We

shouldn't be wasting time," she said again.

"Then eat fast." Britt started on her own food. "But if Camille didn't wake up when Gillian sneaked away to phone us, she's not likely to do so before sunset."

"Are you coming with me? Without Roger and Claude."

Britt suppressed the urge to scold Eloise for that reckless notion. "You know what they'd think of that. They'd say we aren't equipped to handle Camille the way they are. And they'd have an excellent point."

Eloise's eyes hardened. "They don't own us." She took a sip of her black coffee. "You said yourself, they're exhausted. And a point in our favor that they tend to forget—she would sense a pair of vampires coming a hundred feet away. She won't be on subconscious alert against mere mortals."

"What do you figure on doing if we find her?"

"Not if, when. Young vampires need less sleep than adults, right?"

"So I've been told," Britt said.

"Then Gillian may be awake or sleeping lightly. And we know she wants to be found. When she hears us prowling around, she'll come out to meet us, and maybe we can get her away without disturbing Camille at all."

"Maybe." Britt thought the idea sounded farfetched, though not totally impossible. "If it's that simple, why doesn't she just escape on her own while Camille's unconscious?"

"I've wondered that, too. But we can't waste time speculating about it." Eloise's eyes shone with threatened tears. "We can't just abandon her!"

Britt pushed aside her empty bowl and leaned across the table. "Gillian means a great deal to you, considering how short a time you've known her."

Eloise nodded, wiping her eyes with a napkin.

"At the risk of sounding like a shrink," said Britt, "could this feeling be related to the loss of your baby? Because you couldn't save the baby, saving Gillian is especially important to you?"

"Maybe." Eloise gave her a guarded look from under damp eyelashes. "Does there have to be a subliminal reason? Can't I worry about her just because she's a child in trouble?"

"That, too," said Britt. "So do I. But I'm not sure aiding and abetting you in charging to the rescue without weapons or backup is the best way to help."

"If you don't feel able to come with me, I'll go alone."

With a sigh Britt stood up to clear the table. "Blackmailer. You know darn well I won't let you do that."

"Then let's get started."

"Okay, I'll drive, and you navigate." After stashing the dishes in the dishwasher, Britt got dressed, then collected the phone book and a street map of the Annapolis-Baltimore area from Roger's office. She decided against leaving a note for him. If he woke before they returned, he would quickly discover where she'd gone. Leaving a message would neither increase nor decrease his anger at the risk they were taking.

Eloise sat in the right-hand seat of Britt's kelly green Porsche and checked the index against the street addresses of self-storage companies in Arnold, Severna Park, and other communities along Route 2. Gillian, after all, didn't know the area well; she might not have identified the location correctly. "I never expected there'd be so many," Eloise said, flipping through the yellow pages. "Too bad she didn't stay on the phone long enough to give the name of the place."

After making a list of likely hideouts, they visited each one in turn, cruising the parking lots for a glimpse of the car Camille was supposed to have been driving last. At least, Britt reflected as they ticked off prospect after prospect, they had a clear day for the quest, rather than the nasty weather so common in December.

"I'm not suggesting we give up," she said as they restarted the car after a pit stop at a gas station, "but don't get your hopes too high. Look at how many entries we have left to check."

"If you don't have any better suggestion, I'll keep going until I've run out of places. You suit yourself."

Eloise's intensity worried Britt. "Oh, I'm sticking with you. I promised that. But have you forgotten Camille's driving a stolen car? What if the police have already picked it up?"

Eloise said with a wan smile, "Are you telling me the police in your area are so underworked they can afford to give high priority to a missing vehicle? Even one involved in a murder case?"

Britt couldn't help chuckling at that notion. "You do have a point. The car may well be sitting right where she left it when they holed up for the day."

So the two women continued their circuit of a dreary succession of storage complexes, which all began to look alike after a few hours. Britt insisted they break for lunch at one. Eloise would recover from her depression more rapidly with proper nourishment. They refueled on a reasonable facsimile thereof at a fast food restaurant in a small shopping strip. Britt nudged Eloise toward the broiled chicken breast sandwich and overruled her suggestion that they eat on the road.

Tucked into a corner booth with a view of two toddlers spinning on a merry-go-round shaped like a giant hamburger, Britt said between nibbles, "Do you still feel the same way about trying to conceive again?"

"I won't change my mind."

"What does Claude think about that?"

"I haven't asked him." Eloise dispiritedly plucked at a lettuce leaf dangling from her bun. "I know what he'd say. He would endorse the idea out of a sense of duty. I don't want to be an obligation."

Britt refrained from expressing her opinion that Claude saw his bond-mate in entirely different terms. "Have you considered adoption?"

"Are you kidding?" Eloise glanced around and lowered her voice. "Adopting a human baby would be out of the question. I can barely see Claude as a father to one of his own kind. A human child—no way. And what woman of his race would give her baby to an ephemeral?"

Britt had to concede that she had a point. Few vampires were sympathetic to Volnar's interbreeding project. "Surrogate motherhood? If you're convinced that your body can't support a hybrid fetus, what about *in vitro* fertilization—your ovum, Claude's sperm—with the embryo implanted in a vampire mother?"

"Same objection. Where would we find a female willing to have her body used that way? And there's the added complication that they're capable of pregnancy only once every few years."

Britt gave up on the argument. With Eloise in this *yes, but* mood, no rationale would change her mind. Only the healing influence of time might accomplish that.

Tossing her salad with the plastic fork, Eloise stared at Britt with a thoughtful frown that made her uncomfortable. "Enough about me. What about you? I know you had your tubes tied at age thirty-five. But have you ever thought of adopting?"

"I admit visiting my sister, Darlene, and her kids puts me in a might-have-been mood sometimes. On the other hand, the idea of all that responsibility and loss of freedom is pretty scary."

"Physician, heal thyself. How can you blame *me* for being scared?"

"I don't blame you a bit. I never meant to imply blame." Britt crumpled a sandwich wrapper in her fist. "If I'd never met Roger and had married an ordinary guy, I might have considered it. But I don't see myself as the single parent type. As for Roger, even if we lived together, Gillian gives him more than enough to deal with." She forced a smile. "This *road not taken* stuff isn't very productive. We make our choices and live with them. I have no regrets."

"I envy you." Eloise bowed her head on her hands. "Oh, God, Britt, I'm so confused. Maybe you're right, maybe I hope rescuing Gillian will get me un-confused."

After Britt had nagged Eloise into finishing her lunch, they bundled up to face the clear, cold day again. A few steps from the car Eloise stopped to look up at the sign over a bookstore two doors down the row of shops. "Start warming the engine while I run in here. There's something I want to pick up."

Wondering what had suddenly changed Eloise's frantic need for haste, Britt complied. Within a couple of minutes Eloise emerged carrying a small paper bag, which she stashed in the back seat without volunteering any explanation.

In view of her dejected mood, Britt decided not to bug her with questions. They hit the road in silence. The problem wasn't so much the length of their list of possibilities as the travel time from one to the next, with traffic congestion and wrong turns constantly delaying them. By late afternoon, Eloise drooped with fatigue, clearly beginning to accept Britt's estimate of the long odds they faced.

The sky was growing dim with the onset of twilight. Aside from the danger of facing an emotionally unstable vampire after dark, Britt preferred to minimize Roger's annoyance by getting home, if possible, before he awoke.

They crept along side streets, Eloise reading directions from the relevant page in the map book. In the gathering gloom the warehouses and abandoned used car dealership they passed impressed Britt as more threatening than any Gothic haunted mansion.

She was peering ahead, trying to get her bearings on the self-storage billboard they'd glimpsed from the highway, when Eloise cried, "Britt, I think that's the one!"

Braking, Britt checked the license plate of the car parked at the curb against the wrinkled scrap of notepaper bearing the stolen vehicle's description. Not that she needed to, since by now they had both memorized the data. She felt an involuntary grin spread across her face. "Well, I'll be damned."

Chapter Fourteen

AT ONCE THE gathering gloom of dusk felt thicker. Britt flicked on the high beams to confirm her first impression that the car was empty. "Looks like we found them." Her heart raced. She was having second and third thoughts about not having brought Roger along.

She drove around the block and up to the main gate of the storage complex. A white cottage, apparently part office and part home, stood guard just outside the chain-link fence. "You wait in the car. No need to descend in force on whoever watches this place." Britt strode to the cottage and rapped on the door. In the back of her head she felt a stirring as Roger began to rise from the depths of his day-sleep. She ignored it.

No one answered her first knock. She knocked harder. A minute later she heard slow footsteps approaching. A burly man with salt-and-pepper hair and a matching moustache yanked open the door. "What's the matter, can't you read?" He pointed to a hand-printed sign next to the door—*Business Hours, 7 A.M. to 4:30 P.M. Only.* "Christ, you'd think I could eat supper in peace!"

To judge from the TV noise in the background, he was eating in front of the evening news. "I'm terribly sorry to bother you," Britt said, "and I won't keep you long." She reached into her purse for the first bill she came across in her wallet, which happened to be a ten. "A friend was supposed to meet us here so we could help her unload some stuff, and we're getting concerned that she hasn't shown."

The manager's expression mellowed a degree at the sight of the ten-dollar bill. "I ain't seen anybody for a couple of hours."

"She's a tall, thin woman with black hair," said Britt, not sure whether to mention the child. She maintained eye contact with the man; though she couldn't hypnotize instantaneously as Roger might, she hoped to exert psychic pressure to make the manager suggestible.

"Maybe you mean Miss Karnstein?"

"Karnstein?" *Oh, Lord, talk about chutzpah!* "Yes, Carmilla Karnstein. When was she here?"

"Yeah, that's the name. She rented a slot early this morning, right after I opened. I ain't seen her since."

"Maybe she came in while you were busy, and she's waiting for us inside." Britt gave a subliminal nudge, wishing she could do that as reliably as a vampire could. "Which unit did she take? I can go look for her and not bother you anymore."

The man showed no suspicion, just impatience. "She's in B-thirty-seven. Now, can I get back to my supper before it freezes to the goddamn plate?"

"Yes, please do. Thank you for your help. Don't worry about anything."

He slammed the door. Hoping he would stay safely occupied until they were gone, Britt returned to the car. "We don't have the code for the vehicle gate, so we'll just walk in," she said after repeating the conversation to Eloise. Britt extracted a flashlight from the glove compartment. In the alleys formed by the rows of cinderblock buildings, between the infrequently placed floodlights pools of darkness lay in ambush. Her heart raced like a caged mouse in an exercise wheel. Vampires could well be awake by now. Camille, invisible, could be watching them from any patch of shadow.

Roger's nagging presence in Britt's mind became impossible to ignore. She acknowledged him. [Where the blazes are you, and what do you think you're doing?] he demanded.

She told him. [Stop distracting me. I didn't think it was a great idea, either, but we're here now.]

[Good God, Britt, of all the harebrained stunts—Retreat and stay out of sight until I can get there.]

[Absolutely not. By then, Camille will be awake for sure. Now we still have a chance to catch her off guard.]

When Britt refused to answer any further objections, Roger stopped talking. She still, however, felt his disapproval weighing on her.

"Carmilla Karnstein—do you believe it?" Eloise whispered as they tiptoed over the blacktop, imagining that their every step reverberated through the cement canyons. "She's ready for a confrontation. What else could that mean? She's throwing out a challenge."

"Let's hope we can evade it, the way you planned," Britt said. She flashed the light at the nearest row of identical doors, trying to get her bearings. The numbering system didn't follow an immediately discernible logic. She veered in the direction where she thought B-thirty-seven should be.

Six minutes later by her watch, though Britt felt she'd been wandering for an hour, they located the end of the row that included

Camille's storage shed. "Looks depressing, doesn't it?" Britt said. "The humiliation of stooping to this couldn't improve her temper." A blaze of anger from Roger assailed Britt's mind. A reaction to her own nervousness? She reflected it back to him and felt him struggle for calm.

"This time I take the lead," said Eloise. "You stay here for backup. If Camille is awake, we can't give her a chance to grab us both at once."

Much as she hated hanging back while her friend plunged into danger, Britt had to agree. The fact that they hadn't been attacked yet gave her hope. Either Camille was still dormant, or she wasn't there at all. Unless, of course, she was waiting until they crept up to the door to pounce on them.

*Stop scaring yourself. Strong emotion can make you a target. So calm down and quit broadcasting, already!*

Britt couldn't tell how nervous Eloise was. Eloise edged along the building with a faint smile on her lips, as if the joy of taking positive action outweighed all the negatives. A couple of feet from the closed door she reached out to tap with her fingernails and spoke Gillian's name.

No answer. Britt clutched the flashlight in a sweat-slick hand, reminding herself to stay put, not to increase the risk by any rash outburst.

Eloise said, "Gillian, are you in there? It's us, Britt and Eloise. Please come out and talk to me."

The door inched open. Eloise sprang back. The opening widened just enough to admit a human form. Gillian sidled out. She immediately closed the door behind her.

A gleam of red in her eyes, she stared at Eloise, who retreated several yards from the building. "Come with us, Gillian," she said softly. "Hurry, before she wakes."

Gillian took one step in Eloise's direction. "You should not be here without protection. Why didn't Roger come?"

As quietly as she could manage, though painfully conscious of the tap of her shoes on the pavement, Britt walked up beside Eloise. "Don't worry about that. Come on, we have to get you away from that creature."

Gillian's eyes flashed between the two women. "You don't understand. Camille will destroy you. She doesn't care about the risk— she kills. If I go with you, she'll track us down."

Eloise clenched her fists in frustration. "No, I don't understand!

Let's get out of here, and you can explain later."

Gillian glanced over her shoulder at the door she'd emerged from. "I can't escape her. We are bonded. She—forced me." She lowered her eyes as if ashamed of the admission. "I do not want to cause your death."

Eloise stepped forward and clasped Gillian's hands. The girl flinched but neither pulled free nor attacked. "I won't abandon you to that—monster," said Eloise, tears trickling down her cheeks.

Suddenly Britt saw the door behind them swing open. Britt swept the flashlight beam across the space. She saw only a shadow that flitted across her field of vision.

An instant later Camille materialized beside Eloise.

Before Britt could move, Camille wrenched Eloise from Gillian's grasp. Leaping backward, dragging Eloise with her, the vampire woman stood with her back against the wall. One arm encircled Eloise's waist, pinning her arms to her side. Camille's other hand covered Eloise's mouth and bent her head sideways to expose her neck above the coat collar.

"Please," Gillian hissed. "There is no reason to harm her."

For an answer, Camille grinned and leaned over to bare her teeth an inch from Eloise's throat.

AT THE DOOR of Britt's apartment Roger barely paused for a mental probe. The stillness instantly told him Claude was asleep and wouldn't hear a knock. *Still asleep, this far into twilight?* Using his key to open the door, Roger felt a pleasant coolness; they had turned the heat down to sixty or so. He hurried to the main bedroom.

A ghost of Britt's fragrance lingered in the room. Claude lay face down on the queen-size bed, naked, with the sheets flung back to expose him to the cool air. His lack of response to Roger's steady gaze revealed the depth of Claude's weariness. Roger wouldn't have disturbed him for anything less than this emergency.

"Claude, wake up." No response. *This is worse than I thought.* He placed a hand on his brother's bare shoulder and began to turn him over.

Claude exploded out of torpor. Face contorted in a growl, his eyes aflame, he pounced like a rabid tiger. He threw Roger to the floor and landed on top of him, going for his throat. The mindless rage scalded Roger, clouding his mind also. He barely managed to raise an arm to block the attack. Claude's teeth slashed his wrist.

Claude's frenzy detonated inside Roger's skull, blazed through his veins. Unthinkingly he backhanded Claude and leaped on him. Kneeling on Claude's chest, Roger clamped his hands around his brother's neck. He couldn't distinguish between his own panic and rage and the other's.

A silent cry from Britt pierced the crimson fog like a laser beam. Roger let out a long, trembling breath. He shifted his grip from neck to shoulders, digging his nails into Claude's flesh. The scent of Claude's blood, mingled with his own, stung his nose. "Wake up!"

When he saw recognition in Claude's eyes, he stood up. Claude pulled himself cautiously to his feet. "Damn it, you should know better! Can you imagine how close you came to getting your throat ripped out?"

Roger compressed his wrist and concentrated to stop the bleeding. "I didn't realize you were operating on a hair trigger. You were so deep under—"

"Well, you should have!" Claude snarled. He rubbed at the oozing scratches on one shoulder.

*Yes, I should—I saw how edgy he's been the last couple of days.* Cut off from communion with his lover, Claude was suffering from withdrawal like any addict deprived of a drug.

Claude reached for the clothes he'd left folded on the brocade-covered chair. "You've matured, little brother. Ten years ago you couldn't have taken me. Well, what's so damned urgent?"

"Britt and Eloise—"

Claude went rigid, eyes blank. His inner senses blasted open by the violent clash and the shedding of blood, Roger *felt* Claude groping along the psychic cord that linked him to Eloise. A second later Claude erupted into action, scrambling into his clothes. "Bloody hell, what are they doing?"

"Eloise had some farfetched scheme of tracking down Camille and Gillian and using herself as bait. Britt went along to keep an eye on her. It seems they've found their quarry."

Fingers flying down a row of shirt buttons, Claude said, "Why didn't Britt stop her? And her leaving didn't wake me—" His hurt seared Roger's own chest like a raw wound. "Are we really that far out of touch?"

"Not necessarily," Roger said. "I didn't sense Britt leaving either. Both of us are simply worn out."

Claude pulled on a black turtleneck over the half-buttoned shirt and shuffled into his shoes. "If Eloise took the rented car over to your place, we're stuck with your Citroen."

"Yes, and I'm driving. You don't know the area well enough, and Britt has already given me directions."

"Agreed." They raced downstairs and around the block to the cul-de-sac where the car was parked.

All the way across the river to Interstate 97, Claude fidgeted. Early evening on a Monday was the worst possible time to make any speed between Annapolis and Severna Park, but Roger figured they would get there faster by following the freeway to the exit nearest their destination than crawling up Ritchie Highway past innumerable traffic lights. Claude's fear made Roger feel as if he were standing naked in an icy wind. *I'm too open to him—I don't like this at all!* When they finally turned off 97 onto Route 2, Claude cursed under his breath at the line of traffic stretching into the distance. "Can't you step on it? Pass the blasted idiots and get moving!"

"Not unless you want to lose five more minutes dealing with one of Anne Arundel County's finest. And to answer your next question, there's no practical shortcut by way of side roads."

Claude subsided, glaring out the window at the stretch of woods that flanked the highway. Roger said, "Try to relax. You won't do any good by gnawing both of us to death with anxiety. Britt and Eloise are safe thus far. Here's the intersection. We're almost there."

Minutes later, he felt Britt scream inside his head. Through her eyes, he saw Camille grab Eloise.

*I'M NOT PREPARED for this!* Britt squeezed the flashlight, wishing it were a gun. *No, I'd probably end up shooting Eloise. I didn't seriously believe we'd find them, or I'd have thought to bring a weapon.*

"Let her go," Gillian persisted. "She's done nothing to harm you." She fingered the cross at her neck in an oddly human gesture of anxiety.

"Human standards of justice don't matter to us," Camille said. "For my purpose, one ephemeral is much like another." She spread her fingers to cover Eloise's mouth and nose at once. Freeing her other hand, she slammed her fist into Eloise's temple.

Eloise wilted, stunned. Hoisting the unconscious woman in her arms, Camille bounded like a doe toward the back of the complex.

Gillian stared after her, then threw an anxious glance at Britt. "If I don't come with her, she will—" Gillian raced after Camille.

To Britt's eyes, Camille seemed to flicker in and out of existence as she ran from light into shadow and out again. Britt thought she saw the vampire's upper torso sprout luminously pale wings. *Here? She can't be that reckless!* Britt trailed after Gillian, who ran in Camille's wake. Scarcely able to keep them in sight, Britt glimpsed only darting silhouettes.

At the rear of the buildings she caught up in time to witness Camille soaring over the high chain-link fence, still carrying Eloise. With a glint of red-tinged eyes, Gillian glanced back at Britt, then scaled the fence. Near the top her climb merged into a leap, so that for an instant she seemed suspended in the air. She sprang to the ground on the other side running so fast that Britt saw only a blur. Camille, however, gliding overhead in her winged form, provided a clear reference point.

Britt wasted no time staring after the fugitive. She ran for the entrance at an uneven pace, her shoulder purse awkwardly thumping against her side. Her lungs labored; she was used to jogging, not sprinting. Gulping the cold air made her throat sore. Scrambling under the vehicle barrier, she dashed for the car. Her hand shook when she tried to jam the key into the ignition. She knew she needed to collect herself with a few deep breaths but was afraid of wasting the minute or two that would take.

*What's the hurry?* she thought as she whipped the car around. *She'll wait for me. She wants me to follow her; why else would she make such a flashy exit? Eloise is just bait for me and Roger.*

Sure enough, Camille hovered in the sky less than a mile away, circling like a giant, moth-winged vulture. *I wonder how many UFO reports we'll see in the paper tomorrow?* Britt steered the car in the direction of her quarry's flight. In the back of her mind she felt Roger approaching.

The side streets feeding onto Ritchie Highway bustled with going-home traffic. Perhaps, after all, few people would notice the creature gliding overhead; they were too busy watching stoplights and competing for gaps in the passing lane. Camille seemed to be flying parallel to the highway. After several minutes she veered off to the right.

Muttering curses, Britt inched into the right lane of the feeder road she was on and cut through a restaurant's parking lot. An irate chorus of horns beeped behind her. The chase led her toward an unfinished stretch of the projected Route 50 extension. When Camille began to drift downward, Britt found herself pulling up to a spur of roadway blocked with cones and *Do Not Enter* signs. She parked on the shoulder and got out. Camille had sunk out of sight behind the trees. Rather than deal with the encumbrance, Britt locked her purse in the car and tucked the keys in her slacks pocket.

She trotted up the unfinished grade, past the hulks of deserted earth-moving equipment. Blacktop soon gave way to dirt and gravel. Britt caught herself panting again. *Good grief, I thought I was in better shape.* Rounding a curve, she froze.

The site was a future overpass. Vehicle lights and the roar of engines below told her she was standing above a four-lane highway. Camille stood about a yard from the edge, her arms clasping Eloise around the waist. There was no railing. The quiver of Camille's wings suggested she might glide aloft at any second. Gillian confronted her from a few feet away.

Britt wished she had the night vision to distinguish details. Gillian bent forward, her arms reaching, as if poised to spring but afraid to. Her eyes gleamed like Camille's. Eloise stirred feebly in her captor's grip.

"Isn't this what you want?" Camille hissed the words. "Come and take her. She wants to serve you—she will enjoy it. Haven't you been yearning for just this chance?"

"Not like this!" Gillian cried.

"I'm disappointed in you. Haven't you listened to anything I've said? Her life is no longer than a butterfly's compared to yours. Why should a few years, more or less, keep you from sharing that pleasure with her? Come on, prove you deserve to be one of us."

Gillian raised her arms, fists clenched. "Claude is purebred, and he doesn't treat them like animals. I would rather enjoy them the way he does."

"For what? At most, one of their brief lifetimes. And then what are you left with? Nothing but a grief our kind should be above."

"Gillian, don't listen!" Britt called. "Camille, stop playing games. You don't want Eloise. You want me. Let her go, and I'll surrender to you." She felt the pressure of Camille's eyes upon her. "You know I'm not lying. I'm ready to face you. Or are you too much of a coward to handle a donor who's not unconscious or scared witless?"

"Why should I make a trade," Camille said, "when Gillian and I can have both of you?"

RORGER FOLLOWED BRITT'S silent call to the half-finished road. Beside him Claude expelled loud, hissing breaths and exuded a rage that shimmered in the air like a scarlet mist.

"Steady," Roger said as he braked behind Britt's Porsche. "We can't help them by losing control."

The truism was lost on Claude, who leaped out of the car before the wheels stopped spinning. Together they raced up the curve to the incomplete overpass. The tableau that faced them shocked even Claude into immobility.

Camille held them in checkmate. At their slightest move to attack she could fling Eloise onto the highway below. Eloise's eyelashes fluttered. She let out a moan, then suddenly doubled over in Camille's loose embrace, retching. Nothing came out. When she straightened up, she shivered in the frigid wind but met the newcomers' eyes with a weak smile. Roger and Claude flanked Britt, watching Gillian edge toward Camille.

"I don't want this," Gillian said. "If I aid you in stealing Claude's—lover, I'll be as outcast as you are."

With a snarl Camille jerked on Eloise's hair. Eloise emitted an involuntary groan but refused to scream. "Too late, cub, you're already an outcast—as my bond-mate, what else can you be? Our destinies are linked. Come here and satisfy your hunger. Haven't you heard, a knowing victim who's been had by someone else makes the best of all feasts."

Roger felt bloodlust pouring off Camille, immersing Gillian, who inched forward like steel to a magnet. *She craves human blood! How could this happen? She's too young.*

"What's stopping you?" Camille's attention focused on taunting Gillian. She held Eloise loosely, almost casually, as if trusting in her strength to thwart any attempt at flight. "Are you still trying to be part human? It's hopeless, so why waste energy on it? You'll always be a monster to them."

"Not to Britt and Eloise." Gillian panted with thirst.

"Yes, even them. Why do you think they want to feed you? Because they're sorry for you. Poor freak—poor little monster! Is that what you want? To twist your nature out of shape just to earn pity from your inferiors?"

Gillian's lips writhed in a sound between a snarl and a moan.

"Gillian, she's lying!" Britt cried. "My feelings are open to you. You know that isn't how I see you!"

"Are you prepared to spend eternity as neither fish nor fowl?" Camille persisted. "Take her! Don't wait for their pity to give you what is yours by right. Claim what you need—show me you're really one of us!"

In a predatory crouch with her fingers curved like talons, Gillian crept closer. Her mind boiled with such confusion that Roger couldn't sort out the emotions she projected. Grinning, Camille scored Eloise's neck with her index fingernail. The sharp scent of blood pierced the frosty air.

A growl rumbled in Claude's chest. Roger, unable to shut out what Claude projected, sensed his muscles knotted with the agony of restraint.

"Don't do it," Britt whispered.

Eloise rested limp in Camille's grasp. While Camille's eyes bored into Gillian, Eloise tilted her head as if in invitation. She slowly turned in Camille's embrace and put an arm around the vampire's shoulders. Distracted from Gillian, Camille looked down at her unexpectedly cooperative victim.

Eloise reached over Camille's shoulder to the nearer of the shimmering wings. She grabbed the delicate membrane and gave it a fierce wrench. Camille howled in torment. Her pain blazed out, engulfing Roger.

In the back of his mind he was thankful that the traffic noise on the highway would drown out her scream. He watched Eloise break free and run. She lurched out of the vampire's reach and fell headlong on the ground. Instantly Claude leaped between his wife and Camille.

Roger helped Eloise to her feet, keeping one eye on Camille. Simultaneously, Gillian lashed out at Camille with all the force of her revulsion. Along the enforced bond that linked them, the child's rage crackled like a bolt of electricity down a lightning rod. Roger saw Camille's aura coruscate with the untamed energy.

Chained by the tie of her own making, Camille had no defense against Gillian's anger. Collapsing to her hands and knees at the edge of the drop-off, the woman convulsed in agony. Her appearance oscillated from human to beast and back again, finally subsiding into her normal shape. To Roger's ears, the wind that gusted around them seemed shot through with peals of thunder. It took him a moment to realize that the roar sounded only inside his head.

Claude lunged toward Camille. Their auras clashed like a pair of exposed high-tension wires crossing in a cascade of sparks. The woman struggled to rise and face her attacker. She succeeded only in getting up on one knee before Claude seized her. With one hand knotted in the tangle of her unbound black hair, he slashed her throat with the claws of his other hand.

Blood spurted from a severed artery. The metallic scent stung Roger's nose. His head spinning, he hastily let go of Eloise, dimly sensing her stagger but not fall. Out of the corner of his eye, he saw

Gillian double over, stabbed by Camille's pain.

His whole body vibrating with the growl that issued from his throat, Claude gripped Camille's head between both of his hands. For an instant their eyes met, both glowing crimson, one with pain and the other with hate. An image from fourteen years past flashed into Roger's mind—his own hands gripping Camille's brother exactly that way. He envisioned Claude twisting the woman's head off.

"Claude, no!" He sprang to his brother's side. "You do not want to do this!" Roger himself, though brought up with human standards of justice, had scarcely been able to deal with his killing of Neil Sandor. To this day, calling it *execution* sometimes struck him as hypocritical. Once the tide of fury ebbed, how would Claude deal with the fact of being a kin-slayer? All his life he'd been taught to view that deed as the ultimate taboo.

At first Roger was afraid Claude wouldn't even be able to hear him. He lightly touched his brother's arm. Without releasing Camille, Claude turned on Roger with a snarl.

Staring into his eyes, Roger said, "Is your revenge worth the risk of becoming an outcast like her? Is she worth doing this to yourself?"

Though it nauseated him, Roger deliberately summoned up the image of Sandor's death. He gathered all his revulsion and self-doubt and flung them at his brother. He felt Claude mentally recoil as if he'd taken a blow to the heart.

Claude's animal sounds changed to heavy breathing. After a visible struggle, he managed to speak. "You saw what she did to Eloise."

"By vampire law, does that merit death?"

"You'd do the same thing in my place."

"I'd want to," Roger admitted. "But we're talking about you. Do you want that memory for the rest of your life? Claude—do you want to force Eloise to share a memory like that?"

A shudder coursed through Claude. He let go of the woman's head and stepped back.

Too weak to flee, Camille pressed one hand to her bleeding neck and glared up at Roger. He clamped onto her arm. "Listen to me. Volnar is on his way here with your advisor. No matter how many years her bond with you has been dormant, it still exists. They'll track you down. Why make matters worse by continuing to run?"

A gurgle welled up from Camille's ravaged throat. After a couple of seconds, the blood stopped gushing. Roger was astonished that she had the strength to control it. "I won't go back! I won't let them lock me in that living death again!"

Her panic reverberated in Roger's mind like the clang of a giant bell. He shouted over it, "Surrender of your own free will, and that may not happen!"

"Don't lie to me!" In an unexpected surge of energy, she snatched her arm from Roger and kicked out to trip him.

Instantly Claude was at his side. Roger leaped up, and together they held her at bay on the edge of the precipice. "You can't escape capture," Roger repeated. "If nothing else, we can track you through Gillian."

"Gillian—" Camille choked on the name. "Betrayed me—" She gazed past the two men at the child. "Then I'll take you with me, cub!"

Roger expected her to charge at Gillian. Instead, Camille sprang up and whirled in midair. She dove headfirst for the highway below.

Dashing to the drop-off, he watched Camille hurtle toward the pavement. At the same instant, through his bond with Britt, he saw her fling herself at Gillian.

"Gillian, don't watch!" Britt cried. She tackled the girl, caught her off balance, and tumbled to the ground with her.

Camille's skull impacted on the blacktop in the headlights of an eighteen-wheeler. The driver tried to swerve too late. His right front wheels rolled over the woman's head as the truck screeched to a stop. A voice in a numbed fragment of Roger's brain noted, *She chose her moment well. Deliberately.*

A car rear-ended the eighteen-wheeler, while traffic around them skidded off the road onto the shoulder. Roger forced his eyes away from the wreckage. An siren-like wail burst from Gillian. Her claws gouged the fabric of Britt's coat. Britt projected no fear, only a yearning to give comfort.

"Gillian, it's over. Break out of it! Look at me!" She gave the keening child a vigorous shake.

Though terrified that Gillian would strike at Britt in her torment, Roger didn't dare interfere. Eloise and Claude, clinging to each other, also watched, helpless.

Gillian's scream cut off. Immobile, she stared blankly at Britt.

"She tried to punish you with her death agony," Britt said. "Don't let her win! You're free of her!"

Absorbing Britt's words, Roger understood Camille's final threat. Yes, Camille had meant to drive Gillian into madness by forcing the girl to share her death. Roger prayed Britt's intervention had blunted the edge of the experience.

Gillian blinked. The fire faded from her eyes. "Britt?"

"Is she—gone?" Britt asked.

Gillian closed her eyes for a second. "Yes. When I reach for her, I touch nothingness. She is dead." She collapsed on Britt's shoulder.

Chapter Fifteen

SIRENS ULULATED IN the distance. Roger knelt beside Britt and Gillian to put his arms around both of them together. "We can't stay here. We have to get away before the police swarm all over this area."

Britt stood up, pulling an unresisting Gillian with her. "I second that." She dug out her car keys and threw them to Claude. "You two can use my car."

Gillian clutched Britt's wrist. "Stay with me!"

"Of course I will. We're both riding with Roger."

Gillian clung to Britt all the way down to the cars. Just before they separated for the drive, Roger gave Claude and Eloise a long, penetrating look. They meshed with the harmony that had been absent for almost a week.

Correctly interpreting Roger's silent question, Eloise said in an exhausted but serene voice, "Yes, I'm seeing straight again. When we thought Camille was about to—to kill me, I felt Claude's reaction. He wasn't in agony over losing a food source or a drug. And when you said that about his imposing a horrible memory on me—well, I know he cares."

"And about time, too," Claude said as he opened the car door for her. His voice quivered with a strain that belied the teasing words.

"All those doubts—they already seem like a mirage," said Eloise as she belted herself in. She was speaking to Claude, not the rest of them.

Seconds later, both cars accelerated back toward the freeway. This time, Roger took care to stay within a five-mile-per-hour standard deviation from the speed limit. The last thing they needed right now was to draw official notice.

On the way home, Gillian maintained a desperate grip on Britt's hand. So far, Roger's fear that the child would either sink into catatonia or go raving mad and attack proved unfounded. He felt her folding in upon herself as if shielding an open wound. When they turned onto the traffic-free lane leading to the townhouse, her tension slackened. She must have been so sensitized by the psychic detonation of Camille's suicide that the emotions of strangers, even through layers of metal in automobiles, tortured her like breathing poison gas.

When Roger parked the car, he noticed that Claude and Eloise had fallen behind and were nowhere in sight. No surprise there.

Once he and Britt got Gillian inside, with the door bolted, she released her hold on Britt. "Thank you for your help," she said in a subdued tone, fingering her cross. "Perhaps I should not be touching you."

"Why?" said Britt, though she doubtless felt the hunger Gillian projected.

"I might lose control." Gillian's voice quavered. "She—Camille allowed me to taste human blood through her senses."

"She deliberately taught you—" Roger stifled his anger. Violent emotion wouldn't help the girl.

"Yes. I can't be trusted near Britt now." She stood in the middle of the front hall with her head bowed, as if expecting a slap.

Beckoning her to the stairs, Britt said, "Now, stop that! We trust you. If you were going to break out in a feeding frenzy, you'd have done it by now. Go take a shower, and you'll feel better."

While Britt and Gillian went upstairs, Roger headed for the office to check the answering machine. Switching it on in response to the blinking light, he heard Volnar's voice:

"I'm calling from London. I've made contact with Lilias, Camille's advisor. She has agreed—with considerable reluctance—to track Camille for us. We'll be leaving in approximately three hours." He concluded with a telephone number.

Roger dialed the number, which turned out to be a hotel, and was connected with Volnar. "Don't bother bringing this Lilias back with you," he said when the Prime Elder answered. "You're too late."

"Are you saying you've captured Camille on your own?" Volnar's voice conveyed his usual infuriating calm, no sign of surprise or anxiety.

"She's dead," said Roger. "Suicide."

A moment of silence was all the reaction he got. Then Volnar said, "You are absolutely certain?"

"No doubt whatsoever. I saw her skull crushed. Furthermore, she had forced a blood exchange on Gillian, who confirmed the death."

"That's very unfortunate," Volnar said. "Camille is the last person I would have chosen to exercise that crucial an influence over the child."

"Damn it, is that all you can say? There's no telling how deeply she may be scarred!"

"I agree with your assessment," said Volnar, "but there is no point in letting your emotions run amok. We must rationally consider how best to treat her. Did she experience Camille's death?"

"I'm not sure how much of it she shared." Sitting back in the swivel chair at the desk, Roger forced himself to match Volnar's calm, at least outwardly. He described Britt's intervention and explained how Camille had deliberately stimulated Gillian's appetite for human blood.

"That is *most* unfortunate," Volnar said. "Gillian is too young. However, there's no turning back. Once the craving has been awakened, it must be satisfied."

"I was afraid of that," Roger said.

"I shall be landing at BWI Airport tomorrow afternoon, your time. Needless to say, I'll collect her from you as soon as possible."

*Collect her!* "Just like that? You think I'll be glad to have her taken off my hands?"

"Won't you?" Volnar's tone gave no hint of his thoughts.

"It's not that simple. She is my daughter, confound it!" A relationship that meant nothing in Volnar's world-view. "My original resolution stands. I won't turn her over to you against her will. But I suspect she's ready to return, provided you don't terrify her."

"Roger, you must have a very low opinion of my intelligence."

"No, it's your sensitivity I question. If you want me to cooperate, you must promise not to force a blood-bond on her. Not after what she's been through."

"Certainly not. Really, my young friend, do you suppose I've educated hundreds of children by purposely terrorizing them?"

"I don't know you well enough to judge." Despite their bond, Roger had held Volnar at arm's length as much as possible, and Volnar had never insisted on any contact other than superficial. Roger didn't feel up to sparring with his mentor, but there was one statement he had to make. "I've come to a decision. Gillian is not just a vampire. As my daughter, she is part human and deserves exposure to human values. That facet of her psyche needs to be cultivated."

"Indeed? Most of our people would say that such an upbringing would only confuse her." The cool tone betrayed neither approval nor disapproval.

"What the blazes do they know about human growth and character development? That's my specialty, and I'm convinced that Gillian will suffer more if that side of her personality is suppressed. Damn it, do you want her emotionally stunted?"

"On what do you base this conclusion," Volnar said, "aside from the questionably valid theories of psychoanalysis?"

Roger warned himself not to let Volnar prod him into losing his temper. "Upon my own experience. I suffered for decades because you allowed me to grow up as human, totally ignorant of the other half of my heritage. With Gillian, you've tried to bury her human side. I don't believe the result will be much better."

"Strangely enough, I think you're actually making sense," Volnar said.

Ignoring the elder's air of cool amusement, Roger said, "Before I return her to you, I want a guarantee. I demand visitation rights—joint custody—whatever the hell you choose to call it."

"You actually want to share the burden of her training?" Roger could visualize the skeptical arch of Volnar's luxuriant eyebrows.

"I'll manage. And I think Juliette will back me up on this." *Good Lord, I completely forgot!* "That reminds me, Juliette called earlier and said she was on her way down here to help me search for Gillian."

"Opportune," Volnar said. "Very well, if Juliette has no objection, I'll agree to your proposal."

Emotionally flattened by Volnar's unexpectedly easy capitulation, Roger ended the conversation as quickly as possible. *Did I actually talk him into that? Or was he planning to suggest it himself all along?* With Volnar, one could never tell, and at this point Roger didn't care.

Hanging up the phone, he heard the shower and the washing machine running simultaneously. Britt must be washing Gillian's clothes. *Déjà vu all over again, as the man says.* A rap on the front door announced the arrival of Claude and Eloise. In addition to Britt's purse and her own, Eloise carried a small paper bag.

After hanging up her coat, Roger took them into the living room and started a fire. Eloise held the bag on her lap while she cuddled with Claude on one of the matching love seats. Roger didn't bother offering Claude a drink; their sated lethargy made that obviously redundant. He did suggest a glass of eggnog for Eloise, which she accepted.

Licking foam off her lips, she said, "How is Gillian? That must have been terrible for her."

"Too soon to tell," Roger said. "In addition to the shock of witnessing Camille's death, she needs to be fed."

"Well, you have a volunteer," said Eloise. Claude's arm tightened protectively around her shoulders, but he wisely made no verbal protest.

"Thank you, but I believe we already have one donor." The water upstairs cut off. "Gillian will probably be down soon."

Britt, freshly scrubbed and changed, came in and lit a pair of bayberry candles to supplement the firelight and the glimmer of the Christmas tree. "You were talking to Volnar, weren't you?"

Claude, heavy-lidded with contentment, said, "Oh? How did Fearless Leader react to your news?"

"I'll tell you when Gillian's here, instead of repeating everything."

"She needs human blood, doesn't she?" said Britt, taking a seat next to Roger. "And she's afraid to take it, poor kid. Camille couldn't have traumatized her worse in such a short time if she'd planned it that way."

"She probably did," said Claude.

At that moment Gillian walked timidly into the room, wearing a robe of Britt's. She approached Roger and stood with her hands folded and head downcast. "You spoke to Lord Volnar? What's to be done with me?"

"Confound it, you're not on trial!" Roger moved over and gestured for her to sit between him and Britt. "Volnar will pick up your education where he left off, if you're willing to go back to him. No one will force you to do something you aren't ready for."

"That's what *she* said."

"Camille?" said Britt softly.

Gillian nodded. "She promised not to force anything upon me— and then she—" She covered her eyes and shuddered with tearless sobs.

Britt's fingers curled with the urge to comfort Gillian. Roger noticed Eloise leaning forward, straining against the same desire. He, too, knew better than to touch Gillian at a moment like this, no matter how much he yearned to help.

After a while Gillian lifted her head and stared at Roger. "Lord Volnar wants to continue as my advisor? He doesn't think I am irreparably tainted?"

"Oh, good grief!" Britt curbed her anger and modulated her voice to a soothing tone. "Gillian, we call that kind of thing *blaming the victim*. Nobody here thinks that way, and I certainly hope a creature who's lived God knows how many millennia has better sense."

"I shared Camille's—emptiness."

"That must have been terrible," Roger said. "But it doesn't have to shape your entire life. Vampires are highly adaptable, and so are human beings. Both sides of your heritage are in your favor. And another thing—would you like to spend part of your time here? Learn from me—and Britt, for that matter?"

Gillian's eyes glowed. "You don't want to get rid of me?"

"I'd hardly suggest this if I did." He felt an unexpected surge of affection, which he didn't know how to handle. It had taken him long enough to learn how to express his love for Britt. *And now I want to start all over with a child?*

Britt reached for Gillian, then drew back, unsure whether the girl was ready to be touched. Gillian groped for Britt's hand and squeezed it. When Britt winced, Gillian looked stricken. "I hurt you. I knew I shouldn't—"

"Stop worrying, it was an accident," Britt said. "I'm not afraid of you."

"Perhaps you should be. I know I wasn't supposed to crave human blood yet. I don't know whether I can feed safely—whether I can even associate with ephemerals safely."

Eloise said, "Are you thinking of what Camille said about being a monster?"

"Partly." Gillian tensed as she watched Eloise cross the room with the bag she'd been holding.

"Here, I got you an early Christmas present." Eloise sat on the rug next to the coffee table, stroking Gillian's clenched fingers as she might stroke a kitten. "This is one of the most beloved and respected children's books of all time. The heroine is a creature most people think of as monstrous, and she lives on blood." She got out the book and placed it in Gillian's lap.

"*Charlotte's Web!* Eloise, that's perfect!" Britt applauded.

Though pleased at the gift's effect, Roger was puzzled. He knew the story only by reputation. [A fable about a pig and a spider, colleague?]

[You haven't read it? How culturally deprived can you get? Take my word, colleague, it's perfect. I'll bet Volnar never would have thought of this.]

[I'm sure he wouldn't.] Aloud, Roger said to Gillian, "Your mother is on her way here. If she agrees to the plan, we'll arrange to have you stay with me as often as Volnar can spare you from your regular course of training."

"And I do advise you," said Claude, "to accept the bond with him. After the past few days, do you see the advantages of it?"

"Yes," Gillian whispered. "The way she did it was hideous, but there were moments—Yes, I understand why I need that." She swallowed. "When do you think I'll be able to have a bond with a donor, like you and Eloise?" She scanned the two of them, once again nestled together on the couch.

Claude gave her a gently mocking smile. "In a godawful hurry to race in the opposite direction, aren't you? Before you can handle that, you have a damn sight more growing to do. It's a serious commitment. You place your life in your partner's hands." The tender way he absentmindedly caressed Eloise's hair made it clear that he considered the risk well worth it.

"What you need to think of at the moment," Britt said, "is your first—donation." She glanced at Roger. [I hope you aren't going to be difficult about this, colleague.]

[No, I'm resigned to it.]

Gillian made no attempt to hide her trepidation. "Do I have your permission, sir?" He nodded. "You don't think there's a danger I will—harm her?"

"I'm here," Roger said. "I won't allow it. Dismiss the worry from your mind, and enjoy the experience." He envied her that. How would it feel to be initiated by a willing, knowledgeable donor? Nothing like his own confusion, guilt, and fear at that stage of his life.

Britt rolled up her left sleeve to offer Gillian the curve of her inner elbow. Gillian gazed at Britt as if she, instead of her donor, were entranced. Haloed by her disheveled auburn hair, curling with dampness, the child's thin, sharp-chinned face looked elfin in the firelight. Her fingers wrapped around Britt's forearm with the timidity of a wild animal creeping out of the woods to accept crumbs from a human benefactor.

"You needn't hypnotize her," Roger said, "but you must take care not to cause pain."

"I won't," Gillian whispered. But she made no move to feed.

"Would you prefer that we leave?" Claude asked.

Gillian emphatically shook her head. "The more people are watching, the less afraid I'll be."

Britt put her right arm loosely around Gillian's shoulders. "What are you afraid of? Your own impulses?"

"When I shared Camille's prey through the mind-link, she killed him."

Roger bit back a curse. *Hell of a role model!* "That doesn't mean you'll be irresistibly compelled to reenact it. No doubt the victim was entranced. Britt is fully aware."

He noticed Gillian's thumb mechanically caressing the tender spot inside Britt's elbow. "Camille constantly spoke of how ephemerals' lives meant nothing to her, because they *are* ephemeral—

because they always die. But we can die, too. *She* died. We can be destroyed by accident at any moment, just as you can. I have no guarantee that I'll live any longer than you." She looked at Britt, then Eloise. "Or you." This truism, axiomatic for the human race, apparently struck her as a revelation.

"No, you don't," said Britt. "None of us has a guarantee. So don't let it paralyze you."

After one more glance at Roger for reassurance Gillian bent over to fasten her mouth to Britt's arm. Without being told, Gillian remembered to prepare the spot with gentle flicks of her tongue, anesthetizing the skin with the secretions in her saliva. Britt stroked her hair. To Roger's eyes, a rosy mist that mingled hunger and the longing to satisfy it enveloped both of them.

*Is that how Britt and I look together?* No, it couldn't be the same, for Britt's yearning toward Gillian held no sexual overtones. Rather, the mood she projected felt almost maternal.

Gillian's fear dissipated in the joy of the sharing. Her eyelids drooped like a contented cat's as she drank. The resemblance was heightened by the croon, very like a purr, that vibrated in her throat. When Roger touched her gently on the back of the neck, careful not to shock her into a violent reaction, she willingly lifted her head. Her eyes shone.

Instead of the restless jealousy he'd expected to feel, Roger found that he shared her contentment. It hovered in the air like the fragrance of flower petals moist with spring rain. Claude's face, he noticed, reflected the same satisfaction.

Eloise murmured, "If you need more—"

"No, that's quite enough." Gillian looked faintly surprised. "When the donor gives willingly, one doesn't have to drain them to be fulfilled."

Claude chuckled at her air of discovery. "Congratulations, you are a fast learner, little one."

Leaning back against the couch, Gillian closed her eyes as if she might fall asleep despite the time of night. Much as he hated to disturb her, Roger decided he had to voice a warning. "This was for the purpose of initiation. You won't be able to enjoy it often, until you're old enough to find your own—partner. Meanwhile, you'll have to hunt for unwitting donors, which will be more complicated."

Gillian nodded without opening her eyes, clearly in no mood to listen to cautionary lectures.

"You'd better save it, old man," Claude chuckled. "We all need rest, even if it's too early for some of us to sleep." He coaxed Eloise, also on the verge of dozing off, toward the door.

As they prepared to leave, the doorbell rang. Roger sensed a nonhuman but non-hostile presence. Not Volnar yet, so it had to be Juliette. When he let her in, an icy wind laden with sleet howled after her.

"You probably shouldn't have driven in this," Roger said as he took her coat. Uneasiness over facing her at such an emotionally-charged time drove him to hide behind the conventional remarks he would make to a human acquaintance.

"It just started a few minutes ago." Shaking ice out of her sleek, Irish Setter red hair, Juliette gave him a sly smile in recognition of his nervousness. The smile faded as she raised her head like a fox scenting the air. "Gillian is here. What happened to Camille?"

"Dead. I'll tell you about it later." Weariness descended on Roger at the thought of repeating the story over again.

After a nod of greeting to Claude and a measuring look at Eloise, Juliette followed Roger into the living room. Britt stood up at their entry. "How do you do, it's a pleasure to meet Gillian's mother." Silently she remarked to Roger, [Why am I trying to lie to a vampire? This is a little too much like meeting an ex-wife.]

[No, never think that!] He felt Britt wince at the force of his reply. [You know there was never any personal tie between us. I was no more than a sperm donor.]

[I know that's how your kind view it. Being human, I have a little trouble with the concept.]

As if guessing Britt's qualms, Juliette said, "I'm no threat to you, and I appreciate what you've done for my daughter. Though I'm surprised it needed to be done." She gazed at Gillian, who stared up at her.

"Good evening, Mo—Juliette."

Reaching for Gillian's hand, Juliette drew her to her feet. "Let me look at you. I didn't expect to have our semiannual visit in these circumstances." The girl swayed with the languid intoxication induced by her donor's blood.

Roger, watching from a few feet away, knew Juliette couldn't help recognizing Gillian's freshly consummated initiation. The blood scent in the air, the child's behavior, and the hue of Britt's aura made the situation clear. Gillian squirmed beneath her mother's cool survey. Finally Juliette said, "You've grown since I last saw you. I suppose Camille had something to do with that, but your human heritage probably had more. I wonder what other surprises you have waiting for us?"

"I don't know. I am—surprised—too." At a gesture from Juliette, Gillian resumed her seat next to Britt. "You are not—disappointed?"

"Hardly! I'm intrigued. Would you like to go with me to a hotel for the rest of the night?"

Gillian glanced at Roger, who was fully occupied in trying to disguise his reaction to her comments. Damn it, who had made her feel so inadequate and insecure? He'd expected Volnar to do a better job of protecting her! "Lord Volnar is supposed to come here to pick me up sometime tomorrow."

Juliette sat next to Gillian, holding her hand. "So you've decided to give him another chance? Very mature decision. I have an idea, though. Why don't we ask him to let you spend a week or two at my place in Williamsburg first?"

Gillian let out an audible sigh, slumping into a more relaxed pose. "Thank you, I would like that. Also, Roger said—" She cast an appealing look at him.

"I proposed to Volnar that I take part in Gillian's upbringing. Call it joint custody, if you like. I refuse to be excluded from her life any longer. The methods used to date, so far as I can see, haven't been outstandingly successful."

Juliette said with a rueful half-smile, "I concede that point. Fine, you have my support, if that's what you're asking for."

Claude, listening from the doorway, said, "It'll be an interesting experiment—some would say risky. I'm surprised to hear you agree so readily."

Juliette's eyes glittered as she looked over at him. "Why? If I believe interbreeding with ephemerals will enhance our gene pool, isn't this a logical outgrowth of that belief? What's the point of producing a part-human child and excluding her from that part of herself?"

Britt mentally applauded. [I can't exactly claim to like this lady, but I approve of the way she thinks.] Aloud, she said, "I have to give you fair warning that if Gillian spends time with Roger, I'll have input into her education, too."

Eloise spoke up. "So will I. As often as we can visit Roger when she's here. Or maybe we'll invite her to L.A. now and then."

Juliette flashed her feral smile at the two women. "What is our world coming to when the day people start issuing ultimata to our faces? Yes, I'm sure Gillian will be delighted to have your input."

Gillian nodded agreement.

More gently her mother said, "I'll accept anything that may counteract what Camille did to you. Later, when you're recovered, you can tell me about it."

Gillian squeezed her hand. "It was not all terrible. There were times when I—enjoyed her." When no one lashed out at her for the confession, Gillian went on, "She helped me practice flying. And she taught me a number of songs. I now know fourteen verses of something called 'This Land Is Your Land.' Also 'You're the Top,' by Cole Porter, 'Mademoiselle from Armentieres,' *'Die Lorelei'* in the original German—"

"Later," Juliette said. "We shall help you sort out the useful things she gave you from the damaging effects. For the moment, try to put her out of your mind. Rest."

Tension visibly oozed out of the girl. She murmured a drowsy farewell to Claude and Eloise. "I look forward to visiting you in Los Angeles. I want to view your videotape collection and learn more computer games from you."

Eloise was laughing giddily as Roger escorted them to the door. He didn't bother trying to talk Claude out of driving across the bridge to Britt's; he sensed Claude wanted to have Eloise to himself.

While heating milk for Juliette, Roger telepathically remarked to Britt, [Gillian's life won't be as easy as she imagines. Aside from all the other potential problems of balancing her human and vampire aspects, a child of twelve won't be able to hunt the way Juliette or Volnar can. She may have some rough times ahead.]

[No point in scaring her by bringing that up now. One day—or should that be night?—at a time, colleague.]

After serving Juliette the brandy-laced hot milk, Roger retired to his office while Britt went to bed, leaving Gillian and her mother in privacy to talk. Despite his own negative comments, Roger felt an irrational optimism about his daughter's future. *She'll be all right. Among us, we'll make sure of it.*

## Chapter Sixteen

CLINGING TO ROGER'S arm as they picked their way between patches of ice in the parking lot of St. Mary's Church, Britt said, "Too bad Claude had to miss that. You have such a great choir."

Overhead, bells chimed to herald the transition between Christmas Eve and Christmas Day. Roger agreed with Britt's opinion of the choir, which offset the ordeal of congregational singing. Few auditory experiences were more painful to a creature with perfect pitch than listening to amateurs groan their way through "We Three Kings" or "Hark, the Herald Angels Sing." Nevertheless, he persisted in refusing to do his part to ameliorate the situation by joining the choir. He dodged the music director whenever she approached him with pleas about how much they needed another bass. Too late to discourage her by pretending tone-deafness; she'd heard him sing in the Sunday service too often.

Tonight, though, nothing could mar his pleasure. Eloise, latching onto his other arm, said, "But Claude did experience it all through me. He says that's one of the best advantages of the bond." She held out a gloved hand, palm up, to catch the first sprinkle of snowflakes. "White Christmas! That's one thing we never get in L.A."

"We don't get it here too often either," Britt said. "It's been an unusually snowy December for this part of the state."

Roger let the conversation eddy around him. He enjoyed this guilt-free chance to bask in the overlapping auras of two vibrant women at once. Like the service of Holy Communion, their warmth nourished him and whetted his appetite at the same time.

[That verges on blasphemy,] Britt teased.

[Nonsense. You're the one who is always quoting that Talmudic precept that refusing a legitimate pleasure is a sin.]

[I'm glad you've finally made up your mind that it's legitimate.]

Holding the car door for his two companions, Roger reflected on how accurate her perception was. It had taken him years to reconcile his vampiric needs with his religious background.

[Now that the midnight mass is over,] Britt commented, [you can stop fasting. At least I hope you will.]

Quite aside from the pre-communion abstinence, he'd resolutely kept his distance from her since Monday night to give her time to recover from Gillian. Though he drank no more than an ounce or twice each time they made love, the cumulative effect taxed Britt's health. [Certainly, dear colleague. Christmas is a major feast day of the Church. Celebration is a religious duty.]

Britt's thoughts bubbled with silent laughter. His skin tingling with the sensuality she projected, Roger had to concentrate hard to keep the car on the road.

Since the snow flurry had just begun, the streets were clear enough to make the drive home routine. Claude welcomed them at Roger's townhouse with mugs of hot buttered rum, the ingredients for which he'd managed to ferret out on his own. "A trifle too sweet for me," he said, "but it does fit the season." They sat in front of the fire to drink in a soothing dimness punctuated by candles and the multicolored lights on the tree. Eloise snuggled up to Claude as if they were settling in for a long stay. Roger wished they would leave—they were still using Britt's apartment—but couldn't force himself to the discourtesy of saying so.

"I've been wondering," said Claude, "whether you've had a run-in with that county police contact of yours over Camille's suicide."

"He called about it the following day," Roger said. "Fortunately, I managed to convince him Britt and I knew nothing about her death. My car, thank God, wasn't noticed in the area."

Britt set her half-finished mug on the coffee table and leaned against his shoulder. "Roger stonewalled. He's very good at that."

Roger tasted his drink. Yes, too sweet and rich, though he enjoyed it in small doses. "It helped that I went down to Captain Hayes' office and spoke to him in person. I told him Gillian had run away from Camille and called me to pick her up. Hayes believed me."

Claude smiled at that. "I should hope so, little brother, or you'd be losing your touch."

Eloise said, "Have you heard from Gillian since she left?"

"She phoned me from Williamsburg yesterday," Roger said. "She has taken human prey twice under Juliette's guidance, with no trouble. And she's prepared to accept blood-exchange with Volnar."

"That's a relief," said Eloise.

Claude nodded. "Fearless Leader should be able to counteract the negative effects Camille left on her."

"By the way," Roger said to Eloise, "Gillian sent the message that she enjoyed *Charlotte's Web*."

Britt said, "One thing about vampire adolescents, they don't have preconceived prejudices about children's literature versus adult reading material. I remember what a tough time I had getting my oldest nephew to look at *A Wrinkle in Time*. He thought it was for kids and beneath his dignity."

"Yes, our children suffer from an entirely different set of prejudices," Claude said.

Britt finished her drink and, at a silent suggestion from Roger, got up to switch on a Bach cassette. They basked in the music without talking for a while; over the years Britt and Eloise had adopted the vampire habit of dispensing with low-content social chatter.

When Roger eventually disturbed the silence by getting up to add logs to the fire, Claude said, "You know, I've thought a great deal about what flowed between us in the last moments before Camille's death."

"Oh?" Roger had tried to avoid thinking about those moments.

"For a short time, we seemed to commune somehow. Not a full-fledged bond, but a definite link. Don't you agree?"

Roger mulled over his memory of the episode. He recalled the unsettling vividness of his perceptions, how Claude's, Eloise's, and Gillian's emotions had been etched on his brain like the afterimage of a lightning bolt. "Granted, I briefly shared your experiences, as if our minds somehow merged."

"And you imposed yours on me to deflect me from killing Camille."

"I felt it, too," said Eloise, "as if you'd temporarily tapped into our bond. I think that's part of what shook me out of the pit I'd fallen into. I saw Claude's love for me clearly again, sharing how strongly Roger believed in it."

Britt, caressing Roger's hand, which she had captured while he was preoccupied, said, "I felt some of it, too. Thought I was imagining it, under stress."

"No, we actually did—involuntarily—form a sort of network among the four of us," said Claude. "An interesting but not entirely comfortable experience."

"I endorse the last part of that!" Roger said. Merging his mind with Britt's was one thing, both an ecstatic luxury and a fundamental necessity of his being, but even a hint of such contact with anyone else alarmed him.

"Could be worth exploring, though," said Claude.

Again they sat in silence for some time, each assimilating the conversation at his or her own pace. Britt remarked telepathically,

[This intrigues me. I wouldn't mind *exploring* the possibility.]

[Call me a coward if you like, but you know how I feel about that kind of intimacy.]

[Yes, I know, and I'd never push you. Much, anyway.] She rubbed her head, catlike, against his chest. Roger felt himself blushing. Claude and Eloise didn't seem to notice, though. Claude was nuzzling his lover's earlobe as if he meant to seduce her on the spot.

[Doesn't look as if they're planning to leave,] Roger said. [Perhaps we should propose adjourning to the bedrooms.]

[Why?] Britt retorted. [Good grief, it's just Claude and Eloise. Lighten up!] She relentlessly stroked his palm and nibbled at his neck.

Across the room Eloise unbuttoned Claude's shirt to slip a hand inside and massage his chest. They shifted from the love seat to the floor, where they reclined on the deep-piled carpet. Braced against the couch, he rubbed her back in languid, circular strokes, while she lay in his arms with her head on his shoulder.

Roger felt his face growing hot, though not entirely from embarrassment. The sensuality radiating from the other two made him lightheaded. Britt projected tempting images into his mind and teased him with ineffectual nips of her blunt incisors. [Why aren't we down there, too? The rug would be more comfortable than the love seat—more room to stretch out.]

[I prefer privacy.] Roger was acutely conscious of how the words clashed with the desire he couldn't hide from her.

She assailed him with a vision of her nude body aglow in the firelight, undulating beneath his. Slipping onto the floor, she lay on her back and opened her arms in invitation. He burned with thirst, his pulse throbbing in sync with hers. The yearning to merge with her swept away all reluctance.

He lay next to her, side by side for maximum face-to-face contact. He longed to feel the warmth of her skin without the barrier of clothing, but a shred of reticence wouldn't let him go that far in the presence of other people. After a deep, lingering kiss, Britt guided his left hand to her mouth and bit into the flesh at the base of the thumb. Understanding what she wanted, he made a tiny incision in his hand with his razor-edged teeth. Britt's mouth and tongue on the wound felt like the lapping of painless fire on his hyper-sensitized skin. His head whirled; he had the illusion of lying at the center of a huge, pulsing heart.

Britt's inner voice, incoherent with passion, commented, [It's been so long—since it was this intense—and you aren't even touching—]

With no sense of voluntary movement, he found himself sipping from the sweet-scented valley between her breasts as from a chalice. All conscious thought drowned in their shared fulfillment. At the periphery of his awareness, he sensed Claude and Eloise's passion like a distant echo reinforcing their own.

When he opened his eyes, through the red mist that floated before them, he noticed Claude and Eloise moving closer. In Roger's ears their heartbeats formed a counterpoint to the harmonious rhythm of his and Britt's. Britt stirred in his arms.

He felt a hand pressed to his mouth. An instant of disorientation gripped him as he tasted someone other than Britt. Eloise. "It's all right," she whispered. "Claude wants us to."

Britt added her silent reassurance. [If that's what you want, beloved,] he told her. He nibbled Eloise's palm, licking a few drops of her unfamiliar but piquant life-essence. At the same time he was aware of Claude tasting Britt. Strangely Roger didn't react with jealousy this time. The peace that enfolded him prevented that.

He did feel a twinge of apprehension, though, when Eloise broke contact, and Claude reached over her body to offer his bared wrist. Claude greeted Roger's instinctive withdrawal with a warm chuckle. "After all we endured together a few nights ago, you're still afraid of this?"

Half ashamed, Roger said, "It isn't exactly fear."

"A bond between us won't diminish the uniqueness of what you have with Britt. Nor what Eloise and I share. Haven't you learned the difference between friendship and sex yet?"

Bathed in Britt's aura and savoring Eloise's less overwhelming but pleasant flavor, Roger didn't feel threatened by the question. "You may have a valid point."

"When Britt nourished Gillian, that didn't encroach on your bond, did it? Gillian's fear of bonding is natural. She's only a child. By now, you should have outgrown that. If you're going to act as mentor to her, shouldn't you know the full depth of what that union can be?" Claude seemed content with Roger's thoughtful silence as an answer. "And so should I, for the same reason. If you're willing, *mon frere*, I would like to deepen our friendship."

In reply Roger extended his left hand, still trickling blood where Britt had sampled from the incision. Simultaneously he nipped the inside of Claude's wrist. He felt none of the panic he'd barely been able to suppress when he'd made this exchange with Volnar over fourteen years before. Now Roger knew what to expect. The metallic flavor of Claude's blood, the chill brush of his lips, the body heat of Britt and Eloise flowing over both of them like rich red wine on the palate, all blended with the radiance of the fire and the candle flames in a sensory gestalt of aching intensity.

Roger opened himself to the clarity of his brother's mind. Through Claude, like gazing through the surface of a pond, he saw the top layers of Eloise's thoughts and touched their mutual love as well as her unsuspected tenderness toward him. And he sensed Claude tracing the threads of Britt's consciousness through him in the same way.

Roger saw himself through their eyes—not only Britt's, as usual, but all three of them. He witnessed their amused, half-dismayed reaction to viewing themselves as he saw them. Thoughts and emotions sparked among them like fireflies flashing across the landscape of a summer night. Or like the fine-spun filaments of a net in which all four were intertwined. The scintillating web enmeshed them in a waking trance. They nourished one another, each fully himself or herself, yet in a sense new to all of them united as never before.

Chapter Seventeen

FROST-COATED GRASS crunched under Gillian's feet. She ran across the dark field with a light wind lashing her face and ruffling her hair. She wore only jeans and a sweatshirt, no coat, for the thirty-five-degree night felt just pleasantly brisk to her. Two Irish wolfhounds loped beside her, one on each side like an escort. Though she could have outdistanced them instantly with a 60-mile-per-hour sprint, she paced her speed to theirs. The dogs' uncomplicated joy in the exercise made them comfortable companions. Gillian enjoyed the complex flavor of human donors' blood but still found prolonged exposure to their emotions tiring.

She reached the fence at the edge of her mother's property and leaned on it to stare into the dark expanse of the nearest neighbor's pasture. With Juliette's blessing, she had stolen an occasional snack from the horses that grazed there, not enough to affect the animals' health. At this time of night, though, the field was deserted.

Tilting her head back, Gillian contemplated the stars visible in the cloudless December sky. If only she could stay here.

*If I wanted to stay a child.* Vampires past early childhood didn't live with their mothers. This interlude had to end soon.

A stirring of air behind her broke into her reverie. Turning, she saw a black and silver shape glide to earth in the middle of the field. When he alighted and strode toward her, she recognized Volnar. His pale wings contrasted with the dark fur that covered his face, arms, and bare chest.

She folded her arms and waited for him. Her stomach knotted, and her heartbeat accelerated. Impatient with this sign of her anxiety, she willed it to slow down. To her satisfaction her pulse obeyed her will.

When Volnar got within a few feet of her, he reabsorbed the wings into his back and allowed the dark pelt to fade away and his fangs and pointed ears to return to normal. The dogs crouched and edged backward, whining.

"Go home," Gillian whispered to them with a dismissive gesture. They raced toward the house in the distance.

"Good evening, Gillian," Volnar said.

"Good evening, sir." Electricity from his aura crackled over her skin. As usual his mind felt like a sphere of cold metal with no emotions leaking out. She had no idea whether he was about to flay her with his wrath. She folded her arms again, wishing she could shield against him that easily.

"Have you enjoyed your holiday?" His tone remained level, his expression bland.

"Yes, sir." She focused on keeping a tremor out of her voice. "Roger and Claude and their friends cared for me well. So did Juliette."

"I'm aware of that. Nevertheless, you know how foolishly you behaved."

She sensed the razor's edge in that remark. *Here it comes.* "I know." She clutched at the memory of drinking from Britt, thriving on the lifeblood and affection so freely shared. "I shouldn't have run away from you. And I shouldn't have let Camille seduce me. But I'm not tainted."

Volnar's eyebrows arched at that word. "No, you are not. I have never implied such a thing."

"Other vampires have. Purebreds."

"Will you allow others to define you?"

"No." She hugged herself to keep from shaking. "Not even you."

A tinge of amusement crept into his voice. "So you've tasted human blood and now you think you've grown past the need for guidance?"

She relaxed a degree. Maybe he wouldn't flay her alive after all. "No, sir. Both my parents have made it clear to me that I still have a lot to learn."

He stepped closer to her. His metallic scent prickled her nose. "If you find it impossible to learn from me, young one, another advisor could be found. Someone whose teaching style, so to speak, suits you better." The crimson gleam in his eyes challenged her.

Was the offer sincere or some kind of test? Without a crack in his mental shell, he gave her no hint. She recalled how Roger had described his own initiation by Volnar as harrowing but worth the ordeal. She remembered hints dropped by others of her kind about how lucky she was to have the Prime Elder as her mentor. Volnar possessed power and knowledge few of their species attained. If she wanted the strength and skill to build an independent life for herself, his power would prove an invaluable asset.

Camille had forced a bond on her. A wave of chill, far colder than the December night breeze, swept over her. *No! That woman is dead!*

*She has no control over me now.* Gillian drew upon the warmth of more recent memories to dispel that cold. Her family's blood-sharing had blotted out any stain left from Camille's violation. Volnar wouldn't violate her that way. His offer made that clear.

If she could trust him. But without that trust, she realized, she would never finish growing up. "I don't want another advisor," she said. "I want you to teach me."

"You know what that involves."

"Yes."

She closed the last few inches between them. Volnar loomed over her, not moving. Gillian placed her open hand on his chest. He felt like a statue carved of ice. The cilia in her palms vibrated with the energy sparking in his aura. Yet he still made no move. He waited, testing her.

Her throat tightened, and the hairs on her arms bristled. *I can't do it!* Meeting his reptilian stare, though, she felt a surge of defiance. She wouldn't justify his doubts by proving herself a coward.

She rolled up her right sleeve and, inch by inch, forced her arm toward his mouth, wrist turned to expose the veins. At last she touched his lips, parted in a ghost of a smile. But he still did nothing.

She clamped her other hand around his left forearm and lifted it to her own mouth. Shuddering, she pierced the skin. His blood trickled over her tongue. It scalded and froze at the same time. She fastened her lips to the incision and sucked hard to overcome the impulse to tear herself away. The fluid burned down her throat like brandy and ignited a flame in the pit of her stomach.

Only then did Volnar nip her wrist and drink. Closing her eyes, she clung to awareness of herself while her life flowed into him. She felt as if she floated in a void with a cyclone swirling around her.

Phantom hands gripped her and stopped her from falling into the abyss. In her mental landscape she saw a castle whose turrets towered out of sight into a scarlet-tinged mist. When the whirlwind deposited her outside the castle, she stood before a stone wall with a massive door. The portal swung open. An endless corridor stretched before her. As far as her vision reached, door after door lined the hallway, inviting her to explore the chambers they guarded. The chambers of Volnar's ancient mind.

She stepped inside.

Margaret L. Carter

Marked for life by reading DRACULA at the age of twelve, Margaret L. Carter has remained passionate about vampires. With degrees in English from the College of William and Mary, the University of Hawaii, and the University of Califonia (Irvine), she featured a chapter on DRACULA in her dissertation. Her nonfiction works include THE VAMPIRE IN LITERATURE: A CRITICAL BIBLIOGRAPHY and DIFFERENT BLOOD: THE VAMPIRE AS ALIEN. In addition to a werewolf story, SHADOW OF THE BEAST, she has had several vampire novels published, including DARK CHANGELING, to which CHILD OF TWILIGHT is the sequel. She and her husband, a retired Navy Captain, collaborated on a fantasy novel, WILD SORCERESS.

Lightning Source UK Ltd.
Milton Keynes UK
UKOW03f2120140514

231718UK00001B/10/A